DARKWIND

THE STARCHASER SAGA
BOOK I

R. DUGAN

For information contact:
R. Dugan
PO Box 1265
Martinsville, IN 46151
reneeduganwriting.com

Cover design by Maja Kopunovic
Map by Jessica Khoury
ISBN: 978-1-7339255-0-1

Second Edition: May 2020

10 9 8 7 6 5 4 3 2 1

DEDICATION

To Pam
For the song that introduced me to the truth
of who Cistine really was.

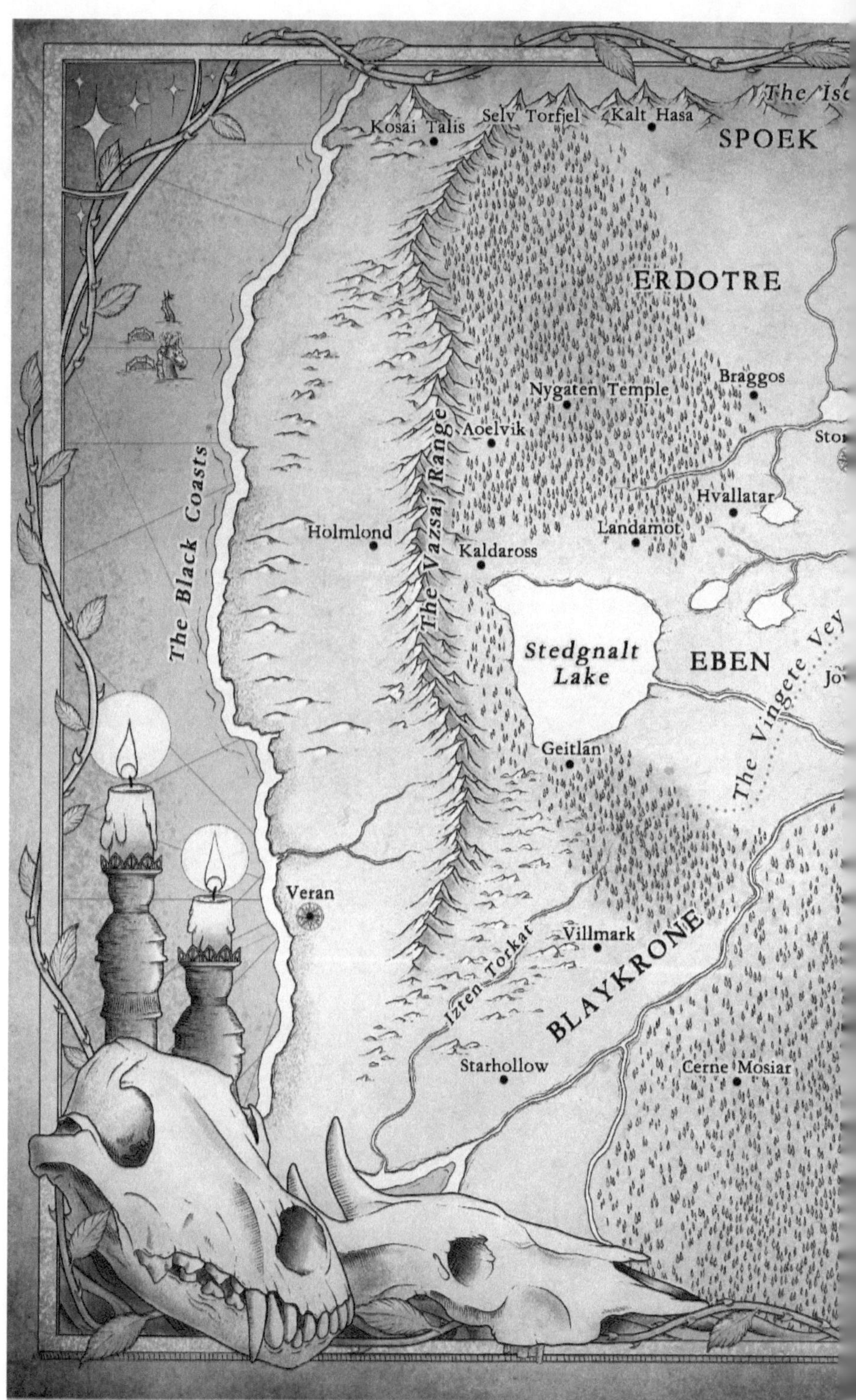

The Isc
SPOEK
Kosai Talis
Selv Torfjel
Kalt Hasa
ERDOTRE
Braggos
Nygaten Temple
Aoelvik
Stor
Hvallatar
The Vazsaj Range
Holmlond
Landamot
Kaldaross
The Black Coasts
Stedgnalt Lake
EBEN
Jo
The Vingete Vey
Geitlan
Veran
Izren Torkat
Villmark
BLAYKRONE
Starhollow
Cerne Mosiar

ange
Siralek
NORDBRAN
Azkai Temple
KROAKEN
Felstrond
ven Hatcheries
Detlyse Halet
Keltei Temple
Nior River
lidom
LATAUS
SVERD
The Wildwood
Soratt Temple
copr. 2020 Jessica Khoury

THE PRINCESS

OF

BOOKS AND BEAUTY

CHAPTER
ONE

CISTINE NOVACEK KNEW something was wrong the moment she woke with her bodyguard's fingers wrapped around her shoulder.

The last vestiges of a bad dream drummed in Cistine's pounding heart as she loosened her white-knuckled grip on her sheets and scrambled up in the disparity of light and darkness. The darkness was one of Talheim's deep nights pressing against the panes of her floor-to-ceiling windows; the light was a ghostlamp, a bioluminescent shell of phosphorus plants glinting in a small jar. Its gentle glow limned the contours of her bodyguard's face as the woman released Cistine's shoulder and straightened, her tan skin, feather-short reddish hair, and mismatched eyes stroked by the teal glow.

Cistine rubbed her cheeks, still itching from the day's cosmetics. "What's wrong, Ashe? Why are you still here this late?"

Ashe threw Cistine's robe into her lap. "Get up and follow me, Princess."

If she hadn't known Ashe her entire life—if some of her earliest memories hadn't been of this solemn-faced girl standing beside her crib in this very room, teasing her with a flash of sunlight along her battle knives— she would've gone straight back to bed. But Ashe was normally a pillar of calm, so it was the nervousness minting her blue-and-green eyes that dragged Cistine fully awake. She tugged on the robe, freed her hair from its collar, and hurried after her guard.

The halls of the Citadel—Talheim's crown jewel—looked no different from any other night. Through the great bay windows, Cistine could barely glimpse two of the four bridges that joined the Citadel's enormous stone plot to the capital city of Astoria. Beyond that, there was a small pocket of coastline visible, glimmering jewel-bright under the full moon's light.

Everything appeared calm. Everything was in order.

Cistine elongated her stride to match her guard's. "Ashe, what time is it?"

"Quarter past midnight. Try to keep up."

Cistine *was* trying, but Ashe set a grueling pace through the empty corridors. "You know, respectable people are sleeping at this hour."

Ashe's mouth quirked. "And *you* know the King's Cadre Wardens never sleep. Especially the one who's tasked with keeping his young, impressionable daughter safe."

Cistine pressed a hand to her breast, privately relieved Ashe had risen to the bait. "Me? What trouble am *I*? All I ever do is gossip in the Citadel and read my many, *many* books. Surely I'm not the reason you look so out of breath and distracted tonight."

"I wish it was your fault," Ashe said. "You know all those distant cousins and lords' wives you've been gossiping with for the past week?"

Cistine smiled. "No, I'm just so blind, I've missed how they've all been fawning over me."

This time, Ashe did not smile. "They aren't here for your twentieth birthday celebration as we've been told."

Suddenly, Cistine was glad of her robe. Though light and soft, it hid the prickle of gooseflesh that reared under her thin shift and traveled along her thighs, down to her ankles.

Her father had made such a fuss over her coming-of-age birthday. He'd sent invitations to the four corners of Talheim, inviting all his relations and the lords who oversaw the smaller provinces, and even convinced the ones in the south to attend. As rumor had it, they all needed a reprieve anyway from the tension of holding the shaky peace with neighboring Mahasar at the border.

King Cyril and Queen Solene had never been sparing in their celebrations of Cistine's birthdays, particularly as she'd grown older. A coming-of-age ball, with all her cousins and aunts and uncles present, and half the kingdom in attendance, was simply to be expected.

But if that was a sham...if there was something else at play here...

"Ashe, what's the matter?" Cistine demanded.

"I'll show you."

They reached a private study that abutted the throne room itself. Ashe ushered Cistine into the cool, dark confines, sliding the door shut at their backs. She went to the wall, motioned Cistine to crouch beside her, and pried loose a small stone, sending a shower of white dust onto the polished boots of her black Cadre uniform.

Cistine wasn't surprised by any of this. After all, the Cadre served as both the King's household guard and his eyes and ears around Astoria. It made perfect sense that Ashe had places to listen in at every wall...even to the throne room.

That room was one of Cistine's least-favorites in the Citadel, possibly in all Astoria. The soaring high-backed seats—one carved of ivory, the other of obsidian—perched grandly on the dais where her parents sat. They stood as stark reminders that one day, as sole heir, Cistine would sit on the ivory throne, someone would sit on the obsidian one beside her, and duty would force her to legislate hour after hour.

It would be the end of all the books and tea, the years spent researching subjects that interested *her*. All the long winters of blazing hearths with no demands on her time but chatting with her people in teahouses and shops...gone. After her twentieth birthday, she would have to focus on matters of succession-planning and law, just as her mother had done when she'd married King Cyril at the tender age of nineteen.

Cistine almost looked away from the room and asked Ashe to describe what she ought to be seeing, but the strangeness she glimpsed inside anchored her gaze and slit a slow frown into her brow.

The thrones were empty.

The King and Queen occupied the head seats of the throne room's long table instead, and Cistine's aunts and uncles were seated on opposing sides of it, along with her remote familial relations and the lower lords to whom she had no blood affinity. Among those men was Lord Rion Bartos, the last Commander to lead the Cadre before his retirement to the estate of Practica when Cistine was thirteen years old. He'd come frequently to the Citadel since then, but always with his wife, Eboni, and his son—and never to sit at the planning table with the King. He'd outright refused to allow political matters to interfere with that friendship.

But there he was, grim-faced, slant-mouthed, scowling.

And wearing his Cadre uniform.

Cistine looked swiftly at Ashe. Her focus was trained on her old commander, too.

Soft murmurs pattered around the table like summer rain, too low for Cistine to hear. She shifted closer to Ashe, balancing her chin on her Warden's shoulder. "What are they discussing?"

The answer came from above their heads: "The South."

Cistine sat back hard on her heels, dragging her robe tightly around herself. "*Julian?*"

"What are you doing here?" Ashe hissed.

The eavesdropper, hidden in the shadows of the room's long, sculpted upper edge, dropped from his perch and landed lightly beside them. "There's another loose brick up there."

Cistine sputtered. "No one told me you were coming!"

"You really think I'd miss your coming-of-age celebration?"

Cistine forgot everything that worried her as Julian Bartos joined them at the wall, moving with the same long-limbed grace—and the same firm set to his heavy brows and high cheekbones—as his father. But Lord Rion's son lacked his father's ruddy countenance. He favored his mother more, with his wing of dark hair and equally dark eyes. Cistine knew this because she'd been studying him from the corners of her eyes every time he and his parents returned to visit the Citadel.

Julian held her stare openly now and flashed a smile that made Cistine's knees turn to lead and changed her heart to a crashing surf. "Princess, it's good to see you again."

His midnight eyes glinted with mirth as he took her hand and kissed it, and in that moment Cistine was glad she was wearing her periwinkle robe, and not the red one that would have accentuated her blush rather than her curves. "You as well, Julian."

He crouched between them, serious again. "So. They're saying the danger has grown near the southern border with Mahasar. Lord Trevar just reported sixteen small raids in less than three weeks."

Ashe skimmed her thumb along her lower lip. "Dangerous."

"Terrifying, if you're a southerner."

Cistine frowned. "What does this mean?"

Julian's eyes slid to her. "It means our neighbors in the Southern Kingdom are flexing. Mahasar is testing our mettle along the border."

"A raid every few seasons, especially after a hard winter, isn't uncommon," Ashe said. "But it's early summer. Usually things would've quieted down by now."

"They're not sacking grain silos or releasing a few paddocks of cattle, either. These are forts they're attacking."

Cistine's blood chilled. The Talheimic forts, framing their borders with the Northern and Southern Kingdoms, were the outlook for any sort of disturbance from their volatile neighbors on both sides. "Mahasar is sending a message."

"Well, if you wanted to raise the notion of war without actually *declaring* one," Julian said, "that would be the way to go about it."

King Cyril cleared his throat, and the muttering at the table stopped. Julian, Cistine, and Ashe pressed themselves closer to the small gap in the wall to hear him speak: "This is a dangerous dance we've stepped into. Mahasar struts, but they have yet to make any advances that would truly constitute an act of war."

Rion nodded. "If we were to attack them now, even in retaliation for the forts, it would make us the instigators. After that, King Jad would have no trouble rallying the support of his entire kingdom, even his laziest magnates, to battle. His ranks would swell to the hundreds of thousands, and that's besides Mahasar's usual army, which far outnumbers anything we've faced in battle in the last two hundred years."

The lords and nobility shifted and muttered. Cistine's throat cooled with dread.

"We can't allow the fate of the forts to go unmentioned," her Uncle Filip said. "There must be some retribution short of declaring war."

"We could invite King Jad and his advisors for peace talks," Queen Solene said, "but don't think for an instant that he would not seize the opportunity to search out this city's weak points while he's here. He's coveted the Citadel as a prize for years."

"Of course he has." Lady Eboni rested a hand on Rion's brawny arm and smiled at the Queen. "You remember the state of *his* old capital city, Solene? What chaos that was."

The King shook his head. "I would not allow King Jad to set foot in my city under any circumstances. I might meet with him in Middleton, if Lord Dorminger is agreeable."

Lord Dorminger nodded slowly as he palmed his red-bearded face. "But to what end? Asking them kindly to cease the border raids?"

"To learn what they hope to accomplish through them."

"Cyril," Solene murmured. "We know what Jad wants."

Cistine's father sat back in his seat, running a hand through his hair. The agitated movement belonged to the reckless prince he had once been, now buried under the threads of silver in his brown hair and the weight of the thin circlet on his scarred brow. "There is another way. A means of frightening Jad into keeping his treacherous fingers inside his own borders."

"What are you going to do, march down to the forts and flash your pale buttocks in his face?" Rion asked.

Cistine was grateful for his irreverent question, because it made her father smile.

"No," Cyril said, "but we could make him think twice before attacking us if we had Valgard standing at our backs."

The rarely-spoken name of the Northern Kingdom whipped through the room, stealing the breath from every pair of lungs—including Cistine's.

"Siding with Valgard," Rion scoffed. "To what end? We defeated *them* in the last war—what good is their strength against Mahasar?"

"Not all strength is strength of arms," the King said. "The North is tenacious and its people are clever. They have certain powers we lack. And perhaps they would stand united with us in friendship if they perceived the threat from Mahasar would bring war to their border once again."

"Stand with us, against Jad," one of Cistine's aunts muttered, "and without their augments. Augments they no longer have because of *us*...because we made them seal the Doors to the Gods."

King Cyril was quiet for a very, very long time.

"Conquest is Jad's goal," he finally said, "to expand his own borders at any cost. If he marches across the Middle Kingdom, do you really think he won't try to take the North as well? Valgard is in as much danger as Talheim if Jad can't be stopped."

"We haven't even spoken of Valgard in years, or allowed the people to discuss it after what happened there," Solene said. "The risk is so great if we broach that subject now, Cyril."

"You know all the reasons this is a terrible idea," Rion added.

Several heads bobbed in agreement, but Cistine didn't join them. Her mind was already racing through all the things she knew of Valgard.

She'd been told very little about the Northern Kingdom or the war between them and Talheim, except that her father, a newly-married prince at the time, had fought alongside Cistine's grandfather against Valgard. King Ivan had died in the last battle before Cyril and Rion led the Wardens of Talheim to the heart of the North.

The rest of what happened was shrouded in mystery, unwritten in any book Cistine ever found. She only knew from Ashe's stories that the closing of the Doors to the Gods and the dissolution of augments—the gifted power of the True God and his lesser vassals to the people of the north—had severed the line of the Northern Kingdom to their vast wells of inhuman power.

No one spoke of that anymore, not even her father. And yet here, at this table, with so much at risk from Jad's movements in the south, the King of Talheim himself ignored the unspoken rule.

Clearly, he was desperate. Everyone was, to even dare mention Valgard in friendly terms.

"Cyril." Rion's vulnerable, earnest tone drew Cistine back from her thoughts. "I fought beside you in Valgard. I saw what it cost them, and us, when they surrendered and closed the Doors. Even though their Chancellors agreed to that ritual and signed the truce, that peace is tenuous at best. We can't risk alerting them that Mahasar is on the move against us. What if they join forces with Jad instead?"

Solene nodded slowly. "We can't hold out against an attack from both sides. Forget the North, my love. They can't help us."

Cyril took his queen's hand, lacing their fingers together. "Then what do you suggest? Jad will only be content with fort sackings for so long. Sooner or later, we all know he'll make a show of his true intentions, whether we instigate or not."

"Or he won't," Rion said. "He may whittle away at us, one piece at a time. He has the madness for it. And the patience."

Cistine watched the weight of the kingdom pressing down on her father's shoulders as he held onto her mother's hand. "If I hadn't seen enough war in Valgard to last me a lifetime, I might say that was preferable to this chipping away." He looked to his left. "Dorminger. How soon can Middleton be fortified for peace talks?"

"Two months," Dorminger said. "But it will be another few weeks after that before an emissary could reach Jad in Arak Shehr. You know their whole capital is seething with paranoia, just like its King."

"Unfortunately. And then another few weeks for Jad to reach Middleton."

"Assuming he doesn't come at his own leisurely pace," Eboni said. "Which I can almost promise he will."

"If we can hold the southern border that long, with minimal loss of life, it will be worth it for the chance at peace," the King said. "Let's begin the proceedings. In the meantime, Rion, if you're willing..."

"At your command."

Julian frowned, pressing his fist to his mouth.

"I want you to travel to the southern border with the other lords," Cyril continued. "There's never been a better warrior in Talheim than you. The King's Sword will be an asset to the defense in the south."

"Consider it done."

Julian let out a shaky breath, bowing his head and squeezing his eyes shut.

"No one may breathe a word of this to Cistine," Solene said. "We all lived our coming-of-age celebrations under the threat of war with Valgard. I won't let Jad's ruthlessness steal my daughter's joy. He's already taken enough."

Ashe reached around Julian to grasp Cistine's hand. Cistine squeezed back until her own knuckles ached.

The lords and noblemen rose, bowing to the King and Queen before they trudged from the room. The bend of every neck and back told Cistine just how weary they were from the secret they kept, and from the fear that after peace talks and costly fortifications, Jad would still march from Mahasar into the Middle Kingdom and take what wasn't his at the tip of a sword.

Soon only the King and Queen and Rion and Eboni remained. Rion cleared his throat. "The moment the last ghostlamp dies on her birthday, I'll ride south."

"Eboni, you and Julian are welcome to move into the Citadel," Solene offered. "I could use your support in the months to come."

"I would be honored, Solene."

Cistine's heart fluttered at the thought of Julian living in the city again, perhaps only a few doors away from her.

Chairs scraped as the King and Queen rose. Solene and Eboni embraced. Cyril laid a hand on Rion's shoulder, then bumped foreheads with him. "Hold the line, brother. Just buy me the months we need to cobble together a treaty that will spare our people."

"With my life, Cyril."

Julian slowly sank back on his haunches. His eyes branded Cistine, full of fear for his father facing the immoral King Jad. Cistine wished she didn't know the sort of man Jad was; that she hadn't heard the stories of his madness, so she could offer Julian some sort of comfort.

But they both knew the tales about Mad King Jad. All too well.

CHAPTER TWO

THE SMELL OF rosemary and freshly-turned soil wafted up from the Citadel's garden as Cistine stood on her balcony, the natural tan of her skin turned silver by the moon. She gazed at the distant slice of the Agerios Sea where the blue skirt of the harbor hugged Astoria's hips, the moonlight kissing the wavecaps.

Ever since her parents first brought her to the coast, Cistine had yearned for the waves. They'd gone back every year the day before her birthday, forsaking legislation and duty, because she'd pleaded so desperately. But tonight, even that faraway surf's song didn't calm her. It tugged at her instead, a beckoning cry that slid along her bones, filling her head with dark notions.

Come, it called. *Come and see.*

She tried to imagine the upcoming celebration ball with dancing and eating, opening parcel after parcel of books and beautiful dresses. Her family and her people all in attendance, her parents smiling and laughing and putting on a show. Then some excuse would be made, and Eboni and Julian would remain in the Citadel while Rion rode south to face Jad's forces. Maybe he would return in a few months. Maybe he would meet the King in Middleton, if the peace talks happened.

Maybe not.

Now that Cistine knew her party was a front for a much larger matter—a secret her parents wouldn't share with her—she couldn't imagine celebrating. She couldn't envision eating a single piece of cake or opening one parcel. She almost wished she was as ignorant as the King and Queen tried to keep her.

"Ashe, why did you bring me to that room tonight?" she asked.

Ashe reclined heavily against the open balcony door. "I don't believe the royal family should have any secrets...especially with you coming of age. I'll take the punishment for that decision if it comes. But out of every generation that's ruled from this Citadel, Cyril's is the first without a stain of scandal or infighting. I'd like to keep it that way."

Cistine had to admire her brash defense of the Novacek family's honor. If only it made her feel better.

"I didn't know how bad things had gotten," Julian murmured from his perch on the bed. "I'm being officiated into the Cadre this summer, and no one ever mentioned this war council to me."

"Or to me," Ashe said. "The King's kept the finer points secret from the Cadre. Until tonight, even I had no idea the ball was a ruse."

And a clever one. It was an excuse to bring all the nobles and lords together without arousing fear among the people or giving Jad an excuse to accuse Cyril of holding council against Mahasar.

"Do you think the peace talks will work?" Cistine asked.

"God willing," Ashe said. "But we all know the stories. Jad kidnapped the prince's betrothed and her handmaiden just to provoke a reaction. And when he got one—a bloody one—he laughed about it."

"Can someone so sick in the head be expected to show for a peace talk?" Julian wondered. "Or to honor the statutes of one?"

In the silence that followed, Cistine knew they were all thinking of the same story: Jad, only a prince at the time, had once hired bandits to capture Solene and Eboni and held them captive in his family's old capital city, Khorraris, as a taunt and a challenge. Rion and Cyril had defied King Ivan's orders and raced to Khorraris only to find it burning already, torn with infighting. Jad's father had died in the ensuing struggle that reduced

Khorraris to cinders, while the prince and Rion fought to free their stolen loves.

And with his feet planted in the ashy wreckage of the capital, with his own father's severed head at his feet, Jad had laughed.

That was the story Rion had told Julian and Cistine as children: Jad cackled as his city burned around him. Then he pointed a finger at Cyril and Rion, at Solene and Eboni, and told them death was coming. Someday, Talheim would be his.

That was the man Rion was going to face: a mad prince who had become a mad king, with plenty of reason to hate the Middle Kingdom.

Cistine covered her mouth with her hands. Her home lay beneath her, twinkling with ghostlamps and candles. How would it look if it burned? How would the four bridges be rebuilt if they were broken? Where would the people go if their houses and shops were ransacked like the southern forts?

And what would become of King Cyril if he faced Jad in combat? What would become of Rion after he left the city?

From the way she found Julian bent with his head in his hands when she turned, Cistine knew he was wondering the same thing.

"Is Valgard really a lost cause?" Cistine asked.

Ashe folded her arms. "It's a moot point. The King can only direct his energy one way or the other: south or north. He's choosing to focus on the peace talks rather than rallying a neighboring army for war."

"But it wouldn't have to be a war! Not if Jad saw us with the might of Valgard at our backs."

"You read too many stories, Cistine," Ashe said. "I was the youngest Talheimic to fight in that war. I wasn't even part of the Cadre yet, and what we endured still haunts me to this day. All I saw in Valgard was death and pain and blood. They have nothing good to offer us."

"Nothing but death and pain, you said. The North is known for that! Which may be precisely what would make Jad think twice about crossing us."

Julian lowered his hands from his face and peered up at Ashe. "She has a point.”

“No, she doesn’t,” Ashe growled. “I know what you’re thinking, Cistine, and *you* are not going to Valgard. What would you tell your parents? And what about your retinue? You can’t bring a stomping clutch of royals north of the border forts. You’d be inviting disaster.”

“I wouldn’t need a retinue. Just you.”

“Oh, that’s a brilliant idea. Visiting a kingdom of former enemies with one Warden in tow. You really haven’t thought this through at all, have you?”

The idea was still forming in her mind. But now that she had to defend it to Ashe... “Two people could move more swiftly and secretively than an entire army.”

Ashe stabbed an accusatory finger toward her. “Stop it, right now. This is just an excuse for you to visit Valgard like you’ve been dreaming of since you were small.”

Julian eyed Cistine curiously. “Why would you even want to go there?”

Cistine tossed up her hands. “I never said I did!”

But the words were a stale half-truth, bitter on her tongue. She knew—and Ashe knew—she’d always felt a tug of curiosity toward their mysterious northern neighbors, a people she knew even less about than Mahasar. The lack of talk surrounding Valgard had piqued her gossip’s heart for a very long time.

“Listen to me. You’re just now turning twenty, Cistine,” Ashe said. “You’ve never seen war. Do you know how old I am?”

Cistine sighed. She hated this argument. “Thirty-three.”

“That’s right, thirty-three. I was twelve when I chased the Cadre north of the border, and I still have nightmares of what I saw there. Augers ripping our Wardens apart with fire and lightning and ice. A cold in the bones of the world that went so deep, no flame could melt it. There’s nothing north of the forts but *suffering*. We’re better off taking our chances in Middleton than with them.”

Footsteps clomped suddenly in the outer hall, and a sizzle of panic jolted Cistine forward. She pointed Julian and Ashe toward the door of the bathing chamber that opened back out into the corridor, and Ashe hurried to it at once.

Julian hesitated, watching Cistine. "Our fathers will be all right, Princess."

He ducked out, shutting the door softly behind him.

Cistine leaped into the bed, shedding her robe and bundling it under the covers. No sooner had her head struck the pillow than her door opened. Pink ghostlight licked her eyelids as feet crossed the room. The balcony doors whispered closed. Then her father's voice, hoarse and low: "Are you asleep?"

"Mmm-hmm," Cistine smiled.

"Liar." Cyril's weight settled on the bed. Cistine rolled over to face him, reading the shadows in his eyes. "What's kept you awake?"

"That dream again. The one with dark halls and chanting men." It wasn't entirely a lie. She *had* been dreaming of those things before Ashe woke her—the cruel recurring vision that always knotted her fingers into fists around the bedclothes.

Cyril's hand shook slightly as he stroked her hair from her brow. "It's only a dream, Cistine. Don't let it trouble you."

Cistine stared at the jeweled rings banding her father's fingers: a sapphire band for marriage. A ruby for his heritage. An emerald for her— the color of her eyes. "Why are *you* awake, Papa?"

He gazed toward the balcony doors. "Royal matters. Nothing for you to concern yourself with."

It hurt deeper than Cistine expected. Her father had never lied to her before. Of all the people she'd ever loved—even Ashe—she trusted his honesty the most.

Tell me, Cistine wanted to beg. *Tell me that you* need *this ball as a part of your strategy. I won't hate you for it!*

Cyril's gaze finally returned to her. "Is this really about a dream, or are you just excited to see Julian again?"

Cistine kicked him from under the covers. "*Papa!*"

Cyril laughed, and even though she was blushing furiously, Cistine was glad to hear the sound. "I'm your father, Cistine. I see everything. And those feelings are nothing to be ashamed of. Your mother and I—"

"*Please*, don't make that comparison." Cistine hid her face behind the blankets.

"I'm just saying that certain things are meant to be. The bond your mother and I share sometimes seems to defy all logic." Cyril turned the sapphire ring around his finger. "In the North, they would call people like us *selvenar*."

Cistine dropped the blanket and sat up against the pillows, intrigue driving out mortification. That was twice her father had broached the subject of Valgard tonight, and neither time did he seem angry. "*Selvenar.* What does that mean?"

"Blended hearts," Cyril said. "Two people whose destinies are so entwined, it seems ordained by the True God that they would come together at any cost. I would have crossed oceans for your mother...I would have died in Valgard to keep our kingdom safe even if she was the only woman in it."

Cistine smiled. "How romantic."

"Well, the romanticism doesn't make it any less true. And you know I would do the same for you, Cistine. If your mother and I are blended hearts, then you're the heart that comes from that blending."

Tears blotted Cistine's vision. "I know, Papa."

He bent forward to kiss her forehead, and Cistine closed her eyes as the scent of sandalwood and citrus washed over her: notes of home and happiness. "I barely slept before my coming-of-age party, either. But try to, all right? You'll be miserable if you don't."

Cistine nodded, burrowing her fingers into the blanket and watching hills and valleys creep along the fabric as her father stood. "Papa...what if I said I didn't want a ball this year?"

Cyril froze. It was an absolute sort of stillness, the kind that made Cistine almost squirm. "You've looked forward to these celebrations every year since you were a child."

"I know. Maybe I'm just growing tired of parties."

"Your twentieth birthday is important, Cistine. It's your coming-of-age, the day you'll be recognized as a fully-fledged adult of ruling and marrying age."

No mention of the war council. No hint at all that he might be honest with her.

"If this is about your future ascension to the throne," Cyril added when Cistine stayed quiet, "we can make adjustments. We'll start slowly and acclimate you to it."

Cistine's heart shriveled at the thought. She nestled deeper into the covers. "I would just...much rather spend this birthday at the coast. Ashe suggested the Bartos estate."

She hoped the quick lie would trap him, force him to tell her why he wouldn't *let* her leave, for the necessity of the ball and the risk of the princess being away from the Citadel's safety while trouble brewed in the south.

She didn't expect her father's face to glow with sudden excitement at that suggestion, or for him to nod. "The Bartos estate. Well, we can't cancel the ball, not after everyone's already made the journey here, but if you wanted to go afterward, we can certainly accommodate *that*."

That shriveled remnant of Cistine's heart slowly wilted from her chest, like a browned leaf drifting down from its stem.

He wasn't going to tell her about the war council, even if she threatened to leave. He would sooner lie to her than bring her into his confidences, despite all his talk about her coming of age. He would eagerly send her away before making her part of this conflict.

Very well. If he wanted to send her off, then she would go.

"If it's all right, I'd like to stay there with just Ashe. A few quiet months to ourselves, before...you know." She let her father fill in the gaps himself: before the peace talks with Jad that he didn't know she knew about. Before she began her ascension to the throne, which they both knew she despised.

Cyril rubbed his bearded face. "That would be unusual, Cistine. But we can accommodate it, on condition: you take Julian with you. You and Ashe could use a guide in that coastal town. It's a maze there. You might be lost without him."

Cistine couldn't coax even a wisp of volume to her voice. "I'll bring

Julian and Ashe, and only them. I'd like to go the day after the ball, if that's all right. And I don't want anyone else there. No servants, no Wardens, Papa. Just for a few months, I'd like to live as the commoners do. Before I rule over them."

Cyril's eyes softened. "You're as kind as you are clever, Cistine. I'll speak to Rion and Eboni. We'll ensure your journey is kept secret. I'm sure they'll be thrilled you want to make use of their second home."

When he'd gone, taking the ghostlamp with him, Cistine couldn't sleep. The wind stirred the wonderful smells of the garden through the seam of the balcony doors: cucumbers and tomatoes, fish oil fertilizer, basil and parsley. She wanted to bury herself among the zucchini fronds and the melon patches, to sink her fingers in the soft, rich Talheimic dirt, so she could imagine her roots were deep enough to keep her here. To protect everyone if it came to war.

But that was no more than a fantasy.

When Cistine finally fell asleep, nearly at dawn, it was straight back into the dream she'd told her father about. She was in a crib, but the barred walls might've also been a cage; people peered through it, their faces strange and distorted in the battle of candlelight and shadows that fought to consume their eyes. And to consume her.

One of these strange people reached out and placed a hand on her head, and her whole body began to glow.

It was Jad. She was certain of it.

When his hand traveled down to clamp her mouth, smothering her where she lay, Cistine woke with a harsh gasp, sweat-soaked and shaking. With every thud of her heart, flightiness crept deeper into her heaving chest.

Come, it whispered. *Come and find salvation.*

It was a familiar pull toward distant waves and deep ocean fathoms. Cistine had never truly listened to that tug before…never more than to look behind when they walked away from the coast each year. And yet tonight of all nights, the pull was strongest.

And in the dim quiet of her bedchamber, with her family's secrets lurking in the corners, Cistine began to plan.

CHAPTER THREE

THE CORSET'S BONING clenched Cistine's ribs like angry hands, her scarlet gown spilling around her in the exact shade of southern borderlord blood—a resemblance she couldn't shake no matter how hard she tried. She could hardly breathe as she sat on one of the fine chairs at the back of the ballroom—still too much like a throne for her taste—with her mother and father on either side of her, watching commoners and distant relations stream in under the glass dome.

There was such a sharp contrast between their faces: the commoners grinning brightly at the festivities, remarking on the paper lanterns, silk garlands, and the violins and pianofortes that saturated the air with tingling notes; and the nobles, Lord Dorminger, Lord Trevar, and Uncle Filip among them, all looking haggard and weary, as burdened by the conversation in the throne room the previous night as Cistine was. It didn't appear they'd slept any better than her, either.

But Cistine couldn't let them see how she shared their anxiety or their secrets. She forced an exhausted smile for the people who came to bow and curtsy before her, to wish her a joyous twentieth year and to compliment her dress. A few of her aunts and uncles paused to speak with the King and Queen, and every syllable rang of false cheer. Their happiness was as much a front as this ball itself while they played at joy for her sake.

Cistine wished every moment of showmanship from her parents didn't twist the knife of betrayal a bit deeper into her ribs, knowing what they kept from her. And that it didn't make her own lie about traveling to the Bartos estate feel easier.

She was not enduring this for gifts or fine food or potential suitors. She was here because her father needed a front for his war council. Tomorrow, she would leave because her kingdom needed her to do that, too.

The stitch in her chest loosened some at the thought of traveling north. But only some.

When the ballroom had reached capacity, the minstrels changed tune, and Cyril swept Solene off to dance. Cistine politely declined the same offer from a cousin and rushed to the tea table instead, where small pots on hot rocks wafted the perfume of lavender, citrus, and sage on the warm air. Cistine poured herself a cup with shaking hands and sipped it slowly to steel her nerves.

"You're going to have to dance with someone eventually, you know." A quiet, familiar voice came from behind her.

Cistine shut her eyes and drew in a deep, herb-scented breath. "I can't pretend all evening, Ashe. Look at my family's faces! This is *horrible.*"

Ashe gripped Cistine by the elbow and dragged her behind a gossamer curtain at the ballroom's edge. In its shadow, Cistine faced her Warden, somber-faced and looking less enthused about this ball even than Cistine. "I know how difficult this is for you. But for Talheim's sake, you need to keep up the ruse. We can't afford the panic if word spreads."

"All the more reason to leave for Valgard as soon as possible," Cistine argued. "Tonight, even! I've already found a captain who'll sail us there."

Ashe dragged a hand down her face. "You're really going through with this. Cistine, I told you, Talheim isn't welcome inside Valgard's borders. It may not have been written into the truce, but it was implied."

"If it's only implied, how can they hold me to it?" Cistine sipped her tea and let its fine floral notes sooth her nerves. "Ashe, I know it frightens you to go back there. But my father thought it was important to try. So even if he can't, *I* have to."

Ashe grumbled. "And this captain. You trust him?"

"He comes highly recommended."

In truth, the man she'd contacted was a seafaring merch to the outlying islands. Little better than a pirate, some said, but a little better was all Cistine needed. That would ensure their safety for enough golden zaltos; and a well-paid merch would keep her movements secret until she returned.

Returned, she prayed, with an army of northern warriors behind her.

Ashe's sigh drew Cistine from her thoughts. "I'm still of half a mind to drag you to your father and make you confess this insane scheme to him."

"You wouldn't dare. You answer to *me*."

"I answer to the royal family, and I'm not certain what I'll tell them if their daughter is kidnapped by barbarians."

"I won't be. My father never would've suggested an alliance if things were that terrible."

"Maybe." Ashe's expression remained guarded with skepticism "But since we both know you'll go whether I'm happy to join you or not, I'll settle for making it to the docks tomorrow without being caught, reamed, and thrown from the Cadre. I've survived plenty of things in my lifetime, Cistine, but I don't want to see the look on Lord Rion's face if he hears of this. You know how he feels about the North."

Cistine's irritation faded in the face of what Ashe stood to lose by accompanying her on such a brash mission. "I'm doing my best."

"I know you are." Ashe squeezed her shoulder. "It's just the one night, Cistine. You'll manage it. And then we'll be on our way."

"What in God's name are you two doing back here?"

Cistine jumped and almost sloshed her tea at the sound of Julian's voice. Immaculately dressed in dark trousers and a white linen shirt and vest to offset the deep tan of his skin and his glittering eyes, Julian positively glowed in the ghostlight.

His suspicious gaze swung between them when neither woman answered him. "You can't hoard her all night, Ashe."

"I'd like to see you try to stop me." Ashe plucked the teacup from

Cistine's hands and nudged her from behind the curtain. "As it happens, I was just telling Cistine she needed to find a suitable dance partner. And here you are."

Cistine could have hit her Warden for that remark. Thankfully, Julian seemed oblivious, offering up a gallant arm, and Cistine took it with a storm of nerves knocking into the sides of her stomach.

"Enjoying the party?" Julian asked as he guided her to the center of the ballroom where their parents danced.

"Not really," Cistine admitted. "How can I after last night?"

"True." Julian's casual tone dropped away, a mirror to Cistine's own weariness. "My father's behaving as if nothing's wrong. Meanwhile my mother is staring into corners and trying not to cry. They're treating me like a child, like I can't stomach a notion of war."

"Well, you are a tender boy of twenty-two."

Julian snorted as he took her hand and laid his own on her waist. "And you look far older than twenty in that dress."

The flush spread down Cistine's neck. To hide it, she sought her parents again among the crowd: spinning and stepping together, their faces broken with smiles she almost would have believed if not for the things she'd learned the night before.

Julian followed her gaze, then tugged her into the steps of the same dance. "Do you think they trust us?"

"I'd like to believe that, but I just don't know," Cistine admitted. "All I'm certain of is that they'll always want to protect us from the worst. From fear. From the same sort of war they faced when they were our age."

"It's not as if we're going to charge headfirst toward danger, swords raised," Julian grumbled.

Cistine had no answer. That was precisely what she was going to do.

And then it struck her, all at once as they made two turns around the dance floor, that she was dancing with Julian Bartos of all people. In her best dress. On her birthday.

Nerves crashed over her and sweat gathered at her hairline. Heart thundering, Cistine cast about desperately for something to say. "How—

how are you enjoying your Warden's training?"

Julian shrugged. "It's fair. Only two of us joined up in Practica, so there's more focus. More time to hone our specific talents."

"That must be nice."

"Most days. But tonight, I'm starting to wish I'd never left Astoria when my parents did."

Dry-mouthed, Cistine felt her knees grow weak. The way he was *looking* at her—

When had they stopped dancing? *Why* had they stopped?

"You're coming of age today. Our parents are trying to stop a war. Everything's going to change, you know?" Julian's dark eyes held her captivated, speechless. "Even us."

And Cistine did not know if the thrill of nerves in her belly came from the look in his eyes, or the thought of her own impending journey.

Julian spun her suddenly away from the other dancers, back toward the refreshments table, and past it. A pair of Wardens drew open the door of the ballroom's balcony, and then they were outside, skin kissed by the cool summer evening. Alone.

"I know what you and Ashe were whispering behind that curtain." The words burst from Julian like he couldn't contain them anymore. "Sailing north to Valgard? After everything Ashe said last night?"

Cistine slipped her hand from his, pulse racing in the side of her neck. Unlike Ashe, Julian had no sworn fealty to her, no reason at all not to tell her father and mother what she was planning. "I know your father says their people are wickeder than Jad. But *my* father thought there was hope in appealing to them, so someone should try."

"And that someone is *you*. The only daughter of the Novacek family, sole heir to the crown."

Cistine's belly writhed at those titles. "Julian, I'm begging you. Don't breathe a word of this to anyone."

"I won't have the chance to." Julian's eyes glinted in the moonlight. "I'm coming with you."

It was impossible to know what to blame her nerves on now. "That's—

you don't have to—"

"Well, my presence here would be difficult to explain to our parents after tonight, seeing as I'm supposed to be your escort to the coastal estate," Julian pointed out. "So I have to make myself scarce. Either I go with you as promised, or else I'm making the journey north alone. Safety in numbers. Isn't that what the Cadre always says?"

"You haven't made the Cadre yet."

"And I may never get the chance to if Jad rides roughshod over this kingdom." Julian wandered to the balcony railing and braced his hands on it, gazing out over the city. "I hear he doesn't have a Cadre of his own. He has people he calls Enforcers, and their purpose isn't to protect, it's to terrorize. If half the stories of what they do to women and children are true, I'll stake my life on keeping the Cadre around. What do you say, Princess?"

Cistine joined him, her voice lodged behind the hard lump in her throat as she gazed across the city's slumbering turrets and shops. She wasn't certain she deserved his loyalty—or his silence. Dragging Ashe with her to the dangerous north was one thing. But Julian...

When she didn't speak, he swiveled his head toward her. "That's my father who's riding south tonight. My father, who's told me stories of the horrors he saw in Khorraris ever since I was old enough to dream about combat. I'm not letting him go without a fight."

And that was something they had in common, which sent Cistine's heart fluttering wildly against her ribs again. "In that case, we'll be glad to have you along."

Julian blew out a long breath. "So, they think we'll be at the coast together. How long does that buy us?"

"Months, if we're lucky."

Julian cast her a smile in the gloom. "We'll be lucky, Princess."

And despite her racing heart and singing nerves, Cistine believed him.

CHAPTER FOUR

THE AGERIOS SEA was a nodding head limned with gold laurels, the shape of its crown dashed apart and rising again in the form of rolling waves Cistine couldn't drink in deep enough.

She ignored Ashe shouting her name as she dashed along the deck, violet skirts flapping against her ankles. She grabbed the rigging and swung up onto the railing, leaning out to catch the waves' violent spray between her fingers as they crested a swell. The sails snapped open with the southerly breeze, bringing the warmth of summer chasing down the crossed straps on the back of Cistine's dress.

She dropped into a crouch on her heels, glancing back at the crew of *The Caffeny*. The merch vessel surged over every wave under the steady command of Captain Burbridge, white-haired and craggy-faced, who manned the helm with the sternness of someone used to facing much rougher seas.

And Cistine was glad they weren't rough, so she could truly take them in.

The small slice of harbor where they'd picnicked during her childhood was nothing compared to the yawning blue expanse around the ship. Several days from Talheim's coast, Cistine could almost believe they would never reach land; that the world beyond her kingdom was nothing but rolling waves, porpoises and whales crashing through the surf, and slender, quicksilver fish streaking along the ship's flanks.

"Cistine!" A hand snared her collar, almost jerking her from the railing. Cistine laughed as she slid back onto the deck, turning to face Ashe's glare. "Are you twenty, or ten? I told you, keep your feet on the deck!"

"What's the trouble, as long as I don't fall in? If I didn't know any better, I'd almost think you feared the sea." Cistine looped arms with Ashe and steered her away from the railing.

"I just don't want to jump overboard and fish you out."

Cistine checked Ashe's hip. "If you're so unhappy, you could ask the captain to ferry you out to the Bartos estate. I hear it's quite pleasant and relaxing there. Julian has been telling me all about it since we set sail."

"Tempting as that sounds, who would protect you while I was busy enjoying myself?" Ashe freed her arm only to throw it over Cistine's shoulders. "Lord Rion's idiot son?"

Cistine followed Ashe's subtle nod, and her mouth dried up.

Julian, shirtless and armed, faced off against a sailor in a friendly duel on the ship's forecastle. Their blades clashed toward each other's ribs and peeled back again, always just short of burying into the skin. Julian's dark hair was knotted back from his face, loose threads framing his strong, stubbled jaw. He laughed carelessly as he doubled back from the sailor's lashes, whirled around the man, and slapped his haunch with the flat of the blade.

Cistine's stomach panged as she watched them strike and twist. It was like the dances from her birthday celebration, but deadlier. So much concentration was required to dart through each other's patterns without doing harm. She remembered—and reviled—the long-ago days when her father had forced her to train in those steps.

A whistle ended the fight as Captain Burbridge surrendered the wheel to his First Mate and descended to join them. The sailor halted his assault on Julian, and they all turned to face the Captain as he stepped up on a barrel beside the mainmast. "Listen up, you lot! We'll sail abreast of Valgard's northern shores in half a day. Ready the skiff for our passengers!"

While the sailors scurried to obey, Julian joined Cistine and Ashe, mopping the back of his neck and perching his elbow on Cistine's shoulder. A casual gesture on his part, but the heat of his muscles practically burned where they touched her skin. "Can't you sail us straight into port?"

"Too much paperwork involved to dock at Veran's quay." Captain Burbridge watched his crew unlash the skiff and swing it over *The Caffeny's* side. "Any particular notion why you chose this wretched spit of land to visit?"

"Professional curiosity." Cistine had told him they were prospectors for a family of wealthy merches. "You of all people should know how much an unmined treasure trove is worth, Captain."

"Aye, but I also know the dangers of one." His eyes cut to her. "Best tread carefully on these shores. This kingdom hasn't always been friendly toward Talheim. Some would say it still isn't."

The captain swaggered back to the helm, whistling a shanty under his breath. Scoffing, Julian scooped his shirt from the railing and tugged it back on. "He's an optimist."

Cistine turned to him, swallowing with relief as the muscled contours of his chest disappeared under the loose folds of his shirt. "Are you hurt?"

"I'm all right, Princess. Nothing a few swigs of grog won't cure."

"Inspirational, your fortitude," Ashe deadpanned.

Julian freed and tousled his hair as they descended the hatch to their quarters belowdecks. "So, this ought to be fairly straightforward, I imagine: travel to the port city, request to see the king—"

"Chancellor," Ashe said. "Remember, they don't have kings and queens here."

"They have Courts and tribunals." Cistine recited the things Ashe had told her from her own vague memories of the North. "Valgard is ruled by five separate Courts, each sitting in session under a different Chancellor."

Julian snorted. "A kingdom with no king."

"Well, we call them one of the Three Kingdoms because they did have monarchs, long ago," Cistine said. "Someone overthrew the last king, and the Courts rose up in his place."

"That must get complicated." Julian flopped onto his cot in their small chamber. "What's to stop one Chancellor from coming to power and undoing everything the last one legislated?"

"I don't know," Cistine admitted. "I'm sure they have laws in place to protect other laws."

"And how do they choose which Chancellor sits when?"

Ashe shrugged. "No one ever told me that."

"The people in the port city should know," Cistine said. "They'll point us in the proper direction."

Julian nodded. "So, we meet this Chancellor, treat with him for aid against Mahasar…"

Ashe kicked the trunk under her own cot, which housed their belongings: Talheimic steel, books from the royal library, and a few other odds and ends Cistine had brought to trade with if the Chancellor needed some plying. "And then it's back to Talheim."

"We'll walk straight past the forts," Cistine said, "with the Valgardan army in tow."

"Simple enough," Julian said. "I take it you ladies will want to sample the finer things Valgard has to offer if we have time."

Cistine grinned. "My wardrobe could use some plumping out."

"And my arsenal," Ashe said. "I wasn't able to bring any Valgardan steel with me when I left last time, but their knives are legendary. Some are rumored to cut through any material, no matter how strong. I wouldn't mind having a few like that in my bandolier when we return home."

Cistine mimed a yawn, rolling her eyes at a smirking Julian. He leaned back on his elbows, propping his head against the wall. "While you're doing that, I'll concern myself with the taverns."

Cistine's excitement faded. The taverns—and the wenches that populated them, no doubt. Valgardan barmaids were legendary, according to Ashe: talented bards, unparalleled drinkers, and irresistible bedfellows.

She fell back against the door, scowling. "*If* we have time for any of this. We are here to prevent a war, you know."

Ashe cut her a sharp look, but Julian remained oblivious, picking up a clay cup from the bedside and tossing it to himself.

"We'll be rowing half the night," Ashe said, "so I'm going to sleep while I can. Cistine?"

"I'd rather see as much of the sea as possible before we move inland again." Cistine glanced at Julian, hoping he would offer to accompany her. But he went on tossing that cup, eyes fixed on the ceiling.

The sight of the sea wasn't enough to lift Cistine's spirits this time. She leaned her folded arms on the railing, plucking a splinter loose from the wood and gazing across the water.

She wasn't here for Julian. She wasn't here *because* of him. But she also hadn't entertained the thought of watching him wine and wench through the port city, either. Particularly after how he'd behaved at her birthday celebration.

She'd thought—she'd *hoped*—

A calloused hand scraped the railing, approaching her. Cistine watched the dying daylight paint its rosy fingerprints down Captain Burbridge's face as he joined her, his posture mirroring hers.

"Beautiful, isn't it?" he murmured. "The sea."

"I've always thought so." Cistine glanced up at his burly, bearded face. "Why did you begin to sail in the first place, Captain? Did you feel a call to the sea?"

"Always," Burbridge said. "I love these waters. Love this ship. They'll sink me off the port bow when all's done."

Cistine smiled. "Well, I feel the call, too. I've always been drawn to the water."

"Or places beyond it." Burbridge watched her with steely eyes missing little. "I've seen you these past few days. Always staring off the bow. Always north."

Cistine frowned. She hadn't realized she was looking in any particular direction when she let her mind wander from the waves.

"A calling's a powerful thing, lass." Burbridge hefted himself away from the railing and started down the deck. "Just be sure you don't lose yourself in it. The first thing they teach you when you take the helm is to never trust the horizon. It can swallow a man whole."

"Captain?" The crash of a wave against *The Caffeny's* hull nearly drowned Cistine's voice, but Burbridge's heavy steps came to a halt nonetheless. "That call I've felt. To the sea, or...north, like you said. It's growing stronger the closer we sail to Valgard."

It was the first time she'd spoken it. The first time she'd acknowledged aloud how, ever since the night of the war council and particularly after they'd cast off from Astoria's docks, that voice had nagged her more and more to come and see just what the horizon offered.

"Is that common?" Cistine added when the Captain didn't speak.

He shrugged. "All depends."

"On who you ask?"

Burbridge swiveled back to her, his eyes like stormy seas cradling secrets in their depths. "On who you *are*."

CHAPTER
FIVE

THE SPINES OF the coastal city of Veran, rising from the late-night fog that hugged the shoreline from horizon to horizon, served as Cistine's first glimpse of Valgard. Crouched in the skiff's belly, she watched the slim spires of quartz and sandstone buildings weave through the dense mist, pulling down the foggy veil to watch the three travelers row into the harbor.

As they neared the coast, a bright, refracted glow cut through the haze. Ashe tensed, and Cistine put a hand on her Warden's knee. "I think it's a light tower—you know, where they prop enormous mirrors up on standees and light fires in front of them. The glare can cut the mist for miles."

"It doesn't seem to be doing its task very well tonight," Julian grunted, fighting the oars as they sliced through the water.

Cistine smiled. "Then we're still too far away."

The mist formed a wide barrier along the outer shoals, and as they rowed deeper into the harbor, they passed through it. The light strengthened, and Cistine caught her breath at the first unhindered sight of the Northern Kingdom.

The rocky black coasts were like nothing she'd ever seen before. The closest might've been the foothills of the Calalun Peaks outside Astoria, where she'd spent some of her earlier summers rock-climbing with her cousins. But the Calaluns were gentle green sweeps broken up by the occasional wind-battered dark stone face. Here, the cliffs were perilously slick and mostly unburdened by greenery except near a waterfall that cascaded from the highest peak, falling down shelf after shelf into the Agerios Sea.

The city itself was cordoned by a winding wall of outer turrets and walkways that faced the sea. Greenery thatched its heart, its outer edge, and even some of its rooftops. Cistine could see the pale spray of smaller falls, perhaps even manmade, surging inside the wall. The buildings themselves—capped with glittering silver domes and spires, or flat and brown like the pages of an old book—grew up from one another's spines, all the way to the height of the mountain behind them.

Cistine surged to her feet, skirts dampened by the splashing oars as she moved to the skiff's single mast. She clutched it in one hand, draping her body out above the dark water as they closed the distance toward the smallest quay along the harbor. "Welcome to Veran."

Julian settled the oars in their locks, got to his feet, shucked off his shirt, and dove into the water, splashing Cistine and leaving her sputtering in his wake.

"At least we don't have to watch him strut around without his shirt on," Ashe laughed.

"Don't say that!" Cistine slapped her arm as Julian bobbed above the surface and towed the skiff toward the quay by its long rope.

"So. Veran," Ashe said while Julian hauled himself onto the dock and lashed their skiff to a bollard. "According to Burbridge, it's the largest coastal city in Valgard. During the war, Rion's scouting turned up a man called the Guide who lives here. Assuming he's still alive, he should be able to point us where to go."

They gathered their belongings, Ashe toting the enormous chest, and mounted the slick stone steps to the first turret along the wall. There were indeed more waterfalls above, tumbling over a thirty-foot drop of stones and lichen and ending in a long canal that followed the wall's curve. Enormous gondolas sliced through the water on a journey around what Cistine assumed was the entire body of Veran, docking and disembarking from the canal's sides.

"Well." Julian fanned a hand back through the wet tips of his dark hair. "This isn't what I expected."

Cistine darted to a lonely gondolier standing at the dock's end. "How much for a gondola ride?"

"For lovely lasses? Free." The gondolier looked her over with a charming smile that left her flushing. "Besides, you don't quite look as if you're rolling in mynts."

Valgardan currency, Ashe mouthed to Cistine behind the gondolier's back.

He helped them into the gondola, one after the other, chuckling when Julian shook off his hand. Cistine gripped the long boat's sides as they pushed off from the dock and cut through the calm water, the city growing up in height to their left and the shore dropping steeply away from under the wall to their right, sliding straight into the sea. The gondolier used his long pole to guide them expertly away from both walls in the wide channel, and for a time the brush of sleek wood in the water was the only sound disturbing the night.

"Tell us about the city," Ashe said.

"There's three districts to the market: the House of Steel, the House of Aliment, and the House of Wonders," the gondolier said. "You'll want to take that chest to the House of Steel if it's weapons you're looking to trade for."

"Aliment," Julian echoed. "You mean ailment?"

Cistine giggled. "No, it's another word for food."

His eyes brightened as he rubbed his hands together. "Taverns."

Cistine pursed her lips and looked up toward the city itself. "And where would we find the Guide?"

The gondolier crouched on one knee beside her, looping his arm around the pole shaft and pointing up toward the city. "You see that enormous house up there, with the violet windows? That's the Guide's home, and you'll want to see him sooner than later. People who stay in the city too long without reporting their dealings make the Guide very nervous."

Ashe tapped her fingers on the chest. "We'll go first thing tomorrow, after we've had a good night's sleep."

"Some taverns might have accommodations above them," Julian said.

Ashe scoffed. "I'm not letting Cistine sleep above a bawdy hovel of brawling drunkards."

"I don't mind," Cistine murmured.

"You can protect her, can't you, Ashe?" Julian drawled. "I don't see what the concern is."

"The concern is that I'm going to be at the House of Steel for hours yet," Ashe argued. "And who's going to look after her until then? You?"

Cistine gripped the gondola's rim more tightly. *Say yes, please, say you will.*

Though she didn't know what she would do with Julian's undivided attention for hours. She'd been a hive of nerves after just a few minutes at her birthday ball.

Julian flopped against the gondola's curve, scowling. "Fine. Have it your way."

They docked below the House of Wonders in an arched recess of stilts crowded with thick shadows. The gondolier pointed them up a flight of steps to their right. "Take the street at the top to the left. That goes on for half a mile, and then you're in the House of Steel."

As Ashe and Julian lugged the chest from the gondola, Cistine pulled out the emerald pin that tamed her hair, letting the hickory waves fall in a gentle wash around her shoulders. She pressed the pin into the man's hand. "For your troubles. No one should work for free."

His brows arched as he stared at the glamorous hairpiece. "Well, stars above! Thank you, lass."

Cistine smiled, gathered her skirts, and hurried after her friends up the flight of steps.

Hemmed in by colorful awnings that braided into a fabric roof, the House of Wonders smelled deeply of foreign spice and perfume. The vending stalls were still open despite the hour, lit by glass pomegranate lanterns and ghostlamps, their familiar sheen a comforting balm in such a strange place. The heat of many bodies pressed against Cistine from every side, and she kept close to Ashe's heels as they passed stalls of trinkets and baubles, games and toys. Cistine stifled a moan of delight when she noticed a boutique selling hand-made gowns of pure silk and taffeta.

"Tomorrow," she whispered to herself. "Tomorrow, you can shop all you want."

Ashe slowed after they'd gone nearly half a mile, frowning at the face of an inn that jutted into the street. It was absolutely crowded with windows. Either there were several to each room, or the accommodations were only as wide across as a man's armspan.

Julian snorted. "*This* is your choice?"

"At least it's quiet here." Ashe shouldered open the door.

The inn was indeed quiet, and cozy. Twin hearths roared on one wall of a parlor dotted with sofas and plush armchairs. A table of refreshments under the front windows wafted the smell of crushed cherries and buttery pastry through the room.

Ashe approached the admission counter. "One room with two cots, please," she said. "We'll pay when we leave, since we don't know how long we'll be staying."

The man behind the counter, balding and bored-faced with a book open before him, gestured to a sign on his left. "Please take note."

Ashe read the sign aloud: "All patrons failing to pay will be hunted down by...what in God's name is a Viperwolf?"

"Something you'd rather not cross with."

The atmosphere grew chilly as Ashe stared at the man. Cistine winced at the tension, stepping up to her Warden's side and leaning her folded arms on the counter. "What are you reading?"

The man flashed the book's cover without peeling his eyes from it.

"Treatises on Romantic Discourse," Cistine mused. "I've never read it, but I think love isn't something you can learn to do from reading a book."

The man licked his thumb and turned the page. "Is that so."

"A treatise can tell you how to seduce women, but it can't tell you a girl's favorite flower. It can't tell you how she loves the sound of rain on the windows, or how her favorite tea to sip while she reads by the fire is an herbal orange blossom blend. Or how badly she wants you just to listen to her talk about *her* favorite books from time to time."

Julian shifted his feet behind her. Flushing, Cistine plowed on, "And it certainly won't tell you that the only way to truly win her heart is by showing her that you're concerned with more than her body…that you desire her mind and soul as well."

Slowly, the man raised his attention from the book. He studied Cistine for a long moment before his eyes flicked to Ashe. "Third level, second door on the right. If you require anything your room doesn't accommodate, ask for Beaugard. I'll do my best to assist you."

"Thank you, Beaugard," Cistine smiled. "And best of luck with your romance."

He grunted and turned back to the book, but Cistine could see he was no longer reading. His brow pinched in a thoughtful frown as Ashe led them up the stairs.

They found the room perfectly accommodating, with its own bathing chamber, a pair of respectably-large beds, and three windows looking out into the street. Julian claimed the bed beneath the windows, and Ashe and Cistine took the one close to the wall. Ashe divested the trunk of weapons, leaving behind Cistine's books, a few changes of clothes, and a small purse of heirlooms.

"I'll sell what we can spare. The rest we'll carry with us to the Chancellor." Ashe slipped from her sheath, the sword that was her most prized possession, and nudged it under the bed. "Don't touch my steel while I'm gone."

"We won't, Ashe," Cistine said. "Be safe."

Ashe kissed the top of her head, shot a curt nod to Julian, and let herself out.

The silence swelled. Cistine drew her legs onto the bed, tucking her skirt over her knees. Julian flopped onto his back, arms folded behind his head. With one leg cocked at the knee, he stared up at the ceiling's dark wooden beams. "I should touch her sword."

Cistine groaned. "She'll tear you to pieces. She's so on edge as it is."

"I know. It must be difficult for her to be back here after the war."

"It's hard to believe there was one, isn't it?" Cistine leaned back against the wall and peered through the window. The glass was frosted with summer steam and whorled with the colors of the lanterns outside. "Veran is so peaceful."

"It's like our parents always told us: peace can shatter as fast as glass."

"And it's even harder to put back together."

Julian rolled onto his side, propping his head on his hand. "That was quite a thing you said to the innkeeper about how to win a woman's heart. Something you've learned from your dozens of suitors?"

"I've only had a handful of suitors. Few lasted longer than a month."

"Your father's wrath?"

"Mine, actually. I don't want to be valued for the crown on my head or the curves under my dress. If a man can't be bothered to spend time learning to know me, I won't waste time being courted by him."

Julian raised a brow. "I'll have to remember that."

They didn't speak again. It wasn't long before Julian drifted into a snoring slumber. As quietly as possible, Cistine padded to the window and cleared the fog with the side of her fist. Despite the color that swam around the inn, her gaze traveled irresistibly toward the dark shoulders of the mountains.

Across their backs, they carried a sky full of stars. There were constellations visible here Cistine had never seen before.

They were so far from home. So far from the weight and responsibility of royalty.

Come. A quiet tug, a whisper. That call moving through her chest. *Come closer.*

Maybe Captain Burbridge had been right—the call wasn't to the sea, after all. She couldn't tell from this vantage point, but she wondered if right now, she was facing north.

A cool stream of unease trickled down the dip of Cistine's spine.

⌒⌒∾

The next day did not go how Cistine planned.

She woke to the blinding rasp of rain battering the windows. A peek outside showed that most market vendors were closed with signs hung up in their windows urging patrons to return tomorrow; despite the empty streets, Julian's bed was made up and empty, cold to the brush of her fingertips, as though he'd left as early as possible.

When Cistine left Ashe snoring and hurried downstairs with a book under her arm to read before the fire, she found a note on the refreshment table, addressed to her in Julian's familiar scrawl: *Gone to find more food. I'll return soon.*

And beside it, still steaming, was a mug of herbal orange blossom tea.

CHAPTER SIX

THE ONLY WAY to reach the Guide's home was by climbing numerous flights of stairs through Veran's residential district. Cistine's thighs and ankles screamed at the torture by the time they arrived at the enormous slab of black granite that bore the weight of the Guide's house, far above the rest of the city.

"Well," she gasped, "at least the Guide knows anyone he speaks to is determined to travel."

Ashe and Julian swapped smiles. Neither of them was half as winded as her, and their loose clothes, while damp, were better suited for this kind of exertion. Cistine's mauve dress was the lightest piece of clothing she'd packed, and it still weighed against her like a ship's anchor, rain-soaked and clinging to her ribs.

"At least the struggle is behind us." Julian squeezed her shoulder. "The downhill trudge will be easier."

Cistine forced a panting smile at his touch. She thought of nothing but orange blossom tea when she looked at him; and when she caught his eyes lingering on her, and he smiled gently, almost shyly, before he turned back to face the house, she wondered if he was thinking of it, too.

Their admittance was a quick affair. Once a pair of guards in gold-threaded navy attire relieved them of their weapons—a dagger each from

Ashe and Julian—the enormous birch doors swung inward by some silent command.

The entry parlor was impressive. Flanked with tinted windows, its white tiles, azure fountains, and potted ferns all paled under the weaving of a thousand threads strung from wall to wall. It was a gentle canopy forged of hundreds of braids: vermillion, coral, marigold and marmalade, lapis lazuli and heather, jade and buttermilk.

"Someone has far too much time on their hands," Julian muttered as the guards ushered them to a staircase at the room's end.

Cistine trailed her fingertip along a braid of cornflower blue and ivy green, and Ashe smiled. "That green matches your eyes. Your mother's, too."

Cistine grinned. "I noticed."

They rose above the canopy, and Cistine looked back on it as the guards unlocked the door at the top of the stairs. From here, she realized the threads wove into a single tapestry: four women, arms outstretched, with a shower of stars above them. Beside them was a man in black attire, bleeding into a figure armed with a bow and sword, bleeding into a formless shadow, and then into a king crowned with a diadem of five stars.

The door creaked open to reveal the Guide's spacious chamber. Its turquoise couches married flawlessly with the gold accents on the walls, the candles in the teardrop chandeliers spraying dapples on a lush fawn rug spanning most of the room. There were no writing tables or bookcases, and only one wall was decorated, if it could be called that, with a floor-to-ceiling map. Against its drab gray background, there were glints of silver snow and citrus sand, green meadows and mulberry mountains, and a long, dark road from the mountains to the distant cities, marked *The Vingete Vey*. Creatures dotted the map's edges in smears of black. Most were animals, but some had the appearance of unnaturally tall, skull-masked men.

Across from the strange map, stationed by a set of bay windows overlooking the harbor, was the Guide himself. He perched on a stool next to an enormous vertical loom, stretched with a pale brown warp thread, and worked in the weft: intertwined strands of green, gray, and blue. The colors reminded Cistine of Talheim's meadows on a cloudy summer day, when the dirt was thirsty and the grass stroked flat by a sultry wind.

The Guide was as surprising as his craft. Cistine had expected a cunning man around her father's age making his home among reams of paper, not this ancient, wizened figure with veins as blue as the weaving skeins in the basket next to him. He didn't look up even when the guards shut the door with a snap.

"Foreign visitors, I see." He said, his voice dry as ancient twine. "What is your business?"

This was the moment Cistine had both anticipated and dreaded, and only she could carry it out. So she cleared her throat and stepped forward, sketching a low curtsy. "My name is Princess Cistine Novacek of Talheim. I've come to appeal to whichever Chancellor currently sits in power in Valgard."

The Guide's hands stilled, and Ashe and Julian shifted their feet.

"A princess. We've never had one visit our shores before." The Guide resumed weaving the weft into the threads. "What have you come to appeal for?"

"That's a matter between us and your Chancellor," Cistine said. "I'm sorry, but I can't discuss it with anyone else. I can only promise we come in friendship, and that we won't ask for much."

"Seeking friendship between the Northern and Middle Kingdoms, you have no notion of how much you truly ask for."

Julian cleared his throat. "The Chancellor will want to hear what we've come to say."

"Only he can decide that." The Guide wove the blue and green in and out of the gray, a hypnotic dance of knobby fingers. "Skyygan Court currently sits in session, but it is Kanslar Court you'll want to haggle with. They come to power in just over a month."

Cistine winced. She hadn't anticipated having to wait for the Courts to change session before they could negotiate, but she also trusted the Guide knew which Chancellor was most likely to heed their plight. "Thank you for your insight."

"And what are we going to do until then?" Julian demanded. "We can't afford a month's boarding at the inn."

Cistine glanced at Ashe. "We could work for more coin?"

"The courthouse accommodates all its guests at no cost," the Guide said. "There is a caravan departing soon for the capital, Stornhaz. You will find shelter there until the time comes for you to present your case to the Chancellor of Kanslar Court."

All these places and people and Court names blew through Cistine, and she clutched them desperately, eager to commit them to memory. "When does the caravan depart?"

"Go to the city's northern gate at dawn, six days from now. It will be waiting for you there."

Cistine curtsied again, backed up to stand between her friends, and froze as the Guide added, "And do not let anyone disarm you again."

A tense stillness emanated from Ashe and Julian. Cistine's chest hitched in response, and she slid another step back.

"Why do you say that?" Ashe asked.

"Far worse things than robbers haunt the road between cities," the Guide murmured. "These days, it isn't wise to travel unarmed."

CHAPTER SEVEN

DESPITE THE GUIDE'S warning and the pressure of passing time, Cistine found it almost easy to enjoy herself during the six days they needed to squander in Veran.

She spent the first four reading at the inn while rain hurled itself against the windows in droves. Ensconced in a blanket, faithful mug of tea in hand and her mind in her books, she only surfaced when Ashe returned from haggling, flashing new steel on her hips, and when Julian came back from the tavern, sloppy, tipsy, and smiling as he waved to her and stumbled upstairs to sleep. And when the innkeeper shuffled off to keep the company of a lovely redheaded maid. Cistine tried not to eavesdrop or notice the girl's blush whenever her hand brushed Beaugard's, but as Talheim's most famous court gossip, it was difficult not to.

On the fifth day, the rain finally ebbed. Cistine woke to sunlight trailing its palm along the curve of her cheek, and she bounded to the window and yanked the drapes wide to the sight of open doors and vendor stalls with their veils turned up. Shoppers already poured through the House of Wonders.

Today, Cistine found Ashe and Julian together, eating pastries and chatting before the blazing hearths in the parlor. She skidded into the room, looped her arms around Ashe's neck from behind, and squeezed her until she choked. "I take it we're going shopping today, Ashe?"

"You have ten mynts to squander, Cistine, and that's *all*," Ashe said as Cistine picked up a raspberry pastry and sank onto the sofa between them. Julian shifted to make room, and Cistine pretended she didn't notice how close he really was, or how he draped his arm along the sofa's backing beside her shoulder.

"Ten mynts. Perfect," she said. "I can make do with that."

Ashe raised a brow. "I mean it, Cistine. Not a coin more."

Cistine bobbed her head furiously as she polished off the tart in three rapid bites. Ashe rose and stretched, shifting the sword strapped across her shoulderblades. Cistine hadn't seen her without it since their visit to the Guide's house.

"I'll be outside when you're ready." Ashe swaggered out, leaving Julian and Cistine alone for the first time in days.

Julian yawned, a vision of unruffled laziness as he stood and offered his hand to Cistine. "I'm off to the taverns again. I don't know much about this Stornhaz, but I doubt it wets its flanks with ale like these gambling houses do."

"Of course," Cistine sighed, letting him help her up.

She blinked in shock as his hand slid away, leaving three more silver mynts in her palm.

"You didn't think I was spending *all* my time just drinking, did you?" He winked. "Gambling turns a profit if you have friends like I did back in Practica."

"What sort of friends?"

"The kind who teach you to win." He kissed her knuckles. "Buy yourself something spectacular, Princess. I'll look forward to seeing it."

He pocketed his hands and strutted out, whistling.

That day passed in a blur of colorful silk, decadent food, sublime jewelry, and sore feet for Cistine. Ashe waited patiently while she donned gowns in every color imaginable. They laughed at hats that spilled over with piles of flowers, tendrils of lichen, and mourning veils the color of a moonless night. They flitted from bakeries to thread shops to book vendors. Cistine spent the most time there, thumbing through page after page of books she couldn't even read.

"Excuse me," she said to the vendor, "what language are these written in?"

"Old Valgardan," the woman said. "Hardly anyone can read them. We adopted the common tongue of the Three Kingdoms centuries ago. The only reason anyone ever buys these texts is for decoration."

Cistine smoothed her palm over a particularly beautiful cover: stitched with gold and wine runes, the pages hand-bound and feathered with time, if not with use. Then she spent her last mynt to take it from the woman's hands.

From there, they traveled to the House of Aliment, where Ashe bought mugs of foaming hot milk spiced with cinnamon and cloves. They wandered from cart to cart, and Cistine shuddered at the fare: braised snakes, bull tongue pate, and roasted rats with sea-pine chutney. "People really eat this?"

"Some eat worse," Ashe said. "When I was here last, our rations were scarce. We supplemented."

"With tongue pate?"

"With anything we could find: old meat dug from augmented ice. Whatever insects survived the snow. Birds we dropped with stones."

Cistine gagged. "No, thank you. I'll keep my pastries and braised meat."

Ashe smiled tensely and draped an arm around Cistine's shoulders. "I hope that's all you're ever forced to eat."

They reached the steps leading down to the House of Steel, and Ashe towed Cistine to a halt. Her mismatched eyes traveled to a vendor's booth nearby, strung with daggers in thigh holsters. "I think I could use another dagger, given what the Guide said."

Cistine groaned. "Ashe, please, no...sword dens are duller than the steel they sell. Can't we go back to the inn?"

"We've been everywhere *you* wanted to see. I'll just be a moment."

"It's never just a moment! You have to touch every dagger, test the balance of *every* blade, and then you lambast the seller with enough questions to make a mother cry. Please, Ashe, not now."

Ashe folded her arms. "Then when? We leave at dawn."

"I don't know! We'll get up early."

"As if! Prying you from bed at an early hour is a feat for the gods themselves."

"Ashe, I'm exhausted," Cistine said. "My feet ache. Can't you walk me to the inn and then come back?"

Ashe sighed. "I suppose I'll have to."

Cistine fought off a stab of guilt at the dejection in her Warden's face. She hadn't lied, after all. Her feet really did hurt.

Ashe didn't speak until they reached the inn, and then it was only to direct Cistine to pack the trunk in her absence. As Ashe checked her mynt purse and marched toward the door again, Cistine said, "Ashe, wait."

She halted, hand on the doorknob.

"Don't be angry, please," Cistine said to her Warden's stiff back. "I'm just tired. That's all."

"You're always tired when it's something someone else wants to do," Ashe said. "We're here for *you*, Cistine. Because you wanted this chance, and you needed friends to help you. But we're not your packhorses. You could do with thinking of what others want for a change."

Cistine frowned. "You think I don't care for what other people want?"

"I think you run from whatever inconveniences you even the slightest bit. And I don't entirely blame *you* for it, either. You've been spoiled—"

"Spoiled?" Cistine barked. "Just because my family loves me—"

Ashe scoffed. "Oh, Cistine, don't be naïve. Cyril doted on you from the moment you were born. He's given you *everything* exactly how you want it."

"He didn't give me the truth, did he?" The words stung as they clawed from her throat. "That's why we're here."

Ashe rubbed her feathery hair. "I'm not talking about recently. I'm talking about all the times before, and how that's taught you to find your way around uncomfortable things instead of through them. You wouldn't survive on your own in any place more dangerous than a teahouse, and that worries me."

Cistine's mouth dropped open. She and Ashe had argued plenty of times, but never so personally. These were accusations tipped with venom, spearing straight to her heart. "Just go look at your precious daggers, Ashe. Maybe their *gentleness* will wear off on you."

Ashe stormed from the room, but her angry words lingered. Cistine couldn't bat them away as she stared at the purchases on the bed, trying desperately to think of how happy they'd made her when she'd bought them: the book of ancient Valgardan stories; a fine jewel-crusted necklace with earrings to match; a formal dress, sleeveless and white, with rich burgundy accents along the bodice and neckline that dripped down the waist into sleek petals pooling along the hem; and a small hand-painted mug for her tea.

It was a fair cache for thirteen mynts, but Ashe's words soured her glee over them. After all, she wasn't here to shop.

Cistine packed the trunk carefully with her new treasures and took the rune-book to the foyer to study it, but she couldn't concentrate. The foreign words all blurred back into the shape of Ashe's accusatory face. Dusk rubbed against the windows when Cistine finally shut the book and stared outside. Blue and green ghostlamps winked at her through the glass.

"Ashe is wrong," she muttered. "I *can* survive places worse than a teahouse."

And she would prove it by finding Julian and enjoying his conciliatory company tonight.

Though it was a spontaneous choice, it made more and more sense as she stashed the book in the trunk, retrieved her embroidered cape, and dipped into their communal traveling purse for one more mynt. Thanks to Julian's gambling, they would still have enough to pay for their lodgings and the caravan.

Julian had described the taverns as an artery between the Aliment and Wonder Houses, but Cistine hadn't expected there to be quite so many on the cobblestone avenue. The street itself was unmistakable, both sides lined with low, broad establishments leaving their doors open, welcoming in the warm night and the drunkards who staggered from one drinking hole to the next.

Cistine paused at the mouth of the street where several helpful vendors had directed her, arguing with herself; she'd only ever visited one tavern in her life, with Ashe and some of her Cadre companions in tow. Cistine had sat on the counter and sipped cider while the Wardens joked and arm-wrestled in the corner. They'd all known Cistine was the princess, so no one had touched her, but these places lacked that sort of warmth. The light in their windows glowed a cold blue, and the patrons coming and going didn't have the look of respectable citizens.

Then again, there wouldn't be much to prove if they did.

Cistine shook her robe forward to hide her trembling hands, crossing the street to avoid a heap of bawdy drunks in the gutter singing an off-kilter tune. When one of them called out to her, she ignored him and skittered inside the first tavern.

On the other side of the tinted windows, this place reminded her much more of Astoria's taverns. Though the pelts and antler racks strung up on the walls certainly belonged to animals that had no place in Talheim—their horns covered in fine layers of velvet and their hair strangely-colored and coarse—the adamant counter and crudely-carved tables and chairs were soothingly familiar. So were the rowdy patrons, none of whom paid her any mind as she went to the counter.

The barmaid's brow creased as she watched Cistine slide into one of the only free seats. "What'll you have?"

"A...a mug of your finest ale." The words stumbled like a bad joke on Cistine's lips. The barmaid quirked a brow, but she accepted the mynt Cistine slid across the counter and hurried away to fill a stein.

Cistine twisted on the stool, surveying the room. Now she had to find Julian, which proved more difficult than she'd expected. Almost everyone in the tavern had the same look: ratty clothing under cloaks ale-stained and pigmented with dust from the dark cliffs around Veran. In fact, she was likely in the wrong tavern altogether. And there had been at least a dozen along this street.

Her mouth suddenly dry, Cistine snatched up the ale and took a gulp as soon as the barmaid set it before her—and coughed violently. The drink was far more brutal than even the most pungent tea. It left her nose burning.

A man several seats down chuckled at her discomfort. "First sip?"

"No, I've had...plenty of ale." In truth, Cistine never had a taste for it, but she didn't want to be laughed off the stool and out of the tavern.

The man slipped from his own stool and came to stand beside hers, plunking his ale down as he leaned one elbow on the counter, close enough for Cistine to smell him. His clothing reeked of strange herbs. "Matthias is the name. Yours?"

"That's none of your business." Cistine tried to insinuate her tone with the same cool aloofness Ashe had mastered long ago. "I'm here to meet someone."

Matthias glanced around the tavern. "Describe him to me. Perhaps I can point him out."

"Oh...thank you! Well, he's as tall as you, and his hair is dark, and his eyes—"

"Haven't seen him," Matthias interrupted. "But how about if we search the other taverns for him together?"

A warning chill drifted through Cistine's body. She swiveled to face the counter, clutching her stein in both hands. "That's all right. I'll wait for him here."

Matthias made an odd tapping motion on the counter next to his stein. "It wouldn't be any trouble at all. I know these taverns like the back of my hand."

The reek of herbs enclosed her from the back as another man sidled up to them. "I'm Roosha. Matthias is my friend. I think I saw the boy you're looking for at the next tavern."

"Go away." Cistine couldn't coax any volume to her voice. "Please."

"Don't worry, we just want to help you find your friend." Roosha's heavy hand descended on Cistine's shoulder, and she flinched out from under it. No one was moving to her defense, not even the barmaid, who was occupied down the counter.

Cistine's stomach plunged, and the ale surged up her throat, scalding her nose. When pushed away from the counter, Roosha's hand closed around the back of her neck, cinching tight as she twisted to free herself. "Let go of me!"

A man's voice cut through the tavern noise, lively but sharp as a knife: "Do as she says."

He'd stalked up on their exchange so quietly Cistine hadn't even noticed him, but now she couldn't look away. His appearance was almost startling, especially his hair: he wore it long and white over the top, falling nearly to his shoulder on one side. The other half was deep black and shaved close to his skull. With his shirt collar undone and a dark vest plastered against his ribs, this newcomer was carved of honed, brutal lines. His fists were wrapped as if he'd been fighting, and loosely clenched, like he might be ready to do it again.

A raven perched on the man's shoulder. Wings snapped close to its body, it watched Cistine with its head tilted.

"You heard her." The man's smile was as cool as his voice. "Let her go."

Roosha sneered. "She's our catch."

"That's not an arrangement she seems pleased about." The stranger slid a hand through his hair, flipping it to the other side of his head, and Cistine sucked in a breath. A long, pale scar bisected his hairline from the temple past his ear, as if someone had slid a knife along his scalp, tucking his hair back. The roots themselves were white. "I'm the friend she was looking for."

Matthias scoffed. "Is that so?"

The man's eyes bored into Cistine's, begging her to play along.

"Yes," she said. "This is him."

Roosha's hand loosened slightly, and Cistine bucked his arm away and slid from the stool, hurrying toward this newcomer. Between the three men, he felt like the safer one to stand beside, especially with the briny sweat of Roosha's fingers still soaking the back of her neck.

"Pity," Matthias drawled. "You can smell the cleanness on her."

The man's arm draped around Cistine's shoulders, and she flinched again. He bristled with raw power, and where Julian's fingers always hovered just short of grazing her, this man's hand circled her shoulder with a casual strength that would've been better suited to gripping a sword. "I think you men had best find another drinking hole for the night."

Roosha folded his arms. "And if we'd rather not?"

The man sucked in his bottom lip in a short, soft whistle.

The raven exploded forward, shooting toward Roosha's head. Talons raked bald skin, drawing blood. The man beat at the air, howling with pain, and the other patrons dove away as the bird wheeled and speared toward Matthias, gouging his cheek. In a flurry of wingbeats and driving claws, the raven rushed the two men toward the door.

"Apologies for that," Cistine's rescuer drawled. "There's really no taming him. Faer...Faer! Leave them alone, you useless bag of feathers!"

The bird stroked back to join them, gliding onto the man's shoulder with a proud squawk. Grinning, the man offered him some morsel from his pocket. His eyes drifted down to Cistine.

"Are you all right?" he asked. "Those were slavers, you know. They like to prowl this street looking for girls who are too intoxicated to fight back."

Cistine grimaced. "I barely had a sip!"

"Maybe so, but with that cloak and those cosmetics on your face, you reek of an easy catch." He finally dropped his arm. "A word of warning: stay far, far away from this part of the Aliment if you're alone. You are alone, aren't you?"

Cistine lifted her chin imperiously, though her heart still throbbed against her ribcage. "I'm here with a friend."

He broke into an easygoing smile, sweeping his hair back to the other side of his head. "Better. You're learning." Then he bowed to her, bracing an arm across his chest. "Quill's the name. And this," he frowned playfully as the raven alighted on his wrist, pecking at the buttons of his shirt, "is Faer."

"Thank you for your help."

"You ought to thank the bird. I was going to let things be, but he insisted I intervene."

Cistine laughed. "Well, thank you, Faer."

The raven tipped his head, croaked, and swooped away from them to perch in the tavern's rafters. Quill glared after him. "First he forces me to be gallant, then he leaves me to make conversation on my own. But if it wasn't for terrible friends, I'd have no friends at all. May I buy your next ale?"

Cistine rubbed her arms, glancing around the tavern. Still no sign of Julian, which she expected. If he'd been anywhere in the vicinity, he would've charged Matthias and Roosha the moment they'd laid hands on her. "I shouldn't be here. This was a mistake."

"That's the spirit," Quill said. "Would you debase yourself to accept an escort, then? I have a feeling those two haven't gone far."

Cistine hesitated. His offer seemed gracious enough...and he had plucked her away from the slavers. But there was no guarantee he wasn't a slaver himself. Her attackers had certainly implied he was out for a catch, too.

When Cistine said nothing, Quill whistled, and Faer descended to his forearm. He offered him to Cistine. "At least take Faer. He'll keep you safe. One short whistle, and he'll attack anyone you point him toward. Once you send him off, he'll find his way back to me."

Cistine swallowed. She'd seen what the raven was capable of, and yet... "I don't want to make the walk alone."

Quill fished out a mynt from his pocket, flipped it onto the counter, and led the way out the door. Cistine followed him, Faer fluttering up to perch on her shoulder.

Just as Quill suspected, Matthias and Roosha stalked the alleyway across the street. Their scowls when they caught sight of Quill beside her were nothing short of lethal. And once again, there was that casual arm around her shoulders, friendly but teeming with power. Cistine wondered what would happen if those slavers tried to cross the street.

To her relief, they didn't. And as the sea wind sighed between the edifices of Veran, Cistine was grateful for the break of Quill's powerful body, too. It kept the bitter, salty wind at bay.

"So, tell me, Stranger," Quill said as they walked, "what's brought someone of your obvious riches to Veran?"

"Trade," Cistine lied. "And you?"

Quill drew something from his pocket, and its strong, familiar odor knocked her chest like a kick, reminding her of her garden at home. She watched in fascination as Quill wedged the cinnamon stick between his teeth and talked around it: "Scouting."

"Is that your profession?"

"You might say that." Quill flashed her an enigmatic smile. "But on the side, I pry lovely women from the hands of swine."

"Well, this lovely woman certainly appreciates your efforts."

Quill folded his arms behind his neck and leaned his head back. "Veran's changed since my last visit. It changes whenever I'm here, but this time is different. It's like a sickness has crept in."

Cistine frowned. "What sort of sickness?"

"Corruption. Greed. Apathy. It all depends on which street you turn down. There was a time when slavers were driven out by the Vassora, but you can't find even one member of the city watch on patrol anymore. So men like the ones you met tonight are as free to conduct business as stall vendors."

It seemed these Vassora had the same duties as the Cadre, then. But Quill was right—Cistine hadn't seen anyone fitting that description in the entire week they'd spent here. "Maybe someone ought to do something about all of this."

"Maybe," Quill's gaze slid to her, "someone already is."

When they reached the inn's familiar avenue, Cistine finally relaxed. "I'm grateful for your kindness. You didn't have to help me."

Quill shrugged. "I told you, it was Faer's idea, not mine."

The inn door shrieked open, and Cistine winced as Julian and Ashe stormed out. When they caught sight of her, with Faer on her shoulder and Quill swaggering at her side, they dashed forward. Ashe reached them first, caught Quill by the front of his shirt and rammed him against the nearest storefront, holding him in place. Before Cistine could raise a word of protest, Julian grabbed her upper arms. Faer flapped his wings and kept his perch with a cranky bleat.

"Where were you?" Julian demanded. "We tore the House of Wonders apart looking for you! We were going out of our minds."

"I was at the taverns, looking for *you*," Cistine said.

Julian blanched. "What?"

Quill chuckled. "I take it they keep you on a snug leash, Stranger."

"Who are you?" Ashe snarled. "What are you doing with her?"

"Quill isn't a threat," Cistine said, though she was barely beginning to accept that herself. "He escorted me here to protect me from...from slavers."

Her knees wobbled as she said it, as she truly fathomed where she might be now, and what might be happening to her, if Quill hadn't intervened. Her eyes swung to his face, tears budding on her lashes.

She knew by the way the humor drained from his features that he was thinking the same thing. He tongued the cinnamon stick across the bridge of his pale lips. Then he spat it onto the street and broke Ashe's grip fluidly, rocking up from the storefront. "It seems you're safe now. I'd best be on my way."

"Let us pay you something," Julian grunted, "for bringing her back safely."

"I wasn't aware she was an heirloom with a reward for her safe return," Quill said, and Julian's fingertips dug into Cistine's arms. "I don't charge for the safety of women. Consider it the day's charitable act. Now, if you'll excuse me, I have business with a pair of men from the Aliment."

His intentions couldn't have been clearer, and despite the strength Cistine had felt in those muscles, her heart pounded with concern.

"Quill," she said as he started up the street. "Be careful."

He looked back, cocky smile fastened in place. When he whistled, Faer squeezed Cistine's sleeve with his talons, took flight, and returned to Quill's shoulder.

The plumaged pair disappeared into the shadows.

CHAPTER EIGHT

FLETCHED WITH SIMPLE wagons peeping like headstones through the dense morning fog, the path beyond the north gate curved between sparse pine groves and vanished into the mountain passes above. That trail would lead them to the Vingete Vey, across Valgard, and into the city of Stornhaz.

Cistine hadn't realized the trail was there before they'd climbed up to the gate just before dawn. Now she stared down its twisting length, letting her exhausted mind wander. It was better than thinking of what had happened at the tavern the night before.

Beside Cistine in the gate's shadow, Ashe fidgeted, laying a hand on her sword, then on her new dagger. "Cistine, I want to apologize."

Too groggy to even feel surprised, Cistine yawned into her hands. "For what?"

"For the things I said to you yesterday. Or...how I said them, really. I meant them, but if that was what drove you to the tavern..."

"It wasn't," Cistine lied. "I was bored of the inn. That's all."

Julian returned from scouting the path in time to catch her words, and he smiled. "Understandable. But if you ever get the urge again, at least wait for one of us to escort you, all right?"

Cistine smiled and nodded, ignoring the biting echo of Quill's remark about her being a guarded heirloom. He didn't know she was a princess, why that made her valuable, or why she needed to be guarded. *Wanted* to be.

Cistine craned her head back to peer up at the gate: broad and mostly plain, hewn of seasoned gray stone that looked almost slippery. Curious, Cistine wandered off to the side while Ashe and Julian muttered about watches and the treachery of mountain paths, and laid her hand to the rock.

And she *felt* it.

Resonance ached within her like a chime had been rung, thudding through the backs of her knees and along every ridge of her spine; as if Valgard itself, in the bones of the mountains, in the hills' hollow ribs, had just marked her presence at the gate. And it welcomed her, beckoning in the breeze that sighed through the pines:

Come, Cistine. Come and see.

"Cistine." Ashe's voice jerked her from the reverie. She and Julian had turned back to face the steps down to the canal. "They're here."

Cistine clutched the book of Valgardan runes to her chest as the caravan of plainclothes merches joined them. Plenty of their kind roamed the city streets and wayroads of Talheim, moving from one place to another with their carts full of merchandise, dressed inconspicuously in colorless attire to avoid drawing attention from bandits.

While their leader shook Ashe and Julian's hands, striking up a conversation, a flock of dark-armored men flooded up the steps. They were armed to the teeth in steel, with flinty eyes to match.

Vassora. The word stuck in Cistine's mind to the tune of Quill's voice.

It seemed they hadn't vanished after all. They'd found work as escorts instead.

The men prowled to the carts and flicked away the hide coverings, exposing more men within who'd watched over the carts during the night. As they traded shifts inside, Cistine spotted enormous crates of supplies nestled in the wagon beds.

Mynts traded hands, and then Ashe and Julian joined Cistine at the arch again. The caravan leader strode past, offering her a cursory nod.

"That was Rolf," Ashe said, "the leader of this merch band. Now that he's bled us for every mynt we had left, he says we're welcome to travel with them to Stornhaz."

Julian offered his hand to Cistine as they approached the last cart in the train. "Are you ready for your next adventure, Princess?"

"Of course I am." Cistine accepted his hand, and Julian helped her up the steps into the wagon.

It was difficult to tell if they made good progress the first day. By Ashe's vague memory, these mountains were part of the Vaszaj Range that girded the entire western coast, longer than it was deep. But when Veran fell away behind them, slowly disappearing into the coastal valley like a freckled gem shoved into a thief's pocket, there was nothing but dark stone fletched with green pine and endless clusters of snow to look at.

Cistine and her friends passed the hours playing card games and making empty bets on what Stornhaz would offer them. They didn't have much to anticipate; the city ahead lay shrouded in mystery.

"What do you remember about the Courts themselves, Ashe?" Julian asked.

Ashe shrugged. "Very little. We weren't here for diplomatic discourse. I know before the fighting broke out, King Ivan tried to make a treaty with whatever Court sat in session at the time, and he was told in so many words to go dig his own grave."

Though Cistine's grandfather had done just that, his military campaign in his last living months opened the door for the peace he'd been told would never come. A tenuous peace, granted, and held together by a written truce, but one Cistine hoped would be enough to convince Valgard to stand with Talheim against Mahasar.

The procession halted as the sun settled at their backs behind the ridges they'd wound through during the day. Rolf directed one cart to each end of the road, creating a bulwark at either side. As the caravan settled in and several people vanished to hunt—Ashe among them, while Julian helped build the fires—Cistine wandered from cart to cart, trying to glimpse what was inside.

No one spoke to her, not even to warn her away, but the guards were keen at their posts behind the wagons. Their eyes flashed whenever Cistine came close, and their hands twitched, preparing to draw steel if necessary.

Cistine escaped their scrutiny at the largest fire, where Rolf consulted maps and charts by the soft light. Cistine sat on an overturned pine trunk across from him, resting her book in her lap and folding her hands over it as she studied him. "Are you a merch, or someone the merches hire to protect them?"

Rolf said without looking up, "I'm the one they pay handsomely to deliver them safely to Stornhaz."

"What sort of wares are they carrying?"

"The sort that meddlesome children are better off not asking about."

Cistine's breath snagged.

Rolf looked up, and his gray eyes glimmered. He chuckled, gesturing with his ink pen toward the caravans. "Food supplies. Garments. Some awful sort of decorations, I suspect. I don't have to know, and they don't tell me. The pay is the same whatever they bring, whether it's clothing or wares or a gaggle of surgeons."

Cistine wiggled her fingers over the fire. "And these guards are yours?"

"Most are. The rest were sent by Devitrius."

"Who is that?"

"Someone you're likely to meet once we reach Stornhaz."

Cistine hoped it was a man less rugged and intimidating than the one before her. "It just seems like quite a number of blades for food and garments."

Rolf's laughter was sharper this time. "Only a cossetted girl would assume rations and raiment are any safer to transport across Valgard's territories than treasure." He nodded to the book in her arms. "Can you read that?"

"Not yet."

"Then you ought to burn it. Ancient stories about wayfinders and shadows are good for nothing but building the flames. And it's going to be a cold night."

Cistine glared at him. "I paid my last mynt for this, and I'll learn to read it someday."

"Filling your head with nonsense. Your loss, really." Rolf rolled his map and strolled away, barking orders to his guards.

Still clutching the book tightly, Cistine caught Julian's eye halfway across the camp. He perched on the driver's seat of a wagon, passing his dagger from hand to hand. When he held her stare, Cistine's heart thundered. She went to join him.

"That looked like a pleasant conversation," Julian remarked as Cistine leaned against the wagon's step below him. "What did Rolf have to say?"

"What you might expect. He has no time for anything that isn't made of steel or coin. He's just an escort for these merches and their trinkets to Stornhaz."

Julian examined his blade's slick edge by the dying daylight. "Interesting. I had myself a look around the wagons while the guards were distracted with the fires. Those aren't trinkets in those chests. They're weapons, Princess. An arsenal."

Cistine glanced at Rolf and his guards, and then at the silent merches who'd barely spoken on the journey. Their procession felt more like a funeral than a caravan, if she was honest. And either Rolf had lied to her about what they were doing, or the merches were lying to him. "Do you suppose the Guide sent us along with them for some reason other than our safety?"

"That's what I wondered." Julian dropped next to her on the path. "But whatever else they are, they took our mynts and let us come along. So for now, we'll play ignorant."

"For now."

Cistine didn't flinch as Julian rested a hand on the back of her neck. Because just then, as her eyes met those of the nearest guard and he flashed her an arrogant smile, Cistine was back in the tavern, facing the slavers.

Facing someone who wanted to do her harm.

CHAPTER NINE

Tension banded Cistine's stomach, making her shy of their traveling companions as the caravan conquered the chilly upper passes and began the descent from the Vaszaj Range to the lowlands, where warmth rapidly returned. Cistine spent most of her time leaning from the last wagon, soaking in the sunlight and basking in the sheer breadth of Valgard around them. The land was a banner of color: gold meadows in the distance, green fields and rocky croppings close by, and pockets of cities all over the valley floor.

They finally reached the Vingete Vey at the foothills, marked by another archway, and started out across the plain. It was dotted with hardy brush that offered little for shelter or sightseeing, and Cistine buried her face in a book to pass the time. Ashe sharpened her weapons, and Julian dozed on the seat.

The sun was sinking below the Vaszaj Range when he spoke up for the first time in hours, without cracking an eye: "Who's going to speak to the Chancellor of Kanslar Court?"

Cistine looked up from her book. "I assumed I would. Unless you have an objection?"

Julian's eyes fluttered open, long lashes feathering his cheekbones, and that molten stare pinned her to her seat. "Given their merches are liars who travel with an armed guard, I'm not hopeful about the sort of man we'll be facing at the end of this road. I'd rather Ashe or I spoke to him."

Cistine frowned. "You believe I'm incapable?"

He swung himself upright on the bench. "I believe you're capable of anything, but that includes being overpowered by someone trained in the blade."

"Julian's right," Ashe said slowly, and Cistine cut around to face her with a disbelieving whine. "Don't look at me like that. We both know you've been shirking your diplomacy lessons for over a year now. Negotiating with this Chancellor may prove more of a challenge than you're prepared for."

"I'm Talheim's princess." Cistine's voice shook with anger. "You can't leave me outside locked doors while *you* bargain with the Chancellor!"

"Look at what nearly happened in Veran with those slavers," Julian argued. "That may not be uncommon in Valgard. Who's to say the Chancellor will even deign to bargain with a—"

"A woman?" Cistine snapped.

"I was going to say a princess who's out of her depth."

"Nothing has to be decided today," Ashe intervened. "But when it comes down to it, we need the best negotiator on the task. That may not be you, Cistine."

Cistine flopped back against the wagon's curve, arms folded. She was a princess by blood if not by choice, and she *would* negotiate for the safety of her kingdom. She would not be useless. No matter what it demanded of her, she would not let Talheim—or herself—be ridiculed or denied.

They entered the shadows of a small pine grove, and Ashe closed her whetstone pouch, turning to peer back toward the dark slab of the mountain, dotted with trees, still filling the horizon behind the wagon. Julian followed her gaze, but Cistine refused to. She looked the other way, toward the cart drivers visible through the canvas flap. They were the only ones in this wagon who hadn't incurred her wrath today.

"What is it, Ashe?" Julian asked.

"I'm not certain."

The only thing Cistine was certain of was how furious she was, and how fiercely she wanted them to know it.

So she was still staring doggedly at the cart drivers when a thick, dark arrow slammed into one man's mouth and broke through the back of his skull, flinging him into the footwell beside Cistine.

Cistine launched herself away from the man's dead body, screaming. The wagon careened left as the other driver fumbled for the reins, a battle he lost when a second arrow strummed the cords of his throat and lodged through either end of his neck.

Cistine wasn't the only one screaming now. Furious, shocked shouts boomed from the caravan as a hail of arrows soared from the trees on both sides. Ashe grabbed Cistine by the arm and threw her into the footwell, landing on top of her, and Julian crouched over them until the barrage slowed. Then he was up, scrambling over their tangled limbs and onto the driver's bench. The wagon shot forward again, and Cistine trusted Julian was driving them away from danger. She lay on her back under Ashe, watching the pine trees skim by, watching the pink sky blur overhead. Between the speed, the sight, the sounds of death and terror—she was going to vomit.

And then an arrow struck one of the horses.

The wagon lurched, peeled over the animal's body, and tilted beyond correction. Cistine and Ashe bounced over the seat, struck the road, and rolled. Cistine cried out as pine needles and rough stones caught and tore her arms and hands. She slammed against a tree; all the air surged from her lungs and she choked, gasping as the wagon overturned on the road, breaking into enormous, jagged splinters. Julian leaped from the seat, landing in a crouch on the dirt path. He was up and running before the second arrow struck the second horse.

Julian pulled Cistine to her feet. "Are you all right?"

"No," she gagged, gripping her belly. They hadn't come far enough to escape the sounds and sights of combat. The assailing archers had spent their arrows and were pouring out into the open to fight. Even at a glance, Cistine knew they outnumbered Rolf's guards.

Ashe limped from the trees beside them. Blood ran from her thigh where a blade of wood protruded, snagging through her pants. Julian eyed the wound. "You can't run on that."

"And I'm not leaving you behind," Cistine panted.

"There are still six wagons," Julian said. "If I can free the horses, we'll have a chance to escape."

Cistine looked between the cluster of combatants and the wagons they'd abandoned at the roadside. Julian risked being drawn into battle if he went, and with no one to protect his sides.

If Cistine only had a bow in her hand...

Julian took a step toward the road, and Cistine grabbed his sleeve, her tongue shriveling as she struggled to craft words for her fear, her longing, in case one of those arrows found a home in his flesh.

And then the battle was over, even while it still raged, because of two men who entered it without warning.

The last gasps of daylight struggled to paint the silhouettes of their bodies, but in armor the color of the granite slopes behind them, it was almost impossible. Cistine only knew they were there by the lick of light along steel as they each drew twin sabers from sheaths on their backs. The pair dropped from the treetops and skimmed forward, falling on Rolf's guards without mercy. The cries of battle turned to screams of slaughter.

Cistine pressed a hand to her mouth and buckled. Only Julian's arm around her back kept her from sagging to the ground as the men cleaved through the guards like a fork winnowing through straw. Blood sprayed the path and the trees around it. Severed heads and broken limbs flopped in the carnage.

Cistine's vision dappled. She vomited all over her hand.

Ashe cursed—not at Cistine's sickness, but because the guards, the merches, even Rolf, who was somehow still alive, broke ground and ran straight toward Cistine and her friends.

Cistine tried to plant her feet, but she stumbled again, terror and sickness plucking the strength from her bones. Julian threw his sword to Ashe and bent to lift Cistine into his arms; but before he could, the guards slammed into them, enclosing them in the middle of the fight.

Cistine didn't know what they were meant to be: fresh blood to spill, a distraction, or a shield between the caravan and these archers and swordsmen—these death-gods, entities of darkness and murder. They moved in perfect synchrony, pulling back and slamming into Rolf's entourage again and again. Two against many, when the archers fell back to guard the road, and yet these attackers struggled no more as two than as ten.

At Ashe's command, Julian spun Cistine away from the fight the same way he'd spun her at the ball, bundling her rapidly toward the trees. But one of the death-gods noticed, his cowled head turning sharply, and then his whole body followed. He sheathed one blade and speared through the fight, straight as a deadly arrow. His curved saber led, swinging toward Julian's neck, and Cistine screamed. Not a plea, not a warning or a challenge, only a visceral cry as the blade sliced down in the sun's dying light.

It stopped, kissing Julian's throat, bringing him to a halt. Cistine tumbled from his grip and fell to her knees in the brush, staring up at the warrior. His free hand slashed up to peel back his hood, letting it fall between the shoulders of his dark armor.

"Stranger?" Quill shouted.

Cistine dug her fingers into the grass and stared at this living calamity. This merciless swordsman.

Her savior from the tavern.

The other man, still locked in combat, shouted Quill's name. Quill looked sharply to the side, where one of Rolf's men darted into the trees.

Cistine prayed he would bring aid.

Quill brought the pommel of his sword down on Julian's head, knocking him unconscious. Then he turned up his hood, shooting after that fleeing Vassoran guard.

By the time Cistine lurched to Julian's side, Ashe was there. She tumbled down beside Julian, touching his jaw. "He's alive. Breathe, Cistine...he's all right!"

But Cistine couldn't breathe. Quill was here—Quill, who'd been nothing more than a laughing protector sent by the True God to that tavern in Veran. Yet today he savaged through Rolf's guards like they were nothing.

Cistine gripped Julian's hand and clung to his inert body until the ringing in her ears faded. Until all she heard was weeping from the path, and only then did she dare look.

Four merches were alive, down on their knees with arms raised in surrender. The second warrior held his blade to Rolf's neck.

"I know who you are," Rolf growled. "I heard you say the other one's name."

The man stiffened, and so did Cistine, as Quill emerged from the undergrowth. Cuts scraped his face, battle bright in his stormy eyes. He swirled his saber in a lazy circle and swaggered up to his companion's side.

A touch of knuckles to Quill's chest halted him. The man kept the back of his hand on Quill's collar as Rolf spit ropes of bloody saliva on their feet. "Tell the mongrel you serve, this changes nothing. He may have come crawling from the shadows after all this time, but he doesn't have the ranks to spread along every road from every coastal city. He can jam his fingers into as many cracks as he likes...the dam will still burst."

The man let his arm fall.

Quill docked off Rolf's head.

Cistine retched, but she had nothing left to give. Eyes streaming, she saw Quill sheathe his blade. The archers converged, arrows retrieved from the wagon skeletons and notched, pointing toward the merches. The other warrior went to the shattered wagon.

Quill jogged back to Cistine and her companions. "Are you hurt?"

"Get away from us!" Ashe lurched to her feet and broke down again, grabbing her leg. Blood pumped steadily between her fingers from the shaft in her thigh.

Quill slowed, hands raised. "You ought to wrap that."

"I ought to wrap my hands around your *throat!*"

Quill shoved Ashe onto her haunches with his foot. "If you don't want to make that wound any worse, I suggest not moving."

Cistine gaped up at Quill. He stared back at her, hood fallen away again, the pale sheaf of his hair spilling over the mottle of black and brown on the underside. His eyes were just as lively from slaughter as they'd been from ale in the tavern.

She wondered if he'd looked just as lively when he'd gone back to finish his business with Matthias and Roosha.

Cistine flinched when the other man tossed aside the wagon's splinters and dragged the chest free. With one swift kick, he broke the lock and pried it open. Rage burned away the shock and horror that pounded through Cistine's body as this stranger rooted casually through her belongings, her fine dress and her jewelry. All her books. Ashe's weapons.

"Get your hands off that!" Cistine surged to her feet. She heard Ashe shout her name, but she still charged forward—uncertain of what she would do, except slap this death-god. Underneath that hood, there must be the head of a man. He certainly had the enormous, terrifying shape of one.

But Quill spun smoothly, catching Cistine's armpit and towing her against his chest. The same muscled arm whose strength had spelled salvation when he'd defended her from the slavers felt like an iron cage as it trapped her elbows against her body. "Not here. This is not the place, and Maleck is not the man you need to have this conversation with."

Cistine ignored him. "Get away from that chest! Those are our trade items—that's all we have to bargain with!"

"And now you have nothing." The man—Maleck—shut the chest and turned to the archers. "Dispose of the bodies. Collect the items into three carts and empty a fourth for the prisoners. Turn the other horses loose."

"Mal," Quill's tone belonged to the easygoing man in the tavern again, not to the bloodstained hand that gripped Cistine's arm at the hinge, keeping her from breaking free. "What about these three?"

Maleck turned to face them, laying his hood back, and Cistine stopped struggling.

His face was a collision of youth and age: narrow and sharp, but lined along the brow and beside the eyes. He sported high cheekbones and dark stubble freckled with grizzle, and grooves framed his full lips. Everywhere Cistine looked, she saw a young warrior at war with a weary man. Gray-streaked black hair, cut to a short weave on top and braided long, hung between his shoulderblades.

But it was his eyes that captured Cistine's attention: hazel-gray, the irises limned with a gentle swirl of green, the right one cleaved by a gnarled ridge of old scarring. They were...empty. Divested of any feeling whatsoever. Cistine had seen eyes like that only once before: when she'd visited the hospital in Talheim, held the hand of a dying Warden, and watched the life fade from him.

Maleck had that calloused look of a new corpse, as though someone had reached inside him, torn out everything that made a man what he was, and left this killing husk behind.

Cistine drooped in Quill's hold, and he grimaced audibly as he propped her up again. "We can't leave them wandering out here, Mal. They could be found. Someone might question them. The Vassora, even."

Maleck tilted his head. His gaze dropped from Cistine to Julian, unconscious on the ground, then to Ashe, who'd struggled to her feet again and leaned against a tree for support, blood oozing from her injured leg. He stared at her the longest.

"Put them in the cart with the merches," he said. "I'll see to the woman's leg once we've cleared the road."

Ashe snarled, "Put your hands on me and I'll kill you."

"If I don't, you will die of blood poisoning before we reach our destination."

"What does it matter to you how death finds me, if you're just going to kill us anyway?"

"If your fate was to die on this road, I would have removed your head already."

Cistine squeezed her eyes shut as Faer soared down from the treetops and landed on the broken lance of the cart's upturned spine, his caw of victory a dire punctuation to Maleck's chilling words.

And just like that, Talheim's princess became a Valgardan prisoner.

CHAPTER TEN

TRUE TO HIS word, Maleck tended to Ashe once they'd traveled some distance into the trees—though Cistine couldn't fathom why he bothered when Ashe made it perfectly clear she wanted no part of his help. The triage itself became a battle requiring an archer on each of Ashe's limbs and Quill pressing his weight on her chest while Maleck removed the shrapnel and cleaned, stitched, and bandaged her thigh. Helpless, Cistine huddled next to Julian's unconscious body while Ashe spat profanities and threatened to remove Maleck's head.

The journey away from the road after that night went much quicker, and much less comfortably, than the one through the mountains. Cistine couldn't sleep with the slap of branches along the ripped hide covering, the jouncing of wagon wheels over the pitted, rocky ground, and the constant stirring of their companions: the merches, bound hand and foot to prevent escape.

Cistine and her friends weren't bound. But they couldn't run.

And then came the commotion when Julian finally woke, a groggy and furious mess, and he and Ashe began to feed one another's rage.

"That bastard lands a good blow," Julian muttered as he knelt in the footwell and Cistine spread the folds of his dark hair to examine his bruised skull. His hair was tacky with blood, but still soft under her fingertips. She tried not to breathe the smell of him too deeply.

"I think there's more to this than what we've seen," she said. "More to why they brought us along. And look—they left us unguarded back here. Why do you think that is?"

"I think you're being naïve," Ashe snapped—still prickly from Maleck's triage. "You've never been captured before, but I have. Waking up in the back of a wagon after a battle never ends well, even if the butchers spare a few bandages for your leg."

Julian scoffed under his breath, moving out from under Cistine's hands to sit on the bench beside her. "The way those two fought...we aren't going to beat our way through this."

"Did you see what they did with my sword?" Ashe asked.

"It went into the trunk." Cistine scuffed her slippers in the footwell. "Along with *everything* we own. And they put on a new lock we don't have a key to."

"Julian," Ashe said, "I want that sword back."

He looked up through his lashes. "What do you have in mind?"

"We have to stop eventually. If I create a diversion, can you pick the lock and retrieve my sword?" Julian nodded. "Good. And then we run."

"They have archers," Cistine argued, "and there's little cover."

"Then we dodge."

"What about your leg?"

"Let me worry about that. Sooner or later, we *have* to run, Cistine. I'm not going home to tell Cyril I let his daughter get kidnapped by a pack of thieves."

Julian leaned one hand on the seat behind Cistine. "It's a good plan, Ashe."

Cistine tossed up her hands. "Fine, then! If it's such a good plan, why settle for only opening the trunk? Why not steal *Maleck's* weapons while you're at it?"

She waited smugly for them to realize how awful their plan was and offer a different solution than stealing and running from men who'd already run them down and stolen from *them*. But to her horror, Ashe said, "He *is* carrying fine weapons."

"You can do it subtly enough," Julian agreed. "Cadre Wardens have quick hands. Cistine can stand watch, and if we knock him unconscious first…"

"What?" Cistine yelped. "No, that's not what I meant!"

"You're brilliant, Princess," Ashe said. "When should we do it?"

"If they ever let us out of this wagon," Julian said. "If they don't, then we take our chances on any night. I'll handle the guard…"

In hushed tones, they started to strategize while Cistine gaped at them.

Ashe, crippled from the wood shard to her thigh. Julian with a head wound. And they *still* thought they could run, and somehow not be shot in their backs by the archers. Worse, their resentment of these Valgardans was making them reckless enough to consider stealing from Maleck, whose stare alone made Cistine fear for her life.

Cistine sucked in her breath and winced. She'd grabbed the bench so hard, splinters jammed themselves into the beds of her fingertips. She jerked her hands back and shook them out, pain singing through her skin.

"Let me." Julian took her hand, turned it over, and slid the splinters out one by one. Callused from holding a blade, his touch was still shockingly gentle. Shivers raced into Cistine's core, filling up her empty belly. "You have to trust me, Princess. I won't let anything happen to you when we do this. I'll keep you safe."

Cistine fought back a disbelieving whimper. He thought her concern was for what Quill's people would do to her, when it was Ashe who'd agreed to steal weapons from a death-god, and Julian to steal them from the trunk.

But she couldn't stop them. They'd already proven they wouldn't listen to her in matters where she knew less than them. And escaping captivity was certainly one of those things. "Promise me you'll do this carefully, at least."

Julian frowned, plucking at a particularly stubborn splinter.

"We'll be as careful as possible, Cistine," Ashe said.

Julian bent his head and used his teeth to catch the end of the splinter. As he drew it out, something in Cistine's middle snapped taut and followed the thread of it to his pale face and bruised irises. And to his laughing mouth as he spat the splinter onto the floor.

The opportunity to act didn't come for many days.

Cistine wasn't certain she could find her way back to the Vingete Vey if she tried. Each morning when she woke from another fitful slumber, she looked outside only to see different patterns in the landscape. She was certain they'd doubled back a time or two, but there was no telling how far they'd come or where they were going now.

By common standards, Cistine supposed they weren't being mistreated. They were given food, bandages for Ashe's wound, and a communal bucket to relieve themselves in. But for a princess forced to squat in the footwell in front of unfamiliar merches and close friends to do her business, the humiliation was torturous.

Because of that degradation, she thought she would be more than prepared when it came time to steal the weapons and escape. But when the day broke that Ashe announced they should strike, Cistine wasn't ready at all.

"Tonight," Julian agreed, scraping the bottom of the bench. He'd been playing with something down there for days. "Our pace has slowed, so we must be close to our destination. And something tells me we don't want to know where that is, or what they plan to do with us there."

"Kill us," one of the merches said. It was the first time any of them spoke since the Vey, and the rasp of that abused voice raised the hair on Cistine's arms.

"Is that so?" Ashe's tone was lazy, but tension bristled along her shoulders.

"Aye. This is what they do. We aren't the first they've captured. We won't be the last."

"What do they want with us?" Cistine asked. "With *you*?"

"It's their leader you ought to be concerned about," the merch said.

"We've heard rumors of him and his band. The pair who sacked the caravan, they're nothing. Dogs on a leash. But their leader...some say Death and Slaughter wear *his* face into battle."

"All these bandits make the roads unsafe," another man said. "They're the reason we're forced to hire guards like Rolf. But if this is the mongrel we've heard stories of, it won't end well for any of us."

"What will he do?" Julian asked.

"Question us." The first man toyed with his bonds. "Then remove our heads and send the pieces of us back to Veran as a warning."

With a grunt, Julian pried something from beneath the seat. He rolled it in his palm, flashing it at Cistine and Ashe: a nail as long as Julian's middle finger, brutally sharp on one end. Capable of doing great harm—and picking a lock.

Cistine looked between her somber-faced friends. "All right. We'll go tonight."

CHAPTER ELEVEN

THE WAGONS TRUNDLED to a halt at sunset, and relief and fear warred in Cistine's belly when the hide flap peeled back, framing Quill in the waning daylight. He looked like the man from the tavern again: dark pants, pale shirt casually unbuttoned, his vest open over his sides and his fists wrapped. He chewed on a cinnamon stick, offering a hand into the wagon. "Ready to stretch your legs?"

Cistine pressed herself between Ashe and Julian on the seat. "Why tonight?"

"Because I said tonight. Are you staying or coming?"

There was something tantalizing about that hand—the chance to prove he didn't intimidate her. To show herself a princess, not a prisoner cowed by what he'd done to Rolf. So Cistine lifted her chin, wobbled to her feet, and walked down the footwell to take his hand.

Quill smirked, wrapping his free arm around her waist and hoisting her out. He dropped her into deep, springy grass that gently embraced her ankles. They'd made camp in a large meadow bordered by trees—not hardy pines anymore, but oak groves.

They reminded Cistine of the Calalun Peaks. Of home.

Ashe and Julian clambered slowly from the wagon, as Cistine knew they would—they couldn't let her face Quill alone. But it wasn't Quill

Cistine was worried about.

Maleck had already built a fire, and he sat beside it on top of Cistine's trunk—on top of her belongings.

Maleck lifted his dead gaze, Cistine's seething a beacon for his blank stare. From anyone else, that look would've exuded quiet authority. But from him, from those eyes, there was nothing. As if she wasn't there, and the trunk wasn't hers. As if such a clear mockery—his seat on her things—meant nothing more than he'd found it a convenient place to sit.

A shadow moved into Cistine's path: Ashe, subtly blocking Maleck's view. Around her Warden's side, Cistine saw Maleck's gaze drop back to the flames.

Quill strode to the fire, whistling under his breath, and Cistine and her friends slowly trailed after him. A full guard closed around the wagon behind them, each man armed with a bow and a full quiver of arrows.

"Why not free the merches?" Cistine asked, lowering herself to the grass. She kept to Maleck's right side, hoping the scar over his eye made his vision cloudy, so he wouldn't watch her quite as much.

Quill dropped into a sprawl, breaking down more kindling for the flames. "Because they're here for a different reason than you."

"And what reason is that?" Ashe growled.

"Questioning."

"And dismemberment?" Cistine asked.

Something almost like hurt flickered in Quill's eyes. "You've been listening to stories, I see."

"Tell me it isn't true. That you didn't take Matthias and Roosha apart after you brought me back to the inn."

Maleck's eyes lifted to Quill this time. Quill spat the cinnamon stick into the fire. "You don't know why I did what I did, so let's not discuss it."

"So, why are we here, then?" Cistine demanded. "Why did you bind Ashe's leg? Why *any* of this?"

Quill grimaced. "There weren't supposed to be any non-combatants besides the merches in those wagons, and you weren't supposed to see our faces. Now that you have, it's not our choice whether you live or die."

Ashe and Julian were right. They needed to escape from these men.

Cistine tugged her fingers slowly through the grass. "You should let the merches out. At least to stretch their legs and relieve themselves."

Quill arched a brow. "Is that what you think?"

"You're going to question them, aren't you? Who do you think will be easier to coerce: a man you've treated like an animal, or one you've shown kindness?"

Quill's gaze turned to Maleck, and Maleck stared back at him. Then Quill got to his feet without a word and strode to the wagons.

Julian winked at Cistine, and she flushed. With the merches free, there would be more distractions tonight...more cover for them to flee under once they were armed.

At least she'd been able to contribute something to their plan.

The archers brought down meadow pheasants and hares in the last threads of daylight, and Cistine looked away when they skinned the meat by firelight. She'd never spent much time in the Citadel's kitchens, and she wasn't eager to see the men who'd slaughtered most of their caravan kill something else.

The tension built once the meat was dripping over the fire and the archers chattered among themselves. Cistine knew their moment to strike rapidly approached, and this was the last semblance of peace, however fabricated, she would experience for some time.

And with that thought, she felt it again, as if it came in answer to her restlessness: the subtle urge to rise, and go...to *come* toward something, out there in the wilderness of Valgard.

And yet, like a bowstring snapping as the arrow loosed, the sensation rebounded—the call itself shooting back toward her.

Cistine didn't realize she'd come to her feet, turning to face east, until the chatter eased around her. And then it died completely as she took a step, tugged by that notion in her middle. Around her belly. In her heart.

From the corners of her eyes, she saw Quill glance sharply at Maleck, who in turn measured Cistine with his deep, intrusive stare. But even these things ceased to matter.

Come. Come and see.

She took another step.

Quill clapped his hands, and Cistine jolted awake from that breathable darkness of wanting to go, of feeling as if somewhere out there, in the wild lands, there was something she *needed* to see. "All right! That's enough lazing around for the night. Time for patrols."

As Maleck doled out orders, Julian lurched to his feet and clasped Cistine's shoulder. "Are you all right?"

She nodded, mortified and mollified at the same time: that he'd noticed her strange reaction to the call. And that he'd cared.

Even when the archery patrols dispersed, Quill didn't return them to the cart, so Cistine and her companions settled around the fire. Night gulped down the last light, and a spray of stars appeared overhead while Cistine listened to Quill and Maleck moving around the camp, checking the horses, rounding up the merches for sleep, and preparing for the morning's journey—abandoning the trunk.

It was either a taunt, or Maleck deciding these prisoners were harmless.

The small sliver of Cistine that wasn't tense with fear was truly looking forward to proving him wrong.

The firelight crackled, blotting out when Quill crouched beside Cistine moments after she stretched out to feign sleep. "I'm leaving for patrol. Aren't you going to tell me to be safe?"

It was the last thing she'd said to him before he'd gone to confront the slavers. Flushing, Cistine rolled over and put her back toward him. Dangerous, perhaps, but it felt good to show her displeasure.

"I didn't mean for you and your friends to be caught up in this," Quill added. "But you lied to me. You said you were in Veran for trade."

"I was. I just didn't say who I wanted to trade with. Or for what."

Silence hung between them. Then, "You were going to make trade in Stornhaz?"

Cistine brushed her thumb over a patch of grassless dirt in the shelter of her body. "You lied to me, too."

"I didn't. I *was* scouting in Veran. I took the night off to have a drink."

"Scouting the caravan, you mean? Deciding when to attack it?"

"You have your reasons for what you do. I have mine."

"Serving a butcher. I know. I heard what Rolf called you."

Quill sighed. Cistine heard leather creaking as he got to his feet, and she knew he was wearing his armor again—anticipating trouble of some sort. "Be safe, Stranger."

Cistine said nothing, and listened for nothing. He made no sound as he vanished into the grasslands.

She counted to twenty. Then she rolled onto her back and looked at Ashe, lying across the fire. Her Warden's eyes were open, bright and grim with determination. At Cistine's feet, Julian stirred, his gaze fixed on the trunk.

Now was not the time to act. Maleck still patrolled the camp, watchful eyes scouring the darkness, even with the archers and Quill on the hunt tonight.

Cistine's skin prickled as she wondered what they thought might be lurking out there.

∽⌇∽

Several hours passed before Maleck settled down against the trunk. Cistine pretended to sleep, watching him through the shadow of her eyelashes until at long last his fluttered shut. After fifteen minutes of unmoving silence, Ashe rolled onto her belly, picked up a rock, and crawled to his side. Julian's fingers danced on the soil, fidgeting with the nail. All Cistine could do was watch and wait.

The nominal role she played in such an important night was nothing short of infuriating. She wanted to loot the other wagons, or take out the archers who were focused on their task and not on Maleck and his three prisoners, or pick the lock herself while Julian kept watch.

God. She wanted to be *useful* for something more than looking over both shoulders. More than being a beautiful asset, guarded and brought back for some reward. She wanted to be better than useless when danger arose.

Shadows rippled as Ashe loomed over Maleck from behind the trunk, keeping its berth between them, and raised the rock high.

She almost made contact with his skull.

Almost.

Cistine squeaked in terror when Maleck's fingers flashed up, seizing Ashe at the wrist. In one deft movement, he caught her armpit and flipped her over the trunk and above his head, knocking her windless on the ground.

Julian leaped up, and Cistine scrambled with him, terror ripping a scream from her throat. Ashe snatched her hand away from Maleck's grasp, crawling backward from him as the death-god, the man of smoke and shadow, unfolded to his feet and drew his sword.

Armed with the nail, Julian pounced and jabbed, but the makeshift weapon did no good except to shred the buttons from Maleck's undershirt. With a backward jab of his elbow, he put Julian down to his knees, clutching his throat, and he turned back to Ashe.

The state of him terrified Cistine. His shirt hung open over his bare chest, exposing his clavicles and pectorals where the skin was nothing but a gnarled heap of scarring—as though he'd been struck by lightning or set aflame.

Maleck wasn't the only one alerted now. The archers abandoned their posts, tearing toward the campfire as a dark shape careened across the night sky.

Faer. Off to warn Quill that Maleck's blade was underneath Ashe's chin now, the point impressing the skin of her throat.

Cistine lurched forward, and when an archer stepped into her path, Julian surged up, tackled the man and disarmed him, took his thin sword, and rendered him unconscious in two blows. But he didn't dare strike again with the blade when the other archers encircled them; when Maleck's steel was ready to taste Ashe's blood.

Helpless, horrified, Cistine gasped her Warden's name.

Ashe's eyes traced the twisted skin on Maleck's chest and moved to his face. "You were an augur." She looked as if she wanted to peel the skin from his bones with her bare hands. "You fought in the war, didn't you?"

Maleck stepped closer, his blade tipping up her head, and Cistine started to weep in fear. In anger. In horror.

But Maleck didn't make the strike. He was frozen. They all were.

At last, shattering the silence, Maleck said, "You can see what I am, and yet you attacked me. And you face me still."

"You think I'm afraid of you?" Ashe snarled. "You augers don't frighten me. You never have!"

Maleck blinked, and in the depths of that blank stare, something flickered. Cistine couldn't put a name to it. But as Ashe and Maleck stared one another down, twin warriors from opposing battlefields, Maleck's face changed. Emotion tried to crawl across it for just an instant.

And that instant was broken by a piercing whistle.

Cistine twisted toward the sound, and Julian stepped back to her, sliding an arm across her front. His fingers curled in the sleeve of her tattered dress as they looked at the wagons. At the figure standing atop the nearest one.

He was another death-god, robed in a dark shirt and pants. His sleeves were rolled to the elbows, baring long vambraces on his forearms, each one buckled with a slender knife. Swords glinted at a cross behind his shoulderblades. His face, angled their way, was hardly older than Cistine's— less than a decade's difference between them—but his hair was white, like the upper thatch of Quill's, and he wore it chopped into unruly layers; some ending above his ears, others traveling down the deeply tanned nape of his neck. A few wild hanks hung into his eyes as he turned toward Cistine, and their gazes met.

She had the sudden sensation of sticking her hands into ice water, and feeling it scald before it stung.

The man dismounted lithely from the cart and strode across the meadow to join them. Julian's grip on Cistine's sleeve tightened, pulling the seams loose. His back, pressed half-across Cistine's chest, vibrated with a growl.

The man halted beside Maleck, who sheathed his sword and gestured to Ashe. "She's a Talheimic Warden."

The man stared at Ashe, and Ashe stared back. No remorse, no pity in their faces.

Not even when the man reached back for his own sword.

Cistine didn't know why she moved. What she truly intended to do. But she saw steel glint, and for the second time that night, Ashe was in danger.

Cistine refused to be useless again. She would do *something*.

She didn't realize what that truly meant until she'd shoved down Julian's arm, ripped the sword from his hand, and lunged over Ashe to meet the man's blade.

Julian roared her name like a battle-cry, and Cistine heard the scuffle of someone restraining him. She barely managed to heft the stolen sword in time to block the steel that sliced toward the side of her neck.

Her arms wanted to buckle under the sheer power behind this man's attack. He wielded his weapon with single-handed grace, while Cistine braced the grip of Julian's sword with all her might, and still sweat gathered in the small of her back.

But she faced him. He was taller and broader than her, and the most frightening person she'd ever seen, with those cold eyes and that grim jaw. Worse than blank, fathomless Maleck, she saw this man's intentions on the clear surface of his face: he wanted to kill Ashe.

"I won't let you touch her." Cistine meant every word, even if they shook as badly as the rest of her.

The man studied her face, as if she was a problem he hadn't anticipated facing and didn't have a precise idea how to solve. Perhaps no one else had ever stepped in the way of his killing strikes before, or told him he wasn't allowed to butcher whomever he pleased.

"Thorne!"

Cistine almost felt relief at that shout, almost let herself believe she had an ally when Quill jogged into the firelight. His weapons whispered as he slowed to a halt at Maleck's side. Wide-eyed, he looked between Cistine and her attacker—Thorne—who still held his weapon with casual grace. Cistine's shoulders ached as she clung to her sword.

"You left them unbound, Quill." Thorne's voice was the scrape of a fallen star slamming into the dirt, heavy with disappointment. By the way Quill lowered his eyes, Cistine knew exactly who this man was.

Her heart stumbled in her chest.

"I didn't think she would make the attempt." Quill shot Cistine a wounded look, as if she'd betrayed him, but Cistine didn't care. They weren't friends, and even if they had been, she wouldn't apologize for where she stood. Ashe was her Warden, her closest friend. Ashe came before everything.

Thorne circled his blade casually, and Cistine's arms gave way. Ashe shouted as Cistine struggled to heft the sword again, to block the next blow aimed toward her legs. She managed it, but only just.

Several archers snickered. Cistine colored in humiliation.

"You don't know swordplay?" Thorne asked.

"I haven't needed to," Cistine said. "I'm a princess."

Quill hissed under his breath, "Nimmus' teeth!"

Thorne's eyes raked over her. "Poor excuse."

"Don't you dare condescend to her!" Julian snarled, and Cistine heard the dull impact as someone hit him. Tears sprang to her eyes.

Thorne's gaze traveled to Ashe, still in a sprawl, now gripping her leg. For the first time, deeper concern pushed through Cistine's immediate panic. Ashe was a Cadre Warden, trained by their commander himself, and if she was still on her back with weapons drawn on every side, then she must have reopened her wound.

There was no hope of fleeing now, even if Thorne dropped his guard.

"A princess." Thorne pressed in with his blade. Cistine's wrists popped, and she sucked in a whimper. "Not a title we hear often in these lands."

Cistine glanced at Julian. His eyes begged her not to give up the secret she was meant to tell the Chancellor, the Guide, and no one else. But Cistine knew words were weapons, and against these warriors with their swords and powerful bodies, she had nothing but her words in her quiver.

She had to use them, and trust her aim was true.

"I am Princess Cistine Novacek," she said, "and I demand your respect and clemency."

Thorne released Cistine's blade. When she stumbled forward from the lack of weight to brace against, he rested his sword against the side of her neck instead. "You demand nothing from me that you haven't earned."

Cistine's bowels threatened to release. "As royalty, I invoke diplomatic protection."

"We aren't diplomats, and this is a kingdom with Chancellors, not kings. Your title means nothing here."

Cistine cobbled together the vestiges of her courage and screamed in his face: "I am Princess Cistine Novacek of the Middle Kingdom of Talheim, and you *will* lower your blade—*now!*"

To her shock, Thorne's sword fell away from her neck. He tipped his head, studying her matted hair and muddy dress, searching for the princess beneath all the filth her capture had brought to her. "And why have you come to Valgard, Princess Cistine Novacek of Talheim?"

"I've come to appeal to the Chancellor of Kanslar Court," Cistine said— and then added for good measure, "I'm under his protection as well. If you harm me or either of my friends, it will be the death of you."

Quill skimmed a hand under the veil of his hair, grazing the scar beneath those mottled layers. Maleck's gaze slid to Thorne, whose eyes narrowed. "You were traveling to Stornhaz to meet with Kanslar's Chancellor, of all men. With no knowledge of how to wield a blade yourself, and with a King's Cadre Warden for a companion."

Cistine sensed she was treading water over an abyss neither she nor her friends had been aware of until this moment—and that Thorne alone knew precisely how deep it was, and what sort of creatures dwelled in it.

But she refused to show him how much he'd unsettled her, or how truly out of her depth she was. She raised her chin and gripped the sword more tightly in her aching, shivering hands. "Yes, I was. Not that my business is any of yours."

"It is when my men find you traveling with a caravan of smugglers." Thorne sheathed his sword, and Quill snapped forward to disarm Cistine with a blow to the wrists, forcing her hands apart. He kicked the sword away and bundled Cistine against his chest, just like the day they'd captured her.

"Do not argue," he murmured. "Do not sass him. Don't even speak."

Cistine gave one painful twist against the strength of his arms as Maleck hauled Ashe to her feet and restrained her by her wrists. Ashe shuddered at his touch as Maleck and Quill marched them after Thorne toward the wagons. An archer led Julian alongside them, also restrained.

Where they stopped just outside the ring of firelight, the other archers met them, leading the merches out from the wagons and thrusting them to their knees in the grass.

The merch who'd told them of the bandit hoards was the first to raise his head. In the flickering firelight, he'd gone ashen. "You. *You're* the mongrel of the Vingete Vey?"

Thorne looked at them with pitiless spite, and Cistine saw in him the man they'd told stories of. "Answer me quickly, and death will also be quick. Waste my time, and I'll make more of it to gut you."

The youngest merch swallowed audibly.

"Who made the bid for your weapons, and why?" Thorne asked.

"Someone in Skyygan," the head merch spoke up. "We aren't foolish enough to tell you a name."

"But foolish enough to transport weapons down the Vingete Vey." Quill's voice was lazy. "Under the guise of garments and food? Really?"

Cistine cut a quick glance toward Julian. That was the same lie Rolf had given them, but Quill had learned, all the way back in Veran, that the caravan wasn't what it seemed.

"Why is Skyygan arming itself with steel from the Black Coasts?" Thorne demanded. "And why is it being done in secret?"

"Ask Chancellor Benedikt," the merch spat. "If you're man enough to walk into Stornhaz and face the Judgement Seat yourself, *bandayo*."

Quill's arms tightened around Cistine, and Thorne's jaw tensed at the strange word. He stepped forward, drawing his sword and resting it against the merch's neck. "Did you know what you were transporting when you set out, or was this Rolf's idea, and his pay kept you from asking questions?"

The merch lifted his chin. "Unlike you, I do my dealings in the open, and with pride. We all knew. We offered our wagons for sparse mynts to serve the Courts. So ask me again if I'll tell you that name."

"No. I know you won't."

Thorne's blade stroked. The merch's severed head fell to the ground.

Cistine arched, bile traveling up her throat. Quill released her, pushing her toward Julian, and as his captor unhanded him he caught her and brought her into the shelter of his chest so she didn't have to see Quill and Thorne bring down the other merches. But she heard their screams, their prayers—and then the deafening silence that meant the only ones still alive in the meadow were Thorne's people and hers.

Cistine peered out from the crook of Julian's shoulder, watching as Thorne sheathed his blade, stepped over the headless merches, and walked toward her. "Look at me, Princess."

Julian's grip tightened around her, but Cistine fought to turn, to face Thorne even while she leaned back into the strength of Julian's chest. If he was going to kill her now, he would not run her through from behind.

With his arms folded, his eyes like chips of ice, Thorne watched her. Behind him, Ashe hung forward slightly in Maleck's grip, taking weight from her injured leg. Quill glanced between them, his eyes dancing just as the firelight danced along his unsheathed blade.

She wondered if Thorne would order Quill to kill her himself, because he'd left them unchained.

"Princess of Talheim," Thorne said. "Do you want to live?"

"Yes," Cistine gasped.

Thorne's eyes narrowed. "Don't take that tone with me. If you want to survive, you'll fight for your life. You won't beg me for it."

Cistine didn't know what he meant, but Quill sheathed his sword.

"Free the horses," Thorne said to the archers. "Bury the bodies. Quill, the chest. Maleck, with me."

He strode toward the grove beyond the wagons, and with Julian's arm around her back, Cistine stumbled after him. With every step Thorne took, and every step they followed, Cistine heard it again: *Come. Come this way.*

And despite her terror, Cistine's feet heeded that call.

CHAPTER TWELVE

THORNE SET A ruthless pace through the dense undergrowth, moving with easy familiarity among the black pillars of the trees, brushing against the night buds blossoming between them. The leaves' veins were a vibrant light-blue, like ghostlight, casting a dim glow along the forest floor. Flowers shivered when Thorne passed them, as if he emitted a palpable energy that sent even nature cowering.

When Ashe's limp slowed them after the first hour, Maleck snapped a branch from a tree and tossed it to her. With that crutch in her hand, they moved even swifter, and Cistine almost screamed with frustration. Her weary feet stumbled over every root and rock, the sharp angles of the forest floor digging into her thin flats.

She was too weary to care where they were going now or what would happen when they arrived.

The pale light of inclining dawn seamed the undergrowth when Cistine stumbled yet again, her sore feet catching in the hem of her dress, and Julian grabbed her elbow to steady her. "I could carry you, Princess."

Cistine shook her head. She was too tired to speak, but she knew she couldn't show that kind of weakness in front of Thorne. He was the bandit leader the merches had feared, and as a princess, as a leader herself, she refused to seem weaker than him.

Any weaker than she already was.

They'd gone perhaps another mile when the rush of falling water reached Cistine's ears. The trees thinned, but the shadows elongated against their faces, and when they finally emerged from the undergrowth she saw the day was later than she'd expected—well past sunhigh. Brown stone hills arrested the light, their great heights propping up a plateau ahead. Water snaked over the lip of it, cascading down a sheer fall and roaring around the rocks at its base into a city of stone-and-wood edifices. Some were built at the cliff base, some hollowed from the brown rock itself. Dirt paths and wooden bridges hemmed the city's fragments together across the river, and small, hardy trees and grasses struggled from the dirt wherever the water touched.

One house, larger than the rest, was wedged against the cliffs, its three hefty watermills churning louder than the echoes of conversation on the wind. These were the sounds of life, the musical backdrop of a normal day. Cistine could've shut her eyes and believed they were in Astoria.

The thought of Astoria, a home she might never see again, stole the last of her strength.

Cistine's knees gave way. Julian grabbed her shoulders and shouted her name, and then she was unconscious.

Cistine wasn't certain how much time had passed, or where she was, when she woke from her dreamless slumber. The first things that struck her were the smells of naked wood and weapon polish—scents that had embraced her for as long as she could remember, thanks to Ashe—and the grainy starch of clean linens.

She was lying face-down on an unfamiliar bed.

She sat up swiftly, then stiffened and moaned. Her head throbbed horrifically with every movement, her mouth dry as sunbaked rocks. The soles of her feet stung from blisters, but at least someone had removed her slippers. Her heels trailed on the scratchy sheets as she slowly dragged her knees beneath her body, surveying the room.

She'd never seen anything like it before. The craftsmanship was immaculate, the wooden posts carved into elegant twists and the archways fashioned into a latticework of knots and angles. Everything was wood—the bedframe she'd slept on, the walls, the rafters, the seats and sofas. Even the empty shelves, sprouting from the walls across the small room, were chiseled from the wooden panels themselves. This room, and the small sliver of hallway beyond it, sprouted from one enormous skeleton: ribs of ornamentation, organs of chairs and couches, and veins of darkwood decoration.

It would have been beautiful if it wasn't her prison.

As the pain in her temples receded to a dull roar, Cistine finally noticed the gentle, throaty chug of the watermills, all turning slightly out of time with one another, right outside the window. She was in the large house at the base of the falls, then.

And beneath the turn of the mills, voices. Murmuring on the other end of the hall.

Cistine glanced shrewdly around the room. No sign of a guard. She was unbound and unwatched. Nothing kept her from walking toward those voices but the fear of what she would face when she did.

She touched a hand gingerly to the side of her neck, where Thorne's sword had tasted the sweat of her skin. The longer she was awake, the more the fear returned. The mongrel hadn't caged her yet, unless his cages consisted of fine wooden walls. But she was alone, with no sight of Julian or Ashe. She was disarmed of everything but her wits. And with a pounding headache, even those were shriveling.

"You're a princess," she murmured to herself. "You will not cower in a room and wait to be summoned."

The vein of strength in those words reminded Cistine of her mother.

She pushed herself up from the bed. Wavering with hunger and thirst, she gripped the small bedside table to steady herself. Then she hobbled quickly on sore feet down the short, dark corridor and into the home's spacious kitchen.

Inviting scents of nuts and berries wreathed this room, but the company was far less welcoming. There were already five people present: one leaning against a wooden counter jutting from the opposite wall, one sitting where the counter cornered into a ledge set with stools, two at the table, and one standing against the wall to Cistine's right, where an enormous blackstone hearth burned with flames. The aroma of baking bread came from its belly.

Every one of these people stopped talking as Cistine entered the room.

Her eyes went to Maleck at once, reclining against the counter. Framed with hanging herbs and sacks of fist-sized potatoes strung up along the ceiling, he almost seemed benevolent. But Cistine tensed at the sheer number of butchering knives and other, smaller preparation utensils arrayed on the counter behind him, all within grabbing distance of his lethal hands.

At the table with Ashe, Julian broke into a relieved grin that shattered Cistine's focus, dragging it away from Maleck. Beside him, Ashe cursed quietly. "Thank God you're finally awake."

"The gods had nothing to do with it." The girl at the ledge swung from her stool and swaggered toward Cistine, the hearth's light brightening the contours of her golden-brown skin. Her bushel of dark curls, tossed casually across the top of her head, sprang against her amber eyes as she halted before Cistine, studying her with arms akimbo. She was taller than Cistine, and slender as a willow switch. "She still looks awfully weak. If I push her, do you think she'll fall over?"

Julian planted his hands on the table. "I wouldn't try."

She smirked. "I'm only joking. I'll admit, she doesn't look quite as fragile without you carrying her."

Cistine's neck warmed as she glanced at Julian. The thought of him having to carry her because she'd *fainted*, of all the mortifying, predictable things—

His smile suggested he hadn't minded, and somehow that made it worse.

"I'm Tatiana." The tall woman shuffled a hand through her hair. "That scowler by the stove is Ariadne. Maleck, I'm told, you've already met."

Cistine risked a glance at Ariadne and found as much glacial cold in her stare as Maleck's. Her upswept eyes, broad features, and full lips were a gentle collage contrasting sharply with everything else about her: dark armor, rigid posture, and a body slung with blades. A sword's hilt peeped over her shoulder. Gnarled scars veined the inlines of her wrists. She didn't seem to breathe as she stared at Cistine.

Cistine feared she might be sick again. "Where are we?"

Tatiana went to the table, sliding out a chair and dropping into it. "Somewhere you shouldn't be, if you ask me: our home."

Cistine edged toward the table, sinking into the seat between Ashe and Julian. Julian sprawled his arm across the back of her chair, his gaze fixed on Maleck—selecting him as the most dangerous figure in the hot kitchen. Ashe's eyes settled on Ariadne. And Cistine, against her better judgement, addressed Tatiana: "*Why* are we here?"

Tatiana blew her hair from her brow. "That, I suspect, was Quill's doing. It would explain why Thorne hauled him out to the falls six hours ago, and they still haven't returned."

Cistine winced. Though Quill had lied to her and helped Thorne capture her, and he certainly wasn't her friend, she still didn't want him to bleed on her account. Or worse. She knew Thorne was capable of worse, thanks to his reputation among the merches and Vassoran guards he and his bandits terrorized.

"What were you discussing when I walked into the room?" Cistine asked.

Julian shifted uneasily. Ashe went very still.

"*Tell me.*"

Julian sighed. "Bargaining for our release."

"Unfortunately, you have absolutely nothing we want." Tatiana folded her arms on her muscled navel as she surveyed them. "Or, at least, nothing *Thorne* wants. I could think of several uses for each of you before we slit your throats. Particularly the dark-haired one."

She bared her teeth in a sleek smile that made Cistine's cheeks flame. "Are you a...barmaid?"

Tatiana raised a sculpted brow. "Take a good whiff of me. Is that mead you smell? Not tonight, it's not. Unlike a barmaid, I only sell my services to people who are worthwhile."

"That hardly includes any of you," Ariadne said. "One wonders why you aren't buried in the field with those merches."

"Buried," Cistine said. "You mean quartered and sent out as a warning to our families?"

Tatiana laughed. "Who's been telling you stories?"

"People that your *leader* beheaded."

"Captives tell tales," Ariadne said. "Not all are true."

"And yet, those captives are dead," Cistine said. "The stories seem true to me."

"Who's telling stories?" The easygoing voice came from behind the counter ledge. Cistine hadn't even noticed there was another doorway there. "Are they about me? They'd better be flattering if they are."

Cistine breathed out a sigh of relief as Quill joined them, damp and smiling, dressed in his casual attire from the tavern again. A bruise marked his left cheek, darkening the socket of his eye, but he didn't move as if he was in pain.

"Are you all right?" Cistine demanded.

Quill ignored her as he passed Maleck and thumped knuckles with him, then grabbed an orange from a fruit basket on the counter.

Tatiana sat up, feet falling to the floor. "Featherbrain!"

"Saddlebags!" Quill swaggered up to the table. "Still looking like something scraped off the bottom of a horseshoe."

"And you still smell like rotten gizzards. Did you bring me a gift?"

"Don't I always?" Quill unhooked a knife from his belt and tossed it onto the table, and Cistine's breath caught as she saw that blood flaked the black blade. "Does this appease your delicate tastes?"

Julian grunted, resting a hand on Cistine's shoulder as Tatiana examined the knife. "Perfection. I love when you bring them to me still dripping in blood."

Ashe growled under her breath, "Barbarians."

Maleck's eyes flicked to her, his arms tightening faintly in their cross. But he didn't make excuses for his brutal friends, bantering over the bloodied blade.

"You mean you don't have a taste for weapons stolen from dead merches?" Tatiana sheathed the knife in her belt. "Pity. Maybe if you did, you wouldn't have gotten captured."

"That's enough," Julian said. "Name your price so we can leave."

"The choice isn't ours," Maleck said. "It belongs to Thorne."

"Where is he, anyway?" Tatiana asked.

Quill dragged out the chair beside her and swung his feet into her lap as he sat. "Where is he always when there's something important to discuss?"

"Brooding."

"If Thorne isn't coming, I'm going." Ariadne shrugged away from the wall. "There are defenses that need shoring up. Quill?"

He yawned, waving a hand. "You go on ahead. I haven't slept in days."

"That's no excuse."

"We aren't going to sit here waiting for one of you to name your price!" Ashe snapped. "We won't be treated like common prisoners."

Tatiana laughed. "As if common prisoners are shown to the kitchen. We don't bake bread for just *anyone*."

"Then why are you doing any of this?" Cistine asked.

"Because I told them to."

Cistine shuddered at the sound of Thorne's cold voice, heralding his arrival through the same doorway where Quill had appeared. His eyes blazed in the warm light, and his knuckles were split bloody.

Cistine glanced at Quill's bruised cheek, her heart sinking.

At Thorne's approach, everyone sat at attention—even Ashe and Julian, more defensive than respectful or afraid as they pressed closer to Cistine's sides.

Thorne spread his hands slowly on the table's edge, bending low. He had the bearing of a predator—something that prepared itself to leap and devour in one swift motion. "I see you've met my cabal: Maleck, Quill, Tatiana, and Ariadne."

"Cabal," Julian echoed. "What does that mean?"

"A small army." Cistine's belly churned with nervousness as she eyed Thorne. A bandit hoard was one thing, but she was beginning to suspect these were not simple thieves. "And that makes you—the prince?"

"High Tribune," Thorne said. "Now give me a reason I shouldn't send Maleck and Quill to dig your graves."

Quill twitched subtly, keeping his gaze on the wall. Ashe leaned forward, resting a hand on Cistine's knee, and Maleck shifted in anticipation.

Cistine didn't doubt her Warden wanted to lunge across the table and bring Thorne down, but she couldn't let that happen—for all their sakes. Instead she swallowed, reaching for the only weapon she had left to wield now that Thorne had parried aside her noble title and her pleas. "I have the name you wanted from the merches. The man who hired the caravan."

Julian stiffened. Quill's head swung toward her, surprise parting his lips.

"That's what you want, isn't it?" Cistine added. "I heard what you said to them. You need that name. And I know what it is."

Thorne's fingers tightened on the table's edge. "Speak it."

"Not like this." Cistine's bowels clenched. "I'll speak to you, noble to noble, not as your prisoner. I'll treat for our lives. Nothing less."

Tatiana brushed her hair from her eyes and held it pinned to her scalp, staring at Thorne. He looked at Ariadne, who held his gaze with chilly immutability.

Thorne straightened, motioned with a tilt of his head, and walked from the kitchen into the dark hallway toward the room where Cistine had woken. A door whispered open, and light illuminated the carvings on the wooden walls.

Ashe's hand tightened on Cistine's knee. "We'll go with you."

"No," Cistine said, though her heart lodged in her throat and made speaking difficult. "It has to be us. Only us."

"Cistine," Julian argued, "you're out of your depth."

Planting her trembling hands on the tabletop, Cistine stood. "Keep watch. I'll be back soon."

She followed Thorne to the door, which opened to a tall, windowless stairwell. The steep climb ended in a loft—Thorne's room, she assumed. It jutted directly above the one she'd woken up in, with a crescent window overlooking the river. Long, low-roofed, and narrow, the space was littered with thick animal hides of colors and textures Cistine had never seen before. There was a small bed, and a tiered writing desk on the window's left, across from a small hearth. A pair of armchairs opposed one another in front of the tinted windows.

Thorne went to them without a word, and sat. Cistine slowly followed, standing behind the chair across from him. She wouldn't face him without something—a table, a chair—between them.

Thorne rested his hands on his thighs and said nothing. Cistine swallowed, then blurted the first thought that came to mind: "You hit Quill."

Those calm, cool eyes narrowed. "Yes."

"Because he asked you to bring us here?"

Thorne brushed his thumb along his split knuckles. "I don't punish my cabal with my fists. I gave Quill the choice: he found you, he took charge of you, so he had the right to fight for your place here. Otherwise, you were mine to deal with."

"He fought for us?" Cistine murmured.

Thorne nodded. "And he lost. So the choice is mine."

That explained why Quill had been reluctant to look at her. He'd been ashamed to leave Cistine's fate, her future, in the hands of the man who'd ruthlessly cut down the merches.

"If I free you now," Thorne said, "and you give me the name, will you go to Stornhaz?"

"Yes," Cistine said.

"Then you'll die." Thorne's blunt retort left Cistine speechless. "Whatever Rolf and his men told you, whatever you heard in Veran, it was a lie. The City of a Thousand Stars will cut you into pieces. Stornhaz will not turn you out the same way it took you in. That isn't what the Courts do."

Temples throbbing again, Cistine gripped the seat rest. "What do you suggest I do, then? Go back to the coast?"

"Just as dangerous," Thorne said. "Word has most likely spread that you traveled with Rolf's caravan, and that we attacked it. When someone takes notice of that, you'll become the target of their suspicions. Anyone who's ever suffered at the hands of my cabal, knowingly or not, will want to flay the truth about us from your bones."

The low ember of frustration in Cistine's belly roared into flame. "Then this is *your* fault. Because I associated with you and your people—against my will, might I add!—now I have no welcome in Veran *or* Stornhaz!"

Thorne scowled. "My cabal has been sacking wagons bound for Stornhaz with food, supplies, and weapons, for years. *Years.* Quill kept an ear open in the taverns all that time, and our names were never mentioned. No one thought we were capable of this...that we were the ones behind these attacks. There are plenty of bandit raids on the Vey, enough that we could cloak our movements among them like one raven in a flock of many. We made certain it could never be traced back to us—by names or by numbers. But because Quill let himself forget the mission, one of the Vassora escaped. Now they know who we are. And word will spread, because my head is a prize any Chancellor would love to catch."

Cistine's breath snagged. She could still hear it in her head, above the splatter of blood, above the crunch of bone under swords: Maleck's shout when Quill had stopped fighting. When he'd stared at Cistine for a heartbeat too long.

And now they knew Thorne's people were the ones who had attacked the road, stopping so many caravans, because of her. Because Quill had let himself be distracted by her, and forced Maleck to call him back to the fight.

Cistine swallowed. "I'm sorry."

Thorne sat taller in his seat. "What?"

"I'm sorry." Cistine pulled her weak legs around the chair and sank into it, holding her head in her hands. "I don't approve in any way of what you do. Bloody knives and dead merches and ambushes on the road. It's barbaric. But my father was a warrior, too, and this...this will make it difficult to keep yours alive. I'm sorry I distracted Quill."

Thorne remained silent. Cistine couldn't bring herself to look at him, to see if there was amusement, or scorn, or even hatred in his eyes.

"I don't approve of what we do, either." Thorne's quiet words were so startling, they brought Cistine's focus back to his haggard face. "But survival in Valgard is not easy. Nor is thwarting our enemies. And I appreciate your concern on behalf of my warriors." He sat forward again, rubbing his palms together. "I understand why you confronted me when I attacked your Warden. I would have done the same for any of them."

Cistine's cheeks warmed at the memory of that humiliating spectacle.

"What training do you have in the sword?" Thorne asked.

It would do little good to lie to him. He'd seen how incompetent she was. "I practiced formally with a blade until I was seven years old."

"And after?"

"I found I preferred books and spending time with people. My father wanted me to be a warrior, but all those hours on the training fields seemed like such a waste. I was inheriting a peaceful kingdom with deep political trenches. I thought it was better to train my mind than my body."

She glanced up at Thorne, searching his gaze for that mockery, but she found only impassive deliberation.

"Go to Stornhaz, and you may match the Chancellor of Kanslar Court for wits," he said. "But sooner or later, he will outmaneuver you. And you're unfit to face him if it comes to blows."

"I have Julian and Ashe. Both are accomplished swordfighters."

"And you're content to rely on that? Who stood over your Warden and faced my blade? Who would've died if I'd let my stroke fall?"

Cistine scowled. "You think I'll be forced to cross blades with the Chancellor of Kanslar Court?"

"I believe that to face *any* Chancellor unprepared invites Nimmus and the Undertaker to your door."

It was the second time Cistine had heard of this Nimmus, the first time as a curse from Quill's stunned mouth, and it sent a chill through her the way both men had spoken it with almost fearful reverence. Worse still was the alarming realization of ignorant she truly was, and how these people could exploit her for it.

"Fine," she said. "If I'm so hopeless and foolish, then train me."

Thorne cocked a brow. "Those are your terms?"

It took Cistine a moment to remember why she was in this room. Why they were having this conversation. "Yes. I'll give you the name of Rolf's employer, and in exchange I want you and your *cabal* to prepare us to face whatever dangers you suppose are waiting in Stornhaz. That includes making certain Ashe can walk without a limp when we go."

"Fair," Thorne said. "On one condition. My cabal's time is precious. You will not squander it through laziness or games. Understood?"

Cistine had expected more of an argument, and she regarded him cautiously. His face betrayed no hint of distrust, not even a glimmer of a lie. His voice was a steady, sure rasp, faintly accented.

She didn't trust it.

"All of that," Cistine said. "Training, and healing for Ashe...in exchange for one name. That's fair by Valgardan standards?"

Thorne stared through the window at the dark land beyond, the distant, roaring falls. "Names carry greater weight here than a Talheimic can imagine. A name can turn the tide of a battle. It can define life or death for a Valgardan."

Cistine believed the low earnestness of his words. But she decided to test him, just a bit.

She reclined in her seat. "If this name has such value to you, then I have other demands as well. I want my trunk back."

Thorne folded his arms, facing her again. "The clothes, the books, and the jewelry, you may have. The weapons are ours. We need every piece of steel we can find."

"Not Ashe's sword. It's valuable to her."

Thorne narrowed his eyes—calculating. "Then I want an heirloom in exchange. Something I can sell to make up the blade's value."

"Done." She was hardly attached to the necklace she'd bought in Veran, anyway. "And I want a tutor. Someone who will train me in the ways of

Valgardan culture, so I'm not out of my depth in *any* way when I travel to Stornhaz."

"I was going to propose that very thing."

"Good. And I want you to tell your people not to touch Ashe."

Thorne tipped his head. "You do realize she fought against us in the war."

"*You* realize we aren't at war anymore," Cistine replied. "And if we were, then as an augur, Maleck would deserve death just as much as you believe Ashe does."

Thorne's gaze turned cold again. "How much do you know about augmentation?"

"Enough to know the Northern Kingdom was dangerous, having all that power. Your augurs were brutal, vicious opportunists."

"You don't know Maleck."

"You don't know Ashe."

They glared at one another, the air between them heating like a forge. Cistine was suddenly aware of how vulnerable she was—how Thorne could leap from his chair and break any of her bones with a cut of his hand.

But to her relief, he receded, drumming his fingers on the armrest. "Let's agree to keep Maleck and your Warden as far from one another as possible. It's in their nature to hate one another. I can give the word for her to remain untouched, but I can't ensure peace between them."

"That's sensible." Cistine ticked off her next words on her fingers: "So, to review: you'll train me, have me tutored, and provide healing for Ashe. In exchange, I'll give you the name of Rolf's employer."

"It seems fair," Thorne said.

It was more than that, so Cistine could barely trust it. But she had the strong sense this man's good graces were a safer place than anywhere else she would find in these strange lands. "I hope your training regimen is quick."

"We'll make you formidable, at least to some degree." Thorne stood, and Cistine rose before him. The High Tribune offered his hand. "We have an accord."

Cistine struck hands with him, holding his gaze firmly—the same way she'd seen her father face the lords and ladies of Talheim over the years. "We do."

And she realized with a jolt as their hands pulled apart that she'd just negotiated her first royal truce.

Everyone came to attention when Cistine and Thorne returned—and judging by the way Julian and Ariadne were glaring at one another, and the murderous look Ashe offered to a stone-faced Maleck, they'd arrived just in time.

"Here are the terms," Thorne announced. "We'll prepare our guests for their visit to Stornhaz. In exchange, their princess will give us the name of whoever bought the steel in Benedikt's Court." His gaze moved to Maleck. "The Warden is not to be touched."

Cistine expected Maleck to protest, to emerge from his cold shell and go toe-to-toe with Thorne over the right to fight his old enemy. But he merely dipped his head in speechless resignation—as if, after everything, killing Ashe meant nothing to him.

Quill stretched and folded his arms behind his head, flashing Cistine a smile. Reluctantly, she returned it. She wouldn't let herself forget that he wore that bruise proudly on his cheek because he'd fought for her and her people. For their right to live.

Ariadne didn't seem so pleased. She watched Thorne narrowly. "You spoke to Kallah while you were out today, didn't you?"

"Ariadne." A faint tinge of warning threaded Thorne's voice.

"Which of us do you expect to waste our valuable time making this cosseted creature into a sapling to face the winds of the Courts?"

Cistine winced at the words, but Thorne smiled. "I expect all of you to. Quill will teach her endurance. Maleck will teach her the sword. And you, Ariadne, will help Tatiana tutor her."

"And what are *you* going to teach her?" Tatiana demanded.

"Nothing. I'll reserve judgement until I'm convinced she's ready to walk into Stornhaz and emerge alive." He turned to Cistine. "What was the name?"

Cistine debated withholding it until her training had begun, to ensure Thorne wasn't tricking her. But as pressing as her need to travel to Stornhaz was, time was just as valuable to Thorne. He needed to shore up his cabal's safety again after Cistine and Quill's encounter on the Vey had broken it.

So she threw a prayer to the gods and risk to the wind. "Rolf told me the Vassora were hired by a man named Devitrius to guard the wagons."

Thorne's jaw clenched, and a flash of anger speared through his gaze. He left the room without another word, and they all stared after him. Cistine wiped her sweating palms on her thighs.

Ariadne and Maleck straightened in silent accord and followed after Thorne. In their absence, as if a band of tension had released, Quill laughed and propped his chair on its hind feet, raking his gaze over Cistine. "Everyone in this city owes their mastery of a blade to one of us, but we've never had the opportunity to train someone together before. Either you'll be the most proficient fighter in Valgard by the time you leave, or you'll be the most interesting, at least."

Tatiana eyed Cistine with cool refrain that made Cistine want to step back from her. "I suppose that means we should welcome you *officially* to Hellidom, the Sanctuary City. And stars help you now, because you're going to be fodder for Nimmus when we're through with you."

CHAPTER THIRTEEN

LULLED BY THE rasping watermills and full of delicious walnut and blueberry bread, Cistine was on the cusp of sleep that night when someone knocked on the edge of the room's doorless entryway.

She'd barely sat up when Ashe entered, followed by Julian. Both were wearing clothes scrounged from the trunk—a certain sign that so far, at least, Thorne was upholding their truce.

"Cistine," Ashe said, "what in the gods' names were you thinking?"

"Training? With *them*?" Julian demanded. "Do you realize how long that could take, Princess? Someone is bound to notice we're missing from my family's estate if we waste time haggling with bandits."

Cistine sighed, drawing the rough blanket tightly around her hips. She was surprised they'd held out against this conversation all through the awkward, silent dinner with the cabal watching them. "It was the only way. Thorne would have killed us. It was either that, or make a bargain to ensure our survival."

"And his bargain is you—a stranger from *Talheim*—well-trained and fed on knowledge of this kingdom?" Julian dropped onto the foot of the bed. "Don't be naïve."

"I'm not! The training was *my* idea. I negotiated a trade. This is what royalty does, Julian!"

"But you hate the blade." Ashe limped slowly to the seat across from Cistine's bed. It faced away from the glass-paned doors that opened up onto a balcony overlooking the river. The moonlight framed Ashe's lean body as she bent over, gripping her swaddled thigh. "Cyril and I tried everything short of threatening you to put a sword in your hand."

"And maybe this Thorne only agreed to training to keep you quiet while he sends a ransom demand to your father," Julian growled. "That would destroy our little ruse, too."

Chills rushed down the backs of Cistine's arms. She fought to endure them, to keep them from creeping into her belly and fomenting into panic. "Maybe so. But I'll pester them until they train me anyway. Whatever comes, I'll leave this city ready to face it."

"Why now?" Ashe demanded. "Why this fight?"

"Because I almost lost both of you," Cistine said. "I had a sword in my hand when I faced Thorne, and I still nearly watched my Warden die. If there's even a chance we'll face the same kind of danger in Stornhaz, then I'm determined to go prepared."

Julian cocked his knees, linking his arms loosely around them. "If that's even a possibility, then maybe we should turn back now, Princess. We can find another way to protect Talheim. Anything might be better than this."

Cistine stared at him, stung. "Do you really think that giving up is preferable to me being trained?"

Julian's brow pinched, and his eyes widened—a wounded look that made Cistine instantly regret her question. "This isn't about you wielding a sword. It's that you shouldn't have to."

"He's right," Ashe said. "You chose books over weapons, Cistine. If these people are right about the dangers of Stornhaz, then we may be safer returning to Veran. Or walking straight back to Talheim."

Cistine shook her head. "Thorne said that isn't an option. Our association with his cabal on the road has already made targets of us. That's why this training is important."

"Then let us be your teachers," Julian offered.

"Ashe is wounded and you're not even a Warden yet yourself. You saw how Quill and Maleck fought. They have years of experience on us."

"And at one time they had something else in their arsenal, which makes them the kind of mentors you *don't* want," Ashe said.

"Augmentation?" Cistine murmured, and Ashe's eyes glittered like steel. "How were you able to tell that just from the scars on Maleck's chest?"

Ashe gazed through the window, as if the reflection showed her life as it once was—life during the war. "Augmentation is a beast. A ravager. Raw, unfiltered power mined from pockets all over this kingdom. It's the reason your grandfather started the war, and he was right to. Valgard was becoming too powerful with all those wells of gods-given energy under their feet."

Cistine shuddered to imagine someone like Jad with that sort of clout behind his blows.

"When we fought the Valgardans, they used conduits to carry the burden of that power," Ashe continued. "No one was able to use augmentation without it taking some physical toll, but the conduits allowed them to pass it along their armor and out from their hands and feet without it burning them alive."

"You think that's what scarred Maleck?" Cistine asked.

Ashe shrugged. "Maybe he was careless. Maybe the conduits in his armor failed. But that was an augmented burn, I'd stake my life on it."

"All the more reason not to let him near you," Julian muttered.

"No," Cistine spoke against her thudding heart. "All the more reason to have a warrior of that caliber show me how to defend myself."

Ashe tossed up her hands, then dragged them through her hair. "Why are you so determined to see things his way? *Thorne's* way?"

"Because we are absolutely out of our depth!" Cistine hissed. "What we understand about Valgard is a patchwork of wartime memory and useless headknowledge. I didn't know about robbers on the Vingete Vey, or about the dangers of Stornhaz. My father never told me any of this...he's suppressed so much talk of Valgard, it's left us at a disadvantage now."

Ashe grimaced. "He has his reasons for that, Cistine. None of us ever thought we would set foot here again."

"I understand that," Cistine said. "But we're here *now*, and if Thorne's cabal can give us some sort of edge, don't you think we're better off with it?"

Julian hung his head. "I don't like it. I still think you should leave the fighting to us."

Cistine's belly fluttered with nerves at his concern. Because he *wanted* to protect her. But it wasn't enough to compromise on. "These were Thorne's terms. We're alive and safe because I agreed to them. I won't apologize for protecting either of you. Ever."

"And you're certain this is what you want?" Ashe asked. "To train in swordplay?"

Cistine blew out a long breath. "Not under better circumstances. But we'll play the hand we've been dealt."

"Spoken nothing like a princess," Julian grinned.

Cistine wanted to laugh at his teasing, but a sudden hollowness set in. She'd simply spoken like herself.

"If you're both ready to accept this," she said, "I'd like to sleep."

Ashe stood from the chair, faltering on her injured leg. And that, more than anything, hardened Cistine's resolve like new steel plunged into cold water. Ashe needed help, and from these people who resented the Cadre, Cistine knew they would find it no other way than through her truce with Thorne.

"Cistine." Ashe's fingers tightened around the chair's headrest. "Thank you for making this sacrifice for us."

"That's what nobility does," Cistine said. "We help the weak. That's why we came to Valgard, remember?"

Ashe's jaw dropped in mock disbelief. "Are you saying I'm weak?"

"Oh, go to bed!" Cistine threw her pillow at Ashe, who laughed as she caught it, lobbed it back, and limped slowly out into the hall.

Julian didn't move. He beat his fist slowly into his open palm, staring at the vacant, sculpted doorway when Ashe was gone.

Cistine's cheeks throbbed with heat. She focused on the bedclothes, acutely conscious that her dress was still filthy, and her hair was a haystack because she lacked a brush. She was no longer the polished princess Julian had always known.

"Ashe is right," Julian said. "That was brave of you, putting your own wants aside to protect us. I'm sorry we let it go so far that you were put in that position."

"What good is a princess if she can't do what's required to defend her people?" Cistine smiled. "She would be useless."

"I've never thought you were useless."

Cistine bit the inside of her cheek, watching as Julian's eyes traveled to the balcony door.

"I swear to you," Julian said, "that after this, I'll do everything in my power to ensure your hand is never forced again. That you never have to choose between your desires and the lives of your friends."

Cistine smoothed the stiff folds of her dress over her bent knees. "Well, I might have to accept that vow."

"Then maybe you'll accept something else with it."

Cistine's breath hitched, and she looked up to find Julian staring at her—those stunning dark eyes twinkling with secrets, like distant stars that burned though they didn't touch her.

"Normally, I would ask permission from your father," Julian said, "but seeing as he's not around, I'll just have to take you at your word."

Cistine still hadn't drawn a breath.

"Cistine..." Julian ran his hand back through his hair and laughed. It was a disarmingly sweet, shy sound, so unlike his usual confidence. "God's bones! I've rehearsed this a dozen times, and it's still not right. Listen...ever since my father moved us to Practica, I haven't stopped thinking about you. At first, I thought I was just missing home and, you know, you were a part of that. I tried burying myself in all these taverns and courting girls over the years, but it hasn't changed anything. I can't forget about you, no matter how many other women I'm with. And when these barbarians attacked us on the Vey, when that one led you back from the tavern...I knew what I was feeling right then wasn't just a Warden's loyalty to his princess. It can't be."

Cistine's heart roared so loudly it half-deafened her.

"I know we can't court officially, not until we go home," Julian rambled, "but I want to make my intentions known, at least. So, Cistine, I'd like to ask permission to be your suitor, and to court you officially when we return to Talheim. If you'll have me."

She stared at him. And stared. And stared.

"Cistine?" Julian's tone dipped with concern. "Breathe. Please?"

She did, and it came in as a humiliating, deep gasp that dragged her hand with it, covering her mouth.

Julian laughed. "Better! And just so you're aware, I'm prepared to sit outside your room all night if I have to, until I hear your answer."

"Yes!" Cistine said between her fingers—and when Julian's brows rose, she amended, "Not that you have to sleep in the hall. But, yes, you may court me. You don't need my father's permission for that."

Julian's crooked smile set her heart soaring. He looked relieved—as if he'd somehow doubted she wanted him. Her heart had yearned for this moment for seven impossible years while she hoped, and even prayed, one of them would find the courage to cross that unspoken boundary and see what lay on the other side of it.

When Julian shifted back on the bed and opened his arms to her, Cistine crawled into his embrace. Though it was more than most courtships attempted on the first night—in the first moment, even—Cistine needed his arms, and his warmth, and his hand smoothing her wild hair tonight.

"Whatever's coming," Julian murmured, "whatever paces they put you through, I want you to know you have me. You won't be alone."

And it was those words—his last before he kissed her hair, slipped from the bed, and left the room—that kept Cistine awake deep into the night. Fantasies, fears, and giddiness took their turns toying with her heartstrings, just as this cabal would soon take turns testing her fortitude. And she couldn't find peace from either.

The moon had passed over the river, painting the sky with milky light, when Cistine finally gave up on sleep and padded out to explore the house.

There were two levels, but the second was separated into rooms accessed by individual staircases, as Cistine had gathered from the lay of Thorne's chamber. Ashe and Julian slept just off the kitchen, through the second doorway. Everything beyond that was a mystery to her.

Cistine shuffled quietly through the kitchen, still smelling faintly of berries and nuts, and into the second dark hall. She glimpsed Ashe's room on the left, doorless, its single window looking out over the river. One of the watermills churned outside, creating soft music in a spray of droplets painted with moonlight like falling stars.

On the right was Julian's room, this one without a window. She could see nothing inside, not even the suggestion of Julian's outline as he slept. She paused for a moment, resting her feet and leaning against the doorframe, and wondered what would happen if she woke him and told him she couldn't sleep.

Before she could act on the raging curiosity that burned in her belly, she heard the echo of quiet voices from beyond the corridor—Quill's among them.

Cistine glanced into Julian's room again. Then she slipped down the hall.

It opened into a round parlor at the end, veined with wooden dividers hewn into branching tree limbs. Stone hearths burned on opposite walls and windows peered out over the home's craggy stone steps leading into the city of Hellidom below. The voices came from a doorway on the left of the home's front entrance.

Cistine hurried to the wooden divider beside the doorway, sinking down behind the tangle of its carved limbs and the gnarled trunk of its body. From this close, she could better hear the conversation.

"Yes, it's worth it," Thorne was saying in answer to someone's question. "We were right about this shipment being different. And now we know why."

"Devitrius," Quill growled. "Nimmus' teeth, Thorne."

"A Kanslar official shouldn't be able to purchase weapons out of season," Ariadne mused in her steel-cold voice. "Kanslar isn't permitted to make trade bargains for another month."

"Then Maleck's reconnaissance was accurate," Tatiana said. "Devitrius is buying weapons from inside Benedikt's Court, when he *should* be relaxing on the riches Stornhaz has to offer out of session."

The ensuing silence held all the weight of a secret. Cistine pressed a hand to her mouth to quiet her breathing so she wouldn't miss a word of what came next.

"Well," Tatiana added, "at least this explains why Devitrius wasn't made High Tribune of Kanslar when everything went to Nimmus in a knapsack. He's still doing his private retinue duties. And now they're planting him in other Courts."

Cistine frowned. Thorne had declared *himself* as High Tribune earlier that evening, placing himself on level with her position.

Had he lied?

"If Mal is right, and the Chancellor has his greatest supporters embedded like ticks in the other Courts," Quill said quietly, "this could become very ugly very quickly, Thorne."

"I know," Thorne sighed.

"It would be one thing if he was amassing wealth or luxury," Ariadne said. "A few trunks of garments bartered out of season, then carried back to Kanslar when the stars rise...that's nothing but predictable greed."

"But not when *Svarkyst* steel is involved," Maleck rumbled. "You remember how it sheared through Quill's armor during the last raid?"

"Like chicken down," Thorne answered.

"What we really need is more dragon scale armor," Ariadne said. "But considering the high cost of that with the last of the drakons hunted out..."

"We'd never afford it," Maleck said. "We were fortunate to steal some for Thorne."

Tatiana snorted. "And who wants to go wandering north of the Isetfells to hunt more dragons?"

"At least we intercepted these blades," Quill said. "That counts for something."

"It counts for very little," Ariadne argued. "Patrols along the Vingete Vey will triple. More Vassora will be pulled from the cities to defend the caravans, and that will leave the smaller villages in the territories with no one to guard them from real bandits when the autumn thefts begin. Not to mention, it will make *our* raids that much more difficult."

"All because Stornhaz will learn it was not only common robbers ransacking the wagons all this time," Maleck said.

Cistine winced. She didn't need to be in the room to know every eye had just turned toward Quill.

"All those years hiding our movements among the other bandit groups...wasted," Ariadne said. "All so you could spare a beautiful woman."

"Leave him alone," Tatiana snapped. "He was following his conscience. And we have a name now because of that."

"You're defending Quill," Ariadne scoffed. "Will wonders never cease?"

"And what is that meant to imply?"

"The only implication you should concern yourselves with," Thorne said, "is what will be asked of us if we can't stop the shipments from now on."

This time, Cistine wished she hadn't heard the silence. It pulsed with the unthinkable.

"We strike the Black Coast mines directly," Ariadne said. "Prevent them from turning up ore...at least for the time being."

"It could never be done without casualties," Tatiana murmured, her spat with Ariadne forgotten. "Miners. Prospectors. Men who provide for their families in Veran as well as the other territories. Every miner worth his rocksalt dreams of harvesting from the Black Coasts."

"Even men from Blaykrone," Quill said, equally soft.

"I know." Thorne's voice sounded heavy, as if the weight of his warriors' fears had moved into his body, pressing his spine and shoulders. Bending him.

Cistine felt the same heaviness bear down on her. It flattened her flush to the divider, dragging her eyes shut with the sheer vastness of it.

"Then we're in agreement," Ariadne said. "The mines are a last resort."

"The very last," Tatiana said.

Thorne drew an audible breath. "Agreed."

Cistine felt a stab of relief that there would be no more slaughters like on the Vingete Vey, no more flashing swords and bloodstained knives—at least for now. And now was all she could think of. One moment. One step before all the rest.

Smiling, she pried open her eyes—

—and found someone staring at her from across the room.

Cistine slapped a hand to her mouth again, this time to muffle her startled shriek. The woman almost blended with the shadows, she was so still. In fact, it was only her eyes Cistine saw, and a hint of her profile, both embossed in threads of moonlight.

The woman held Cistine's stunned gaze for a moment, then slowly shuffled into the middle of the room, leaning heavily on a cane. She was old, her face stamped with sun lines, her stern brow ridged from years of frowning. In this household, Cistine could hardly blame her. But it wasn't her face that made Cistine's stomach churn; it was the state of her left leg.

The limb was a twisted mess, an unwieldly tool strapped to the old woman's body, the foot mangled in half a dozen places and dragging uselessly with every step. Cistine had to force her attention up from the devastated limb to the old woman's face when she halted before her.

Despite her wizened countenance, her thick silver braid, and that leg, her gaze gouged like a blade, snaking rapidly between Cistine and the doorway—perhaps judging how much she'd heard.

Cistine had been caught eavesdropping many times for gossip in Astoria, but this was different. It would mean death for her. For Julian and Ashe.

Her lips parted, but no sound escaped past her shaking hand.

The old woman stared at her for a moment longer.

Then she winked.

While Cistine still gaped, the woman hobbled into the room where the cabal gathered, shouting as she went: "Thorne! How often must an old woman beg? Hold your meetings somewhere else...I can hear you across the hall and past four doors!"

The moment the old woman passed her hiding place, Cistine tore from the room as fast as her blistered feet would carry her, sailing back down the hall, through the kitchen, and into her own room. She collapsed face-first on her bed and listened with heart throbbing in her ears.

But no one came to confront her. No one brought accusations, angry shouts, or drawn blades to her doorway.

Still, her mind churned beyond the last hope of rest. So many names...so much significance hanging on every word spoken in that room tonight. More than ever, Cistine yearned to train her mind, to learn what Blaykrone and the Isetfells were and what they had to do with Thorne's cabal, and this steel. These blades that could cut through armor like bird down.

Shuddering, Cistine rolled onto her back. Clutching the pillow to her chest, she stared up at the ceiling with its web of different wood grains woven together. Just like these matters of caravans and Courts were woven together.

In the darkness, she whispered words and phrases, memorizing them until she could write them down: Isetfells. Blaykrone. The territories. The Black Coasts. Devitrius. High Tribune. Nimmus.

And that old woman...

Cistine had to find out who she was.

CHAPTER FOURTEEN

WELL, AREN'T YOU a gleam of sunlight on a cloudy day, Princess?"

Quill's greeting coaxed no more than a faint snarl from Cistine as she toppled into the chair across the table from him and helped herself to the heel of the bread loaf—all that remained from last night's meal. It seemed she was one of the last ones awake, though the sun had barely peeked over the horizon. Quill sprawled against the table, gulping a mug of something hot and chicory-scented. Tatiana sat on the counter behind him, dressed to start the day and leisurely plucking apart her own portion of bread. When she caught Cistine's eye, Tatiana slid off the counter and sauntered from the room.

Cistine stifled a sigh. That was how it was going to be, then.

Quill didn't seem bothered by Tatiana's sudden departure, finishing off his drink in two deep gulps. "If you want breakfast, you ought to at least attempt to be an early riser."

"If this isn't early, what is?" Cistine grumbled, buttering and devouring her bread in a few rapid bites.

"Let me say it this way: none of us has missed a sunrise in ten years."

Cistine almost choked on her bread. "How can you *stand* that?"

He shrugged. "You acclimate, like with anything. From now on, it's dawn revelry and training with me until the heat of the day. Afterward, Tati will have her way with you. Then you'll rotate to Maleck, then Ariadne. I can't begin to guess what she has in store for you, so…good luck, Stranger."

His tone was casual, but he flopped his hair restlessly across his head. Cistine watched the ravage of mismatched locks, white eclipsing black and brown. "Why is your hair colored that way?"

Quill swallowed, his throat bobbing sharply. "A cosmetic accident. I don't like to talk about it."

"I'm sorry, I didn't mean to offend."

Quill palmed his locks again. "Hardly your fault. I'm particular about my hair is all. It happened a long time ago—before we came to the Den."

"The Den?"

"That's what we call this place." Quill indicated the walls with a wave of his hand. "Because every savage creature needs a den to dwell in." He got to his feet, tossed his mug into a wash bucket under the counter, then beckoned and strode from the kitchen, leaving Cistine to cram the last few bites into her cheeks and follow him.

They'd barely stepped foot into the outer corridor when Julian appeared in his room's doorway. At the sight of his sleep-blurred eyes, the long sleeves of his shirt tangled against the heels of his hands while he stretched and yawned, Cistine's stomach turned over with a delicious flutter.

"Off to train?" Julian asked, with a hint of scorn directed at Quill.

The warrior holstered his thumbs in his belt with a lazy smile. "That's the intention."

"I'll be all right," Cistine interrupted before machismo escalated the tension. "I'll be back before noon."

"Too long." Julian took her hand and kissed her knuckles. "Be careful, Princess."

"You as well." Though Cistine didn't have a single notion what Julian would spend his morning doing in the city of Hellidom.

Quill led the way to the Den's enormous veranda. The sky was pastel blue, the distant, daydreaming colors of a whimsical life lived in peace. Cistine couldn't believe she walked beside a bloodstained warrior under that forgiving sky.

"What happened to Faer?" she asked as they descended from the veranda.

"He's on an errand for me," Quill said. "I expect him to come back soon. I'll let him know you asked."

"Please do. He has the best manners of anyone I've met in your kingdom so far."

Quill thumbed his nose, smirking. "I'm not sure if you just insulted us or complimented him."

Cistine made a face at his back. There really was no shaming these cocky Valgardans.

Quill remained quiet as they crossed the city, offering perfunctory nods to a handful of townsfolk but keeping his gaze forward. That unbroken focus made Cistine's knees lock with dread. No doubt he was thinking ahead to whatever rigorous regimen he had in mind for her.

This was going to be painful.

They reached a flat top of rock that overlooked Hellidom from the southern edge of the town, directly across from the Den with the breadth of the shops and homes between them. Under the shadow of the plateau above, Quill motioned Cistine to a halt and circled her with slow, lanky strides, keeping his thumbs hooked in his belt.

Cistine fidgeted. "What are you doing?"

"Trying to get a measure of what I have to work with. Are you really going to train in a dress every day?"

"I don't have any other clothes."

Quill snorted. "I'll have a word with Thorne about that. But you might want to avoid disclosing it to Tatiana. She'll drag you around to raid every merch in Hellidom."

"Or she would more likely laugh at me for the rest of my life."

Quill frowned. "Tati is a difficult character, but she wouldn't want to see you suffer through training in a dress. Besides, she'll take any excuse to visit the shops."

While Cistine tried to reconcile that notion with the aloof girl who'd admired bloodstained knives and ignored her over breakfast, Quill finally halted, facing her. He pulled a spool of long white cloth from his pocket and wrapped his knuckles.

"How much formal training have you had?" he asked.

Cistine huffed at the tired question. "With the blade, until I was seven. I had tumbling and defense until I was nearly ten—hold breaks and such."

Quill nodded absently, jerking the cloth taut with his teeth and tying off the ends. "And then?"

"That was the end of it."

His eyes flashed to her face. "How old are you now?"

"Twenty."

Quill cursed. "You mean you haven't had any training in the last decade?"

"In my kingdom, we don't make a habit of raiding caravans or beheading merches," Cistine said. "We have peace."

"We have peace in Hellidom, too," Quill countered, "but you don't see our muscles growing soft."

"If you want to train your muscles so Thorne can brag of how you're good for them and little else, you're welcome to it," Cistine snapped. "I prefer to be known for my mind rather than my fists."

"It's not just about what your reputation is," Quill said. "It's about having the strength to fight anyone who challenges it. Whether you're known for your mind *or* your body."

Cistine blinked, lost for a retort as Quill planted his feet apart and put up his hands.

"Land a blow here," he tapped his left middle finger into his right palm, directly over the wrappings, "as hard as you can."

"And that will teach me endurance?"

"It will tell me just how much we *both* have to endure before you're competent."

Cistine knotted her jaw, balled her fist, and lunged, driving her knuckles into the meat of his palm with all her might. She didn't expect the pain that stabbed through her thumb and spiraled all the way from her wrist to her shoulder at the impact. She yelped, stumbling back, and Quill barked with laughter.

"Nimmus, that's worse than I thought," he said. "Have you ever had to actually land a punch in your life?"

"Princess, remember?" Cistine shook out her throbbing hand.

"And Thorne is High Tribune, but he could dismantle me in six strokes, and that's if I was giving it my all." Quill swaggered over to her, taking her arm gently and pinching his fingers around the skin. "You have no muscle tone. And the way you hit me, it was like you were trying to defeat *yourself*. Never punch with your thumb inside your knuckles. You'll break it. And you have to step into the blow—roll it from your shoulder to your fist. It's all in the shoulder and elbow, not really the hand. That just happens to be the part that lands."

This close, Cistine couldn't look away from the hideous purple-green dapple along his cheek. "Like Thorne landed his fist on you?"

Quill's eyes flicked up to her face, then returned to her hand. "He told you about that?"

"I asked," Cistine said. "You fought for us."

"I wasn't sure what else was being negotiated. It's like Tati and Ari said...we don't take in many visitors."

"What would you have done if you'd won rights to us?" Cistine was almost frightened to ask, but she needed to know.

"Most likely, I would've gotten you killed." Quill released her arm. "I would've turned you out into the wilds. And judging by the state of your friend's leg and the way you land a hit, you would've been dead inside a week."

So he'd deduced the same thing Cistine had: that the safest place for her, for now, was Hellidom. "Thank you for making the attempt."

Quill shrugged. "I told Thorne he had to make a choice, either way. He couldn't hold you captive. We aren't slavers."

"And he listened to you?"

"Thorne may be dense as a tree about some things, and moodier than Maleck, but he listens." Quill backed away from her, spreading his feet a shoulder's width apart and gesturing for her to do the same. "All right. We'll make this simple to begin with. Stretches. Then we'll jog. After that, core-strengthening exercises."

"That's all?" Cistine said. "Three things. And that will take us until noon?"

Quill smirked. "I'll be surprised if you survive that long."

Perhaps because he'd challenged her—or because he'd fought for her, and he deserved some show of gratitude for that, even if it was only that she would try—Cistine mimicked his stance. "I'll survive until fifteen minutes past sunhigh."

Quill laughed. "Then we shouldn't waste a single precious second."

In the end, Cistine fell far short of her own goal—and Quill's. She couldn't touch her toes or straighten her legs completely for the stretches. She could only jog half a mile around Hellidom before she had to walk, with a stitch throbbing in her side and her blisters pinching against the sides of her toes and the balls of her feet, and inside another mile she begged for relief. After only one set of core-strengthening exercises, she was dizzy and out of breath.

To his credit—and quite possibly to spare his own life—Quill didn't remark on her failures. He simply accommodated her pace, and assured her, as they made their way back to the Den well before noon, that she would do much better tomorrow in actual training attire. But Cistine doubted she would ever manage more than the half-mile jog or the dozen squats and lunges before she toppled over in a heap.

It was a relief when they climbed the short flight of rock steps to the door of the Den. Cistine tumbled inside, sweating and out of breath, and nearly collided with Thorne on the other side. His hand touched her elbow, steadying her, and his cold gaze jumped from her face to Quill's, asking a silent question Cistine didn't want to hear the answer to. She stormed to the kitchen instead, and nearly wept with joy when she saw both Ashe and Julian there.

"Finally!" Ashe pushed out a seat for Cistine with her good foot. The strong smell of herbs hung over her body; Cistine identified the crispness of a salt poultice and something oniony that made her nose wrinkle.

"How was training?" Julian asked, deceptively casual as Cistine took up the seat beside him instead of the one Ashe had offered her.

"An absolute disaster." Cistine glared at Ashe when she snorted. "What was that for?"

"Am I no longer allowed to clear my throat in your presence?"

"Not when it implies—Ashe," Cistine interrupted herself, leaning forward. "What is it?"

The humor crumbled from Ashe's features. "I'm still not comfortable with this. Sending you away with one of these murderers every morning, where we can't keep watch over you."

"You can come along with us if it will make you feel better…if your leg can manage it. But it won't be good for much other than your amusement."

"Not everyone is built for life with a sword in hand," Julian said.

"I haven't even touched a sword yet! It's the jogging and stretching that I'm terrible at."

Her friends traded amused smiles, but they didn't push the subject as Cistine helped herself to a plate of carved pork shoulder that took up the center of the long table. Her early retirement from training with Quill gave her more time to eat, and she managed to devour two helpings while Julian and Ashe discussed the city and their plans to scour it for information.

Cistine was glad she didn't have to engage in their schemes. She was already rooted too deeply in reliving the humiliating morning and wondering what the rest of Thorne's cabal could possibly do to make it worse.

She'd barely finished her second helping when Tatiana sashayed into the room, wearing thick, baggy pants that hugged her ankles, and a shirt that was little more than a handkerchief covering her breasts and gesturing down to her navel. Cistine's cheeks warmed with embarrassment, and she glanced at Julian. To his credit, he only scowled at Tatiana.

"Seems like it's my turn with you." Tatiana plucked an apple wedge from the pork platter and jammed it into the corner of her mouth. "I hope you're ready to listen and learn, because I'm not going to waste my time on a princess whose only concerns are fabric patterns and beautiful boys."

"I'm ready." Cistine rose slowly, and winced. Her abdominal muscles and calves had seized up while she sat, and now she had to limp to join Tatiana in the doorway. Cistine threw a helpless smile back at her friends; Julian returned it, but Ashe only grimaced as she picked up Cistine's plate and tossed it in the wash bucket.

Tatiana led her through the hall and to the right of the main parlor, and Cistine caught a brief glimpse across it to the doorway where she'd eavesdropped on the cabal the night before. She only spotted a sliver of the room beyond—a dark table, no chairs, and curved walls—before Tatiana opened a door down the opposite hall and thrust her inside.

Cistine liked this room at once. It was an amalgam of stone and wood like many of the homes in Hellidom, the broad, dark beams overhead forging a cozy atmosphere. While there were no windows, plenty of light burned from the hearth on the wall; and there were clothes everywhere.

Cistine's mouth practically watered at the sight: dresses laid out on the bed, shirts and pants hanging from hooks on the walls. All the seating was buried under glittering flats, silk robes, and thick wool coats.

Cistine ran her fingers over a sheer aquamarine dress on the bed. "Where did you buy all these?"

"Wherever I could find them. Caravan raids, shops in Veran, here in Hellidom—don't touch that, it's worth more than your life. Why am I not surprised you love clothes?"

"Apparently, so do you. Some of these patterns...I've never seen anything like them before. The corset is so thick—"

"Armored," Tatiana smirked. "Because even at a Valgardan ball, someone might try to kill you."

Cistine snatched her hand back. There wasn't a hint of jest in Tatiana's eyes, or in her smile. "Has that happened to you?"

Tatiana raked a palm up the length of her bare arm, along a faint scar from her elbow to her shoulder. "When you live this life as long as I have, you accumulate a few wounds. Not that you would know anything about that."

"I'm not here to compare scars with you," Cistine said, "no more than I'm here to hurt your city, or this cabal. I just want to learn what I need to know, and then be on my way. That's *all*."

"It's not about your intentions. It's about the danger your presence poses. Quill obviously didn't think of that. *Thorne* didn't care. And even if Maleck did, he wouldn't say anything. Which means as usual, Ariadne and I are the only ones thinking clearly."

Cistine perched her hands on her hips. "Well, now *I'm* in danger from associating with you. But I'm willing to make the most of it, and I gave Thorne the name he wanted. So I'd like it very much if we could survive these sessions without killing each other."

Tatiana's brows floated upward. Her lips twitched. "All right, then. Where would you like to start?"

Cistine selected a plush chair, moved the shirts from its cushion, and lowered herself gingerly into it. Her aching muscles thanked her with a slim edge of relief, and she watched as Tatiana shut the door, stoked the hearth, and settled onto the bed. Its beige-and-cream linens complimented both the wooden walls and Tatiana's skin as she settled, cross-legged and comfortable, among the pillows. "I can ask about anything?"

"Whatever you like," Tatiana said. "And I can choose whether or not to answer that question."

Cistine quirked her lips to the side, surveying the room. "Do you have something to write with? And on?"

"You want to know if Valgard has writing utensils?"

Cistine scowled. "I want to know if I may *use* them."

"I know what you meant." Tatiana unlatched the drawer of her bedside table and withdrew an enormous, thick book. She tossed it to Cistine. "Do what you want with that. I've never written in it."

Cistine couldn't fathom why. The embossed cover, fletched with what looked like real gold shavings, had to be worth a heap of mynts. She told Tatiana as much, and the warrior shrugged. "It's too sentimental to part with, but the memories are too heavy for me to write over them, either."

Cistine caught the fountain pen Tatiana flicked to her and paused with the tip to the paper, considering her many questions. "Start at the beginning. How is this kingdom laid out?"

"Why do you want to know?"

"Oh, for God's sake! Not to conquer it! If I'm going to navigate through it, I ought to know where I'm going!"

"Fair." Tatiana rolled from the bed and retrieved a scroll from the bookcase beside the hearth. Flopping onto the arm of Cistine's chair, she unrolled the map across their laps. "Valgard is one entity with different limbs." She traced her finger along the map, tapping the middle of it. "This is Stornhaz, the beating heart of Valgard. If our kingdom is like a wheel, then Stornhaz is the hub, and the borders of the territories are its spokes."

Tatiana pointed to the boundaries, one after the other. "Due north of Stornhaz, you're in Spoek, named for the Ghost star at the crown of the territory. It encompasses the Isetfell Mountains. Northeast from Stornhaz is Nordbran, under the North Fire. It's a brutal place, especially up near the steppes before you reach the mountains. Winter nights are cold enough to kill you. Summer days are hot enough to burn."

Cistine jotted notes rapidly, struggling to keep pace with Tatiana's succinct descriptions. "And due east?"

"Kroaken," Tatiana said. "Under the Crow. These are the drylands, lower than Nordbran, and more fertile…especially as you travel closer to the southeast. That's where you'll encounter Lataus, under the Mist. It's all forests and cliffs, mostly. The Nior River that turns our watermills runs down from Lataus into this territory."

"And which territory is this?"

"Unsverd," Tatiana said. "The Scythe of the Undertaker. It extends from Stornhaz all the way to the southern border we share with your Middle Kingdom, but it's mostly uninhabitable fens and a wilderness called the Wildwood."

Cistine resisted the urge to shudder at Unsverd's cruel name, and the cruel star under which these cruel people lived. "What about the southwest?"

Tatiana brushed a gentle fingertip along the map. "Blaykrone."

There it was again: the name that had brought Thorne's voice so low and inspired so much concern from Quill the night before. But Cistine couldn't give any indication she'd heard either of those things, so she let her pen hover patiently over the page while she waited. And waited.

When Tatiana didn't speak, Cistine murmured, "Is that one important to you?"

Tatiana shook herself. "No more than any other. Blaykrone is under the Blood Crown. It extends from Stornhaz to the Vaszaj Range, before Veran, which is under the Loom. It's the only city that governs itself. Due west of Stornhaz is Eben, under the River. It's watered by tributaries from the kingdom's second-largest river, the Ismalete, so it's mostly wetlands."

"And the northwest?"

"Erdotre," Tatiana said. "From Stornhaz through the Sotefold Forest. Not a friendly place. Most of the rugs in the Den are pelts from creatures unique to that territory."

Cistine compared the markings on the map to what she'd written down. "And each Chancellor oversees all eight territories?"

Tatiana snorted. "Politics are for another day. I overheard Quill and Thorne discussing things earlier. I take it you're in need of new threads?"

Cistine bit back a groan. "I'm perfectly capable of shopping for myself."

"Of course. You look as though you've bought plenty of armor in your lifetime. So, tell me which is better: steel silk from the Skurkopp spiders of the forest, or dragon scales? Or the hide of the Farkas wolves in Kroaken?"

Cistine shut the journal and folded her arms on it, glaring at Tatiana, who smiled back.

Cistine knew which of them would inevitably win this staring match, because she'd heard what Thorne had said to his cabal. His warning rattled in her skull about *Svarkyst* steel and what it could do to armor, nevermind the flesh beneath it. "Do you have any dragon scale armor?"

Tatiana's mouth turned down at the corners. "Not enough of it. But we'll find you something fitting, I have no doubt about that. Just come to the market with me tonight."

"Why would you want to help me find armor? You clearly don't like me."

"Oh, I like you well enough for a spoiled, soft Talheimic princess," Tatiana said, "which is the problem. But if Thorne wants you here for now, I might as well have my fun with you. What do you say?"

Cistine looked Tatiana over, fighting the fear that this woman would find a way to dispose of her in the city tonight and solve the little problem Thorne and Quill had created by bringing Talheimic visitors into Hellidom in the first place.

But when she considered another day of sweating and panting around the jogging circuit in a dress, she found herself agreeing despite her fears.

CHAPTER FIFTEEN

T HE PROSPECT OF training with Maleck absolutely terrified Cistine. When he came to retrieve her from Tatiana's room, she almost begged the other girl to come with them, if only so she wouldn't have to spend a moment alone with the colder of the two death-gods.

But Maleck was also quieter than Cistine had expected. He led her to one of the Den's upper rooms, accessible by a small door in the corridor that housed Julian and Ashe, leaving it open behind them.

Like Thorne's room, this stretch of attic space was long, peaked, and covered in furs; but here the dark walls sported lines of weapon racks, everything from shining blades to dark flails to polearms. Each one was familiar, but sparked no excitement, No joy. Only dull resignation.

She trailed after Maleck to a rack of daggers, and he gestured her to sit on a bench before it. While he browsed the knives fastidiously, Cistine knotted her fingers together and pressed them into her lap, trying not to think of what she'd seen him do on the Vingete Vey. With his bare hands, he could deal more damage than Cistine could with all the weapons in this room.

After several minutes, Maleck's stony silence became unbearable. Cistine cleared her throat. "Is there something I should be doing?"

Maleck turned and offered her a knife. "Hold this."

Cistine curled her fingers over the grip's ridged wrappings. Maleck stared at her as if he was waiting for something, so Cistine shrugged, avoiding his gaze.

He picked up another knife, and they traded weapons. "Quill tells me you gave up the sword when you were seven. Why?"

Cistine handed the second knife back to him. "Ask Quill. I told him that, too."

"I want to hear it from your mouth."

With a sigh, Cistine recounted the story to him.

"Training the mind over the body," Maleck said as he handed her a third knife. "If I'd possessed the freedom to make such a choice, things would not be for me as they are now."

Cistine finally dared to look up at him. His face was still stony, but something had shifted. His jaw, perhaps. The angle of his eyes. "And...how are they?"

Maleck shook his head, taking the knife back. "I don't want to frighten you."

It was very likely a thinly-veiled threat, yet Cistine had the sense he was truly sparing her from something terrible—and the gossiping, curious part of her wanted to know what it was. "I don't frighten easily."

"Nor do I, but my word stands." Maleck lined the knives on the floor at Cistine's feet. "Which was lightest?"

Cistine shrugged again. "I don't know. They all felt the same."

Maleck blew out a long breath through his nose. Then he gathered the knives and handed the first one to her again. "What of your Warden, Ashe?"

Tension corded Cistine's body at once, curling her toes and sending fresh pangs into her abused muscles. She gripped the knife tightly, her knuckles crackling. "What about her?"

"She was unafraid to face me."

Cistine chose her next words carefully, with the sense that withholding truth from Maleck was just as dangerous as answering the wrong way. "Ashe has always been fearless, as long as I've known her. As long as she's served my father, at least...since she was twelve."

"She fought here, in the war?"

"Yes," Cistine said. "It may have surprised you she could face you even with her leg injured. But not me…that's just who Ashe is. It's what all the Cadre does."

"Why did she join the Cadre?" Maleck passed her the second knife.

"You should ask her. It's not my story to tell."

Maleck nodded as they traded knives again. "And Julian. What is he?"

Cistine almost choked. Her answer today, as opposed to yesterday…fathoms of difference. The two were hardly comparable. "He's a…a friend. The son of a lord in my kingdom."

Maleck took the knife back from her shaking hand and laid them all out again. "Which one was the heaviest?"

Cistine frowned. "I don't know. I told you, they all felt the same."

Maleck regarded her quietly for a moment, then scraped the weapons together. "You're free to go."

Cistine leaped to her feet, torn between a feeling of elation and a stab of guilt. "Did I pass, or fail?"

"Neither. This is not the test. That comes later."

"Then what was the point of the knives?"

"Training." He turned to the rack and replaced the blades. "Tomorrow, we'll try again."

Though her curiosity nudged her to ask what they were trying *for*, her rumbling stomach interrupted the bevy of questions. She only had an hour or so before Tatiana dragged her off to the market. She wasn't prepared to face the evening on an empty stomach.

"Very well." She hoped she sounded composed rather than confused. "Tomorrow it is."

Maleck didn't turn when Cistine thundered down the steps and ran to the kitchen.

It was deserted this time, but Cistine's disappointment melted rapidly into glee when she saw someone had left her a plate of roasted potatoes, steamed vegetables, and wild game. She planted herself and picked up her napkin—and froze when she realized there was no cutlery.

"Unfortunately, they're all dirty." The papery voice was an echo from last night's greatest moment of fear. "You'll just have to use your fingers."

Cistine jerked around in her seat as the old woman stepped from the shadows of the hall the same way she'd emerged into the foyer the night before, masked by darkness until she chose to be seen. "Oh—I don't usually—that's not how I was raised..."

The old woman chuckled, limping slowly to the table and drawing out a chair for herself. "It's all right. I won't tell a soul."

Cistine didn't know if she was referring to eating without cutlery, or Cistine's spying on the cabal. She slowly popped a potato into her mouth as she watched the old woman, and almost moaned at the rich notes of browned butter and hot herbs that burst across her tongue. Though she'd just eaten lunch before her tutoring session, the morning's training had left her deranged with hunger.

"Did you make this?" Cistine demanded through a mouthful of crisp pea pods and cooked asparagus. "It's absolutely delicious."

"Well, when you're old and crippled, you find new ways to be useful. Cooking is a favorite of mine. And I can dust everything from this high, downward." The woman gestured to the line of her bosom, and Cistine laughed against the side of her wrist. "And sometimes, I catch travelers listening in at doors in the dark."

Cistine froze. The old woman's silvery brows rose.

"Are you going to tell Thorne?" Fear rattled Cistine's voice.

"If I was one of his warriors, I would have to," the woman said. "But I'm not, am I?"

"I don't suppose so." Cistine watched the old woman reach over and pluck a potato from her dish. She was as out of place as Cistine herself in this home of lethal warriors—but unlike Cistine, she clearly felt she belonged.

"Just between us," the woman said, "what do you make of it? The Black Coasts, the mines...all that *Svarkyst* steel?"

"It's not my place to say. It isn't my kingdom."

"And they don't allow women to have opinions where you come from?"

"No, I have plenty of opinions!"

"Then let's have one."

Cistine picked up a fire-roasted tomato and nibbled the fleshy shell, buying herself a moment to think. "It sounds to me like Thorne is facing someone who outmatches him in weaponry and resources. I don't think raiding wagons will always be enough to keep him and his people safe."

"Then what do you suggest?"

"I'm not—"

The woman tipped her head, and the rest of the words—*a warrior*—snagged in Cistine's teeth. She forced down another bite while she considered the old woman's question. She owed her that much for the meal—and for her silence. "I don't know. I don't understand your kingdom well enough to say what he should do."

The old woman thumped her cane on the floor. "Honesty in a ruler. What a rare and welcome thing that is."

Cistine's skin tingled with unease and the feeling of being watched. She glanced up swiftly at the doorway behind the old woman, and found Ariadne standing there, eerily still, a hand on her hip. Her eyes took in the setting, and the two women speaking to one another, with a kind of muted tension that set Cistine back from the table.

"It must be time for me to return to my room." The old woman clearly sensed Ariadne's burning stare, but she gave no hint of concern as she slowly stood. "It was a pleasure to speak with you, Princess Cistine."

"You as well." Cistine watched the old woman hobble past Ariadne, who turned to let her by, squeezing her shoulder in passing.

And then they were alone.

Cistine rose, giving up on the rest of her meal as she approached Ariadne. "I'm ready. What do you have in mind for me?"

Ariadne's eyes flicked past her. "Your plate."

Cistine glanced back. "I thought I was done."

"Then dispose of the plate."

Cistine frowned. "Doesn't Thorne have people who tend that for him?"

"Do you see any servants in the Den? We're all responsible for our own affairs. That includes our rinsed plates, our clothes-washing, and our clean quarters."

"I didn't know that."

"And I wouldn't want you to forget it." Ariadne traced the kitchen with a calculative look. "You're going to clean this entire room. Wash every dish and cookpot. Carry the scraps out to the garden for compost."

Cistine resisted the urge to toss up her hands in frustration. There was no sense in arguing. She'd accepted during her conversation with Thorne the previous day that this abuse was what she had to endure to save her kingdom.

For that, she could shoulder Ariadne's scorn. She could shoulder anything.

"All right," she snapped. "Show me where to begin."

Cistine's fingertips and knuckles ached by the time she finished scrubbing muddy bootprints from the kitchen floor. Ariadne's presence was the only thing that kept her from stalking from the kitchen and leaving the menial labor behind. Perched on a chair she'd dragged into the mouth of the hall by Cistine's room, the warrior thumbed through a book, ignoring Cistine except to grunt the occasional use of a tool or the proper hanging of some household item on the pegs around the room. Cistine had never realized how many utensils were dirtied in a single meal; it was no wonder her father's kitchens were some of the most popular and highest-paid positions in the Middle Kingdom.

Darkness hugged the windows as Cistine sat back on her heels, examined the polished floor, and snaked a glance at Ariadne. She didn't comment on it, just as she hadn't commented on Cistine's dish-washing or counter-wiping. Not a glint of praise. Not even a nod of approval.

A throat cleared from the doorway behind her, and Cistine's stomach writhed as she looked up.

Julian leaned against the curved wooden entryway, arms folded. One brow peaked smoothly, and that was the only sign of his shock as he saw his princess down on her knees, polishing the floor like a scullery maid.

Cistine lurched up, knees cracking, her abused haunches, legs, and hands tingling. "What are you doing here?"

"Searching for the princess," Julian said. "Have you seen her?"

"Very funny." Cistine hurled her polishing rag at him. The simple heft and sling of her arm sent a lance of pain down her muscles, and she groaned.

Julian's smile slipped as he approached her, rag in fist. "Take a walk with me?"

Cistine's heart sprang at the notion of their first courtship stroll—then wilted just as quickly. "I can't. I promised Tatiana I would shop for some suitable training threads with her tonight."

Ariadne snorted as if the thought of Cistine in training attire was absurd, but she missed Cistine's retaliatory glare as she turned the page of her book.

"I could accompany you," Julian offered. "You shouldn't visit a market after dark without an escort, anyway. Not after what happened in Veran."

Cistine motioned him quiet, glancing at Ariadne, uncertain of which troubled her more: the thought of Ariadne knowing about Matthias and Roosha, and how Cistine had needed rescuing, or the reminder for any of the cabal of how Quill had failed them by rescuing her.

Ariadne gave no indication she'd even heard them.

"I'd welcome the company," Cistine said. "We should invite Ashe, too."

"I've been with her all day. She's having her leg seen to right now. She's supposed to stay off it for a day or so."

Cistine's relief that Thorne was keeping his word melted into guilt. She'd been too busy to even visit her Warden after the midday meal. "I'm glad you were there."

"She's my friend, too." Julian led her to the door. "Besides, I needed the distraction. Otherwise I would've been shadowing you all day."

"Did I say you could leave?"

Ariadne's quiet question stopped Cistine midstride. The warrior hadn't moved from her seat, but her eyes were fixed on them now, the book forgotten.

"Tatiana needs me," Cistine said. "If you have a grievance, take it to her."

Ariadne went on staring, her gaze as cold as the heart of winter. Cistine wondered if that stare was perfected by everyone in the cabal.

Finally, Ariadne returned to her book. "Take the compost with you."

Cistine snatched up the tin of crushed eggshells, potato skins, and other half-rotten miscellanies, slipping out before Ariadne could think of another servant's task for her to fulfill.

Julian plucked the tin from Cistine's arms the moment they were out of Ariadne's sight. "I can't believe this. Princesses shouldn't do the work of maids."

Cistine had spent the past hour thinking that very thing, but hearing someone else say it, she bristled defensively. Somehow, her own words in Julian's mouth sounded far more selfish and self-important than she could bear.

She took the tin back from him. "She wanted to see me react. I didn't give her the satisfaction. I'm sure things will be different tomorrow."

"And if they aren't?" Julian asked. "A whole month of this, Princess..."

"I know." Cistine's calves throbbed at the mere notion. "But I have a duty to my kingdom. And I'll fulfill it, whatever it takes."

Tatiana waited for them at the door, her belly and arms covered with a thick wool cardigan. She grinned as she saw Cistine's burden. "We've been making bets for weeks on who would finally be fed up enough to take that tin and dump it. I think I owe Quill and Maleck a few mynts."

"And who were you betting on?" Cistine asked.

"Thorne. He's always been a stickler for cleanliness. Why do you think we stashed that tin in the cupboard?"

They emerged into a sticky, sultry twilight. Insects chirred near the Nior River and the watermills cranked their quiet music as Cistine and Julian followed Tatiana around the Den. There was a small, paddocked garden behind it, under the shade of fruit trees and berry bushes. It reminded her of the garden outside her window in the Citadel—a small pocket of home in an unfamiliar land. "This is beautiful!"

"*We* don't think so," Tatiana said. "Tending it is a waste of valuable energy."

"But it gives you food." Cistine slipped through the garden gate. "You should be more thankful for what you can grow with your own hands."

"It's hardly enough food to make up for how much time we spend pulling weeds and laying soil every spring."

"Don't argue with Cistine about this," Julian warned. "She has a special love for all things green."

Cistine hadn't expected him to notice that. A smile dimpled her warm cheeks as she spread the compost among the plants and bushes.

Tatiana leaned against the fence with a groan. "Are you ready yet?"

"Unfortunately, yes." Cistine plucked a few berries from one of the bushes and thumbed them into her mouth as Tatiana led them toward the market.

"It's good to see you smiling like this again," Julian murmured to Cistine. "Ever since the Vey..."

"I haven't felt like smiling since then," Cistine admitted. "Well...except last night."

Julian wove his fingers between hers, and Cistine flicked a berry to him. He caught it in his mouth with a rakish grin.

A surprise awaited them at the front of the Den: Quill, propped against the porch railing and munching on a cinnamon stick, his arms folded. "I heard someone was going shopping without me. I'm wounded, Tati! I don't know that I'll recover this time."

Tatiana perched her hands on her hips. "You look as lively as ever to me. Annoyingly so, even."

"Why don't I give you a better look all night, then? Someone's got to carry your shopping bags. As usual."

"We don't need an escort," Julian said.

"If it was an escort, I'd be armed," Quill grinned "Can't a man enjoy the finer things without having his motives questioned?"

"Not if he's a featherbrained cutthroat, no." Tatiana swaggered ahead of them down the path, calling over her shoulder: "Coming, or not?"

Quill winked at Cistine and hurried to catch up with Tatiana. Julian swore under his breath, and Cistine squeezed his hand. "Think of it this way: at least they'll distract each other."

Julian's smile crept back into place, slow as a sunset. "I can appreciate that."

They descended into the market together, and Cistine knew that even with Quill and Tatiana for company, she was going to enjoy herself tonight.

CHAPTER SIXTEEN

THOUGH HELLIDOM SEEMED quaint from afar, especially on the paths Cistine had walked on the outskirts during training, Quill and Tatiana showed them inner pockets that dazzled in the night. Few shops sold superfluous wares—there was little to speak of in the way of jewelry or fine dresses—but the food was delectable, and the clothing they did find was like nothing Cistine had ever seen: scarves and shawls of some foreign beast's wool, both cool and warm at once, their colors winking like a dream in the pomegranate-lantern light; trousers like Tatiana's that billowed from the tight waist strap and clung at the ankles; blouses with long sleeves and high midriffs; long shirts woven with armored vests, practical and stylish.

And, most importantly, there was no lack of training and battle armor.

"There is a difference," Tatiana said as they browsed a brightly-lit shop she'd dragged Cistine into. "There's light training armor for the inexperienced and armor weighted like battle-ready threads without wasting the actual resources."

"You mean the steel silk and such?" Cistine asked.

Tatiana smirked. "So you *were* listening today. That's precisely it. Once you've progressed through training, you're ready for true battle armor with its reinforcements."

Julian ran a hand over a set of black fighting armor: a long, loose-sleeved undershirt, vambraces, calf-guards, a chestplate, and a weapon's belt. "What about me? Do you think I'm ready for a set of armor like this?"

"We would have to see you fight," Tatiana said.

Quill rubbed his chin. "That just might be entertaining, come to think of it."

"Then I just might try."

"If you have the stones, my sword is ready for yours."

Much to Cistine's relief, Julian didn't take Quill up on his offer.

They returned to the Den well after dark, Julian and Quill weighed down with bags. They'd left the market with more than just training armor: Cistine had two new scarves, one of which Julian picked specifically for its vibrant gold-and-blue threads. Tatiana purchased several outfits, complaining to the shopkeeper while she paid that she had no room left in her closet for any of it.

"Then why do you keep buying?" Cistine asked as they ducked from the shop.

"Because Tariq has seven children to feed," Tatiana said. "They're Blaykrone refugees. They need the mynts."

"Why not just give it to them, then?" Julian asked.

"Thorne doesn't give charity," Quill said. "He just encourages us to look for our clothes at Tariq's shop before anywhere else."

Cistine pondered that as they passed through the ghostlit paths: the ruthless High Tribune who gave no charity but found other ways to ensure the people of Hellidom had a living. She wondered if that was generosity, or his way of ensuring everyone in the city pulled their weight.

Perhaps it was a bit of both.

"Also," Tatiana added when the silence became thick with thought, "I do love clothes."

That kindred interest had Cistine laughing despite her sore feet as she, Quill, and Julian left Tatiana with the bags in her room, facing the challenge of cramming five more outfits into the overstuffed space.

"We're going to find her buried under a landslide of threads one of these days," Quill lamented, ducking into his own room across the hall.

Cistine caught a glimpse of an open, uncluttered floor, and many windows ushering in the glittering light of Hellidom below, before Quill shut the door.

"They should encourage her to donate to the poor," Julian said as they left the corridor. "She could clothe an entire village with that closet."

"True," Cistine said. "But did you notice, Julian? There doesn't seem to be anyone poor or unfortunate in Hellidom."

They paused before his doorway, and Julian shrugged. "Maybe our benefactor doesn't allow anyone without mynts into his town."

"I heard that."

The quiet rumble came from the kitchen. Though it was dark inside, not even a candle lit, Cistine had no doubt Thorne was there in the shadows, lurking between her and the sanctuary of her room.

Julian bristled. "I'll walk you to bed."

Cistine sighed, taking her bags from his fists. "No. I won't let him intimidate me."

"It's not intimidation that worries me. It's that he'll hurt you."

"He could've done that already," Cistine said. "He could've killed me rather than making peace."

Julian ruffled a hand back through his hair. "Just be careful."

"I will be." Cistine stretched up on her toes to kiss his cheek. "I had a good time tonight."

"So did I," Julian said. "But don't get too comfortable with nights like these, Princess. We're not here on retreat. Time is still working against us."

Cistine bit back the retort that he hadn't seemed so worried about wasting precious time when he was flirting with barmaids and gambling for mynts in Veran. It wasn't the right time for an argument, anyway.

But his comment put her in the perfect mood to face Thorne.

The cabal's leader occupied the head seat at the table, nursing a bowl of stew. Something about the sight of him eating—after she'd seen him with a blade in his hand, or commanding a room of bloodthirsty warriors— seemed unusually domestic.

It was the face of his companion that made her heart truly sink.

The old woman occupied the same chair as when she'd kept Cistine company during her meal earlier that day. The same calm smile turned her features, too. But she and Thorne were eating in the darkness together, so close to Cistine's room—as if they'd been waiting for her return.

Cistine avoided their eyes as she sidled past the table and hurried toward sanctuary.

"Baba Kallah tells me you two became acquainted today," Thorne said.

The name stopped Cistine in her tracks.

She'd heard it before: Ariadne had asked Thorne if he'd spoken to Kallah before he'd treated with Cistine.

Slowly, she turned back toward the table.

Thorne's face was impassive as ever. He didn't lay into her with accusations, so it seemed Baba Kallah had kept her word, and Thorne had no idea Cistine had overheard his clandestine meeting.

The old woman speared her cane across the table, pushing out a chair. "Come. Sit."

Her tone was warm, but the words were steel. Cistine clutched the bags in her shaking fist and slowly sank down in the offered chair, keeping her eyes on Baba Kallah. "We've met. She made me supper."

"Good," Thorne said. "She seems to approve of you."

"Someone with manners in this house of bandits?" Baba Kallah laughed. "Oh, I more than approve."

Cistine flared her nostrils, fighting a smile. Thorne shook his head and returned his focus to the stew.

"And how was your shopping excursion, *Yani?*" Baba Kallah asked.

Another word to add to the list stashed under her pillow, which reminded Cistine of the merches Thorne had slaughtered and the name they'd called him. She tucked both away for later questioning. "It went well, once Tatiana warmed up to me. She's certainly...loquacious."

"No more than the woman who describes someone as *loquacious,*" Thorne said.

Cistine resisted the urge to jut her tongue at him. "At least I won't be fighting in a dress tomorrow."

Thorne's eyes flicked up, gleaming with cool interest. "Let's see them."

Cistine laid the training armor on the table, relieved to know it was clean since she'd wiped and polished it herself. Thorne cleaned his mouth on his wrist and got to his feet, moving beside her to peer down at the threads.

Cistine braced herself to be told that armor from his kingdom wouldn't fit a body from hers, but at least she knew these were quality threads—Tatiana, Quill, and Julian had all assured her of that. She'd almost chosen a pair of winter pajamas, assuming the floaty material was meant for training in the hot sun.

Thorne smoothed his hands over the lightweight vambraces, guards, and belly plate. His thumb followed the curve of the sternum cover, which angled down between the breasts. He frowned as he rubbed a shred of fabric between his thumb and forefinger. "Good. But leave off the bracers and coverings when you wear it at first. They'll weigh you down, and you won't need them until you learn to take a blow."

Cistine almost tipped over in shock. "*Take* one?"

Baba Kallah nodded. "Everyone must take a blow if they're going to give one."

"I didn't agree to bruises and broken bones!"

"And your opponents will never ask you to. So take the blows well," Thorne said. "Don't worry. Quill will come down lightly until you're truly ready to fight."

Cistine's blood throbbed in the creases of her elbows and the backs of her knees. The thought of standing before Kanslar's Chancellor with a bruise like Quill's on her cheek—the thought of walking through this kingdom, sore from blows as well as from physical strain—was humiliating beyond belief.

Oh, she would be wearing the coverings. Anything to spare herself from having her kidneys rehomed by a kick from one of Thorne's death-gods.

She forced herself to smile as she peeled the armor from the table and folded it back into the bag. "Thank you for your advice, High Tribune."

Thorne frowned at the title, and Baba Kallah thumped the tip of her cane slowly on the floor between her feet. "And how was the rest of your evening, Princess?"

"Well, I cleaned the kitchen." Neither of them commended her for it. "Oh! And Tatiana showed me the garden."

Something in her face—or perhaps her tone, which broke with excitement despite her best efforts—made Baba Kallah laugh. "And I take it that was to your liking."

"It was stunning." Cistine sat again, sliding her chair closer to the table. "How many varieties of fruits and vegetables have you planted there?"

"Too many." Thorne returned to his seat as well. "Every year, I warn her and Ariadne we don't have the resources to delegate to tending that gardening patch. And every year—"

"You eat the produce like a starving man," Baba Kallah said. "Don't think I haven't seen you wandering the trellises, eating peapods off the vines."

Thorne shrugged. "They're a fair substitute if you don't have time for a meal."

"Well, watch where you step," Cistine warned. "Those trellises are next to the potato mounds. If you flatten them, you'll bury the harvest."

Thorne raised a brow. "Are you a gardener?"

"It's a hobby of mine, yes."

Baba Kallah stared at Thorne with wide, earnest eyes, until the silence in the kitchen became uncomfortable. He sulked in his chair, giving no indication he sensed the way her gaze traveled repeatedly between him and Cistine.

"You should retire, Princess," Thorne said. "Quill will want you at the rock top, fed and dressed, at sunrise."

Baba Kallah gave up conferring intention to Thorne to smile at Cistine instead, and a rush of warmth stirred her as their gazes met. Baba Kallah reminded her of her own grandmother, who'd helped raise her while the Queen was bound up in royal affairs: a kind, unassuming old woman whose only interest was to help everyone she met.

"If Quill tries to hit you before you're ready to take the blow," Baba Kallah purred, "put your knee into his groin."

Thorne choked on his stew. Cistine burst out laughing, then smothered it with her hand.

No, Kallah was not only a kind old woman. She was an ancient fox in a den of wolves.

CHAPTER SEVENTEEN

THE TRAINING ARMOR proved far more flexible and breathable than Cistine's heavy dresses, though she found it clung to her curves in uncomfortable ways, baring angles she was used to having covered or tamed by a corset. Quill gave her little time to dwell on those things as he forced her to focus on her breathing: how she inhaled when she stretched, when she jogged, and when she labored through the core-strengthening exercises. She was able to walk a bit farther around Hellidom the second day before her blisters drove her mad again, and when Quill slapped her a congratulatory high-five at the end of training Cistine grinned all the way back to the Den.

True to her word, Tatiana was prepared to discuss politics after lunch—but here the conversation adopted a different cadence. Cistine had grown up around legislators and lords; she knew how skillful tongues danced around sensitive subjects, and she quickly realized there was some—perhaps even much—Tatiana kept from her about the inner workings of the Courts.

But the basic sketch was something they could at least lay over the map: five Courts all subsisted within Stornhaz, but only one sat in session at a time. The rest were relegated to weaving connections among the people during the other seasons, cobbling together favors they could call on when their Court sat in session again.

"Each Court has eight Tribunes." Tatiana tapped the map blanketing their laps as they sat cross-legged on the sofa. "One guess as to why."

"Eight territories." Cistine sipped her cup of jasmine tea. "One Tribune to represent each."

"Precisely," Tatiana grinned. "Since each territory has five different Tribunes, you're always bound to have ones you love and ones you hate. Some territories wait an entire year to appeal to the one Tribune they trust with their requests."

Cistine frowned. "They really have to wait that long?"

Tatiana sighed, tapping her groomed nails gently on the side of her cup. "How much Valgardan lore were you able to get your pampered fingers on before you came here?"

"Not as much as I needed," Cistine confessed.

"Obviously," Tatiana chuckled. "Well, I know it's done differently in your kingdom, but here in the Courts our time doesn't rise and set with the cycle of life. Stornhaz moves by a different pace, you might say."

"Show me."

"I'm not sure I can do justice to it. Even when we lived in the City of a Thousand Stars, let's just say I was shouldered from the political circle."

Cistine cocked her head. "You lived in Stornhaz?"

"Yes, but that's not a story for princesses." Tatiana tugged the map from Cistine's legs. "Anything else you want to know?"

Cistine sipped her tea and weighed her words carefully. "If there are eight Tribunes in each Court, which one is *High* Tribune?"

Tatiana tossed the map onto the bed. "I wondered when this was going to come up."

Galvanized by her unhostile reaction, Cistine pressed in: "What is Thorne, exactly?"

"Once, he was a successor. High Tribunes are groomed to replace the Chancellor of their Court. They school for ten years or more in Valgardan law. Train with blades. Accrue favors, sit on the Tribunal. And then, when the Chancellor has served as many terms as the Court deems fit for him, he turns over the Judgement Seat to his High Tribune."

Cistine traced the rim of her mug with her fingernail. "Do all High Tribunes live in cities like Hellidom?"

Tatiana snorted, polished off her own teacup, and set it on the floor. "Not most of them, no."

"Then why is Thorne here?"

"That's not my story to tell."

Cistine tried a different tactic. "As High Tribune, is he the one I should approach about politics?"

"If you're feeling brave." Tatiana sprawled out and leaned her neck over the armrest, her nest of curls spilling against the floor. "You seem like a sweet girl, Cistine, so I'll give you one more piece of insight for free: you should be careful about the questions you ask. There's probably a very good reason Talheim never told you about us."

Cistine frowned. "What reason might that be?"

Tatiana lifted her head, peering at Cistine with hooded eyes. "Maybe because, as a whole, this is not a happy kingdom, and there aren't many happy people in it."

"Quill seems happy enough."

Tatiana snorted. "He's a good liar. If you hit him in the right places, that cheerful armor starts to crack, just like the rest of us."

"Even you?"

Tatiana's eyes gleamed. "Unlike the others, I've lost little and have less still to lose. That makes life easier."

Cistine slid her legs from under Tatiana's, resting her chin on her knees. "I have everything to lose if I fail. Should I be unhappy?"

"No." Tatiana let her head fall back against the armrest again. "But you should be careful you don't end up like us. Doing the things we do."

Something lurked behind Tatiana's bright, flippant words. Like a lockbox, there was a secret trapped inside. "One more question."

"Just one?"

Cistine rubbed her hands over the coarse fabric of her training armor. "Was Valgard always unhappy like this? Or was that...our fault? After the war?"

Tatiana gripped the seatback and lifted herself up to look at Cistine. Her eyes were fathoms deep, searching for something. Perhaps for sincerity...or worthiness. Weighing out whether Cistine deserved to know.

Then she went to the bedside table, opened the drawer, and pulled out a small, square note. She returned to the couch and leaned against its sloped back, handing the note to Cistine. "Have you ever seen something like this?"

Cistine studied it closely: it was a drawing of the cabal, all younger, perhaps even younger than Cistine, and it was almost too detailed, too pristine, too colorful to be real. They all had their arms around each other, and there was another girl there, and a man Cistine didn't recognize.

"Who drew this?" Cistine asked.

"No one," Tatiana said. "It's called a photograph. Something you don't have in the Middle and Southern Kingdoms. Something we don't have anymore, either."

"But how is it made?"

"By a lightbox that bends an image and makes an impression on special paper. But you can't make that much light in a small space naturally. You needed an augment to do it."

Cistine dropped the note. "This was made with augmentation?"

"Most of Valgard owes its shapes and angles to augments, one way or another." Tatiana picked the picture up. "We used it to power our cities. Our machines. They harvested it by the vat back when I was a child. Now we're relegated to ghostplants and candles again. We have to use watermills to filter our rivers."

"So do we."

"And that's all you've ever known, so you're used to it. I used to know what it was like to turn a knob on the wall and trigger an auger-light that would burn until I turned the knob off again."

"But that was unnatural," Cistine said.

"Talheim always thought so. That's why they marched here with their army and told us to shut the Doors. What they didn't know was how an entire way of life would change when the way to the gods was gone."

Cistine glanced at the door. Tatiana's voice was still level, still calm, but Cistine suddenly felt trapped between the warrior and her memories. "Do you want augmentation to come back, then?"

Tatiana laughed as if the question was absurd. When Cistine didn't join in, Tatiana's eyes widened. She stroked a hand through her curls, lifting them and dumping them over the far side of her head. "Unlike some Valgardans, I saw the worst side of what augmentation can do. Was it necessary for the way we lived before? Yes, but it's not necessary anymore. Believing otherwise is one reason Valgardans can be such miserable, feckless people."

Cistine let out a slow breath. "I thought you were angry with me."

"Why would I be? You clearly know nothing about our kingdom. You didn't march up to Valgard and single-handedly shut the Doors." Tatiana returned the photograph to the drawer. "It was a mutual agreement between our kingdoms...before you were born, I'd bet."

"Then why do you sound so..." Cistine trailed off, gesturing helplessly. "Why mention it at all?"

"Because you asked. And because you ought to know what you're getting into if you're really going to stand before the Chancellors, like Thorne says." Tatiana folded her arms and propped her haunches on the small table. "I've gotten used to living without auger-lights and augwains. I'm glad I fall asleep to the sounds of the mills instead of harvesters tapping into the augment well below Stornhaz day after day. But not everyone feels that way. Some might even want to make an example of King Cyril's daughter because he was the one who convinced us to close the Doors at the tip of a sword."

Cistine rubbed her clammy palms on her armor. "That's why Thorne agreed I need to train."

Tatiana's brows knitted. "Thorne has his reasons for accepting your terms. But training is just common sense. You don't walk into Stornhaz inexperienced and unarmed, especially if you're Talheimic."

It *was* common sense, and Cistine should have known it. Her steps in this kingdom should have been far better-mapped from the beginning. She certainly would have prepared differently for this mission if she'd known what to expect of Valgard...if her knowledge had come from more than Ashe's childhood memories and a lifetime of threadbare whispers seeping from behind the Citadel's closed doors.

Why had her father told her nothing of this place beyond a few tales of war? Cyril expected her to be queen someday, though he knew she resented the throne—and a queen would be tasked to uphold the tentative truce between the kingdoms. Why had he prepared her with a wealth of knowledge about Mahasar, who until recently had been of little threat, and yet left the North so deeply guised in shadow?

Was it because of his guilt, knowing the truce had destroyed an entire kingdom's way of life and abandoned its struggling people to find a new means of survival?

"Some of us wish things could be safer between Valgard and Talheim," Tatiana said when Cistine didn't speak, "but truces aren't the same as friendship. I knew someone who took a truce once, thinking it made him an ally of the Courts. It didn't end well for him. For *anyone* he cared about."

"What happened?"

Tatiana's gaze flicked to the door. "There's a reason Quill sleeps in the light. And why Maleck doesn't like to travel alone."

With that, she ended the day's lesson.

CHAPTER EIGHTEEN

RELENTLESS DAYLIGHT POUNDED on Cistine's aching skull, crawling down the dry cracks of her lips and her parched tongue as she unfolded from her core-strengthening exercises, resting again after five grueling repetitions.

Quill loomed over her, head blocking out the sun. "Cistine, I know you can do better than this."

"No," Cistine groaned, prying herself from the rock top, "I really can't, Quill. I'm sweating, I'm exhausted, I'm famished—"

"When you're all those things in battle, that's when you find the strength to beat your opponent down." Quill curled his wrapped hands twice, beckoning. "Don't give up on me now."

Cistine gasped for breath, shaking her head as she rubbed her throbbing middle. "That's it. I'm done for the day."

He frowned. "You're going to unleash Thorne on me. Tati says you're soaking up her knowledge like a sponge, and Maleck has you balancing blades every afternoon. You never say no to cleaning the Den. So why am I the one you can't stand to work with?"

"It's not you! It's these exercises. I'm no good at them."

"That's why we *train*."

"We are training. At *my* pace."

"At your pace, you might be in shape to stand in the Courts when you're Baba Kallah's age." Quill's lively eyes flashed a challenge. "But if you have that long to spare, so do I."

Cistine batted sweat from her eyes, scowling. "For today, I'm done."

Quill sighed, running a hand down his face. "At least tell Thorne you tried for longer than a fifteen-minute walk and five core exercises."

"Done," Cistine grinned. "Thank you, Quill."

"Don't thank me, I'm not doing you any favors. I have my own reason for quitting early today. Faer is waiting at the Den."

"Finally back from wherever you sent him?"

Quill smiled broadly as they slid from the rock top and made their way into the heart of Hellidom. "And with a letter I didn't have time to read before we left this morning."

"You would have more time to yourself if you let me sleep past sunrise."

"If a better sleeping schedule is the only lesson I manage to teach you in all this, then my work is done."

By the time they climbed the steps to the Den, Cistine ached for a glass of cool water. She followed Quill to the kitchen where Ashe and Julian waited, just as they did every morning. Julian brushed out the chair beside him, and Cistine settled into it. Quill sauntered to the window, where Faer perched, cleaning his feathers. Picking up a muffin from the basket on the counter, Quill munched and removed the scroll from the raven's ankle.

Julian gripped Cistine's hand beneath the table, and his brows rose in a silent question. Cistine rolled her eyes and gagged. Ashe snorted into her morning tea—some spicy concoction she claimed would help stave off infection as her wound healed.

Quill finished his muffin, tossed the note into the oven, and dusted off his hands. His expression was torn between a crooked smile and a frown.

"What was that?" Cistine gestured to the oven.

"Something that's going to require my absence," he said.

Before Cistine could interrogate him further, Maleck and Thorne swaggered into the room. Maleck went to the opposite side of the table, setting down a small glass jar in front of Ashe. "More poultice for your leg."

Cistine fought back a smile. At least one of them was trying to keep the peace.

Ashe didn't take the jar. She folded her arms and looked somewhere over Maleck's shoulder. "Thank you."

And only one of them, it seemed.

Maleck turned away from the table without so much as a blink, and Ashe added, "I need someone to train me, too."

Maleck froze as if she'd offered him a biting adder. Quill's brows peaked. Julian scoffed under his breath.

"Poultices will only go so far," Ashe went on. "If I'm too gentle on this leg, it will never be as strong as it was before. So one of you is going to help me strengthen it."

Cistine stifled a giggle at Ashe's brusque tone. Quill jammed a cinnamon stick between his teeth and surveyed her. "I'll do it. Since my other student is doing *so well*, it seems I have more free time on my hands."

Cistine jutted her tongue at him. He grinned.

"No." Maleck's soft word speared Cistine's heart with tines of ice. "Not you. Let me."

Ashe scoffed. "You think you can go slow enough for me?"

Maleck didn't rise to the biting words. "You will need a very specific kind of training if you wish to walk without a limp. I can provide that training. I've been injured like this before."

Julian's hair grazed Cistine's cheek as he shook his head, but Ashe stared Maleck down with that same fearlessness as when she'd faced him in the meadow with his blade against her throat. "Fine. We start at dawn."

Maleck dipped his head and wandered to the basket of muffins, only to be intercepted by Quill, who swung an arm around his neck, pulled him forcefully away, and pounded him on the ribs. "Look who finally has someone to train again! Do you think Ariadne will be jealous?"

"Ariadne knows better," Maleck said. "Let go of me."

"Make me, *Storfir*."

Maleck grabbed Quill around the knees and flipped him, dumping him over the table and onto the floor. Cistine yelped, scrambling to her feet as chairs sailed. But Quill was laughing when he picked himself up, and he dove at Maleck's belly, slamming him against the counter. They started wrestling in earnest, knocking the muffins across the floor.

"Maleck! Quill!" Thorne thundered. "Not in the kitchen."

They stopped at once—Maleck with his hand fisted in Quill's hair, his arm cocked back to throw a punch into the other man's face. Quill's nose was already bleeding, but he grinned as he swiped away Maleck's arm. Faer floated from the window and perched on Quill's shoulder, ruffling his feathers and glaring at Maleck.

"Savages." Ashe slid the poultice jar safely from the table.

Thorne picked up the basket and helped himself to a muffin. "What do you want, Quill?"

"Who says I want anything?"

"You only pick fights with Maleck when you want to show me you're capable of holding your own—which means you want to go off alone somewhere."

"Ah, you know me so well," Quill chuckled. "There's a valley out there that's calling my name."

"No."

"Thorne!" Quill groaned. "It's been months!"

"I know. But we're down one as it is." Thorne's eyes traveled swiftly to Cistine. "I sent Tatiana off this morning."

The laughter went out of Quill's eyes, and he became so still, Faer stopped swaying. The raven was as tense as his handler—as tense as Cistine.

She hadn't spoken to Tatiana since the previous day when they'd discussed territory borders and revisited the map over cups of tea. There'd been no mention of any absence. She hadn't even bothered to say goodbye.

"Where?" Quill asked.

"Nowhere she hasn't been before," Thorne said. "You can relax."

"What about my training?" Cistine asked. "Tutoring?"

"I'll fill in the holes until Tatiana returns," Thorne replied. "In the meantime, no one else is allowed an absence. It will have to wait, Quill."

"Understood."

"You'll divide her patrol between the three of you." Thorne pulled the muffin apart and consumed it in quick portions. "Whatever is left falls to me."

Quill and Maleck snapped their heels together, saluted with an arm across their chests, and left the room. It wasn't until they were gone that Cistine realized Maleck hadn't eaten. In fact, she couldn't remember ever having seen him eat.

"Tonight, at sundown," Thorne said to Cistine, "meet me at the garden. We'll begin your lesson there."

Julian bristled as the High Tribune left the kitchen. "I don't like this. Tatiana is one thing. But that bastard..."

Cistine sighed. "Julian, we've been over this. Everything he might do to me is something he already could have done."

He flattened his hair with a trembling hand. "I'm growing sick of sitting in this house. It gives me too much time to think of what they might to do you."

"Then don't sit. Wander the city. Find small jobs to do. See if you can find out where Tatiana went, and why."

"You want to listen in on Thorne's business?"

"Court gossip, you remember?" Cistine said.

Julian scoffed quietly, getting to his feet. "Be careful today, Princess."

He squeezed her hand, then followed the others out. Cistine hurried to the muffin basket and helped herself to an orange pecan scone. She'd barely taken a bite when Ashe murmured, "How long has he been courting you?"

Cistine almost choked. Pressing her smallest finger to her lips to stifle an unladylike cough, she rasped, "Four days."

"And how far has it progressed? Are you taking the proper herbs?"

"Ashe, for God's sake! I haven't even...we haven't...not even a *kiss*."

Her Warden hummed low in her throat. "When were you going to tell me?"

That question threw cold water on the heat of Cistine's face. She set the scone down, plucking several bite-sized pieces off but not eating them. "I don't know. I was worried what you would say. What Papa will say. Princesses don't usually choose their own suitors without royal approval."

"True," Ashe said. "But you're playing ignorant if you think King Cyril and Lord Rion haven't discussed this union since you were born."

Cistine looked up swiftly from quartering the last half of the scone. "Really?"

"It would make a strong marriage bond," Ashe said, "linking the northern holdings with the Citadel itself. And don't you think the King would be thrilled? His daughter, with the son of his closest friend?"

Cistine started to smile—basking in that idyllic image—when another thought tugged her lips back down. "Does Julian know there was talk of it?"

Ashe shrugged. "I don't know if Lord Rion and Lady Eboni were forthcoming with the subject. I was told never to mention it to you. The Queen especially never wanted you to feel your hand was being forced."

Cistine stared at the scone crumbs, her stomach suddenly in knots while she studied her memories of her birthday ball, of their journey here— even of Julian's company on this mission—in a different light.

What would she do if Julian had known what their parents discussed…if he'd asked to court her *because* of that, because it was expected, or a gainful step for the son of a northern Lord?

Ashe hobbled up, clutching her wounded thigh. "It was bound to happen sooner or later, is all I'm saying. Just be careful, Cistine. The last thing you need to carry back with you from this kingdom is a broken heart."

Cistine nodded, watching as Ashe limped away. A fit of melancholy settled over her like a dark curtain pulled across her heart.

She knew better than to sit and fester in that, so she gathered her wits and went to find Ariadne. For once, she was looking forward to the mind-numbing brutality of cleaning the Den.

⁓⁓

Dinner was a rushed affair of dry meat and bread Cistine cobbled together before Ashe or Julian could find her. She knew she was being cowardly, but after her conversation with her Warden, she was reluctant to face Julian. There was a question she knew she had to ask, and she wasn't certain how to frame it in a way that wouldn't wound her deeply if he answered the wrong way.

So she ate standing up, chased down the food with two cups of warm water, and then hurried outside, massaging kinks from her shoulders where they'd knotted up during her session with Ariadne. Cleaning cobwebs from the upper corners of the hallways was no simple task.

It was a warm evening, the first caress of twilight's gloom gracing the sky when Cistine reached the garden where Thorne waited. He didn't look up when she joined him, mirroring his posture with arms folded on the fence, and it was several moments before he spoke: "Why the garden?"

Cistine considered her answer while her eyes roved over the small, fertile patch. "Because it's convenient to purchase your wares at market, but there's satisfaction in growing it yourself. In having the power to sustain life with your own hands."

"Not a particularly royal notion."

"Is everything *you* do suitable for a High Tribune?"

Thorne's jaw tightened. Whether he'd clenched it out of annoyance or because he was trying not to smile, Cistine couldn't be sure. "No. I feel less like a High Tribune every day."

Cistine danced her fingertips along the fence bar as she stared into the garden.

"Ask," Thorne said.

Cistine drew a deep breath. "Is it the caravan raids that make you feel that way?"

"It's everything. The things I'm forced to do to keep Hellidom a secret. To keep my warriors alive. These aren't political choices. They barely fall short of warfare."

Cistine shivered at the memory of how smoothly Quill had decapitated Rolf. "I'm not certain they fall short at all."

"You may be right," Thorne agreed. "What's your favorite thing we grow in this garden?"

Cistine studied the familiar rows of herbs, the mounds of carrots and potatoes, the fruit trees. "Oranges. They're versatile. They can be used in baking, cooking, and tea-making, or they can be eaten raw. They're sweet and tart. A bit of everything."

"Versatile," Thorne echoed.

"What about yours?"

"Lemons."

"Of all things," Cistine laughed. "Why?"

Thorne tipped his head. "It's time to begin your lesson."

He led her down from the Den and toward the edge of Hellidom. Cistine trotted after him, keeping a healthy distance—glad she still wore her training armor. Where Thorne was concerned, she felt safer that way.

"Thank you for doing this," Cistine said. "I wouldn't want to delay my training while Tatiana is gone."

"This was Baba Kallah's idea. Apparently, I could use something other than weapons and strategizing with Ariadne to occupy my free time."

Cistine grimaced, wondering if that was a jab at his own reputation, or a careless offer of the savage truth.

"Tatiana tells me you've already discussed the lay of our land," Thorne went on, "and augmentation, to some extent."

"The bare minimum of both. I have the feeling she keeps some things from me."

"If I marched into the Middle Kingdom demanding an audience with your father, would you tell me all your kingdom's intimate secrets along the way?"

"I would tell you to get out and never come back."

Thorne offered her a faint nod. "I don't doubt that."

They wove between the shops and made their way up to the opposite bank of the Nior River, toward the falls. The climb was perilous with evening encroaching, but Cistine found her way by following the shock of Thorne's pale hair before her.

"Tatiana also said you're interested in Valgardan politics," Thorne said. "That she told you about the Courts and the Tribunes. That isn't enough for you?"

"Not if I'm going to appeal to the Chancellor."

"You're learning." Thorne motioned her to a halt on a flat spear of rock jutting out over the Nior. Cistine was half-deafened by the roar of the falls to their right, and it took her eyes a moment to adjust to the glow of candles and ghostlamps in the heart of Hellidom, below and to their left. She sat, folding her legs beneath her, and Thorne lowered himself at her side, leaning his head back. He watched the stars emerge from the veil of night as if the gods had pierced their fingers through the dark shroud, letting a glimpse of their mysterious dwelling bleed into this one.

Cistine stole a moment to study Thorne while his focus was on the sky. He still hadn't changed from his rumpled attire from the day they'd met— or else all his outfits were the same. Gouges of exhaustion framed his eyes, and his wrists and neck were strangely lean despite his powerful arms and broad chest. But he didn't so much as sway where he sat, straight-backed and composed.

Still the same man she'd faced in the meadow, with a sword in her weak hands. Yet she was beginning to see different angles of him now, after learning how he treated Tariq and the people of Hellidom—and the way his cabal respected him.

"Would you have really killed Ashe the day we met?" she blurted out.

"If she'd harmed Maleck, yes," Thorne said.

"I'm not so certain Maleck of all people needs defending."

Thorne traced the sky with unhappy eyes. "Maleck is...set apart. He's the oldest of us. He spent the most time with augments. Because of that, he's also endured things the rest of us will never comprehend."

The hitch in his voice surprised Cistine—the way he struggled for words to define what had happened to his warrior. She thought of Maleck's eyes the day they'd first looked at one another on the Vingete Vey—the cold, fractured detachment there, like something had stolen the light from his depths.

She shuddered at the memory—not with revulsion, but with pity. "Was he injured by augments?"

"By people who abused them," Thorne said. "Augments were a resource that could be tapped by those willing to try, as long as they had the proper tools. But Maleck was being forced down a path no one should have ever walked. He barely escaped with his life. The scars of that...you can imagine."

Cistine really couldn't. She'd been born after the Doors had shut, and she'd never entertained the notion of what augmentation was like...what it was truly capable of. "Is Maleck glad the Doors were shut, since the augments caused him so much pain?"

"Closing the Doors didn't solve all Maleck's problems. I think you've perceived that."

Cistine sawed her lip between her teeth. "Should I be worried that he offered to train Ashe's leg, then?"

Thorne didn't answer at once. When he finally did, his voice was strangely soft. "I didn't expect that offer, either. It seems we won't have a choice about keeping them apart, after all. But Maleck doesn't like to be told how to feel. He...regrets the war. Regrets the things he was forced to do in it. It's possible he offered to help Ashe in penance for that."

"That didn't seem to be his opinion when he had his sword to her throat the night you and I met."

"From what I'm told, Maleck did not start that fight."

Cistine looked down at her hands.

"If Ashe attacks him, he'll reciprocate," Thorne added. "Any one of us would. But Maleck has always been determined to make his own choices, and he chooses to see Ashe as a person he can help, not as an enemy to leave crippled on the battlefield."

Cistine frowned. "But they're so different."

"Differences can be conquered." Thorne silenced her next words with a shake of his head. "Look up."

Cistine did—and caught her breath.

While she'd been distracted by the conversation, and by watching the town, the river, and Thorne's face, more stars had joined the host above.

They crowned the sky in a glistering trail, fine as powdered sugar on a dark chocolate cake.

"It may seem strange to a Talheimic princess," Thorne said, "but these stars cast the boundaries of life in Valgard."

"How do you mean?"

"In our legends, the stars are the seals of the gods—one star for each vassal. To swear by the gods or curse by them is considered in poor taste, inviting the Undertaker's wrath."

"I noticed your cabal swears by the stars," Cistine admitted. "Mostly Tatiana."

"We do far more than swear by them. We live by them." Thorne braced his weight on one hand and pointed with the other toward the eastern horizon. "Do you see that constellation there?"

Cistine squinted at the curtain of stars. "I think so."

"That's Skyygan," Thorne explained. "The Shadow. It's continuing to set, and Skyygan Court will sit in session until it does. After that—"

"Kanslar will rise?"

Thorne nodded, sweeping his arm to the west. "And as long as that constellation crosses the sky, the Court of the Conqueror will control the laws of Valgard. When its time sets, Traisende—the four Wayfinders—will rule. And so forth."

"And how do you keep a Court from dispelling all the laws their predecessor made?"

Thorne smiled. "We have laws to protect laws. No ruling can be overturned within a stellar cycle, which is a full Valgardan year. If, after that time, a law is challenged, the Courts will review it together and decide by majority rule whether to strike it from the lawbooks or maintain it."

Cistine drummed her fingers on the cool, damp rock as nervous excitement traveled through her. "You just named three of the five Courts. What are the other two?"

"Yager and Tyve," Thorne said. "Hunter and Traitor."

"Why those constellations? And those names?"

"It comes from an ancient story." Thorne linked his arms loosely around his knees and kept his eyes on the stars. "Long ago, the gods sent four women, the Wayfinders, to search the four points of the compass-star and choose a hunter who would deliver the people from the cruel tribal leaders of Old Valgard. For accepting this charge from the True God, the hunter was considered a traitor among his kind, one who brought trouble to the old way of things. Cast out and scorned, guided only by the Wayfinders, he lived as a shadow, infiltrating the tribes and killing their leaders."

"And I suppose that made him the conqueror?"

Thorne nodded. "Valgard's first Elder King. Those kings ruled until the Courts came to be."

"I like that," Cistine grinned. "It's a good story."

"It was my favorite as a child."

"You were a child once?" Cistine teased—then clapped a hand over her mouth. "I'm sorry, that was rude."

"No, it's a valid question." Thorne's tone was so flat she couldn't be certain if he was joking. "My childhood in Stornhaz does seem like a lifetime ago."

Cistine let her hand fall into her lap. "Tatiana mentioned that, but she wouldn't say much about the city."

"None of them do. It's a sensitive subject," Thorne said. "We were born in Stornhaz, and we all left together."

"May I ask why you left?"

"I would prefer if you didn't."

Cistine bit the skin on the side of her thumb as she thought her way around the question. "Well, the cabal refers to you as High Tribune. Tatiana said you were being groomed to replace a Chancellor. Is that really what you are?"

Thorne sighed. "It's complicated. I was preparing to become a Chancellor, but the closer I rose to the Judgement Seat, the more apparent it became there were...injustices being done from it. Territories were taken advantage of. Weaknesses were exploited, both in the tribunals and among the people. When I expressed my concerns, they were overruled. So I began to consider I could do more good on my own than I could from the Judgement Seat."

"How so?"

Thorne dusted off his hands on his knees. "It doesn't matter. I was wrong. To effect real change in Valgard requires a strong voice in a Court. I had one then, but I don't have it anymore. Now it's nothing but wagon raids and skirmishes, year after year. And in the end, it changes nothing."

"But you have some sort of plan, don't you?"

Thorne glanced at her. He was quiet.

For nearly a half-hour more, they sat in silence, and though Thorne was no longer teaching her, Cistine wasn't eager to end the night. She might have stayed for hours longer, watching more and more stars emerge, had Thorne not suggested they return to the Den so he could take patrol.

They made the journey back in that same contemplative silence, and Cistine's eyelids were heavy as they climbed the steps. She was the first to reach the door—and tensed as Thorne stretched an arm past her, holding it shut.

"Why did you come here," he said, "to this kingdom, when you knew of the animosity between our people?"

Cistine's tongue knotted between two answers, both of them true. One was about the pull in her chest, strange and inexplicable...and somehow damning. She chose the other. "Because Talheim is in danger from enemies in the Southern Kingdom, and I thought Valgard could help. I'm its princess. Those lives are in my hands. What other choice could I make?"

"Talheim has warriors." Cistine could tell Thorne was trawling for answers the same way she'd searched them out in him tonight.

"Yes," she said. "It has warriors who can bleed and die on battlefields."

"You would bleed in their stead?"

Cistine swallowed against the sudden dryness in her throat. "I'm praying it won't come to that."

Thorne's limpid eyes searched hers in the dimness. Cistine couldn't be certain, but she thought a flicker of distress tightened his jaw. "And if we told you that you shouldn't go to Stornhaz, or to Kanslar's Chancellor? That it was too dangerous, or that the outcome would not be what you'd hoped?"

Cistine's fear guttered as a headwind of indignation swept through her. "You're not going to intimidate me with talk of bleeding and danger. I've told you, my kingdom needs me to appeal to the Courts. Whether that involves Kanslar's Chancellor or not, I'm going, and you won't convince me not to. If you have any respect for me at all, you won't try to discourage me again. I am doing this, Thorne. Either help me prepare, or get out of my way."

She hadn't expected such strong words to leap from her tongue, but now that they were spoken, they filled her with a steely conviction that made it easier to hold Thorne's gaze with a glare of her own.

Under that frosty look, Thorne rubbed the back of his neck. He opened his mouth and shut it again. Then he said, "I'll teach you some of our language tomorrow."

And he finally let her open the door.

Cistine was unsurprised to see Julian sitting on one of the polished wooden benches in the entry room. What did startle her was that she was more nervous than glad to see him. Nervous when he inclined his head, keeping his eyes on Thorne as the High Tribune strode past. Nervous when they were alone, and his attention was fixed on her.

"That was quick," Julian said. "How did it go?"

Cistine shut the door, propping her weight against it. Her abused backside thanked her for her consideration. "The same as it goes with Tatiana. They're keeping something from us."

"I might have an idea what it is. From what Quill and Ariadne were discussing behind closed doors today, it seems there's another caravan traveling somewhere. It's different from Rolf's. Tatiana is surveying without engaging."

Cistine wondered if Thorne would've given the order to engage had their movements not been betrayed by Quill's brief moment of weakness on the Vey.

Julian pushed himself up from the bench. "Are you all right? You look upset."

"I'm fine. Just tired."

"You don't have to let them push you so hard." Julian crossed the room to join her. "You're not going to be battle-ready by month's end, anyway. You don't have to murder yourself trying to make that happen."

Cistine rubbed her arms, looking away from him.

"Cistine." Julian gripped her elbows, prying her arms gently apart. "What's wrong?"

"Did you know our parents had...intentions for us?" Cistine blurted out.

Julian's fingers tightened. "My father mentioned it a few times."

Cistine bit her lip, gnashing her teeth as tears branded her eyes. "Is that why you asked to court me? Because it's the expected thing?"

"No." Julian took her elbows and turned her to face him. "I asked you because you're brilliant, and clever, and beautiful. And because whenever I'm near you, I feel like I could fight forever. Like I have something to fight *for*." He trailed his knuckles along the arch of her cheek. "It's hard to find anything to be excited about, being Lord Rion's son. But when I'm with you...I feel like myself again. I feel like I finally remember who that *is*."

Cistine's heart had begun to clatter the moment he'd called her brilliant; now it simply melted, and she melted with it. She sank into his arms, and Julian held her against him, his fingers finding paths through her tangled hair.

"Just remember not to overextend yourself," he said. "Ashe and I would rather see you happily reading a book than killing yourself every day on our account."

Cistine didn't argue. She was already half-asleep in his arms.

CHAPTER NINETEEN

J ULIAN'S REASSURANCE RESONATED in the chambers of Cistine's heart that were already weary of lessons—and spurred her to take action. She cajoled Quill into shorter training sessions—and he must've been distracted, his thoughts on Tatiana or the letter he'd burned, because he let her excuses slide through. Maleck had her progressing to holding different pikestaffs, shields, and swords; when she told him she couldn't feel any difference between the weight of those weapons—which she really didn't—he let her leave within a half-hour, and trained with Ashe in the kitchen instead, working on exercises to strengthen her leg. And that was more important than whatever they were doing with the weapons.

When it came to working with Ariadne, things were trickier. Scraping by on the bare minimum was difficult when the warrior watched her as keenly as Faer. Cistine resorted to scrubbing doorframes and polishing the Den's main level only as long as Ariadne was watching her. If her attention flickered for even a moment, Cistine rested.

When guilt massaged her muscles at night, she reminded herself Julian was right: she wasn't alone, so there was no reason to shoulder her burdens as if she was. The lessons that aligned best with her purposes in Valgard were those from Thorne. Learning the language of Old Valgard and researching its customs and territories seemed like true progress toward helping Talheim, so that was where she placed her strength and the majority of her focus.

Over bowls of stew and open books, Thorne explained how Old Valgardan was a language of runes, not letters—one symbol for every word. Cistine transposed these lessons over the book she'd bought in Veran, and by week's end she knew enough to understand that the first story was about the four Wayfinders Thorne showed her among the stars.

She learned other things, too: that Baba Kallah's favorite name for her, *Yani*, meant *sweet*, and that Quill liked to call Maleck *Storfir*, a taunt aimed toward his muscles, which always earned him a pounding on the ribs.

Finally, Cistine asked Maleck what a *bandayo* was.

She'd learned to fill up the empty silences with him, feeling the cold pressure of his quietness, and when she finally mustered up the courage to ask the question, Maleck's silence was deafening.

"I don't know if Talheim can translate it," he murmured at last. "It calls into question everything about a person's origins: their mother and father, the nature of their creation, the place of their birth. Everything."

The translation, even spoken in Maleck's quiet voice, stung Cistine's heart. "Is Thorne a bastard?" Some of her uncles were of that nature: King Ivan's sons with scullery maids and noblewomen across Talheim. Cyril had given them lordly titles when he'd returned from the war, smoothing out relationships with half-siblings across the Middle Kingdom out of compassion for their mistreatment and concern for the throne's wellbeing.

It truly didn't matter to Cistine how any of the cabal had been born, least of all Thorne, but curiosity wouldn't let her sit silent on the question.

"Thorne," Maleck said, "has the purest blood of us all. But in his own eyes, that makes him the least of anyone. Whenever he was called *bandayo* before, it was to remind him that whatever he is, he can't run from it. Some would say Thorne is cursed to walk the footsteps of a father he despised and cursed to follow a Chancellor he never wished to imitate."

Which made him a man welded to his future, his name inseparable from his title.

Cistine pondered that as she held different buckler shields at Maleck's command, trying her best to look invested. She thought of what it was to carry the expectations of a kingdom on your shoulders, to be bound to a calling when something else called to you instead.

Come. Cistine hadn't felt the tug in her chest since she'd arrived in Hellidom, but now it stirred again. *Come and see.*

She finished training with Maleck, thundered down the steps two at a time, and told Ariadne precisely what she wanted to do in the kitchen that day.

In the evening, when the cabal and Baba Kallah gathered to eat at the dining table, Cistine slinked away from the counter where they fought over platters of venison flank. She placed a lemon poppy-seed muffin on Thorne's plate, in front of Thorne himself, who hadn't risen to retrieve his portion yet.

"I know why you like lemons," Cistine murmured under the commotion at the counter. "Because they're sour and unpalatable, just like you. They may be part of the citrus family, but you'd hardly know it. They're completely their own sort of fruit."

Thorne looked up from the muffin, and Cistine smiled.

"Thank you," Thorne murmured slowly, as if surprised to hear the words himself.

Cistine tossed her hair over her shoulder. "No need to thank me. I like a good lemon, too."

The would-be rulers, lashed to their positions by name if not by heart, smiled at one another over the lemon poppyseed muffin. And they went to retrieve their supper.

The Den's undercroft was a dry, airy place, humming with the watermills' steady grind at one end and sheltered in a deep, cool stone undercroft at the other. This was where the Nior's flow turned the gears and millstones that powdered the grain into flour. Cistine knew all the muffins she and Ariadne had baked the previous day, and all the loaves of bread and scones Baba Kallah made, were blended from the mill's flour and the garden's produce—but she'd never seen the enormous round casks of grain before, hidden under the Den.

Ariadne brought her down to the undercroft after lunch, forgoing her lesson with Thorne. Cistine tried not to miss it too much as she folded her arms, observing the mills and the handful of Hellidom's residents who worked them. "What are we doing here?"

Ariadne gestured toward the casks kept far from the water in the dry, stony side of the undercroft, and when Cistine went to the nearest one, Ariadne removed the tamped lid. "We do our best to keep the grain as dry and cool as possible. But in the summer, that task becomes difficult. We've lost two casks to mold already this year. I want you to make certain there isn't about to be a third."

"You want me to search the grain for mold?"

Ariadne nodded. "Thorne claims you have a keen eye. Let's see if he's right."

Cistine looked helplessly around the undercroft. "There must be at least a hundred casks here."

"One hundred and thirteen, to be precise. It would take the average person three days to sort through them."

Cistine perched her hands on her hips, swiveling to face Ariadne. "And what makes you think I have three days to spare?"

"Well, since you seem to have so much free time after your lessons with Quill and Maleck these days, I thought you'd welcome an involved task."

Cistine raged quietly as she stared Ariadne down. She'd clearly noticed Cistine's lessons were growing shorter, her days filling up with Ashe and Julian more than with the cabal, and she would exploit that if Cistine didn't comply. She might even tell Thorne. And if he suspected Cistine was putting forth the minimum effort, he would no doubt halt the rest of her training on the grounds she was wasting his cabal's valuable time.

"Very well," Cistine said. "Three days it is."

"I said the average person would need three days." Ariadne strode back to the steps. "I'll see you in five. Cassaida, she's yours now."

Cistine kicked a wad of straw at Ariadne's back, though it fell far short of even grazing the woman's boots. Then she turned to face one of the workers who approached with an enormous dish in her arms, heeding Ariadne's summons.

As the light slanted across the woman's body, Cistine fought not to stare.

Half her face was badly burned, as cratered as Maleck's chest. It framed her smile into a grimace as she halted beside Cistine. "You must be the servant Ariadne told us about."

"I must be," Cistine said through gritted teeth.

"Strange...I've never known High Tribune Thorne to employ servants." The woman flashed a crooked smile. "Well. I'm Cassaida. This way, please...I'll show you how to sift the grain for imperfections."

Scowling and batting her untamed hair from her eyes, Cistine followed.

The workers were pleasant, if mostly-silent, company. They shared their water skins with Cistine and helped her lug the larger casks from the corners to be sifted. But the effort of working the sieve, as Cassaida showed her to do, was arm-buckling and rigorous—as though Ariadne placed her here to make up for all the abuse she'd avoided with shorter training sessions.

Cistine passed the hours sifting and marking as the streaks of sunlight on the water through the mills settled lower and lower. Dinnertime came and went, and she was contemplating leaving one barrel of the first batch unfinished and calling an end to the day when a raspy chuckle stirred her focus from the sieve.

"It's arduous, I know." Cassaida planted a basket full of milled grain on the waist-high ledge girdling the undercroft and swept the hair from her gnarled brow. "But just wait until winter, when hunting is scarce around the falls and we have nothing but honeyed cakes to eat. It will all seem worthwhile then."

Cistine had grown used to Cassaida's half-scowl from across the undercroft by now, had learned to see the beauty in her tan skin and gray eyes instead. But this close, she noticed just how deep the furrowed scars ran. A pale streak cleaved through the nut-brown threads at her temples.

"Does that happen often?" Cistine asked. "Scarce hunting?"

"Well, with so many mouths to feed..." Cassaida shrugged. "But we make do. Ariadne and Thorne have a ration plan in place. It goes into effect when the last leaves fall from the trees."

It was really no wonder Ariadne was so concerned with the grain, then. "Where does all this come from?"

Cassaida pursed her lips. "That's a question for Thorne. It's really his choice how much we divulge to strangers."

"Can't anyone in this city answer a straightforward question?" Cistine grumbled.

Cassaida laughed again, tipping the freshly-milled flour into burlap sacks strung from the low roof beams. "Not really. Hellidom is a well-kept secret full of secretive people. That's how we survive."

"That wouldn't happen to be because you're harboring bandits, would it?"

"We have an understanding." Cassaida's smile slipped to a grimace as she hoisted a full bag from the hooks and knotted its mouth. "People like us keep Hellidom fed and watered and in good health. And the cabal keeps us safe."

Cistine opened the last barrel of the day and slowly began to sift it while she considered that. The way Cassaida spoke of Thorne and his people reminded her of how the citizens in Astoria spoke about her father: with reverence and respect, and a hint of affection. "You're not afraid of them, are you?"

"The stories are certainly fearsome," Cassaida said. "And we believed them at first. But when our city in northern Blaykrone began to raise unpayable taxes, High Tribune Thorne sent Maleck to bargain with us. He explained the truth behind the tales—why they stole from the wagons and what they'd built here. He said if some of us agreed to help tend the mills and see to the people's needs in Hellidom, then at every full moon we could send untaxed rations back to our families."

Cistine frowned. "That's illegal...but generous of him."

"I was more concerned with the former, at first." Cassaida nudged Cistine's arms up and loaded handfuls of grain into the sieve. "But then some very unhappy Vassora came to our city and asked us if we'd had anything to do with the bandits from the Vey. When no one would answer them..."

She touched two fingers to the side of her face, and Cistine's stomach plunged.

"Let's just say they were not interested in having tea with liars," Cassaida murmured. "That was the day I realized the Courts were not entirely for us, and whatever Thorne had to offer couldn't possibly be worse than their cruel suspicion."

"I don't suppose much could be."

They lapsed into silent work, and Cistine's heart throbbed for this woman, whose punishment for mere association with Thorne's people had been the destruction of her face. But a part of her was envious, too: that instead of crumbling when they'd hurt her, Cassaida had planted her feet in defiance. She'd done the very thing they'd suspected her of doing in the first place, and now she laughed in their faces with every bag of flour she carried back to her family from Thorne's stores.

Under such circumstances, Cistine would've been too frightened to leave her home, much less march into Thorne's and work clandestinely with his cabal.

And yet...here she was. In a house of known bandits and murderers, with whom her mere association left her marked. And day after day, she chose to stay and train with them.

Before she knew it, the barrel was entirely sifted, and not a speckle of mold had been found. Cassaida tamped down the lid again, smiling. "Tomorrow will be easier, as will the day after that. The key to any task is to find a rhythm, and I think you've struck yours. Now go and rest those arms...you've done enough for one day. I expect to see you again at midday tomorrow."

Kneading her biceps, Cistine climbed up the steps and emerged beside the iron stove to find the kitchen quiet. Only Maleck and Ashe were there, and as usual, they weren't speaking. Instead, Maleck leaned against the table, and Ashe stood with her hands braced in the doorway of the hall to Cistine's room. Her crutch was gone. Sweat swirled her hair against her neck and forced her to squint as it ran into her eyes. Her muscle-banded arms shook as she clung to the sleek wood, keeping herself upright with her weight distributed to both legs.

"Ashe?" Cistine said. "Are you sure you should be walking without a crutch so soon?"

"She shouldn't," Maleck said. "And yet, here we are."

"I'm going to do it," Ashe snapped, "so I can punch that smug look off your face, augur."

"I've told you, I am not an augur." Though Maleck's tone was smooth, there was that strange flash in his eyes. "There is more to me than what I was before."

"Such as?"

Maleck blinked, tipping his head. "I'm a proficient cook."

Ashe barked with ragged laughter, sliding her wounded foot across the floor. "Ha! With or without using augmented flames?"

"Without. I have medico training, as well."

"Good for you. I'd clap, but..." Ashe released the doorposts and sagged forward, stumbling a half-step. Cistine winced, but Maleck didn't move.

"I also collect weapons," he said. "Though I suppose that's hardly a talent."

Ashe grunted, pressing her knuckles against her thighs as she struggled to keep her balance. "Well...so do I. Maybe we're both talentless savages."

"That's good," Maleck said. "Only savagery will defeat your wound."

Ashe flashed him a smile that made Cistine recoil. It was devoid of any of her Warden's familiar kindness, yet it fit here, in this house. In an offering to Maleck almost like a truce. "Anything else?"

"I was an artist once."

Ashe snagged the wall with her palm, staring at him wide-eyed. "You're joking."

Maleck shrugged. "I had spare time."

"Imagine that. Were they oil canvases, or lewd sketches of women?"

"I'll tell you, if you can reach me without clinging to the wall."

Ashe slowly slid her hand to her side. She limped toward him—one step, then two, buckling when she pressed weight on her injured side. Maleck watched with arms crossed and eyes inscrutable as Ashe shuffled toward him, one step after another. Inches away, she stumbled forward and punched Maleck's arm.

"Tell me," she panted, grabbing his sleeve to steady herself.

Maleck touched her elbow lightly. "They were ink sketches of old mountain halls and dark places."

"Pleasant."

"I was not in pleasant places when I drew them," he said. "I only copied what I saw."

"Icy holes and battlefields?" Ashe looked up, and there was something in that glance between them—something Cistine would never understand. Would never *want* to understand. It was a grim memory shared between warriors who had fought on opposite sides of the same battlefield, who had each ravaged the other's ranks. Who had killed one another's brothers and sisters.

Cistine was twenty, and Ashe only thirty-three, but for the first time Cistine fathomed that gulf between them. Not only the difference in their ages, but the war that separated them.

"I am sorry," Maleck murmured, "for whatever part I play in your nightmares."

Ashe let go of his sleeve and looked away. "And...you. For your drawings."

Maleck moved away from her, as if Ashe's presence suddenly stifled him. "It wasn't the war that sketched those pictures."

He ended their training as abruptly as he always ended Cistine's.

CHAPTER TWENTY

THE NEXT THREE days were grueling, but Cistine was determined not to spend a minute longer than necessary doing Ariadne's work—not when the warrior expected her to fail so miserably at the end. She had something to prove to this cunning strategist.

So Cistine cleaved back her time with Quill even more and poured herself wholeheartedly into sifting grain; and with Cassaida for company, it was much less of a chore. When Cistine asked the right questions, the grain mistress became an open book of stories. She told Cistine about the village where her family still lived, on the banks of an enormous lake dividing Blaykrone from Eben. Cistine lost herself in the warm days as she envisioned the place Cassaida described: lovely huts and windmills on the water's edge, framed from behind by mountains.

It made her miss the yearly visits to the Calalun Peaks she'd forfeited in favor of days spent gossiping in the Citadel's glass courtyards. If Talheim could avoid war, she would have to return to those rolling green mountains as soon as possible.

On the fourth day, there were only five barrels left to sift, and Cistine was determined to finish them. Even managing to complete the task one day short of Ariadne's haughty assumptions would be enough to compensate for Cistine's sore arms and stiff haunches; so she shoveled porridge into her mouth after another short session with Quill and sprinted toward the steps beside the brick oven.

"You're in an awful hurry."

Thorne's voice stopped her with her hand on the doorpost. She looked back to find him standing in the mouth of the hall, and the state of his face startled her: that stern jaw tight, those limpid eyes cloudy, almost unfocused. He wandered to the table and plucked an apple from the basket of fruit there, palming it from hand to hand.

"Ariadne has me sifting grain," Cistine said.

"I'm aware."

Cistine licked her lower lip slowly, curiosity plucking her thoughts. This was the first time she'd seen Thorne since she'd begun her task with the grain, and now a question hung on the tip of her tongue—something she'd wondered for four days. "Cassaida said I should ask you where the grain comes from."

Thorne caught the apple on another pass and lifted his gaze to her. Cistine stroked her chipped, abused fingernails along the doorframe and held his stare without blinking.

"They're Blaykrone imports," Thorne said. "We pay for them handsomely."

Cistine cocked her head. "Where does the money come from?"

Thorne arched a dark brow. "Why do you suppose I needed weapons to sell?"

"But the cost to feed an entire city on grain for the whole winter..."

"Is exorbitant. Which is why we raid the wagons. For steel...and also for items that fetch a high price elsewhere."

Suddenly, the dresses Cistine had clung to, the Talheimic baubles, the necklace she'd traded to him for Ashe's sword...they were nothing. Their personal value to her was nonexistent when weighed against the empty bellies they could fill with purchased grain. "You should take everything in our trunk. Even the trunk itself, if you like. I can replace the dresses and jewelry. Just leave the books, that's all I ask."

Thorne's other brow rose now, completing the vision of surprise.

"Really?"

Cistine thought of Cassaida and the four half-grown children she'd left behind. "I have plenty of those things in my home. Others have less. I can't let people starve while I worry about a few silly trinkets."

Thorne palmed the apple again, slower this time. Still watching her. "If you're certain, leave the items in the kitchen tomorrow."

He was giving her one last chance to graciously renege—but she wouldn't.

With Cassaida's cheerful, scarred face in her mind, Cistine descended to the undercroft. And with all the things she was giving away, she felt lighter.

It was not Cistine's favorite day in the undercroft; not because of the labor itself, which was no more or less taxing than any other day, but because of what they found in the second-to-last barrel, and the look on Cassaida's face when they opened the lid and found the black taint among the grains.

"This one is infected," Cassaida sighed. "It's frightening to think how such a small blight can devastate a whole crop."

"Just like that, then?" Cistine said. "The entire barrel is worthless?"

"We can't risk it. We tried to mill tainted grain one year when we were desperate. We lost more people to mania and gangrenous tissue than we would've lost to starvation."

Cistine watched a pair of strong millworkers haul the barrel away to the stone ledge running alongside the mills. She didn't know how they would dispose of it, if the barrel could be salvaged. She prayed it was possible, so at least some recompense could come of this.

"Cheer up." Cassaida knuckled Cistine's chin gently. "One in one hundred and thirteen isn't so bad. It means more food to send to my children. You can smile about that."

Cistine tried to; but after what she'd discussed with Thorne, and after Cassaida's stories about bone-breaking winters and frighteningly hungry bellies, she could muster nothing but melancholy while she sifted out the last barrel. Cassaida joined the workers at the mill, leaving her alone with her thoughts of harsh seasons and starving people.

Company arrived unexpectedly at the base of the steps after nearly an hour, startling Cistine from her dejection with the tap of a cane on stone.

She couldn't imagine how Baba Kallah maneuvered down the short but steep flights of steps, or how she would climb back up again. But here she was, her voice floating through the music of grinding cogs as she limped to join Cistine: "Minding grain is like herding kittens. But it's a good time to think, if you're open to that risk."

"All I can think about right now is how tired my arms are," Cistine groaned as she sifted the last of the grain—and, to her relief, found no moldy patches.

"Pain is good," Baba Kallah rapped her cane on the cask as Cistine tamped down the lid. "If you don't feel pain, you ought to check you aren't dead."

"Is that how you feel about your leg? That it means you're still alive?"

Baba Kallah balanced her hands on the cane's head and slowly lowered herself onto the short ledge that girdled the undercroft's wall. "I have to, or else I'd go mad."

Cistine sat beside her, intrigue dulling the soreness from her muscles. "How did it happen?"

Baba Kallah chuckled. "You're a curious one, aren't you? And bold, no less."

"I didn't become Astoria's most famous gossip by keeping my questions to myself," Cistine smiled. "But if you don't want to tell me, I understand."

A grimace transformed Baba Kallah's face. From the serene, smiling old woman, a pained and angry survivor crawled out. Her jaw was set, her eyes flashing. For a moment, she looked almost like—

"This," Baba Kallah rubbed her leg, "was not an accident. The only accident, I think, was that he wasn't able to finish my other leg before we escaped."

"Who wasn't?"

"My son."

Cistine cupped her hands over her mouth. "Your own *son* did this to you?"

"There was too much of his father in that boy," Baba Kallah said. "Too much anger, too much fear. When the two come together and you put a weapon in their hands, any terrible thing you can imagine becomes possible."

Cistine couldn't fathom ever lashing out at her own mother. Even disappointing her was a burden almost too great to bear. "I'm so sorry that happened."

"So am I." Baba Kallah gripped the cane again, her lips taut. "Not for myself. I still have both legs, after all. But for my boy, my Salvotor...for that rage and terror he endured, and I could never protect him from any of it. For that, I'm forever sorry."

Cistine gently covered the old woman's hands with hers. The skin was surprisingly soft, seamed with gentle knolls and ridges of gathered skin. These hands had known a lifetime of hard work—hands so unlike Cistine's.

These hands had fought harder for survival than Cistine ever would. Baba Kallah had earned every inch of strength she exuded, injuries or none—and that power made Cistine feel strong in turn. It made her ache to wipe the shadows from Baba Kallah's face, to see the smile return to her lips.

"I never thanked you for fighting for us in your own way," she murmured. "For the things you've said to Thorne, and...for the things you haven't said."

Baba Kallah's gaze, which had dulled at the horrific memories of the abuse she'd suffered, brightened again. "I like to think I'm doing some good for him. For both of you."

"You've certainly done good for me," Cistine said. "I don't know where I would be right now if he knew I'd listened in on his cabal's meeting."

"If you suspected the consequences of that, why did you do it?"

Cistine smiled sheepishly. "Because I'm curious."

Baba Kallah unwound one hand from under Cistine's, capturing her fingers tightly. She thumped the cane soundly on the floor, enunciating her words: "*Never stop being curious.*"

"I won't. But I also don't think I'll ever stop being hungry. Would you like to eat with me?"

Baba Kallah chortled. "Oh, I'll never make the climb back up those stairs!"

"Then why did you come down here in the first place?"

"I like to listen to the water. To the mills. It can be too noisy up in that Den...especially when everyone is worrying over Tatiana."

"They're worried?"

"They don't show it like you show your concern for your Warden," Baba Kallah said. "Reading this cabal is like learning a different language, but it *can* be learned if you make the effort."

There was almost a dare in those words—tempting Cistine to look closely enough to see them. Truly see Thorne's people.

She leaped to her feet. "I'm going up. Should I send someone to help you?"

"I'll wait. Sooner or later, Thorne will notice I'm missing. Then he'll come to carry me upstairs." Baba Kallah's eyes sparkled with mischief as she batted Cistine on her way.

Cistine went to the steps, pausing at the bottom to look back. "Thorne listens to you. He seems to value your opinion more than anyone's. Even the cabal's."

She was careful not to frame it as a question, but she knew Baba Kallah would perceive her raging curiosity.

Brows flicking up, the old woman grinned. "He ought to. I'm his grandmother, after all."

CHAPTER TWENTY-ONE

TWO MORE STEPS," Maleck said.

Ashe gripped the table, her arms trembling and her injured leg bearing no weight. "I can't. I'm done."

Cistine pushed her sprouts and potatoes around her plate, watching her Warden struggle to keep her balance. Maleck leaned against the dining ledge, offering no support but his quiet voice. "Just two more steps. That will be two more than yesterday."

"Will it count as a third if I put my foot up your backside?" Ashe panted.

"Yes, if you can make it that far."

Julian nudged Cistine and slid his napkin to her. It took effort to rouse herself enough just to look down. Concluding her brief sabbatical with sorting grain, she'd spent most of the evening rearranging furniture, dusting, polishing, and scrubbing the entry parlor, in addition to upkeeping the kitchen, which was now a daily task. Her back muscles, elbows, and hands were tied up in knots, and her neck cramped. She could barely turn her head to read Julian's handwriting.

Two mynts says she can't do it.

Cistine took the pen from Julian and jotted back, *Do you even have the mynts?*

His eyes gleamed as he wrote, *Where do you think I've been all day? I was helping out in the village, like you suggested. They pay good coin for an extra pair of hands at the shops.*

Cistine smiled. *How heroic of you.*

Julian coughed to hide a chuckle, taking the pen back from her and scribbling, *I'd be lying if I said I didn't do it to impress you.*

Cistine looked up sharply as Ashe stumbled and cursed. Maleck twitched, but kept his feet planted and his arms folded.

She knew Ashe and Maleck had been working at this every day, coaxing Ashe's injured muscles not to seize up when she put pressure on them. She also knew the struggle it had been, Ashe leaning on a cane like Baba Kallah's when she limped back to her room every night. She wondered if Ashe had allowed Maleck to train her because her resentment toward him made her energy blaze brighter; if hatred coaxed her feet forward when her leg wanted so badly to give out and send her sprawling on the floor.

Julian tapped the pen against his chin. Then he wrote down, *Three mynts.*

Cheater.

Ashe slid her foot forward, leaned—and crumbled. Her knees struck the floor and Cistine scrambled to help her, but Maleck darted up his hand. His eyes were the death-god's eyes again, cold and firm, ordering her away.

"Is this what Talheim's Cadre has to offer?" Maleck asked. "Do its warriors amount to so little they crumble at a simple injury?"

"Watch your mouth!" Julian launched up beside Cistine, but Maleck paid him no attention. He focused on Ashe, pulling herself up against the table, clutching her wounded leg with her free hand.

"This is what defends your king," Maleck said. "It's a wonder your people ever defeated us."

"Shut up," Ashe spat.

"It would be a different world by far if Talheim sent the likes of you to win its wars now," Maleck plowed on with more venom—more emotion overall—than Cistine had ever heard from him. "Why did Cistine even bother bringing you along if all you're good for is polishing the floor with your knees?"

Cistine's mouth sprang open in shock at the ruthless question.

And then Ashe moved.

She gripped the table and launched herself off its side, shouting in pain with every step. But she still moved—to the edge of the table, where she let go. Where she thrust herself forward with all her might and led with her fist.

The *crack* of her knuckles on Maleck's jaw rang through the kitchen.

Julian winced. Cistine slapped a hand over her mouth.

Maleck's head turned with the blow, and then he slowly looked back at Ashe. If Cistine had been standing where Ashe was—if she'd just struck Maleck with her bare hands—she would already be stepping back and begging for mercy.

Ashe did neither. She carried all her weight on her good leg, and glared up Maleck, silently daring him to speak again. Maleck stared right back at her.

Julian settled his hand on the small of Cistine's back. She felt the tension in his fingertips, waiting for something to happen, preparing to leap to Ashe's defense.

Maleck sidestepped so the ledge was no longer at his back, and retreated two steps. "Without the table."

Ashe sucked in a hard breath. Cistine didn't see it leave her as she stumbled one step toward him. Then another.

Maleck opened his mouth, and Ashe said, "Step back."

He took one pace away from her, and she matched it, keeping the same distance between them.

"Again."

They moved step-for-step through the kitchen, almost to the doorway, before Ashe's leg finally had enough. She tried to close the distance to Maleck, and her injury yanked her off-balance. Maleck caught her elbows, steadying her against him. He helped her stand upright, still favoring that leg.

"Talheim's Cadre," he murmured. "Unexpected, indeed. And not without its strength and nobility."

Cistine stared at Maleck's hands as they gripped Ashe's arms, supplementing where her strength failed. He wore dark, close-fitting gloves, even while indoors. Though he didn't have any armor on today, his buttonless shirt hid the scars of augmentation across his chest; those permanent markings of a path he'd been forced to walk against his will, gathering wounds and scars for which he was still coddled and pitied, with no other choice but to find the reserves of his own strength to lean into.

The harsh words he'd used to draw out Ashe's strength were already forgotten. And Cistine was glad Ashe had him.

The Den's front door boomed open, jarring them all in place. Someone shouted for help.

Maleck let go of Ashe and sprinted down the hall, and Julian darted after him. Cistine pulled Ashe's arm around her shoulders, and they hobbled together into the front room.

Maleck was already at the door, laying hands on Tatiana. She clung to the polished wooden frame as blood pumped from her shoulder, soaking and staining her filigreed vest and trousers. A dark arrow protruded from her back, the serrated tip punching a hole through the front of her arm.

Cistine gripped the wall, her stomach turning over as Ariadne dashed from the bedchamber corridor. A belt of knives whispered on her hips as she slid to a halt beside a wide-eyed Julian.

"Into the kitchen," Maleck ordered. "Now."

Tatiana cried out as Julian and Maleck pulled her away from the door. Her feet dragged against the floor like a drunkard's, blood spotting the wooden beams. Cistine pulled Ashe's waist, and they ducked out of the way. Ariadne trailed behind Maleck and Julian, her face soaked white. Cistine had never seen a living person so pale.

Under the kitchen's gentle ghostlight, Maleck motioned Julian away. He swept Tatiana up easily in his arms and ordered them to clear the table. Cistine grabbed the food platters and tossed them into the washbasin as Maleck settled Tatiana on the table's edge. She wobbled in place, almost pitching to the floor, and Ashe lurched forward to prop her back up with such care that the arrow hardly jostled.

Ariadne jerked toward the table when Tatiana groaned, and Maleck spun, catching her by the shoulders.

"Not this one," he said. "I need you to find Thorne and Baba Kallah."

Ariadne's eyes were wet and wild, lashes framed with tears as she stared at Tatiana; then she dipped her head and fled the room. Cistine heard the front door bang closed behind her.

"No time to wait for Kallah," Tatiana gasped. Her fingers clutched Ashe's sleeve so tightly, Cistine thought the flimsy seams might separate. "Get it out of me, Mal."

"I have triage training," Ashe said. "I can help."

Maleck stared at her over Tatiana's head. Then he pointed to Julian. "My bedchamber is the last in the hall to the right of the front door. Bring me one of the black daggers in the chest at the foot of the bed."

"Cistine," Ashe said as Julian disappeared, "are you still with us?"

Cistine bobbed her head faintly. Though the old-meat reek of blood turned her knees to water, she knew Ashe needed her. Tatiana needed her.

The thought pushed at her feet, forcing her closer to the table.

"Maleck will have to separate the arrow," Ashe explained. "You hold Tatiana, and I'll brace the arrow while he does it."

Cistine nodded again. In an unsteady fumble, she took Ashe's place, holding Tatiana upright on the table's edge. Long, slender fingers gripped just above Cistine's hips as Tatiana anchored herself in place. "Fancy meeting like this, Princess! Here I was hoping to make an impression when I came back. I had so many plans to make you love me."

"Save your flirting for someone else." Worry cracked Cistine's humor in pieces. "I'm spoken for."

"That can be fixed." A small grunt of pain rolled through Tatiana's voice. Cistine wrapped an arm around her, bracing the back of her neck and pulling Tatiana's face into her shoulder.

Julian darted back into the room, carrying a black dagger wrapped with red cloth. One look at its razor edge, sharpened to a brutally-fine thinness that looked capable of cleaving a piece of parchment dropped onto it, and

Cistine knew what it was: *Svarkyst* steel from the Black Coasts.

Maleck caught the dagger from Julian's toss and brought the edge to the arrow's shaft, testing carefully.

"How quickly can you saw through that?" Ashe asked.

"In moments, so long as she holds still."

"I've got her." Cistine wrapped her arms more tightly around Tatiana.

Ashe gripped the arrow at the fletching and just below the head to steady it. And Maleck started to cut.

Tatiana's scream was deafening. She slammed her fist into Cistine's ribs so hard tears sprang to her eyes. Cistine loosened her grip for an instant, and Maleck roared at her to hold on as Tatiana started to convulse, the arrow chafing and rolling inside the nest of her flesh.

Cistine squeezed her eyes shut and clung to Tatiana again as Maleck sawed through the arrow shaft with armor-shredding steel. The moment the last threads of wood gave way, Maleck barked Ashe's name. They slid the halves from Tatiana's shoulder, and she sank heavily against Cistine, all her breath rushing out in a sob.

The front door slammed again, and this time it was Thorne who rushed into the kitchen: windswept, eyes wide, and wearing a dark blue shirt and pants fletched in silver. The faint smell of food and strong spirits hung around his body as he gripped Cistine's arms, plucking her away from Tatiana. He took his warrior's face in one hand and tilted up her head.

"Tati," he said. "Did they follow you?"

Tatiana's glazed eyes flickered, trying to focus on Thorne. "No. Too...far. Lost them in the trees, right after they...sh-shot me."

"What's wrong with her?" Julian demanded. "Why is she slurring?"

"Check the arrow tip," Thorne said.

Maleck rolled it in his palm, examined the shaft, and flicked a bit of white dust onto his thumb. He rolled it between his fingertips and growled, "Rifandi."

"Tyve poison." Thorne slid his hand around Tatiana's neck and laid her out on the table. "The weapon of the Shadows."

"Stars-damned poison studies," Tatiana gasped.

As Thorne tore apart the shoulder of Tatiana's fine shirt—and the warrior whimpered in protest—Ashe leaned heavily on the table. "Tell me the properties of this poison. I might be able to help."

Maleck raised skeptical eyes to her.

"I've taken poison studies myself," Ashe said. "King Jad of the Southern Kingdom is obsessed with the idea of medicinal warfare. All the King's Cadre has this training."

Julian's fingers curled over Cistine's shoulders, and that steady grip was the only thing keeping her from falling. The thought of King Jad with poison in his arsenal...poison he could turn against Cistine's family—

"It's a paralytic sedative," Thorne said, "with numbing and inhibitive properties."

Ashe frowned at the tabletop, and Cistine's mind trawled through a harbor of knowledge gleaned from her books. "It sounds like Shadowroot."

Ashe nodded slowly. "It does. Shadowroot is used to silence spies so they make it back to their dispatchers without a voice to tell secrets before they die. It's a warning message."

"Message received," Thorne growled. "Can you help her?"

"Yes."

Julian pulled Cistine back from the table as Ashe went to work: calling for hot water and cloths, and some sort of counteragent she and Maleck argued over for several minutes before he deduced Valgard's name for it. Silent tears ran down Cistine's cheeks, her gaze fixed on Tatiana's hand burrowing against the tabletop as she fought for control of her body.

Though they weren't quite friends, and Tatiana was as brutal and secretive as the rest of them, Cistine knew if Tatiana died tonight, if she bled to death or her lungs were paralyzed, if her heart quit beating, it would never stop haunting her. That beautiful, impatient, vibrant fire, snuffed out...it would be such a waste, a loss, and Cistine would never stop mourning it—even though Tatiana wasn't Talheimic.

More kingdoms than Cistine's were suffering now. More people than hers were in danger.

Ashe continued her work silently. At some point the front door whispered open and shut. Baba Kallah shuffled in to join them, leaning heavily on her cane. She was dressed as frivolously as Thorne, the sequins of her pine-green dress catching the light in a beautiful garland. She limped to the table, halting beside Thorne, and she said nothing while Ashe ground leaves and packed them into Tatiana's wound for the fifth time—drawing out the poison, Cistine suspected.

But she could only suspect that, because there was so much she didn't know—things Ashe had been taught that Cistine had never bothered to learn. Her knowledge from books was sparse, and knowing the properties of Shadowroot did not tell her how to treat it. If she'd been alone in the Den tonight, she would have held Tatiana while she died with an arrow in her shoulder and poison in her blood. Useless. Helpless.

Just like the night they'd tried to escape from Maleck and Quill.

Cistine shrugged Julian's hands away, and to her relief he let them fall. She stepped closer to the table, gripping Tatiana's hand in both of hers. The warrior's eyes had long since fallen shut, turning her focus inward to the battle raging inside her body. But when Cistine squeezed Tatiana's hand, to her relief, Tatiana squeezed back.

"Will she be all right?" Julian asked, and Cistine wanted to kiss him for his concern, and for his comforting presence at her back.

Thorne propped himself against the table. His enormous hand covered Tatiana's brow, his thumb brushing the sweat-soaked curls from her eyes. The movement was shockingly tender, and Cistine wondered if it was a grounding habit; if he was reassuring himself, through touch and quiet attention, that one of his warriors would not die tonight. "It's in God's hands. But I suspect she will be, thanks to our Talheimic poison study."

Ashe's mouth twitched, and Cistine knew how glad she was to be useful, given all the ways her own injury held her back.

At last, Ashe hobbled back from the table, shaking the wet herbal pack from her fingers. "We'll have to bind that dressing to the wounds and change it every hour for the first two days, then every four hours for another week. But since the wound was above her heart, she should live."

"Show me what you made," Baba Kallah said. "I can mix up enough of that dressing to garnish our salads for years to come."

The sly joke cracked the tension in the room. Everyone laughed except Tatiana; under Ashe's ministrations, she'd fallen asleep, but her grip on Cistine's hand remained tight like a promise she would recover in time.

"You should teach me, too," Cistine said, and held Ashe's stare as amusement paled into surprise.

"Gladly, Princess."

Thorne's gaze lingered on Ashe, too, and he dipped his head. "Thank you." He scooped Tatiana up from the table and carried her down the hall toward her room, which had been far too quiet in her absence.

Quivering from the exertion of the last several minutes, Ashe yanked out a chair and sank into it, gripping her leg. Her face was pallid. She put her head in her other hand.

Maleck stared at Ashe, and went on staring even when she ignored him. Cistine wondered if her Warden was too exhausted to even feel the brand of Maleck's gaze.

"You have talents," Maleck said, "not only for war."

Ashe bobbed her shoulders. "The war has been over for more than twenty years."

"Yes," Maleck said. "That's true."

The silence waxed, and Cistine's skin prickled with gooseflesh as she glanced between Ashe and Maleck.

"I think," Maleck added, "we often carry the battlefield with us far longer than it needs to live."

"That's true," Ashe echoed.

Maleck turned on heel and strode from the room. Ashe dropped her hand—watching him go.

CHAPTER TWENTY-TWO

CISTINE AND THORNE were the last ones awake that night; she wiped blood from the table without being asked to, because the sight of it made her stomach turn, and she knew she wouldn't be able to sleep one room away knowing Tatiana's blood still soaked the knots in the wood. Thorne drank some kind of Valgardan spirits, and though he offered her some in a silent toast, Cistine shook her head.

She went on wiping as she watched him sprawl out in his chair, still dressed in his fine threads, now stained with his warrior's blood. Cistine wanted to tell him he could still save the clothes if he soaked them overnight, but her tongue cleaved to the roof of her mouth, silencing the words.

She needed to sleep, but in her exhausted mind she could still hear Tatiana slurring, still see the blood pooling from her shoulder and back. And she could only think of King Jad doing the same thing to her people, to innocent families all across Talheim.

She wiped away the last drops of blood, folded the rag neatly, and pulled out a chair. Thorne didn't lift his gaze from the window across the room when she sat beside him. "Where were you tonight?"

"Eating," Thorne said, "with Baba Kallah. We make it a point to meet away from the Den every other week to discuss things."

"Because she's a war councilor? Or because she's your grandmother?"

Thorne's eyes did flick to her then, full of caution. "She's told you much."

"Because she trusts me."

"On what grounds?" Though he spoke the question calmly, not cruelly, it still stung. As if he thought she was unworthy of that trust.

"Because she knows I didn't come here to harm anyone," Cistine snapped.

"And yet, here we are." Thorne spread a broad arm. "One of my warriors wounded, months of sieges on the Vingete Vey ruined, and my cabal divided over the subject of you."

Guilt warmed Cistine's ears, then burned away quickly into defensiveness. "None of that would have happened if I had known what this kingdom was really like. If someone had told me!"

"It's Talheim's responsibility to teach you the things a princess needs to know. Don't place that blame on me."

Cistine could think of no protest. He was right—Talheim had not prepared her for any of this.

When the silence elongated, Thorne's stern expression softened. "If you knew the first measure of strife, no one would have to warn you about Valgard's nature. You would have been able to see it for yourself the moment you made port in Veran. And that's what you've been preparing for: to recognize what you're up against, so you can decide if it's worth the risk of allying with us to secure aid for your kingdom."

"Why not just tell me what I'm going to face?"

Thorne leaned forward, placing his cup on the table. His breath wafted against her face as he murmured, "Because knowing isn't enough to prepare you, or to save your kingdom. I thought I knew...and my cabal wears the scars of my pride."

Cistine opened her mouth to ask him what he meant—and then the front door banged open for the third time that night. Thorne cursed, lurching to his feet, unsteady from the alcohol. Cistine grabbed his elbow as she rose beside him. They both turned toward the doorway as Quill barged inside.

Cistine had never seen him so disheveled—not even after combat. His hair was askew, the mottling and the white clashing together on both sides, his eyes wide and his clothing mud-spattered as if he'd been running along the Nior's banks, stumbling and rising again and again. He'd outrun Faer—the raven swooped through the doorway and perched on his shoulder after a moment, calling balefully and gripping Quill's shoulder so tightly, blood spotted his pale shirt.

"Where is she?" Quill demanded.

Thorne folded his arms. "Easy, Quill."

"Where *is* she, Thorne?"

"She's alive. Resting. Maleck is on guard and Baba Kallah is with her."

Quill slid a hand through his hair, mussing it even worse. There was something half-mad in his appearance, in the gleam of his eyes. "I want to see her."

"Not yet," Thorne said. "Not until your head is clear."

"It *is* clear!"

"Never when she's hurt. I know you."

Cistine looked between them: Quill, shaking with tension, and Thorne as immovable as a stone wall. They were going to clash, right here in the kitchen she'd worked so hard to clean. There would be more blood on the table, possibly. More wounds they couldn't afford.

"Quill." The steadiness of her own voice surprised her. "I held Tatiana's hand while Ashe treated her. That grip was so strong...as strong as always. She's going to be all right."

Quill's gaze flicked to her. Cistine mustered a smile she hoped was encouraging. Her entire face sagged with tiredness.

"What was it?" Quill asked.

"Rifandi," Cistine and Thorne said together.

Quill's hand shook as he pulled a cinnamon stick from his pocket. He put it between his quivering lips, fumbled, and dropped it on the floor. Cursing, he cracked it in half with his heel. "Tyve poison. Out of cycle."

"That's twice now," Thorne said, "if you count Devitrius."

"They're dead, Thorne. I want them dead."

Cistine's blood ran cold—not at his tone, which belonged to the death-god and her savior from the tavern; but it was his eyes, and the look in them, and the way he stared at Thorne when he said it. She knew that face, not because she'd seen it before, but because she'd felt it. She'd *felt* that hollowness, that desperation burning hot and cold at once through her blood: when Thorne's blade had been at Ashe's neck; and whenever she'd seen Julian with a sword in his hand, ready to step into danger.

And now she knew why Quill had run. Why his hands and knees were caked in mud. Why he'd left patrol to return to the Den when someone brought him the news.

"The hunt is yours, Quill," Thorne said, "*after* Tati recovers."

Quill dipped his head in consent. His gaze turned back to Cistine, and she said, "I'll see you on the rock top tomorrow morning."

"Don't bother."

Though Cistine knew he was allowing for his own distractions, not for the way she'd slacked in her training lately, it still hurt. "No. Quill, I...I want to be there." As she said it, Cistine realized it was true. "And I'm going to be there at sunrise, whether you are or not."

"Meet with her, Quill," Thorne said. "That's an order."

Quill's jaw tightened, but he nodded grudgingly, then turned and vanished back down the hall. Cistine knew he would be sitting outside his own room all night, watching the door across from his.

Thorne swung his seat around and sank down into it, picking up his cup again. "That was good, what you did for Quill. You knew what to say."

"I've stood where he's standing before," Cistine said. "I know how it feels to want your friends to be all right so badly you feel like it might break you."

Thorne looked at her over the rim of his glass. "That's why you're here."

"I think it's why we're all here, in one way or another."

Thorne nodded slowly. "Get some rest. Quill is going to make your life so miserable tomorrow, you'll beg for Nimmus to take you."

Cistine made it to the hall before she lost the battle with her curiosity. Leaning her hand and temple on the thick wooden doorframe, she looked back at him. "What is Nimmus?"

Thorne had gone back to staring at the window beside the brick oven. At her question, he frowned, setting down his cup. "Perdition. The Mad Kingdom, they call it. A realm of ravishment and destruction where the wicked are banished when they die. They wander those brutal plains for millennia, until they're driven insane. And then they become specters of mist and cruelty, driving other deadmen to madness when they pass through the Sable Gates."

Cistine shuddered. They had no such myths of disembodied fiends or dark otherworlds in Talheim. Death was simply the end for them, a brutal plunge into eternal shadow without thought or reason. That notion had always frightened her as a child, but hearing Thorne's alternative made her almost grateful for the prospect of an absolute, peaceful end.

"What about the people who aren't wicked?" Cistine asked. "What happens to them?"

Thorne balanced his fingers around the rim of his cup and flexed them slowly. "Cenowyn. The Infinite Haven."

Cistine shut her eyes. Even the name brought peace, like a cool cup of water on a parched throat, after so much chaos that day. "Tell me."

"There aren't many stories. Not half as many as we have about Nimmus. But Cenowyn is said to reflect Valgard in its perfect state. Mountains, rivers, and fields untouched by the scars of war. Joyous settlements inhabited by those worthy of a peaceful eternity. A realm of light and laughter."

"That's all you know?"

"The old epics left it shrouded in mystery, unlike Nimmus. Fear of eternal madness is a better motivator than the promise of paradise, I'm told."

"That's a shame," Cistine said, and meant it. "A place like Cenowyn deserves more stories."

"If there are any, I haven't found them yet."

Cistine pried open her eyes and watched him spin the cup: a restless movement that betrayed just how deeply the notion of eternal madness or eternal bliss weighed on his shoulders. "Then maybe we should write our own."

Thorne stopped the cup turning. Cistine knew he was about to look at her, and he was going to say something. And for no reason she could put into words, she didn't want to know what it was.

So she said, "Goodnight, Thorne," and retreated to her room.

Exhausted, her heart still thumping from nightmare after nightmare, Cistine dragged on her training armor and went out to the rock top before dawn. Quill was already there when she arrived, looking as sleepless as Cistine felt. He sat cross-legged, wrapping his hands, and didn't look up as she crawled onto the stone beside him.

"Good morning," Cistine said.

Quill grunted, focusing on the wrappings.

Cistine started her familiar stretches as she faced away from him, looking down into Hellidom. So much about the small city she didn't know—hadn't *wanted* to know. But her ignorance was as dangerous as her complacency, and she knew she didn't have to be useless the next time something happened. She didn't have to cower or question herself. She could make a different choice.

Muscles loose, Cistine turned and offered her hand to Quill. "Teach me to land a punch."

Surprise tweaked Quill's brows. He accepted her hand, and she hauled against his weight, feeling the shift when he took the burden and boosted himself up.

"All right, Stranger." He spread his legs and put up his hands. "Remember what I told you: thumb out. Roll the punch forward from your shoulder. Now hit my hands, one after the other."

Cistine sucked in a long breath.

This was going to hurt—badly. It would keep hurting day after day, but she was going to do it. They both needed it.

She drove her right fist into his right palm, and Quill shouted, "Switch!" She shifted her aim, her left hand plowing into his, striking his palm with all her might. Quill's mouth quirked. "Again."

Cistine kept hitting him until her knuckles ached, until her arms felt like wilting flowers and her eyes burned with sweat. And then she punched his hands again, and again, correcting whenever he critiqued her form, lifting her fists when they started to droop. Every blow landed on King Jad. On the men who'd poisoned Tatiana. On Roosha and Matthias and everyone else who'd ever made Cistine feel like a prize on a shelf to be guarded and paid for.

As if the stone they danced and bobbed across had cracked open, Cistine felt the girl she used to be slip over the edge, tumble into the crack, and vanish as the hours wore on.

The person who crawled out with the rising sun...she was someone else. Someone determined, someone who'd made a different choice, who wouldn't let anyone—not even herself—turn her feet from this path toward strength.

Cistine didn't know that princess—not really.

But she was dying to make her acquaintance.

THE STUDENT

OF

BONE AND BATTLE

CHAPTER TWENTY-THREE

CISTINE WOKE IN a frenzy, fists flying—still lashing out at the figure who'd bent over her bed in her dreams, fingers twining around her throat. She didn't recognize the gentle hands gripping her wrists at first, or the frantic voice speaking her name. It wasn't until Julian cupped her cheek that she realized he was the person standing over her—not King Jad—and that she was one flailing movement away from punching him in the face.

Cistine recoiled, dropping her hands. Julian half-knelt on the bed, one foot on the floor, his head haloed with strong sunlight blazing through the windows of Cistine's room.

Daylight...*strong* daylight...

"I'm late!" she groaned.

Julian's mouth twitched. "You can relax. You made it to training this morning. Ashe and I were waiting for you to have lunch with us, but you never showed."

The morning's events came trickling back like water through mud. "That's right. I met with Quill this morning, and I decided to nap instead of having lunch."

"*You* decided to skip a meal?" Julian frowned. "You're sure you're not pushing yourself too hard?"

Cistine sat up the rest of the way, pressing a hand to the small of her back. She'd spent hours doing push-ups with Quill's foot against her spine, correcting her form whenever her body eased into a less-strenuous position. Everything hurt, from the palms of her hands to the soles of her feet. Sleep had been a blessed relief. "I'll be all right. As soon as these nightmares stop."

Julian's brow creased deeper. He climbed onto the bed and sat with his back against the wall, opening his arm to her, and Cistine decided everything else could wait. She sank into the warmth of his side, and he rested his stubbled cheek against her hair. "Do you want to tell me?"

Cistine played with the cloth loops securing the hand guards over her middle fingers. Already, the dream's finer points were fading, but she'd had the same one so many times this week it wasn't difficult to weave the pieces together. "Ever since Tatiana was poisoned, I've dreamed about King Jad doing the same to our families."

Julian's fingers tightened on her shoulder, and Cistine shut her eyes. Part of her was relieved he'd been the one to wake her, and not Ashe. Her Warden was stern and caring, and loyal to a fault, but her family wasn't tangled up in the contention with the Southern Kingdom. They were peaceful if unpleasant people, a baker and a confectioner who ran a joint venture on Astoria's main thoroughfare. The only front lines her family ever faced were the ones forming to purchase their sweets.

It was different for Cistine and Julian. Their parents were groomed for conflict.

"I have dreams about my father, too," Julian admitted. "Usually where he dies in the southern forts before I see him again. I'm always running, I'm always right there, but...I'm never close enough to reach him."

Cistine shivered, curling closer to his ribs. "In my dreams, it's usually me who dies. Jad poisons me, but I don't notice it until it's taking over my body."

Julian flexed his fingers around her arm. "That will never happen, Princess. Not while I'm alive."

But even as his words coaxed a blush to her cheeks, Cistine knew it was an empty promise. He hadn't been there in Veran, with Matthias and Roosha. And that was why she had throbbing muscles and a tongue shriveling with thirst: because Julian couldn't be everywhere at once, and Cistine couldn't leave her fate, or the fate of her kingdom, to chance anymore.

"I'm sure your father's all right," she said—eager to lift the subject from herself. "The treaty talks haven't even begun yet...and if King Jad had done something warranting attention, we would know it. Even this far north."

"Maybe," Julian said. "But I can't stop thinking about it. We need to be on our way as soon as possible."

"I know. And *you* know I'm doing everything I can to make that happen. Which is why I should go." Cistine planted a kiss on Julian's cheek before she slid off the bed.

"Don't you want to know why I came halfway across the Den to find you in the first place?" Julian teased, sprawling his legs out on the bed.

Cistine stuffed her feet into her boots, which she'd managed to kick off haphazardly before sleep had suffocated her. "If you can tell me quickly."

"Ashe walked from the kitchen to the front door this morning."

She spun around to face him, almost toppling as she tripped over the pile of books beside her bed. "I *missed* it?"

Julian shrugged. "I told her to wait, but there was no stopping her."

Cistine groaned. She'd been watching Ashe slowly limp further and further from the table each day at lunch, goaded and coaxed by Maleck. Cistine couldn't place what it was, but something about saving Tatiana together had caused a shift between these warriors of rivaling kingdoms. Ashe's focus had grown keener while they'd practiced, and Maleck's flavor of encouragement had changed. He'd learned Ashe needed a battle in order to walk upright again.

"How was her leg?" Cistine demanded, struggling into her second boot.

"Sore, after. I offered to help her back to the table, and I really think she might've killed me if they'd given her a weapon."

"Still the same Ashe," Cistine grinned, but guilt tightened her core. She'd missed something so important...her rigorous training regimen and Ashe's time with Maleck were slowly unbinding them from one another.

"I've got one other piece of good news for you," Julian sat forward, draping his arms over his knees. "Tatiana's asking for you."

Relief bloomed through Cistine, a sudden wildfire. She'd waited days for that report. For Tatiana to be awake for longer than a few minutes at a time—and to be summoned to see her.

She planted another kiss on Julian's cheek and tore down the hall.

She wasn't the first one to arrive in Tatiana's room. Thorne was already there, leaning against the wall beside the door with his arms folded. Cistine ran past him to the bed and sat on the edge, looking over Tatiana's fine silk shirt and thickly-bandaged shoulder. "How do you feel?"

"Nevermind any of that," Tatiana said. "Let's hear it, Cistine, since Thorne won't tell me: could they save the shirt?"

"I'm afraid not. Maybe if you'd had the decency to bleed less…"

"I'll bear that in mind next time I have a poisoned arrow jammed through my bone plates." Tatiana reclined against her pillows. "Thorne's just been catching me up on your progress. Personally, I think he's been going easy on you. Court politics are all fine and good, but who's teaching you about the difference between Erdotre and Nordbran threads? You're going to find yourself with a terrible wardrobe at this rate."

"She isn't here to collect garments, Tatiana," Thorne said.

Tatiana flicked her fingers dismissively, like casting water from her sculpted nails. "Just because *you* wear the same two shirts over and over."

"I knew it," Cistine laughed. Thorne rolled his eyes.

"Anyway," Tatiana said, "I'm glad to see these *allotoks* didn't drive you away with their uncivilized company while I was gone. I'm just starting to like you, I think."

"Well, they're not *all* absolute heathens. Baba Kallah is lovely."

Tatiana sputtered with laughter. "Oh, so you *have* been learning our language!"

"Just fragments," Cistine said modestly. "Are we starting training again today? Now?"

"Not yet," Tatiana said. "I still have a report to give."

Cistine glanced at Thorne. "Should I be here, then?"

He cinched his arms, meeting her stare with unruffled calm. "If you believe that would be in the best interest of your kingdom."

An offer—a hand of trust. And also a choice, for her to decide what would profit Talheim and what would only profit her curiosity.

Cistine knew whatever she might hear between these walls was not fodder for gossip. It wasn't something she could whisper about with her friends among the market streets. Not when it had brought Tatiana back to them with an arrow through her shoulder and poison in her veins.

Some secrets had to be kept at any cost.

Before Cistine could decide if she was ready for such a responsibility, the door burst open again. This time Ariadne entered, striding straight to the bed. She gripped the back of Tatiana's neck and pressed their foreheads together, her breath leaving her on the shakiest sigh Cistine had ever heard from her mouth. "You scared the life from me, *malat.*"

The Old Valgardan word for a sister filled Cistine with as much warmth as if she'd been the one called it. Even tucking herself back on the bed to avoid Ariadne's attention, the warmth between the two women wrapped around her. It made her miss Ashe even worse.

Tatiana gripped Ariadne's forearm to steady herself, eyes floating shut. "Feel free to pummel me within an inch of mine once I can move around again."

Ariadne withdrew, pressing a kiss to Tatiana's curls. "Not this time."

Maleck arrived, blank and dark as ever, and took up post across the door from Thorne. Quill was the last into the room, heralded by Faer, who perched on Cistine's shoulder. Tatiana folded her hands over her belly—an effort, Cistine suspected, by the way her legs tensed under the blanket—as she looked Quill over. "Still ugly as ever, Featherbrain."

"Go soak your head."

"That's the best you have?" Tatiana laughed. "I've endured worse insults from my dead mother, stars rest her spirit."

Ariadne raked an exasperated glance between them. "Are you two finished?"

Quill and Tatiana held each other's stares for a moment. Then Quill grinned and dropped onto the nearest fainting couch, draping his arm over its carved frame. "I think so."

"Absolutely," Tatiana agreed.

"Good," Thorne said. "You've kept us waiting for your report, Tatiana."

She grimaced and sat up straighter against the pillows. "I spied on the caravan, as ordered—followed it from the foothills almost to Eben. I never engaged of my own volition."

"Then why was there an arrow through your shoulder?" Ariadne asked.

"I came too close...and maybe they expected that. The caravan was almost too ordinary. A handful of Vassora. That was all."

Thorne bounced his fingertips against his elbows. "A perfect temptation."

"I decided to take a better look at what they were transporting this time." Tatiana's attention drifted cautiously to Cistine.

"And?" Quill prompted. "What was it?"

"No weapons," Tatiana said. "From what I could deduce, they were carrying surgeons."

"Surgeons," Ariadne echoed flatly. "As in medicos."

"You mean the kind that treat ill people," Quill said.

"Unless there's another kind," Tatiana replied tartly.

The words jarred something loose in Cistine's memory—something about roadsides and campfires and wagons, and— "Rolf."

Maleck's shoulders bristled. Thorne tilted his head. "The escort from the last caravan?"

Cistine nodded. "He mentioned the dangers on the Vingete Vey are all the same, whether you're transporting weapons or wares, or...surgeons."

Quill sat up abruptly, all traces of humor gone. Maleck spoke in that deep, unsparing rumble: "This has happened before."

"Surgeons being escorted from Veran to Stornhaz," Ariadne mused. "And with a guard armed in poisoned arrows."

"The arrows might be a new development," Thorne said. "A lash back against our attacks. But the fact remains they're guarding these medicos *heavily.*"

"Precaution like that can only mean one thing," Quill said. "Sickness in Stornhaz."

The cabal looked around at one another, and Cistine struggled to grasp the weight of those stares. "What does that mean?"

"One of the Chancellors must be badly sick," Tatiana said. "And they're keeping it a secret from the territories."

"If they've been smuggling surgeons in and out for stars-know how long," Ariadne added, "it could be more than one Chancellor. It might be all of them."

"In which case, they're weakened," Quill said. "Thorne?"

Thorne covered his mouth with one hand and cradled his elbow with the other. His gaze was remote, parsing out the report, searching for a path through the possibilities and noting the dangers of each one. "It could also be a trap. They could be calling surgeons into the city to make us believe they're weaker than they really are."

"Why should they care how you perceive them?" Cistine asked.

"It's a complex matter," Maleck said. "Our steps and the Courts' are bound up like a dance. How they move determines, in part, our countermoves."

"And it's our move now," Quill added.

Thorne dipped his head. "The hunt is yours."

"We leave Hellidom," Quill said. "Leave Baba Kallah in charge. The next time there's a caravan, we'll all attack it together. I want to know what these surgeons are up to."

Thorne nodded. "If we establish a camp in Villmark, close to the foothills, we can easily receive reports from Veran. We'll know which caravans are carrying the surgeons."

"Tati," Quill twisted his head to address her, "how long do you need?"

She touched her shoulder. "Another week, at most."

"We can spare that. Just make sure you're rested, all right?" Quill lurched up from the sofa, hesitated as he watched her, mouth ajar. Then, with a fond half-smile, he hurried from the room. Thorne shrugged away from the wall and followed him out.

"Training?" Cistine murmured to Tatiana.

"Not today," she said. "Go with Maleck. I need sleep more than you need knowledge if I'm going to avoid being left behind."

Cistine smiled as she stood. "I doubt Quill would leave *you* behind."

"I don't know what you mean." Tatiana nestled down in the covers and put her back toward the door.

Cistine found herself almost sad to go. It hadn't been until Tatiana was gone—and until she'd returned in such a mortal state—that Cistine had realized how, if they'd met in Talheim, she would've gravitated irresistibly to her. Tatiana was fierce, lovely, and clever, despite her bouts of temper. And Cistine had missed her.

"You'll have to entertain yourself this evening as well," Ariadne said as she led Cistine and Maleck from the room. "Quill and I need to discuss a strategy for this hunt of his."

Cistine tried not to break into a full grin. She didn't mind cleaning as much now as she had in the beginning, but her muscles still beamed with joy at the notion of a night's rest.

Ariadne parted from them, walking through the doorway opposite the bedroom corridor while Maleck and Cistine ascended to the weapon room. It wasn't until they'd reached the cool loft that Cistine noticed the depth of quiet. Maleck was never talkative, but today, after their conversation with Tatiana, that stony silence became a shroud. Not even his breath stirred the dust on the wooden racks as he took down daggers and lined them up on the floor before Cistine.

"What's wrong?" she asked after several uneasy minutes.

In typical Maleck fashion, he didn't answer at once. He gestured to the knives, and she picked them up and put them down again, as she did every day. But this time, she kept her focus on the task and away from Maleck's face, giving him what little privacy she could.

"There's danger in Quill's plan," Maleck finally said. "And danger in staying. I don't like being enclosed on both sides."

That frank honesty, even in his calm, unruffled voice, sent a chill burrowing down Cistine's spine. "You think you should stay?"

"Yes. But we have no choice but to explore this variance. Which is what concerns me: we *have* no choice."

Cistine frowned, setting down one dagger, picking up the next—and hesitating. For the first time, with her muscles still sore from training with Quill that morning, she noticed the subtlest difference in weight.

Maleck's eyes fixed on her. "Which one is lightest?"

She set down the last dagger and picked up the one before it. She curled her fingers over the notched, wrapped grip, almost like wood, but not quite, and weighed it in her hand. "This one. It's the lightest of all."

"It's yours to keep," Maleck said. "And now I'll show you how to use it."

"I passed the test?"

He nodded. "Anyone can wield a blade, but one only becomes proficient when she can feel the difference in her weapons...when she becomes attuned to them. As you are."

His quiet praise sparked a glow of pride in Cistine's heart. She jumped up from the bench and hurried to another rack. "Maybe I should try the polearms next."

"One weapon at a time," Maleck said. "From now on, this dagger is your companion, and you are its keeper. Never let it leave your sight. Wear it. Hold it. Sleep with it at your side."

Cistine gripped the handle so tightly her knuckles cracked. It was unlike any accessory she'd ever worn, and yet it suited her in this place. It fit with her training armor, which matched with her scuffed knees and cracked hands from scrubbing floors, and her sore muscles from training.

A small trill of panic found its way through her, but she clamped down on it with savage determination. She would not feel guilty for changing herself; not when the girl she used to be was cosseted and naïve to a fault, and too inexperienced to protect Talheim.

"I think it should have a name," she said. "Something beautiful and intimidating. Brutal Fang, maybe. Or Death-Bringer."

Maleck rested a hand on her shoulder, and Cistine was surprised both by the weight and the warmth of his touch—so startled she forgot to pull away. "Its name is Nail. Come, let's find you a sheath."

Cistine trailed after him, still weighing the dagger between her hands. It was so simple in make, yet so obviously cared for: its handle polished, its steel sleek. "Did this belong to someone before me?"

Maleck hesitated for a moment. Cistine would've barely noticed the movement on anyone else, but because Maleck moved so pointedly, sparing no inch of muscle, she caught his subtle flinch, and the brief instant he froze with his hand on the hook full of harnesses and straps along the wall.

"Yes," he said. "Aden."

And then he was quiet again, except to grunt at her to turn as he chose a sheath for her and ran it around her hips, buckling it at the waist. He demonstrated how to grip the dagger properly and pull it smoothly from its resting place across her body, against her left thigh.

He finally released her several hours later. In all that time, he never told her who Aden was.

The Den's windows were dim by now. Cistine hadn't realized how long she and Maleck had been in the attic practicing with that dagger. Hunger gripped her belly as she padded down the hall, pausing to peer into Ashe and Julian's rooms. Both were already snoring.

With a twinge of sadness, she stepped into the kitchen—and clapped a hand to her mouth.

An enormous bouquet—wildflowers, summer fronds, and some specially-grown blooms that could only have been purchased from Hellidom's sole florist—sprawled across the tabletop, throwing shade on its even planks. The night blooms' spicy, exotic scent clashed with the gentle aroma of day lilies, tulips, and pale pink roses. There was a note leaning against the vase, and Cistine only had to glance at it to recognize Julian's handwriting.

The scrape of a spoon on wood startled her, and her gaze flicked past the fern fronds jutting all around the vase.

Thorne sat on the other side of the bouquet, mostly obscured, the shadows and light of the flowers cast along the planes of his face.

"I believe these are for you," he said.

Heat consumed Cistine from knees to cheeks, and she rushed forward to read the note:

You seemed busy with the cabal after our talk this afternoon, so I decided to keep myself busy, too. Hopefully this makes up for the lack of time we've spent together this past week. I look forward to seeing you at lunch tomorrow, Princess. Affectionally, J.

Cistine clutched the note to her breast as she breathed in the smell of lilacs and jasmine. She wished Julian was awake so she could hug him—and then kick him for leaving such a personal gift on the kitchen table, where Thorne, of all people, was forced to eat around it.

"I'll move these, I'm sorry..." Then, as her stomach growled, Cistine amended, "after I eat."

She helped herself to two orange bran muffins from the basket Baba Kallah prepared the day before and sat down in her usual seat. Thorne gestured to the bouquet with his spoon. "What's all this about?"

"It's Julian, being the extravagant son of a wealthy lord," Cistine grinned. "They don't know how to do things like this quietly."

"Things like what? Herbal poultices?"

Cistine blinked. "This isn't for poultices. It's a gift."

"They're going to die in a matter of days. I don't see the purpose."

"I feel sorry for every woman *you've* ever courted," Cistine laughed. "What did you give them...the hearts of your enemies on stakes?"

Thorne pushed his bowl away and reclined, tapping his fingers on the table. "Courted."

It was that careful tone again—questioning, without truly asking a question. Cistine stared at him, and he gazed back at her. His eyes betrayed quiet confusion.

"You don't know what courtship is?" she demanded. "When two people are curious about pursuing a future together, they do things for each other like they would do in a marriage...gift-giving, quiet time together, acts of service..."

Thorne shook his head. "That isn't the way it's done here. In Stornhaz, men choose a woman to blend blood with—a *valenar*—usually to create alliances within other Courts. In the territories, most *valenar* join together for survival. But more commonly a man joins with multiple women and never forges the *valenar* blood-bond with any of them."

Cistine scowled. "How romantic."

He nodded to the flowers. "Does this mean you and Julian are joined?"

The blunt question made her jaw drop. "Gods—no! No, that's the reason for courtship. We're learning if we're even capable of being…*that*. For each other."

"And you can tell simply by giving gifts?"

Cistine glowered at him. "The gifts show we're *trying*. That we're thinking of one another and taking time to learn what the other one wants."

"Then what will you give him in return?"

With the second muffin halfway to her mouth, Cistine froze. She glanced at the flowers. Then she slowly lowered her hand. "I don't know. Princesses receive gifts more often than we give them. I was never with my past suitors long enough to learn what they wanted."

Thorne took his bowl to the washbasin. "I have a fairly good guess."

Cistine rolled her eyes. "I'm sure you do. But Julian isn't like that."

"Then he would make a poor Valgardan. We don't strain ourselves to wait and court. We select our *valenar* and consummate the same day."

"Well, it's no wonder you don't have one of your own, then."

Thorne cleaned out his bowl, set it aside, and turned to face her. "I almost did. We chose to wait until she was…prepared. Which was unusual in itself. And in those few months while we waited, everything fell apart."

A cool wash of sympathy snuffed Cistine's indignation. She cleared her throat. "Well…I suppose I really don't have any right to accuse you for your customs. Courtship is a respected Talheimic tradition, but sometimes it does put a strain on a couple if they court for too long without marrying."

Thorne folded his arms. "And I'll be the first to admit Valgardan customs aren't considerate to our women. Unhappy unions come from them every day."

In the heavy silence, Cistine folded the note smaller. Thorne shifted his weight. "It's a good gift," he said at last. And then he disappeared up the stairs to his room.

CHAPTER
TWENTY-FOUR

LEFT HOOK—RIGHT hook—now, bring up that knee!" Quill's commands reverberated across the rock top. Cistine fought the drag of her sore leg, slamming her knee into his cupped palms.

Nail bounced against her thigh as she followed Quill's instructions again: two more swings, one more jab with her knee. The pattern was rapidly becoming familiar to her mind, but her body still struggled to keep pace. Sweat poured down her back and stung her eyes when she pivoted on heel and drove her foot into Quill's waiting hands.

His fingers tightened around her boot. She knew what was coming, but there was no time to correct her stance. He flipped her like a grainsack, and she barely caught herself with her hands, sparing her chin from cracking against the stone.

"Your balance still needs work." Quill circled around her, his boots grazing the rock lightly. "But your endurance is already better. I'm impressed."

The affirmation was enough to get Cistine's hands under her body. She pushed herself upright, sitting back on her heels. "Again."

"Your palms are bleeding."

"I don't care. *Again.*"

"Have I mentioned how much I admire this side of you?" Quill spread his feet and beckoned with his wrapped hands. "I'm at your mercy."

Cistine rushed him with two jabs, left and right, that he easily blocked; but this time, when he shoved her knee aside, she drove her elbow toward his ribs. Quill caught her arm in two places—at the lower hinge and behind her bicep—and twisted it behind her back, forcing her to her knees before him.

Pain fizzed through Cistine's body. She bucked against his grip, but the pressure he was exerting absolutely dizzied her. Gasping, she pounded her hand against the stone three times—the signal that she was done. Quill loosened his grip at once, stepping back, and Cistine massaged her shoulder and stumbled to her feet.

"Don't tell me," Quill laughed. "Again?"

Before Cistine could reply—with words or fists—the sound of a gravel shower reached her ears. Her shoulders loosened, her hands fell back to her sides, and she turned as Julian heaved himself onto the rock top.

"What are you doing here?" Cistine hissed.

Julian straightened, smiling. "You've been inviting us to watch you train since you started. Today, someone wouldn't be quiet about the idea."

Cistine's breath caught as Julian turned back to offer a hand to Ashe, pulling her, cane and all, up to safety.

Cistine didn't know whether to feel mortified or excited that Ashe would watch her train. It had been different before Tatiana's return—before she'd realized this growth was worth the sweat and blood, worth the uncomfortable twinges and cracking joints and strange noises her body made when she pushed it to its limits. Quill laughed off or ignored these things. But when Cistine had invited Julian and Ashe to watch her train before, it'd been when she'd gladly given less than her all; when she'd been able to retain a princess's poise while she walked simple half-crescents around Hellidom.

Seeing them here made her forget everything.

She wasn't ready to share this part of herself with anyone but Quill. This ugly, graceless, undignified slice of her life belonged to them, and them alone. It was a part of her ascension too private to share even with her closest friends.

Ashe's smile faded. Julian frowned. "Princess?"

"Bad timing," Quill drawled, stepping up to Cistine's side. "We just finished the day's exercises."

"It's not even noon," Ashe protested.

"We started early." Quill nodded to Julian. "But I'm glad you made the trek. I've been dying to see what kind of steel is under all that pampered skin, *tajall*."

Julian cocked his head. "What did you call me?"

"To respectable ears?" Quill grinned. "An infant."

"Fighting words."

"Only if you've got the stones to swing a punch."

Cistine pressed a hand to her gut, trying to stifle the lift of her belly when she took a silent breath of relief. Julian stepped forward, and Ashe beckoned Cistine to join her. They basked in the sun together on the edge of the rock as the two men started to circle.

"What's your training?" Quill asked.

"Formally?" Julian smirked. "My father used to lead the King's Cadre. I know my paces."

"And informally?"

"Let's just say I've ruffled a few backs in Talheimic taverns."

"My kind of man."

They both shot forward like arrows from bowstrings, and the thump of fists on meat made Cistine wince. She'd been hitting Quill all day, but she'd never willingly sat by and watched someone strike Julian. Clashing blades was one thing; this was downright uncomfortable.

"That boy can take a hit." Ashe's good foot jumped against the stone, and Cistine knew her still-healing leg was the only thing that kept her from flying forward and tangling herself up in the fight.

"How are you feeling?" Cistine asked.

"Better," Ashe said. "The cane is just pretense, really. Julian thought it would be foolhardy not to bring it along."

"You really don't need it?"

Ashe shrugged. "Only in snatches. Those strengthening exercises

Maleck's given me...they work wonders. I'll have to teach them to the Cadre for our wounded."

Cistine was relieved not to hear the usual disdain in her Warden's voice when she spoke of Maleck—almost as relieved as she was to know Ashe was making such good progress.

Guilt stole through her as sudden and dark as a black-clad thief, blotting out some of her happiness at seeing Ashe here and watching Julian fight. "I'm sorry I've been absent lately. I've missed so much of your recovery."

Ashe snorted. "That's like apologizing for not taking time to watch grass grow. You have plenty to keep you busy so we can get on with our mission. If I had my way, we'd already be gone, but...I see the change in you since we came here, I have to admit."

Cistine swiveled on the stone to face her. "You do?"

Ashe nodded. "And I don't just mean the muscles you're building on the backs of your arms. Yesterday, you took every dinner plate from the table, washed them, dried them, and stacked them without being asked. And the day before that, you were up even earlier than I was, weeding that garden behind the Den."

Cistine played with Nail's hilt. "I didn't think anyone was around to notice."

Ashe draped an arm around her shoulders. "That's my point."

Cistine wasn't sure what washing dishes or weeding meant to Ashe, but she wasn't about to argue when her Warden's embrace was so warm. "Ashe, do you think you could stand a visit to the city tonight?"

"If I had the proper motivation. What did you have in mind?"

Cistine smiled. "I'd like to see the weapon vendors, and I can't think of anyone I'd rather go blade-shopping with than you."

Ashe squeezed Cistine's shoulder so tightly, it almost made her yelp. "It would be my pleasure. I can hardly wait."

Cistine propped her head against Ashe's shoulder and watched the men spar on the rock. Julian fought like an ox, holding his ground and deflecting or absorbing each of Quill's blows. By contrast, Quill was flighty, dancing erratically around Julian's retaliatory strikes. They grappled for several more minutes before Quill tripped Julian and knocked him onto his back. Crouching over him, Quill pinned the younger man with a hand around his throat.

"Not a bad performance," Quill panted. "You managed to last twice as long as Cistine did before I got her into this position yesterday."

Julian stopped struggling. "What did you say?"

Cistine rolled her eyes. "It wasn't *quite* the same position."

"You're right. I had my other hand here." Quill braced Julian's hip, pushing his leg flat to the stone.

"Bastard," Julian said softly.

"Let it go," Cistine sighed. "He's baiting you."

"Maybe so," Quill said. "But he wasn't here. So that thought is just going to eat away at him until he does something about it."

Julian bucked, slamming his knee into Quill's groin and heaving him off. They were both on their feet in an instant, and Julian shed his shirt, thoroughly distracting Cistine from the verbal berating she'd mustered for Quill. The tension in Julian's body accentuated the cut of his muscle, which hadn't wasted during their stay at the Den.

Julian's first punch landed squarely on the hinge of Quill's shoulder, jerking him backward; his laughter cut short when Julian socked him in the mouth. Cistine flinched as Julian plowed in against Quill, assaulting him with a flurry of blows. It wasn't that Quill couldn't take it, or that she hadn't hit him plenty of times herself; but that was with wrapped fists, and it was designed to pull back at the last second.

She wasn't certain Julian was holding back at all.

The two men swirled across the rock, concentration twisting their faces. Cistine knew Quill had chosen his words specifically to release Julian from that calm, armored temperament, to see what was truly lurking under the surface. And Julian had let himself be baited, perhaps because he wanted the fight. Perhaps he wanted an excuse to hit these people, who he'd never fully trusted, who he believed were wasting Cistine's time.

"Relax," Ashe said against Cistine's ear. "They're not going to kill each other. I think they both respect you too much for that."

Cistine's laughter came out more frenzied than she'd intended as Quill slammed an elbow into Julian's ribs, doubling him up. "I don't think I'm the one with the power on this rock."

"Then find out. Tell them to stop."

Cistine pushed herself to her feet and shouted, "That's enough!"

Quill froze like she'd aimed an arrow at his head. Julian, however, made one last deft maneuver: cracking Quill's chin and snapping his head back so forcefully, he fell to his seat on the rock.

"Julian!" Cistine snarled.

"Never talk about my princess like that again," Julian seethed.

Quill chuckled, massaging his chin. "She's lucky to have such a loyal caretaker."

Julian snapped up his shirt and sauntered over to Cistine and Ashe, smirking. Cistine didn't look at him; she watched as Quill shifted his jaw, winced, and thumbed the bruise under his chin. Their eyes met, and she glared—projecting silently she didn't appreciate his last remark, much less the one he'd used to bait Julian in the first place.

Quill's brow furrowed as he took in her posture, her gaze, her scowl. And then he mouthed, *I'm sorry*.

Cistine's hands slid from her waist. Mollified, she smiled.

Julian slipped an arm around Cistine and grinned down at her. "How did you like that? Maybe *we* should train together some time. Seems like I could teach you a thing or two about putting mouthy Valgardans on their knees."

"Maybe." Cistine extricated herself from his grip. "But right now, I should eat. Tatiana won't wait forever if I'm late."

CHAPTER TWENTY-FIVE

"WELL, DON'T YOU look ruffled," Tatiana greeted Cistine as she slipped into her room an hour later. "Whose life should I fear for tonight?"

"It's not that terrible," Cistine grumbled, though these were the first words she'd spoken since the rock top.

Tatiana turned the book she'd been reading face-down in her lap and picked up her tea from the bedside table. "I've lived in this Den long enough to know better. Who upset you?"

Cistine flopped on her back on a sofa. "Quill and Julian."

"No surprise there. Discussion, or distraction?"

"Distraction, *please*." Cistine draped an arm over her eyes.

"What would you like to know today?"

Cistine pondered the question, sheltering in the darkness of her arm. She and Tatiana had discussed a handful of small, inconsequential details about Valgard over the past two days. But one subject had nagged her ever since Maleck had given her a weapon of her own.

"I want to know who Aden is."

Certain silences were indescribable: the quiet after anyone in Talheim mentioned Valgard; the heavy, unspeaking emptiness around Astoria's Citadel the second time Cistine learned she wouldn't have a younger sibling to play with; the day her grandmother died.

This silence reminded her of that: strange and deep, full of sorrow.

Cistine heard the drawer on the bedside table slide open. Shifting onto her side, she watched Tatiana retrieve that captured image and stare at it in the lamp's soft peach light. "Aden...is a sore subject."

"A friend?"

"That's the complicated part. He is, and he isn't. He's Thorne's cousin, from his mother's side. Also, Aden is the reason we're here."

Cistine propped herself up on the sofa. "In Hellidom?"

Tatiana nodded, smoothing her thumb along the photograph. "Stars help me...how do I say this in a way that won't give you nightmares?"

Cistine's pulse sped like a runaway horse as she watched Tatiana's countenance darken.

"We knew we would leave Stornhaz," Tatiana said. "We didn't know when, or how, exactly...but we knew. Thorne was preparing. Most of us had decided by then we were going with him. We all took necessary measures. We distanced ourselves from our families. Thorne did everything in his power to separate himself from his territory. We thought we were ready."

"What happened?"

"Aden made the wrong choice. He told the Chancellor what we were planning, and...Cistine, that's the nightmare I never want you to have."

Cistine shivered at the bitterness in Tatiana's voice. "I want to know. I need to know what these Chancellors are capable of."

"Not yet. Not if you want to stand any hope of staying and appealing for your kingdom. Until you can face them with that puny dagger in a steady hand, I'm telling you nothing except Aden was responsible for what happened to us."

Cistine bit her lips together. She'd learned by now that when the cabal wanted to keep something secret, she'd have better luck picking a lock. "Fine. But where is he now? In Stornhaz?"

"He's not *that* stupid. He betrayed us, but he still faced the consequences for every step he took at Thorne's side before that. Maybe it rattled him, seeing how we were punished. With Aden, it's difficult to tell. Anyway, when we escaped, he ran with us. I really thought Thorne was going to kill him for trying, but Maleck got between them. He and Aden were close back then. But after we reached Hellidom, everything changed."

Cistine moved to the bed, sitting at Tatiana's feet. The warrior propped her heels on Cistine's lap and reclined against the pillows. Again, Cistine waited.

"Aden and Thorne used to be close, too," Tatiana said. "More like brothers than cousins. Aden's older, so he used to watch Thorne when he was little. Quill and me, too. His parents might as well have been ours, and Thorne...Thorne worshiped the ground Aden walked on. So when Aden betrayed us, I saw a shift in Thorne. He stopped trusting everything he'd ever believed in. Lines were drawn, and eventually we all ended up on Thorne's side. Aden knew we didn't trust him anymore, not even when he helped train us. He knew we were all damaged because of him. So he asked Thorne how he could prove himself...and Thorne gave him a choice."

"Which was what?"

"I don't know. But Aden's been gone for a while now. He's out there in Valgard somewhere, working to prove himself to Thorne."

"Do you know where he is?"

Tatiana shook her head. "I think Maleck does. Sometimes, when he disappears to do reconnaissance for Thorne, I wonder if he's looking in on Aden. But we all know better than to ask. Aden's a stubborn ass, and he'll come home when he's ready. When *he* feels like he's atoned for what he did."

Tatiana laid the photograph between them on the bed, and Cistine turned it so she could see their faces, each one so different from how they looked today. She paused to take in the boy standing next to Thorne, with an arm around his neck and a mischievous smile on his broad lips. "He does look like Thorne, a bit. In the eyes." Cistine tapped the other unfamiliar face—the grinning girl beside Ariadne. "Who is this?"

Tatiana's lip curled. "Another sore subject. And not my story to tell."

Cistine accepted that, and grazed a hand against Nail. "Should I even be wearing this? It must make you so uncomfortable, seeing one of Aden's weapons on another person's body."

"You should absolutely keep it," Tatiana assured her. "You've probably realized by now Maleck plans everything in life six steps ahead. He knows more about Aden and the rest of us than I think we'd all be comfortable with if we understood it. So if he let you walk out with Aden's knife, maybe he sees something in you that makes you worthy of it. That makes you like Aden."

"Are you saying I'm a traitor?" A nervous thrill cracked Cistine's teasing tone.

Tatiana slid the photograph closer, staring at the smiling faces in it. "I'm saying that, like Aden, you seem willing to do whatever's asked of you if it means redeeming what you consider precious. Even if that puts you in harm's way."

CHAPTER
TWENTY-SIX

A QUIET COUGH drew Cistine away from the soil she'd spent several hours tending. She drew back in the dusk light, wiping her sweating face on the sleeve of her drab shirt and surveying her work.

A corona of slow-releasing fertilizer enclosed the lemon trees, and the tomato plants basked in a pile of heaping compost she'd thrown together from scraps while cleaning the kitchen. She'd weeded as much as she could, but it was too dark to keep going. Evening wrapped its tender arms around Hellidom, coaxing a muzzy glow from the distant shop windows.

Cistine rocked onto her feet, groaning and pressing both hands to the small of her back as her muscles burned in protest. She turned to face the fence, where Thorne stood with one foot propped on the lowest bar, both arms draped over the top. He coughed again, and this time Cistine wondered if he was trying to get her attention, or if that sound was genuine.

She sidled between trellises and potato hills to reach the fence. Climbing over it brought a stab of pleasure and pride; she certainly moved more fluidly without a dress encumbering her legs, and after weeks of working with Quill and Ariadne, it hardly cost any effort to swing herself over the high slats.

"Your plants were horribly underfed," she remarked as she dropped down next to Thorne. "When was the last time anyone composted this garden?"

He frowned. "I don't know."

Cistine groaned. "Well, no wonder your soil is hard as rock! You should be composting every season...every time you pull up a plant. Nevermind watering. You can't just rely on rain. Someone should build an aqueduct to feed the soil."

Thorne stared at the garden, then looked back at her. "I haven't had the time to research these things."

Of course he hadn't. He was too busy keeping this city secret and his people alive.

Cistine leaned against the railing beside him, her face heating as she tucked her hair behind her ear. "Talheim must seem so simple compared to this."

"No. It seems quiet. And a quiet life is all any of us wants in the end."

Cistine tried to imagine any of them living quietly. The notion was so absurd, she couldn't remark on it. "What are you doing here?"

"Delivering a message: Ashe is waiting for you at the Den."

Cistine glanced up swiftly at the purple sky. "I suppose it's time already, isn't it?" She leaned away from the fence—then hesitated as Thorne sank his chin onto his folded arms. "Are you all right?"

"Fine," he said. "Tired."

Cistine only gave herself a moment to wonder if she was going mad before she pressed her palm to his forehead. "You're warm. When was the last time you slept?"

Thorne shrugged, pressing his shoulderblades against the tight fabric of his dark shirt. "Patrols have become more complicated with Tatiana out of commission."

"They'll be even more complicated if you run yourself into the ground, too. What if Julian and I took a patrol tonight, after Ashe and I come back? Would you sleep?"

"You aren't familiar with our patrol patterns."

"Quill could tell me," Cistine argued. "You leave for Villmark in a few days. I'm sure you won't sleep then, either. At least take care of yourself while you're here."

"I can manage my own affairs."

Cistine perched her hands on her hips. "Do I need to speak to Baba Kallah about this?"

Thorne's eyes narrowed as he straightened. "I don't think you would dare."

"Try me, Thorne. High Tribune or not, you're still human. Every man needs rest."

Thorne's fingers curled sharply over the fence, but his expression was inscrutable as he stared down at her in the gathering darkness. Cistine flexed her fingers on her hipbones to release nervous energy, and held his gaze.

"Go with Ashe," he said, and strode back to the Den.

Cistine jutted her tongue at his back.

"And don't make faces at me," Thorne added over his shoulder.

She dropped her tongue as far from her mouth as it would go and crossed her eyes for good measure.

⌒⌢⌒

As they descended from the Den into the dusty, packed streets of Hellidom, Ashe admitted it was her first time visiting the village after dark—and her very first time at the shops.

While they moved slowly to accommodate Ashe's limp, Cistine was the happiest she'd been in days. The pair meandered between the huts, drinking in the smell of herbal tea and pastries, and Cistine asked Ashe about the best herbs for poultices and wound packs. When that subject lulled, Cistine told her Warden everything she'd missed about training and gardening, and the things Cistine had learned from Tatiana and Thorne.

"There was so much we never cared to know about this place when we waged war here," Cistine said as they stopped at a small booth to buy whatever delicious-smelling fare its vendor was selling.

Ashe shrugged. "It didn't matter to us."

"It matters to me." Cistine accepted two leaf-wrapped bundles from the man at the booth. "Not just because I need the knowledge to appeal to the Chancellors. But, gods, Ashe...the things Talheim did to these people. I feel as if I owe them a debt. We trampled on their culture and left them with ultimatums. And not everyone was part of the war. I wonder if we were seeing more of a threat than was really there."

They wandered to a wooden bench nearby and sat to eat their food. It was some sort of soft, baked flour-disc stuffed with seasoned nuts and pesto that practically melted in Cistine's mouth.

"I think you can afford to wonder that, since you were raised in the peace your father helped make," Ashe said at last. "As someone who fought in the war, I don't think it was simple. You can argue for their culture all you like, but the True God and his vassals never intended for augmentation to be used the way these Valgardans did. It wasn't right for them to hoard and weaponize that power."

"But was that really our place to say? Maybe regulation would've been better than sealing off the wells. Maybe we acted from fear, not common sense."

Ashe shook her head. Cistine finished her food in two ravenous bites, then crumbled up the leaf platter and hurled it as far as she could into the street. A gaggle of hens appeared from between the buildings and pecked the treat apart.

"Anyway," Cistine said, "I just think there's more to these people than I ever considered. And how can I expect them to ally with us if I won't make the effort to know them as they are—not as I've been told? Their hopes, their secrets, their fears..."

"I'll leave that to you," Ashe grunted. "My only interest in them is ensuring they don't hurt *you*, Princess."

When Ashe finished her meal, they walked among the huts and past Tariq's door, where Ashe paused. "They have scarves. Do you want to go inside?"

"Not at all. The weapon shop isn't far from here. I'm saving all my paltry mynts for that."

Ashe's radiant smile cut the gloom as she wrapped an arm around

Cistine's waist and leaned on her, more playfully than tiredly, all the way to the smithy's forge.

Cistine had only glimpsed the shop from outside when she'd come here with Quill, Tatiana, and Julian. She and Julian had waited on the steps that night, sharing a small, sugary confection, while the warriors browsed the wares. Now Cistine led the way into the semidark, high-roofed structure, and the first thing she noticed was the smell: a sweet, almost honeyed tang underneath the powerful odor of coal.

Then she noticed the sound: a hundred blades, some girdled by handles and guards, some not, whispering in the wind as they hung from heavy coils of rope in the rafters. And then there were the sights: swords stuffed in barrels, axes crossed on the walls, shields as tall as a man or as small as an arm-guard strung up on thick wooden support boards, and polearms and daggers neatly lined on racks throughout the room.

"God's bones, look at that halberd!" Ashe towed Cistine toward the back of the forge, ignoring the keeper behind the counter.

Cistine laughed as the balding, bespectacled man watched them go. "May we look at your wares?"

He smiled and waved a hand. "Oh, have your fun. My name is Jostein. Call if you need anything."

For nearly an hour, they browsed the smithy's stock, balancing weapons in their hands and chatting about their different uses, their advantages and disadvantages. Cistine had never heard Ashe talk so much, or so enthusiastically, about anything before. Perhaps because Cistine had never shared her passion about the weight of a polearm versus a halberd and the proper tactical uses of each.

It was only when Cistine's tiredness caught up with her and she had to sit on an overturned barrel that Ashe finally paused for breath. "You must be ready to go back to the Den."

Cistine waved off her concern. "I'll last as long as your leg does."

"Oh, good! Because I'm going to die if I don't look at these bows."

Cistine shut her eyes as Ashe limped away and simply drank of the warm atmosphere, taking in the sounds around her: the street outside churning in motion; the door sliding open and shut again, steel singing as something stirred it; Ashe exclaiming to herself over the finely-crafted bows and matching sets of arrows.

With a thrill of curiosity, Cistine considered joining her to look at them after all. She'd been thinking lately of how much her fingers itched for a bow.

And then she heard the familiar murmur of Maleck's voice: "May I see your daggers?"

Cistine's eyes flicked open. She spotted the warrior at the counter with Jostein, who stared at the bandolier of knives strapped across Maleck's front. "You seem to have plenty. Is this a special commission?"

"Not at all. I need to replace a dagger that was given as a gift."

Cistine touched Nail's hilt as Jostein shuffled to retrieve an entire display box of daggers from a nearby shelf. The man's stride dragged like mud sucked at his boots, and when he returned, he pushed the box toward Maleck and withdrew as if he was afraid their hands would meet.

Fascinated, Cistine leaned forward on the barrel to watch Maleck work, uninterrupted, within the passion of his craft.

Maleck snapped the case open and observed the weapons inside. From her vantage point on the barrel, Cistine couldn't see the daggers, but she saw how Maleck's sensitive fingers floated over their hilts and blades, skimming for some sort of imperfection. Then he tested the weight of each one, as he'd showed her how to do.

"These are well-made," Maleck said, "but a bit smaller than what I need. May I see some others?"

This time, Jostein plucked several daggers from a display rack and laid them out handle-first toward Maleck. The process started over again: Maleck tested the weapons, weighed them, then asked to see more. This happened two more times, and by then Jostein's face contorted as he laid out the weapons for Maleck to test.

"Beautiful," Maleck murmured. "But, again, not what I need. What else do you have?"

Jostein mumbled something as he shuffled the daggers together.

Maleck tilted his head.

"I'm afraid I didn't hear that," he said in his unobtrusive monotone.

A throat cleared, and the towering shape of a third man approached beneath the canopy of unfinished swords at the shop's rear. Cistine didn't have to look twice to know this was the smithy: a man absolutely cut with muscle, bearded and bald, with piercing gray eyes.

Somehow Maleck—though several inches shorter—still outmatched the man in sheer casual strength. But when the smithy walked behind the counter to join Jostein, their unified front made Cistine tense slightly.

"He said," the smithy growled, "you should leave. And send someone else to make the purchase for you."

Cistine couldn't fathom what he meant. No one in Hellidom seemed as knowledgeable about the use and make of a weapon as Maleck. She knew he was being selective about his choice because every facet of the blade's design was important to him—and, as a blacksmith, this man should've taken pride in the challenge of sating Maleck's meticulousness. He shouldn't be turning a customer away.

And then Cistine looked at Maleck's face.

She couldn't say what changed—not his eyes, precisely, they were as cool and calm as ever. But the lines around them, serving the age of his face rather than the youth, slowly deepened. "It wasn't my intention to make you uncomfortable."

"I'd think you'd be used to that by now."

The time for observing in silence was over.

Cistine slid off the barrel and started forward—and Ashe gripped her shoulder, towing her back.

The Warden's face was an unaffected mask, but a storm rioted in her eyes as she limped toward the counter herself, interrupting the conversation with her abrasive presence as clearly as if she'd shouted. "What kind of dagger are you trying to replace?"

Maleck blinked slowly. "A bronze antler blade."

"The one Cistine's carrying now?" Ashe cast a critical eye over the daggers on the counter. "Elk or deer?"

"Neither. A beast from the Kroaken drylands."

"Well, that's a lost cause. Don't look for another antler handle...elk and deer won't measure up," Ashe said. "Try a birch grip dagger. I've weighed Cistine's blade. Birch should be about the same."

Maleck cocked his head. "But birch is weak wood for a grip."

"Not if you reinforce it with steel bands. Especially if the pithy core is framed with bonding metal. I assume this forge is capable of doing that?"

The smithy grimaced at the direct question. "I've never tried."

"Well, maybe you should," Cistine interjected, joining them at the counter. "You can consider it a custom order. And you should also consider how it can hurt your business and reputation when you're rude to your customers."

Jostein's mouth hung open, and his face turned red.

"Ashe, how long should a birch dagger take to forge, do you think?" Cistine pretended not to notice the man's disbelief.

"Less than a week, if his skills are worth the high price of his weapons."

"Let's say three days?" Cistine offered the smithy. "We'll pay handsomely, of course. Assuming my instructor approves the weapon's weight."

"Fair is only fair," Maleck said.

The smithy folded his arms, his throat jerking as if he'd been forced to swallow one of his own creations. "I can manage that."

"Wonderful," Cistine smiled. "We'll see you in three days."

She grabbed Maleck and Ashe by their elbows and towed them from the shop.

"Absolutely ridiculous," Ashe snarled as they descended the steps into the deserted street.

"I agree," Cistine huffed. "I can't believe he spoke to you that way, Maleck."

"Well, I was referring to the cost of his goods, actually."

Maleck stared down the dark avenue. His arms hung loose at his sides, and his shoulders bowed forward slightly. For him, as good a posture of defeat as if he'd put his head in his hands. "It's to be expected by now.

Perhaps I shouldn't try anymore. They only ever see the augur I was. A savage, mindless creature, and nothing else."

Cistine exchanged a glance with Ashe. They both knew the violence Maleck was capable of—they'd seen it on the Vingete Vey. But they'd also seen him tend to Tatiana. And he'd helped Ashe walk again.

Always two more steps. Just two more.

Two steps put Ashe at Maleck's side this time. She didn't look at him as she squinted into the darkness of Hellidom. "They say the same thing when a confectioner's daughter picks up a sword. But we don't apologize for what we are. We answer to the True God and no one else."

Maleck slowly dipped his head.

"Those bows were completely useless, anyway," Ashe added. "Let's go back to the Den."

"May I escort you?" Maleck offered. Cistine knew if they gave so much as a hint he frightened them, as he'd frightened the men in the shop, he would be gone into the dimness of the village as swiftly as he'd appeared from it tonight.

"As long as you don't mind trudging the whole way," Ashe said.

"It's good to slow down on occasion," Maleck said. "To notice things."

He was right—it was good to notice things. And people. In the ghostlit glow from the shops along the path, that was all Cistine could bring herself to do now: to take stock of Maleck's face. The hard planes of it. His scar. The hurt in his eyes.

He looked so different from the boy in Tatiana's photograph. She imagined they'd all looked different before the war, too—though most of them hadn't fought in it. Augurs, walking away with scars. Children, walking away with nightmares. The same sort of nightmares she'd been afraid to see unleashed on her own people by King Jad and the might of Mahasar's Enforcers.

Sickness stole suddenly through Cistine's belly, turning the night's meal sour in her gut.

She only knew how the cabal had been before Hellidom because augmentation had given them the power to preserve their smiles forever in a picture. Augments had given them scars, but also abilities. Things her grandfather had feared.

But had he known about young grins captured in a flicker of time? Had he known about the precious things, like Aden's smirk, Maleck's laughter, and carefree Tatiana smiling with her friends? Had he even *cared* to know—the way his granddaughter someday would? Or had he seen all the northern people, even the children, as vicious defenders of the power from the gods—a power Talheim feared?

Determination blazed through Cistine. Like Maleck, with his deadly eyes and the sensitive spirit beneath, and like Tatiana, with her fierce love of weaponry and clothing and her honest heart behind it all, there was more than just the brutal outer shell of Valgard to behold. Cistine would find a way to understand its true spirit and ally herself to that, not only to its vicious might.

And she would find that spirit through this cabal.

***

The Den was quiet when they returned. Maleck bade them goodnight just over the threshold. "I hope my intrusion was not to the detriment of your evening."

"We've had worse," Ashe said.

Maleck nodded. "You're walking quite well."

Cistine watched him disappear down the corridor to his room. A faint tug pulled at her heart and her feet, as if she should go after him.

Come. That whisper again. That call. *Come and see.*

Instead, Cistine let Ashe tow her into the broad, curved hall where her room and Julian's lay open. They lingered outside Ashe's chamber, and Ashe kissed Cistine's cheeks before she embraced her. "I had a lovely time tonight. It was good to have you all to myself, if only for a few hours."

"Even with uppity shopkeepers involved?"

"Especially then." Ashe smiled mischievously when they drew apart.

"Long before you were born, I met people like that every day in my parents' store. They thought there must be something wrong with me because I preferred battle over baking. A sweet girl from a good family who dreamed of joining the King's Cadre? It was unheard of."

Cistine cocked her head. "Did you ever consider giving up because of that?"

Ashe snorted. "You know how I am, Cistine. They only encouraged me to prove I was good at what I'd chosen to be."

"And now you guard the King's daughter. I'd say it's been proven."

"That, or the gods are punishing me." Ashe mussed her hair. "Sleep well."

Smiling, Cistine waved goodnight and went into the kitchen—and found Thorne slumped over against the table, his head buried on his folded arms. He snored softly, his back rising and falling in steady breaths. He didn't rouse even when Cistine tiptoed past him into her room.

It was already occupied: Julian sulking in the chair and Quill lying on the bed, reading one of her Talheimic books. They both snapped to attention as she entered, frowned when she snatched a blanket from her bed, and mercifully didn't follow her back to the kitchen.

Cistine fluffed out the blanket and spread it over Thorne's shoulders, careful not to touch him. He didn't rouse except to sink his head deeper into his arms with a quiet sigh.

"I suppose I won't tell Baba Kallah after all," Cistine whispered.

He didn't stir at that, either.

Grinning, Cistine padded back into her room to meet Quill's crooked grin and Julian's smile of relief, which only spread when Cistine took his hand and perched on his knees.

"Don't you both have your own rooms?" she whispered.

Quill switched his long hair from one side of his head to the other. "I'm supposed to give you instructions on how to manage a patrol. Ariadne will be back in an hour, and then Hellidom is yours to protect until sunrise."

"Apparently, we're being punished for something," Julian growled.

Cistine grinned at Quill. "Just tell us what to do."

CHAPTER TWENTY-SEVEN

THE WEEK PASSED in a blur, each day almost the same as the last. Cistine trained with Quill, navigated Valgardan language and customs with Tatiana, practiced proper grip, toting, and slow strokes of weapons with Maleck, and continued to clean the Den under Ariadne's watchful eye. But she also took up poison studies with Ashe and patrols with Julian—a short, uneventful duty that rapidly became her favorite pastime.

It wasn't for the endless walking, and not even for the beauty of Hellidom—which was undeniable as she traveled its outskirts, crushing ghostplants beneath her boots to light the way—but because these were the moments she had Julian all to herself, with very little distraction.

Under the bright moonlight, they walked with hands clasped, discussing Talheim, and particularly Astoria. He told her about life in the estate of Practica and how dull it had been in the country before he'd begun formal Warden training, with only a handful of small taverns to amuse himself in when he wasn't killing pheasants with a sling.

"That must've been terrible for you," Cistine said one night when they paused to drink water and rest on a small pile of stones among the trees bordering the Nior.

She leaned her head against Julian's shoulder, and felt him shrug. "No worse than it was for you."

"How do you mean?"

"Well, a princess who loves to read, relegated to boring necessities of rulership," Julian said. "I respect your father with all my heart, but I think he should've respected *your* wishes more and not forced you into meetings and parties you had no use for."

"I suppose..."

"I used to watch you when we came back to visit," Julian chuckled, "when you were forced to take your seat next to your mother in the throne room. You always had a book hidden in the folds of your dress."

Cistine flushed with embarrassment. "I once read an entire story in there, sneaking glances when my parents weren't looking."

Julian brushed the hair behind Cistine's ear. "So clever. And attractive."

Cistine didn't think she'd ever felt so content as when they walked back to the Den that night, fingers linked. But after they'd said goodnight, and she lay in bed, trying desperately to sleep—knowing dawn would come too soon—she was suddenly restless. Memories climbed into the bed with her, crowding her awake.

It was true she'd despised those royal meetings and couldn't wait to leave them. She'd groaned dramatically to Ashe whenever King Cyril summoned them both to the throne room. But the fragments she'd taken to heart—pieces of intelligence and council she hadn't blocked out by chasing the glimmers of dust with her gaze through the shafts of sunlight, or sneaking paragraphs from books—had followed her here. That wisdom had allowed her to speak with Thorne as a ruler, had helped her decide when to listen, when to stay, and when to walk away.

She owed her survival in Valgard thus far to her parents as much as herself. Their unwillingness to let her retreat into her own head—their insistence that she must know something of rulership, whether she wanted to or not—had helped her navigate in the treacherous landscape of Thorne's prickly secrecy and the Northern Kingdom's mysterious customs. Perhaps they hadn't taught her enough about Valgard to make this simple; but what she did know about being royal had kept her alive.

Cistine didn't sleep at all that night. She lay awake, missing her parents so desperately her belly ached. And her melancholy only increased at dawn, when she dragged herself out of bed and trudged all the way to the rock top only to find it empty.

"Wonderful." She perched her hands on her hips and scowled at the absence of her mentor. "The first time Quill is ever late...why today?"

She waited several minutes for him to arrive, and when he didn't, she started her exercises alone. Let him take his time reaching the rock top and see her already working. Maybe he would think twice about keeping her waiting in the future if he saw she didn't need him.

That determination carried her for half an hour in solitude before a shadow fell across the stone, and in the middle of a push-up, a small weight settled into the middle of her back. Faer cawed against her ear, ruffling his feathers as Cistine sank down on her belly, fighting to catch her breath.

"Now he's sending messenger birds?" Cistine slung out her arm, and Faer hopped down to the hinge of her wrist so she could pluck the roll of parchment from the band on his leg. Rolling onto her back, she cocked her knees up to rest her aching abdomen, and held the strip above her head so she could read it. Faer fluttered onto her knee and preened.

I hope you're not at the rock top already, Quill had written. *With Tati now. Today's the day.*

Cistine's stomach dropped. She sat up so rapidly, she dislodged Faer. The raven circled the stone, squawking indignantly, as Cistine read the note again.

They were leaving for Villmark.

Cistine had never run so fast in her life—not even during training. She sprinted back to the Den with Faer banking overhead, keeping pace, and arrived at the veranda just behind Ashe and Maleck, who were arguing as they mounted the steps. Maleck's breed of argument mostly involved a series of long-suffering headshakes. Ashe was fuming, hands clenched and nostrils flaring. They both stopped as Cistine jogged up to join them, and raised their eyebrows in silent question.

Cistine slapped a hand to her sweaty forehead. "The smithy! I forgot we were supposed to go back today!"

"We just came from there, actually. Now, it's time to prove once and for all that I was *right*." Ashe snatched Nail from Cistine's sheath—ignoring her protests—and thrust it into Maleck's hands. "There! Feel it. Tell me they're not the same weight."

Maleck sighed, freeing the birch-handled dagger from its scabbard on his thigh. He held the weapons out before him, one in each hand, then blinked in surprise. "You're right. They are identical."

Ashe smirked. "I told you so. I know my weapons." She studied Cistine as Maleck returned Nail to her. "You look ragged."

"I just ran here," Cistine said, "all the way from the rock top. Quill says you're leaving today, Maleck?"

He nodded. "In one hour."

Cistine sheathed Nail in choked silence and hurried inside, letting Ashe and Maleck trail her slowly over the threshold. She went straight to Tatiana's room, and found Quill and Tatiana were still there: Quill lying on a sofa, Tatiana cramming things into a bag. They were dressed in their armor—real battle armor, not the training threads Cistine had grown used to—prepared to face trouble the moment they set foot outside Hellidom.

Tatiana whirled to face her as she knocked, and a charming smile erased the crease that had stamped her brows a moment before. "Look at you! I knew Faer would find you on the rock top. Pay up, Featherbrain."

Quill rolled his eyes, fished a mynt from his pocket, and flipped it to her. "My mistake, Cistine. I thought I warned you yesterday."

"You probably did. I don't remember much of anything before patrol with Julian last night."

Tatiana burst out laughing. Quill arched a brow. "That scintillating, was it?"

"Oh, stop it! He just brought up things I hadn't thought about before." Cistine joined Tatiana beside the bed and peered into the bag, full of weapons, clothes, and several small glass bottles. They reminded Cistine of novelty-shop items branded with promises to increase one's luck or allure. One was red, one bright lavender, the third deep aquamarine.

There was something strange about them, almost familiar; enticing, like the appeal of exotic spices—a sizzling brine on the back of Cistine's tongue. She dipped her hand into the bag, reaching for the red jar, certain for a moment it was shaking, vibrating somehow, under a strange duress that called out to her.

Tatiana slapped her wrist, and Cistine yanked her hand violently from the satchel. Tatiana pulled the drawstring shut. "Did you come to steal my things, or to see us off?"

Cistine shook her head to clear it. "I wanted to see if you needed any help packing."

"Clearly, I have that under control."

"And how's your shoulder?"

Quill turned his head toward them sharply, his keen eyes missing nothing.

"Stings," Tatiana said. "Nothing I can't live with. Your Warden's poultice pack worked wonders. Besides, I can fight with my right hand better than my left. They didn't strike fast enough to cripple me."

"Lucky for them," Quill growled, "otherwise this would be a different hunt."

Tatiana busied herself slipping the pack over her shoulder and didn't look at him. "Don't worry about us, Cistine. Concentrate on your training. Kanslar Court takes power in a little over a week. Your window of opportunity starts to shrink after that."

Cistine trapped a flutter of panic beneath a deep breath. "I know. I'll keep reading and exercising and cleaning the Den. I promise."

"Look after Baba Kallah, too," Quill added. "We all know she does too much already. She needs your help."

Cistine nodded, startling slightly as Tatiana threw an arm around her. "You'll be fine, *Yani*. And we'll see you in a fortnight at most. You'll barely have time to miss us."

"I wouldn't miss you anyway."

But that was a lie. She *would* miss the long afternoons drinking tea and discussing Valgardan politics, and the early-morning runs and grappling sessions, and the weapon room's musty, calming quiet with Maleck as her only companion. She would even miss the burden of Ariadne ordering her to clean room after room.

Quill stretched to his feet. "Do us a favor? Go and tell Thorne the rest of us are ready. He's holding up the hunt."

"As usual," Tatiana drawled.

Cistine smiled and hurried out into the hall, suddenly eager to be away from their armor and that satchel and the reminder that they were all leaving, and she was staying behind.

"Aren't you going to wish me good luck?" Quill called after her.

Cistine stuck out her tongue and shut the door on his laughter. She passed Maleck and Ashe again, still talking about knives in the front room. She tiptoed by Julian's chamber, where his snores echoed despite the late hour. Then she slipped by Ariadne in the kitchen, who was cramming bread loaves and vegetables into a sack.

"I expect this place to remain spotless while I'm gone," Ariadne said without turning.

Cistine gritted her teeth. "I assumed as much."

"Don't take a tone with me. This is for your own good."

"I'm aware." Cistine sidled toward the hall.

"One more thing: stay out of our bedroom corridor. I don't want you snooping through our personal belongings."

Stung, Cistine paused and stared at her back. "You really think I would?"

"Gossips are capable of anything."

Biting back a harsh retort, Cistine dashed up the steps to Thorne's room.

It was almost eerie the way the quiet enveloped her there. The pelts on the floors and walls muffled all sound from the Den below, like stepping into a different house entirely. Cistine wondered if that was why she'd found Thorne sleeping at the table rather than in his own bed: close to every movement and capable of hearing every sound. The collision of peace in his chamber against the chaos in the Den made it seem like a sanctuary. The furious knot in Cistine's guts loosened slightly as she shut the door.

And then she saw his scars.

It knocked her speechless for a moment: Thorne standing beside his bed, his damp hair trailing water down his bare back. At first, it was the sight of him shirtless that left her flustered; and then it was the markings on his flesh that brought her hands to her mouth.

She'd read so often about scars: how they puckered the skin in places, creating small mountains in the flesh. Ridges that could be followed like maplines. But Thorne's scars were sunken hollows in his tan skin—craters where something had been taken away. And not only taken, but chiseled out. They looked as if they had never healed properly.

Cistine knew she'd made some small sound—that even the tiniest whimper of sympathy and horror had escaped her lips—because Thorne froze. The return of that absolute, predator stillness she'd witnessed in the meadow the day they'd met startled her from her stupor.

"Thorne," she whispered. "Are you all right? What happened?"

He dragged on his shirt, rolling it down over the scars and fluffing the hem several times. "Contrary to what Quill and Tatiana might have taught you, it's actually polite to knock before entering in this house."

"I'm sorry," Cistine said. "But what *happened*?"

He picked up his leather chestpiece from the bed and buckled it into place. It was the same armor the others wore—the first time she'd ever seen him dress for battle. "What do you need, Cistine?"

Cistine pouted, frustrated with her curiosity and concern dismissed twice. "Quill and Tatiana wanted me to tell you they're ready to leave."

"Good."

"And you're holding everyone up."

"As usual." Thorne secured his vambraces and picked up a satchel from the floor, checking its straps and buckles meticulously, as if he was waiting for her to leave.

Cistine stepped toward him instead, burying her feet in the thick vermillion rug skinned from some beast in Erdotre's massive forest. She wondered if that was where he'd gotten his scars.

"It's a good thing Ariadne is packing light fare to eat," she teased weakly, "because you're all so well-fed on secrets, you don't have room for anything else."

Thorne's fingers went still.

Cistine halted behind him, close enough that she could reach out and touch his back, if she wanted to. But she was afraid to know what those pitted scars felt like...afraid her stomach would rebel if her fingers slid into the cracks of his skin, where some of his darkness and ferocity seeped out.

"At least tell me you're all right," Cistine said. "I've never seen scars like those before."

"Then you should know the answer to that question."

Her breath hitched. Of course he wasn't all right. Whatever had left such terrible wounds in him couldn't be simply forgotten.

"I don't keep this tale from you for lack of trust." Thorne's voice was so soft—the quietest Cistine had ever heard him speak, "but because it haunts me. *I* can't return to that place. I can't take anyone else there with me."

"I'm not afraid to go."

Thorne shook his head. "Then ask Baba Kallah."

When Cistine didn't step away, Thorne turned, looming above her, and in some ways his eyes matched his voice...hollow and quiet and exhausted. Even though he'd slept during the nights Cistine and Julian took patrol, he looked weary. To varying degrees, they all did—alternately spending their energy being relieved, and then uneasy, over Tatiana's return and her report of the surgeons.

And though she wasn't a warrior herself, Cistine knew it was dangerous to go wearily into battle.

"Keep everyone safe," she said. "What would I do without my teachers?"

"I'll gladly guard them with my own life."

And Cistine knew—despite how often he came down on them harshly, despite the times he commanded them as a High Tribune rather than as their friend—he would do it. Even if it cost him everything.

The thought twisted her stomach into a slippery knot. "You be careful, too."

Thorne nodded, hitching his pack higher onto his shoulder as he stepped past her onto the rug, where he paused, his dark boots clashing with the red pelt. The perfect mixture of old and new blood.

"The garden," he said. "It smells different today. Crisper."

"It's flourishing," Cistine couldn't help but smile. "It's amazing what a bit of watering and fertilizing will do for the soil, isn't it?"

Thorne glanced over his shoulder, his gaze raking her gently from head to foot. "Yes, it is."

Cistine's smile broadened into a full-toothed grin as Thorne strode to the door and slid it open. His parting was brief, with his foot over the threshold. "The garden is yours. Do whatever you like with it."

He shut the door before Cistine's mouth had finished tumbling open in surprise.

Cistine spent several hours in Thorne's room. She didn't snoop, though she desperately wanted to; instead, she sat in the armchair by the window and gazed down at the garden.

She didn't believe Thorne had tricked her. He stood nothing to gain from offering the garden and then snatching it away. So it was really hers to plant and tend as she pleased. And as she peered down at the hedges and rows, she dreamed a future for it in the few weeks she had left in Hellidom.

She plotted a watering and harvesting schedule, made plans to purchase enough baskets and storage barrels for all the food, and decided she would write detailed instructions for Ariadne on how to nurture the plants and store the harvest when she left.

The notion of retribution after so many days and nights of grueling labor around the Den made her giggle.

When Cistine's growling stomach finally dragged her into the kitchen, the quiet absolutely engulfed her. She'd grown so used to hearing some sort of movement—Ariadne patrolling the Den, Maleck sharpening weapons, Quill and Tatiana chattering—that the silence made her uneasy. It was a relief to see Baba Kallah plodding around the kitchen, though she was mouse-quiet as she cobbled a meal together.

Cistine pulled out a seat for herself and made sure to scrape the feet on the wooden floorboards, announcing her presence as she sat. Baba Kallah didn't speak, limping to the enormous oven and ladling up a heaping bowl of stew. While she grated fine cheese over it at the counter, Cistine fidgeted. Finally, desperate to break the silence, she asked, "Where are Ashe and Julian?"

"In town, training her leg. Hm..." Baba Kallah examined the grater. "When you have a wound you can heal from, it's amazing the steps you'll take to restore your mobility."

Cistine gazed at the old woman's mangled left leg. "Healed or not, I think Ashe may have a scar."

"Scars are funny things. Some people are defined by them. Others define their scars for themselves."

"Which one is Thorne?"

Baba Kallah set the grater aside. With a sigh, she gathered up the stew bowl and shuffled slowly to the table, where she placed it before Cistine. Then she pulled out a chair for herself and sank into it, flexing her gnarled fingers on the head of her cane. Cistine busied herself eating, avoiding the old woman's piercing stare.

"Did he tell you himself?" Baba Kallah asked. "Or did he hope I would?"

"The latter," Cistine admitted.

Baba Kallah stared at the oven. "I told you how my son had me beaten, and my leg broken."

Cistine winced, shoveling a bite of hot stew into her mouth so she could only nod.

"Well, that punishment was not only mine to bear." Baba Kallah massaged her leg with absentminded strokes, feeling out the injury despite its age. "When Salvotor broke my leg, he did it in front of Thorne. When he whipped Thorne, he did it in front of me. It was a warning. Punishment for us both."

Cistine's appetite shriveled up like a crisped corpse. She set down her spoon and pushed the bowl away. "Why does your son hate you so much? Why does he hate *Thorne*?"

"Hatred was too strong a word for it back then," Baba Kallah said. "Or, perhaps not too strong—too *invested*. There is a curse in the men of this bloodline, in how they're raised. In how they treat their wives and sons."

Cistine tipped her head. "I'm not sure I understand."

"When I said there was too much of Salvotor's father in him, I meant it," Baba Kallah croaked. "Just as there was too much of my *valenar*'s father in him, and his father's father in him, and so on. In this family, men are treated like dogs. They're shown no love, no mercy, no kindness from their fathers. They're taught indolence and hate from the fists of the men who raise them, and then they turn and teach it to their wives and their own sons until their knuckles run bloody. Salvotor was no different."

Cistine pressed a hand to her belly. "And Thorne?"

Baba Kallah stretched out her damaged leg and propped her cane between her knees. "I tried to spare Salvotor from this curse. I tried to rear him as a good man. But my *valenar*'s hold over him was too strong. Salvotor was nursed on hate and fed on despair, and by the time I realized just how tightly his father controlled him, it was too late. So, when Salvotor's son was born, after my *valenar* died, I set myself on the promise that I would never allow my grandson to become the savage man his father would try to make of him."

"How did you manage that?"

"I showed him love in all the ways my *valenar* forbade me from loving Salvotor," Baba Kallah said. "I dried his tears when they hit him. I fostered his interests when they were mocked. I showed him all the goodness I could, in as many cunning ways as I knew. But when Thorne's father learned..."

She pressed her wizened lips together, shaking her head.

"That was when he broke your leg?"

"Salvotor very much wanted Thorne to become a Chancellor. When he realized Thorne planned to leave Stornhaz, and I'd encouraged it, and the *ways* I had encouraged him...he had Thorne brought before Kanslar Court on a charge of treason. It was a unanimous vote for Thorne to receive the lash, and for my punishment to be just as swift and fierce."

"Holy God." Cistine's stomach churned, threatening to spew the few bites she'd eaten across the table.

"I don't think it went how Salvotor predicted," Baba Kallah continued. "The lash might've broken Thorne, if they had left it at that. But when my son took the honor of breaking my leg himself...well, that was a side of Thorne I hadn't seen before. Nor have I seen it since."

"Will you tell me?"

"I'm not certain it can be described. There was pure rage there. He broke his chains to come to my aid. He shed more blood that day than the courthouse had ever seen within its walls."

Cistine cupped her mouth in both hands. New angles of Thorne's savage reputation—and of his struggle against the Courts—loomed into focus with every word from Baba Kallah's mouth. "Was that when you all left Stornhaz?"

Baba Kallah nodded. "And now look...I've spoiled your appetite."

There was no sense denying it. Cistine couldn't even look at the stew as her insides writhed with horror and fury toward Baba Kallah's pitiless offspring. "I'm glad I know. And I think it still pains Thorne. That's why he can't talk about this."

"Yes," Baba Kallah sighed. "But, that he sent you to me...that seems like progress, doesn't it? He's at least letting the story be told, even if he can't tell it himself."

Cistine nodded. "Is that the whole story?"

Baba Kallah's gaze was shrewd, suddenly avoiding Cistine's face. "No, it isn't. But Thorne would not like me to tell the rest of it. It's his to tell, really, and I won't say it for him. I cannot betray his confidence."

Cistine had expected that. Her stomach cramping at everything she'd learned today, she stood, sliding her chair back into place. "Do you need help returning to your room?"

Baba Kallah flapped a hand. "I'm perfectly fine where I am. Go."

Cistine hurried through her own room, straight to the balcony. The garden lay beyond the wooden railing, smelling just how Thorne had described: crisp and fresh, budding with life. The Nior churned to her right, spinning the mill wheels. The day was calm and peaceful, the sky bereft of even the memory of clouds.

Somewhere out there, Thorne was leading his cabal toward Villmark. He was leading them to battle, wearing scars none of them could see.

Scars his own father had given him. A legacy he fought to escape every day.

Cistine sank down with her back to the door. And as she stared at the falls, she cried—silent, heavy tears, painting her lips and dripping from her chin.

She cried for Baba Kallah's pain, and for Thorne's. Because she wasn't certain anyone else ever had.

CHAPTER TWENTY-EIGHT

AFTER THE CABAL'S departure, Cistine found herself entertaining a friend she hadn't seen in some weeks: boredom. Even following Quill's training regimen, reading the tower of books Tatiana had left for her, keeping the Den clean and weighing out the weapons with Ashe and Julian in the loft, she was through with everything by mid-afternoon each day.

She hadn't realized how much of her training was interaction with her mentors—even Maleck and Ariadne. With little to focus on but her exercises, her breathing, and chores, time sailed by.

Julian and Ashe clearly appreciated her newfound freedom. With the midday humidity pressing down over the Den, they sought relief swimming in the shallow pools at the base of the falls, reading by sunlight, or walking Hellidom by ghostlight.

"If this one small place has so much to offer, imagine what Stornhaz must be like," Julian remarked one night as they strolled the avenues between the shops.

"We'll know soon enough." Ashe kept pace with them easily now, barely limping thanks to the poultices and stretches Maleck had left for her to do. "And then we can finally go home."

Home. The thought led Cistine into a tangled thornbush of emotions. Even if they returned with the Chancellor's blessing and a host of

Valgardan warriors at their backs, they still had to endure months of waiting for King Jad to accept or deny the offer to meet for the peace treaties. And if he refused, then the Middle Kingdom would soon feel no safer than these northern wilds. Less, even; if her home became a battleground, Cistine would never truly feel safe there again.

"Are you all right?" Julian tightened his arm around her shoulders. "You're shivering."

"It's cool tonight," Cistine lied.

"Well, your hair's still damp." He threaded his fingers through the damp locks and gave them a small, affectionate tug. "There's a tea shop at the end of this street. Why don't we stop in and see what they have to offer?"

"I'll never say no to tea."

Julian's answering laughter warmed her insides better than any herbal blend.

"The weather really is strange in this little valley," Ashe remarked. "So hot in the day, and so cold at night. It's almost unnatural."

"It's the landscape," Cistine explained. "Lataus is mostly plateaus and Unsverd is all wildlands. So below the cliffs, everything is cooler. We just happen to be at the border where they meet."

"You've really gotten to know this place, haven't you?" Julian said.

"I like to be familiar with my surroundings."

And that was the truth—if not the entirety of it. She'd broken her promise to Ariadne and crept into Tatiana's room to study the map of Valgard again the night before. First to look at the territories; but then, sitting cross-legged on the bed, she'd followed the small slice of land along the Nior's banks from Hellidom all the way back to the Vaszaj foothills. There she'd found the tiny encampment of Villmark, and she'd spent hours wondering what was there, and what the cabal was doing.

She couldn't fathom why her heart was so heavy. She had everything she'd come to Valgard with: Ashe and Julian. She had days of laughter on the riverbank, and books to read, and even a garden to tend. She had tea in the morning with Baba Kallah, who told lovely stories, and afternoons wrapped in Julian's arms, her head on his chest as they basked in the sunlight.

And yet, something was missing.

They settled in at the small tea shop, and Julian ordered a kettle of orange-blossom tea for the whole table. Cistine drew Nail and followed the wood grain with it, shaving off moldy curlicues in a perfect crescent.

"We should have invited Baba Kallah," Ashe said as they waited for the tea.

"I like that woman," Julian agreed. "Hard to believe she's related to Thorne."

Cistine stopped scraping and glanced up at him. "Why do you say that?"

"Because she's kind, for one thing. And gentle."

"And not as frigid as the northern permafrost," Ashe added.

Julian shrugged. "They're as different as night and day, that's all."

Cistine returned to her dagger and hid her scowl with a sharp bite to the fleshy inside of her cheek, digging in so hard tears sprang to her eyes.

She hadn't told them about the garden Thorne had given her, completely unprovoked and asking for nothing in return. It was a strange kindness, the oddest thing that had happened so far in Valgard. Stranger than the pull in her heart...stranger than how comfortable she was growing in her training armor every day.

Or perhaps it wasn't strange at all that the man who'd endured the whipping bar, who'd broken free to save his grandmother, had given Cistine so small a gift that meant so much. That he'd run himself to a fever compensating for Tatiana's absence so his cabal wasn't overworked. And he'd given this hunt to Quill, knowing how badly he needed it.

"I don't think Thorne is how you think he is," she said.

"Really?" Ashe's tone lilted with skepticism. "And how is he?"

The sommelier returned with the tea, placed it on the hot tray, and left again before Cistine settled on an answer that didn't betray Thorne's confidence: "He's like me."

They were much quieter when they were full of tea and scones, and they walked back to the Den beneath a thick veil of clouds. It was too overcast tonight to see the stars, but Cistine wondered if the cabal could see them in Villmark, and if they were plotting their steps according to those figments of distant light as this whole kingdom plotted itself to the turning constellations.

"I'm going for a bath," Ashe announced when they entered the Den, and she disappeared down the hall. Cistine started after her toward the kitchen, but Julian snagged her hand, sending her heartbeat skipping when he twirled her to face him.

"I'm sorry if I upset you in the tea shop," he said. "I didn't mean to drag the High Tribune's name through the dirt."

"Are you sure about that?" Cistine asked.

Julian's mouth twitched. "All right, well...I didn't think it would bother you if I did. With or without his acts of charity, Cistine, we're still at his mercy."

"I'm not so sure we are. He left us here alone. If we wanted to leave, we could."

"So, why don't we? The days are wasting away. If we leave for Stornhaz now, we should arrive right as Kanslar rises. Why not finish our mission while the cabal is gone, and then go home?"

"Because I'm not quite ready to bargain with Kanslar Court yet," Cistine said, "and Thorne knows I know it. This isn't mercy. It's trust."

"And do you trust him?"

Cistine wasn't certain why that question felt like a trap.

The front door jammed open with a bang, startling Cistine so badly she shrieked. Julian swooped an arm around her waist and brushed her behind him, but they both relaxed when they realized the newcomer was a commoner, not a warrior. Clad in the same combination of vest, trousers, and a filthy undershirt as Julian, he hardly cut an intimidating figure.

And then Cistine saw the fear in his eyes, the way he gasped with panic, and her cheeks grew cold as the blood drained from her face. "Julian, go fetch Baba Kallah."

"Where's the High Tribune?" the man demanded. "Has he left yet?"

"Calm down." Cistine strode toward him while Julian broke away down the corridor full of rooms. "What's your name?"

"Nevermind that! Is the High Tribune here?"

Cistine braced her hands on her hips. "If he was, he would make you identify yourself, wouldn't he? Now tell me who you are."

The man scowled, dragging a hand down his face. "*Orrin.* I'm a vendor of fine foods and spices here in Hellidom."

"Well, Orrin, the High Tribune isn't here. He and his cabal left two days ago. Why do you ask?"

"Where was he going?" Orrin demanded. "Villmark?"

"Does it matter?"

"Of course it does!"

"What's going on out here?" Ashe reappeared with clothes and soap weighing down her arms, her sharp gaze leaping between Cistine and Orrin.

Cistine turned toward her Warden. "This man has a report for High Tribune Thorne, and he's being very rude about it."

"*Eiskan kas corvat,*" Orrin spat under his breath.

Cistine stiffened and revolved slowly back to face him. "Think what you like, but this *worthless little barmaid* is trying very hard to help you calm down so you can present your case clearly to Baba Kallah, who is in charge in the High Tribune's absence."

Orrin's mouth dropped open, but no sound emerged. Before he could apologize—before Ashe, her eyes gleaming like chilled steel, could *make* him apologize—Baba Kallah shuffled into the room on Julian's arm. Despite the slowness of her gait, the old woman bristled with the same power Cistine both feared and admired in the rest of the cabal. It peeled back the creases of her face and brought youth to her glittering eyes.

Orrin dropped to one knee with an arm across his chest. "Kallah. This woman tells me the High Tribune is gone. Is he bound for Villmark?"

"Yes. He's been gone two days now, Orrin," Baba Kallah replied. "Where have you been? Still trading with the villages near the Vey?"

Orrin sprang back upright. "That's right. And I heard stories there: the caravans are all going armed these days...*heavily* armed. Twenty Vassora to a cart, at least."

Baba Kallah frowned. "How many carts in a caravan?"

"The last was made of three. A surgeon to each cart."

"And twenty guards to a surgeon," Baba Kallah murmured. "This sickly Chancellor is taking no risks."

"There's more," Orrin said. "These men carry an entire store of flagons now."

Baba Kallah lurched heavily against Julian's arm, forcing him to catch her weight. His gaze flashed to Cistine, but she couldn't look away from Baba Kallah's face. She saw something in her chalky complexion and quivering lips that she hadn't seen before...not even when Baba Kallah told Cistine about her wicked son. Not even when she'd told the story of her shattered leg.

Panic.

"What's a flagon?" Cistine demanded. "What does that mean?"

"Something very, very dangerous," Baba Kallah croaked, "for which Thorne is unprepared. They've faced worse odds before, but not in such perilous climes as the mountain passes near Villmark. And never with so many flagons at the enemy's disposal."

"Are there any scouts we can dispatch to tell Thorne?" Cistine asked.

"He's taken most with him, and the rest we cannot spare, or else we risk leaving Hellidom undefended."

Woozy with horror, Cistine dug her nails into the wall's deep wooden grooves. "What about Thorne? The cabal? Someone has to warn them."

"If Thorne was with us, he would make the same choice: Hellidom over the cabal, every time," Baba Kallah said. "Orrin, you may return to your shop."

"By your leave." He flashed his arm across his chest again, cast Cistine a withering glare, and retreated from the Den.

"Baba Kallah." Dampness swam across Cistine's vision as she stepped closer to the old woman. "We can't just let them go."

"Listen to me, *Yani*." Baba Kallah took Cistine's hand and squeezed it until her bones twinged. "We cannot spare the *men*."

Cistine held her gaze for a moment—those intelligent, sharp blue eyes.

Then they parted ways: Baba Kallah hobbling after Orrin toward the door, and Cistine striding down the hall, through the kitchen, into her room.

"Cistine!" Ashe shouted, hurrying after her.

"What was that?" Julian demanded.

They both halted in the doorway as Cistine pulled a small, beaded bag from under her bed—one of half a dozen Tatiana had given her, freeing room in her own closet for newer satchels—and started stuffing clothes into it. "I'm going to Villmark."

Ashe braced her hand on the doorframe. "Excuse me?"

"I have to warn them about the caravans. I'm not ready to defend a city with just Nail and my fists, but I can go to Villmark and tell Thorne what's coming."

"Have you lost your mind?" Julian barked. "The foothills are days away!"

"I know. That's why I'm leaving *now*." Cistine buckled on her vambraces, chest and leg guards, and Nail's sheath.

Julian slammed the side of his fist against the wall. "We don't have time for this! We're here for Talheim, not for them."

"And there will be no negotiating without their help! I'm not done training yet—I'm not finished with them." Cistine brushed past her friends, back into the kitchen, where she threw dry onions, cured meat, bread, and baked fruit chips into her satchel.

"You don't have to go, Cistine." Though Ashe's tone was calm, concern glinted in her eyes. "Let them send someone who knows this terrain."

"I've studied the maps every day for weeks. And you heard Baba Kallah. They can't spare anyone else."

"It's not worth the risk," Julian insisted. "Your life—"

"Don't say it." Cistine heard him catch his breath at her barely-tempered rage. "Don't tell me my life is more valuable. *Every* life has value, even Valgardan life. Besides, they're in these straits because of me. Because Quill let himself be distracted...because of *me*."

She knew Ashe and Julian were looking at one another. She knew the choice they were weighing, and she couldn't force them to make it one way or the other.

"I'm going." Cistine jerked the satchel shut and turned to face them. "Are you with me?"

Julian sighed, blowing out his temper like a candle wick. "You don't even have to ask, Princess. Whatever you need, whenever you need it...I will *always* be there."

And he punctuated that promise by stepping around the table, taking her face in his hands, and pressing his lips to hers.

Softness was the first thing that struck Cistine. Not just his grip, but his mouth—a sanctuary for her agitated breaths to hide in, where her fears quieted.

She slid her hands around his waist, locking them in the small of his back as his kiss spun her head into sugary ropes and her knees buckled. She'd been kissed plenty of times before, but this was the kiss she'd waited years for; the one she'd giggled about with her maids and dreamed of in the darkness after they'd left her chamber. A kiss more than half a decade in the waiting.

When Julian released her, his night-dark gaze sparkled with stars. Cistine turned a tipsy smile toward Ashe, who rolled her eyes. "Well, I'm going, too. But don't expect me to kiss you."

CHAPTER
TWENTY-NINE

During their journey to Hellidom from the Vingete Vey, when fear and exhaustion had choked her sense of wonder, Cistine hadn't been able to appreciate the beauty of Valgard's landscape: the thick jade undergrowth, silvery birch trees and small, sparkling streams weaving together in the filigree of a priceless storybook. Eventually, all those streams coagulated into a narrow river Cistine vaguely remembered wading across on that long, horrible trek. Once they conquered it, careful of Ashe's leg, they traveled due west.

Cistine brought along the map from Tatiana's room, but she still had to rely on Julian and Ashe to help her keep the course. Julian monitored the sun, quietly altering direction whenever they strayed. Ashe kept pace determinedly, one hand frequenting the sword lashed between her shoulderblades, that suspicious gaze marking every shadow.

Cistine knew they set a good clip for Ashe's leg, but to her it felt too slow, knowing they raced to keep the cabal from a trap. She didn't breathe easily or rest well until the day she finally spotted mountains crowning through the trees ahead. At the sight of those foothills—which meant they must be close to Villmark, judging by the map—she began to hope they would find what they were searching for: the cabal unscathed.

They stopped that night in the foothills' shadows only when darkness stifled their momentum. Tucked against a small hill in the undergrowth, one of many that sprouted among the trees, Cistine felt Julian's breaths lifting his back as he lay on one side of her, and Ashe on the other. Sitting up with her arms around her ankles, she watched the stars and allowed herself to relax for a moment, to simply breathe the cool air, and to think no further than this quiet grove and her friends beside her.

Julian shifted in his sleep, slinging his arm over her knee, and Cistine smiled down at him. Their kisses since the Den had been fleeting and few, but they still made her stomach flutter. It was a hopeless cause, trying to disentangle her elation and joy from her nervousness on this journey. Too much was happening all at once.

Ashe groaned low in her throat, startling Cistine's attention away from Julian. "How are you still awake, Cistine?"

"Nerves, I suppose," she whispered.

Ashe patted the slope between them without opening her eyes. Cistine sighed as she sank down onto her back, and Ashe flung an arm over Cistine's belly, trapping her to the ground. "Sleep. You need it."

Cistine traced the stars with her eyes, her mind wandering into doubtful conjectures that chased sleep even farther away. "Which Chancellor do you think is sick?"

"Take your pick. I just hope it isn't the leader of Kanslar Court. It will be more difficult to convince a sickly man to fight than a healthy one."

Cistine bobbed her head. "I'm glad *you're* healthy again."

Ashe's arm tightened around her. "So am I, Princess."

Enveloped in warmth, Cistine finally shut her eyes. Exhaustion swept over her at once, and she slept so deeply that in a blink of time, it was already morning.

Cistine woke to a hand over her mouth.

She swung wildly, grabbing for Nail, waking Julian and Ashe with a thrash of limbs. The hand peeled back at once, and Cistine flipped over to face her attacker.

His stippled hair hung rakishly into his eyes as he crouched on the embankment, one wrist balanced on his bent knee. Head cocked, Quill grinned. "So, *that's* why no one ever wants to wake you up in the morning."

"Quill!" Cistine roared.

The foliage rustled as Ariadne stepped in from their left, and Thorne from the right. Both gripped their weapons, their imposing figures shattering the sunlight and casting long shadows toward Cistine and her friends.

Quill stretched, popping his back as he rose. "You're the last people we expected to find bedded down in the hills like fawns."

"Why are you here?" Thorne asked.

"We came to warn you about the caravan. It's a trap," Cistine said. "It's carrying more than a hundred Vassora."

Quill blew out an exasperated breath. "We *know* that."

"You...you do?" When Quill nodded, a hot rush of embarrassment traveled down Cistine's spine, pooling in her belly. "Did you know they also have an entire store of flagons?"

Quill's attention skated to Thorne.

"What do you know about flagons?" The High Tribune's voice was soft, but the muscles leaping along the sides of his neck were not.

"Nothing," Cistine admitted. "But I saw the look on Baba Kallah's face, so I assume they're dangerous."

Thorne's gaze was cold, clear, and relentless—an icy avalanche barreling down on her from straight ahead. "Where did you hear this report?"

"A merch named Orrin." When Thorne didn't reply to that, Cistine added, "Baba Kallah sent me."

It was almost a lie. But Julian and Ashe didn't contradict her, and at his grandmother's name, Thorne's rigid posture loosened, and he smoothed a hand through the air. Quill and Ariadne stepped back, though their faces remained as tense as their leader's. "You could have sent a scout."

"And left Hellidom that much weaker?" Cistine said. "We both know you prefer it this way. Your city stays protected, and no lives are at risk but ours."

Thorne stepped closer. "And how do you prefer things?"

A loaded question trawling for the deeper answers, like always. Cistine cinched her arms as she faced him. "Ask what you're really wondering."

Thorne took another step, and this time Cistine caught the gleam of daylight on the inlaid threads of his armor. "Did you leap at the *first* opportunity to follow us, or did you wait for the most convenient one?"

Julian scoffed. "We came here to help you, and this is how you're going to speak to us? We should've let you charge off and get slaughtered."

Cistine stared Thorne down, unmoved by his challenge. "I waited until the garden could last a few days without me."

Thorne's jaw flickered at the reminder of the gift he'd given; what he'd done for her...why she cared. His gaze was steadfast, branding her with his curiosity and surprise. This man whose own father had brought him before the Chancellor to be whipped, whose flesh and blood had broken and betrayed him, was surprised anyone had made this journey for him. For his people.

"Message received," he said. "You're free to go."

Another challenge. This mission in Villmark was not Cistine's. It had nothing to do with her training, or with Talheim or her people. The most she could hope to do here was sate her curiosity and reassure herself the cabal was safe.

And that was enough.

"It's a long walk back to Hellidom," she said, "and Ashe needs to rest."

"Cistine, I really don't."

"I'm your princess, and I say you really do."

"Quill?" Thorne said.

Grinning, Quill stuffed a cinnamon stick between his teeth. "Let them stay. It will do us some good to see what a Talheimic princess is made of without a soft bed to fall into every night."

Ariadne rolled her eyes. "You're a fool, Quill. These hills will eat her alive."

"Only one way to know for certain." Quill extended his arm in a low bow, gesturing them up the embankment. "The camp awaits."

It was good the cabal found them when they did. Once Cistine saw Villmark, she knew she would never have discovered it on her own.

Buried in the foothills half a day's walk from the lower passes of the Vaszaj Range, she nearly strode straight past the camp's entrance. Only when Quill caught her arm and drew aside a curtain of lichen to her left did she realize they'd arrived.

Villmark was little more than a brutally-carved clearing surrounded by heaps of stone which at first glance looked like runoff from landslides. But there were people emerging from them, these huts of a sort where the archers sheltered—men and women like the ones who'd sacked Rolf's caravan. She wondered if Quill and Maleck had left from these same grounds to intercept the merches and their cache of *Svarkyst* steel—and Cistine and her companions.

"Welcome to Villmark," Quill announced with a broad sweep of his arm. "Some of these people might try to convince you they don't like it here. Don't believe that. They actually *hate* it."

"I can't imagine why." Cistine rubbed her arms and stepped onto the barren stretch of rock that marked the camp's boundary. It hardly looked lived-in, and she knew if an enemy passed by, the warriors could pull back into those stone shelters and blend with the rugged terrain. There was no warmth here except a pocket of small fires kept low beneath the shroud of mountain trees hanging stubbornly from the cliffs above, and those could be easily doused if needed.

Maleck tended one of those fires. He was focused so intently on the flames, he didn't look up until Faer floated over to the tree above him and let out a loud squawk. Then his gaze snapped to them, and his eyes blew wide.

Cistine smiled as Maleck leaped to his feet and hurried to join them. "They followed us."

"I know. Shocking, isn't it?" Quill draped an arm around Cistine's shoulders. "Apparently, someone took Tatiana's maps to heart. Or just took her map."

Cistine smiled sheepishly as Maleck's gaze dragged almost irresistibly to Ashe. "You *all* came."

"Are you surprised?" Ashe's tone was casually cool, daring him to mention her leg.

"Yes," Maleck said. "I am surprised it took you this long."

"We were checking over our shoulders the whole way from Hellidom." Quill gave Cistine a playful shake. "Looks like Tati owes me a few mynts."

Cistine craned on her tiptoes, searching for a glimpse of Tatiana's fine clothes or curly hair among the archers. "Where is she?"

"Leading the other patrol in the mountains," Thorne said. "Maleck, watch for her. The moment she returns, gather the cabal in my shelter."

"What about us?" Julian asked.

Ariadne arched a brow. "Are you part of the cabal?"

"This is one conversation that does not concern you," Thorne said to Cistine. "I'll escort you to your living arrangements."

"Just call them what they are," Julian muttered. "Hovels."

"There are some people who would murder each other for shelters like these," Ariadne growled.

"That doesn't make me feel any fonder of them."

Cistine sighed. "Julian, please, let it go."

Julian rolled his eyes, stalking silently after Thorne across the camp to one of the rustic stone caves.

The interior surprised Cistine. After Quill's remark and Julian's disdain, she'd braced herself for a bed as cool and unforgiving as the rock top where they trained; instead she stepped onto a velvety carpet of dense, dark pelts, framed with unbroken ghostplants in glass jars.

"My quarters are in the shelter to the left," Thorne said as Cistine dumped her satchel on the floor. "Maleck and Quill are to the left of that, and Tatiana and Ariadne are to your right. I'll warn them to keep their games to themselves. Faer has a knack for finding mountain scorpions and leaving them in the hovels as a gift."

Cistine shuddered. "Thank you for that. I don't think I'll ever sleep again."

The High Tribune folded his arms. "You would have slept better if you had stayed in the Den."

Cistine curled her toes in her boots as she faced him, anchoring herself to her choice. "No, I don't think I would have."

Thorne's eyes flickered. Cistine thought they softened. Then he nodded, told them to send for him if they needed anything—and he was gone. Retreating just as quickly as when he'd given Cistine the garden, as if he didn't know what to do with himself if he wasn't doling out orders or giving long, sizzling looks to people.

Julian cracked his knuckles. "All right. Let's search every inch of this place for scorpions."

Cistine laughed, placing a grateful kiss on his cheek as he started to lift the pelts and search underneath.

"Interesting that his warriors are spread out," Ashe mused. "This shelter should belong to the women, so there's no gap between Thorne and his cabal."

Trust Ashe to think of that. Cistine's heart twisted as she looked around the small cave, comfortably able to house three. Clearly, the living arrangements had been this way for some time, with the cabal neatly divided into pairs—except for Thorne and one other. One who had been forced to sleep alone and encased here, where Thorne could keep an eye on him.

This shelter had once belonged to Aden.

Cistine barely had time to sort through their rations from Hellidom—or remove her boots from her tired feet—before Tatiana returned to the camp. Cistine knew she'd arrived by the sound of Quill yelling insults across Villmark. Tatiana shouted him off, and then Cistine heard her storming closer to their shelter.

"I'll be right back." She hurried outside and nearly slammed into Tatiana in the entrance.

"What are you doing here?" Tatiana snapped.

Cistine grabbed her elbow. "If you want to have this conversation without someone leaping to defend my honor, let's talk in your shelter, not mine."

Tatiana's mouth clamped shut. Hands in fists, she stalked to the tumble of rocks on the right. Cistine hurried after her.

It was easy to tell who slept where in this shelter: one half was pristine, not even a hair of the speckled pelt displaced. The other was disarrayed with piles of clothes, weapons, and half-finished rations in leaf beds. But the pillows met in the middle, and Cistine could envision the two women lying with their heads together, talking deep into the night.

Cistine skirted the mess on Tatiana's side and sat. "How did you know I was here?"

"Quill sent Faer with a message," Tatiana said. "I thought it had to be his latest prank. I told myself there was no conceivable possibility a stars-forsaken *princess* was foolish enough to run her hardly-trained hide off to the Vaszaj Range and intercept a battle brigade. It just wasn't possible. Or so I thought."

"Did Quill tell you *why* we're here?"

"It doesn't matter! Cistine, listen to me..." Tatiana shifted and grimaced, massaging her still-healing shoulder. "The Vassora put an arrow into me. This is not training. These are not *games*. This is a real mission, where lives can be lost. What do you suppose King Cyril would *do* to us if his precious daughter died on Valgardan soil?"

Cistine wavered, sinking her fingers into the pelt to steady herself. Death was terrible enough—hers or her friends'. But she hadn't entertained the possibility her father might hold Valgard at fault if the unthinkable happened. That the possibility of war against King Jad might somehow be made to marry with a blow of retribution against the North for the death of Talheim's only princess. "I didn't think of that."

"I'm beginning to understand that's a habit of yours." Tatiana dropped cross-legged before her, taking her hands. "Cistine, you *must* start thinking of your life as a prize. Stars know the entire rest of the world does. Either they love you, or they love the power that comes with your title. I'm going to tell you the same thing we always tell Thorne: get a hold of yourself and stop believing you're expendable."

"I don't..." Cistine paused. "Does Thorne really believe that?"

"His father certainly didn't inspire him to think any differently. The number of times he's almost died, pulling one of us from a raid...too many to count. We have enough on our hands with that. Stop trying to best him for recklessness."

"I'll keep it in check," Cistine said.

"Good. Because you are too pretty and far, far too amusing to waste on an early grave."

Cistine rolled her eyes. "Tatiana the Flirter has returned."

"Admit it. You're flattered." Though Tatiana's tone was light, her face remained stern. "But hear what I'm saying, Cistine. You're better-trained, you're wiser than you were, but this is still a dangerous kingdom. Especially in a place like this."

Cistine tilted her head. "How so?"

Tatiana shifted to sit next to Cistine so they both faced the hovel's entrance. "There's a reason these archers aren't trusted members of the cabal. They're trained, and they've agreed to help Thorne, but they're also unpredictable. They're not loyal to peace or justice, just to the thought of paying back the Courts for slights over the years. So you have to be careful where you step and what you say to them."

"Where did they come from?"

"Territories all over," Tatiana said. "When Thorne's reputation as a bandit leader grew, it attracted people from every corner of Valgard. Quill trained them in archery mostly, because aside from him, none of us are particularly good shots."

"But...Thorne trusts them. So they must have good character."

"Let me put it this way." Tatiana brushed the hair from Cistine's shoulder. "If they'd been the ones to find you in the forest, they might've shot you without question."

Cistine's stomach clenched. "Oh."

"That's what I mean about knowing what you're getting yourself into.

It's why I'm frankly ready to drown you for setting foot out here."

"But what's done is done," Cistine said. "We aren't going back. So you're just going to have to find a way to accept our presence here."

Tatiana's tongue poked from the corner of her mouth as she measured Cistine. "Spending time with Thorne hasn't been good for you."

Cistine laughed. "At least we can still agree on *that*. But I am flattered you care."

"Not about you. About what it means to the cabal if you die. So many wasted hours."

Cistine scoffed. "You do care! Admit it."

"Never."

Boots scraped the stone outside, and Quill shouted into the hovel, "Thorne's called a meeting! You're holding everyone up, Saddlebags!"

"Now that you're out here, you're holding them up, too!" Tatiana barked back. To Cistine, she added, "Just stay in the camp unless one of us is with you. And try not to ruffle any feathers."

"That, I can promise."

Tatiana squeezed her shoulder and swaggered out to meet Quill, engaging in a festival of banter that trailed away as they walked to Thorne's shelter. Cistine slipped out after them and stood embraced by sunlight, trying to think of things she could do: change into comfortable clothes, sort out her armor, maybe eat something. She might even try to be friendly with the archers and learn what it was like to serve as scouts under the command of a High Tribune in hiding.

But she found herself crossing the camp anyway, kicking over a stump near Thorne's shelter and planting herself on it. She pulled out Nail and examined its edge, trying to look busy to any passing archers while she listened to the murmurs coming from the stone hovel.

"Obviously, flagons considered, we can't attack them in the passes," Ariadne was saying—Thorne had clearly laid out Cistine's report already. "We'll have to wait for them to descend into the lowlands now."

"Blaykrone lowlands, Ari," Quill said. "Think about it—a battle on that terrain, with flagons...especially where the road leads?"

"Casualties are almost guaranteed in that scenario," Thorne said. "And I for one am not prepared for that."

"If we fight in the mountains, casualties are *absolutely* guaranteed," Ariadne snapped.

"But we asked for this fight," Maleck said. "The people of this territory did not."

"Then what do you suggest we do? Traipse into their trap?"

The telltale sound of a snapped cinnamon stick echoed from inside, and then Quill's voice: "Cistine gave us something valuable here. It is still a trap...but now we know what to expect from it. That gives us the advantage."

"We can choose the battle on our own terms," Tatiana agreed. "We decide how and where we confront these guards and their flagons."

"Keep the battle high," Thorne said, "up in the mountains, where we can outmaneuver them."

Ariadne murmured, "You're not suggesting what I think you are."

"The Izten Torkat," Quill said. "We'll send them down the Throat of God."

"If we trap them in that pass, they'll have very little room to move," Tatiana said.

"That's brilliant—but neither will we," Ariadne argued. "There's a reason most caravans take a week to cross the Throat *alone*. You've all seen how narrow that pass is."

"That's where we hold the advantage, Ari," Quill insisted. "We'll swoop in ahead and lay a trap of our own. Cluster all the carts together and break them in half, one by one, while they're still expecting us on the lowlands."

"The advantage of surprise, and of preparation," Thorne agreed.

"Not to mention," Tatiana said, "the flagons. If we manage not to rupture them...and if we can kill the Vassora before anyone uses them..."

"Stop talking," there was a grin heavy in Quill's words, "or I'll start drooling."

"It would be a windfall," Thorne said. "But our focus isn't on the rewards. We need to capture the surgeons for questioning. Everything else, even the flagons, comes second."

"But you still won't have this fight in the lowlands," Ariadne muttered.

The silence was frigid. Cistine tensed.

"Don't let this face I wear fool you, Ariadne," Thorne said. "You know what lies behind it."

Cistine sheathed Nail, got to her feet, and hurried away. She didn't know if that ended the conversation, but she didn't think she wanted to know anything more about the face Thorne wore—or what was lurking under its polished surface.

CHAPTER THIRTY

A HAND ON her shoulder rocked Cistine awake from that dream again: King Jad stalking her with a vial of poison in his fist, a shadow following her from the Den, never content to allow her a moment's peace. She was almost glad to roll over and see Maleck crouched beside her, his quiet eyes half-masted in the shelter's dimness.

"Patrol," he murmured. "Thorne's orders."

Cistine groaned, pushing herself up on the thick pelt. Despite its softness, she felt the hard ground beneath—and that, just as much as the conversation she'd overheard outside Thorne's shelter, had kept her tossing and turning all night. Now her joints were stiff and her muscles ached as she reached for her training armor. "Is this his idea of punishment?"

"Mine. And it isn't punishment. It's a privilege."

Unsteady movement behind Maleck caught Cistine's eye. Ashe was also awake, pulling on her boots.

"I'm going with you," she said at Cistine's questing whine. "Hellidom was one thing. But here in the wilds, where we were attacked before? Not a chance you go alone, Princess."

Maleck drew himself swiftly to his feet. "I'll wait for you outside."

Still bemoaning her exhaustion, Cistine yanked on her training armor and crawled to Julian. He still slept soundly, as if he was already used to these conditions, and barely stirred when she brushed his hair aside and planted a kiss on his temple.

"Ashe and I are going on patrol," she whispered against his ear. "We'll be back soon."

He grunted, burrowing his face more tightly into the soft fur. Grinning, Cistine ducked outside to join Ashe and Maleck in the bruise-blue darkness before dawn.

Though it was early, Cistine immediately spotted Quill and Ariadne limbering up with several archers for training. Tatiana sat outside her shelter, wrapped in an emerald robe and sipping a cup of tea while she browsed a map. Thorne was nowhere to be seen.

"What *is* this place, exactly?" Ashe asked as Maleck led them into the thick shawl of foliage that wrapped the hills around Villmark.

"During the war against the Middle Kingdom, there were training camps like this one all over Valgard." Maleck held aside a low-hanging branch for the women to pass under. "Most were never plundered. They remain good outposts for people like us."

"To what end? Another war?"

Maleck squinted into the trees. "This is where the lesson begins." He gestured them to a halt, then nodded to Cistine. "What do you hear?"

Cistine put several paces between herself and the two warriors. She closed her eyes, fending off exhaustion and surliness at the early hour. And she listened.

At first, the silence was all she could focus on, because she knew it was a trick. She knew Villmark was behind her, and she ought to be able to hear movement of some kind; but not even a whisper of conversation passed through the trees six yards away.

Another gift Thorne was unwittingly giving to her: silence so she could concentrate.

The wind stirred the pines, humming through the steep crags, resonating like a woodwind instrument. Somewhere in the gaps between the thick, gnarled trunks, something rooted among the fallen needles. Distantly, water burbled along a streambed.

Cistine whispered these things to Maleck as she noticed them. Of the wind in the mountains, she told him the most.

"It reminds me of a symphony my father took me to in Astoria," she said. "Those different peaks and rises in the sound...it's just like instruments. Like the mountain passes are God's own symphony, playing for anyone who has time to listen."

Maleck sighed, and Cistine's ears heated; perhaps she'd said too much or hadn't sounded enough like a warrior. She turned back to face her companions and found Ashe already staring at Maleck—who'd closed his eyes and turned his face into the wind, a faint crease seaming his brows.

"There are times," Maleck said, "when I realize I am...not as much a part of this world as the others. I don't notice everything. Sounds, I don't always hear. I'm too much in my mind."

Ashe frowned, but Cistine didn't move. She couldn't. Her heart was slowly breaking in her chest.

This was what Thorne meant when he'd said Maleck was broken in places. But until this moment, she hadn't realized he knew. That perhaps he even understood just how different he was, and how differently the others perceived him because of it.

"But," Maleck went on, "the way you describe it, I can hear it...like the orchestras that play in Stornhaz. Long ago, I made my home in the rafters above the music hall. Their practices lulled me to sleep each night."

"Which instrument was your favorite?" Cistine asked.

"The piano. Such power in its make, and yet the music it produced was sweeter than any other."

Cistine smiled. "I liked the violins, myself. I asked my father to buy me one after my first symphony."

"And you were terrible," Ashe teased. "It put a bad taste in my mouth about music for weeks."

"There are no terrible students, you know...only terrible teachers."

Maleck finally stirred from his reverie, facing Ashe. "You taught her?"

"I tried," Ashe said. "But I hadn't picked up an instrument in years. I was rusty, and she was a nightmare."

"I thought you played beautifully," Cistine protested.

Ashe laughed. "Which was all the proof I needed that you were unteachable."

Maleck led them into the trees. "It's good you have one another. An anchor of that nature is invaluable. It can keep you from drifting if you forget who you are."

Cistine wondered how far he had drifted. How lost he truly was, and didn't let the others see.

"Don't be dramatic," Ashe said. "You have an anchor, too."

"Do I?"

"In Thorne, yes. You're here to guard his back. I can tell by the way you move around him...always trying to get between him and any kind of threat. Even if it's someone talking about him when he's not in the room."

Cistine stared at Ashe. She hadn't noticed Maleck's movements so keenly. In fact, many times she'd tried *not* to notice him.

"You're watching out for him," Ashe continued, "just like I watch out for Cistine."

Maleck said nothing. But the way his mouth twitched, it seemed he fought not to smile.

Their time on patrol passed with the climbing sun, but Cistine barely noticed, her attention consumed by Maleck and Ashe's instructions: how to track by pawprints, scat, and broken branches through the undergrowth, and which berries were poisonous and which could be eaten.

"I remember some of this from my books," Cistine said as they paused to gather handfuls of blackberries from a thorny bush. "But it's good to see it in practice."

"Knowledge is a powerful ally," Maleck said, "but, unapplied, it can leave a person puffed up and useless."

Cistine pondered that as she followed the warriors up a sharp incline behind the bush. Perhaps Maleck was right—and perhaps she herself had been the most puffed up and useless pupil in all the kingdoms combined.

She'd always craved knowledge...but to what end? She'd never imagined herself applying the things she knew. She'd never even considered how her knowledge might serve the people when she became queen. It was simply how she'd passed the time, made friends, and kept up conversation in the Citadel: by being the woman who always had an answer for everything, the smartest one in the room, brimming with arbitrary facts her handmaids and guests tittered over.

Embarrassment stabbed Cistine so sharply, she caught her breath, then whispered to herself, "No," just to halt her mortification in its tracks.

How *simple* she was. A child who'd desperately wanted approval from those she would one day be forced to rule. She'd abused knowledge and gossiped endlessly to make herself feel important and secure in a kingdom where everything was being chosen for her. In the symphony of Astoria, she'd been a cymbal clashing loudly off-beat, while everyone was beholden to tell her she made the loveliest music.

"Cistine?" Ashe called. She and Maleck had reached the top of the slope, their bodies framed in daylight from a gap in the foliage. "Do you need to rest?"

Cistine gritted her teeth, shook her head, and jogged up the slope to join them. Fresh determination burned in her belly, slamming every step down hard on the incline.

She would do better from now on. She would make use of her knowledge, and only in ways it was needed. And she would not make knowledge her shield against feeling inferior.

She would make it a weapon to safeguard her kingdom.

When Cistine reached the peak of the hill beside Maleck and Ashe, the world opened before her, an embrace of light that seemed to reflect the fire of conviction blazing in her core.

The cliff dropped steeply off before them, plunging into an enormous gorge. On the far side were tall, rolling hills, and beyond them, the back of the Vaszaj Range, spreading out as far as the southern coasts, a brown-and-white scroll unfurling from horizon to horizon where snow still capped the tallest passes. Early-morning mist braided into the river's spray below, weaving a modest skirt around the foothills and the mountains themselves.

"God almighty, this is gorgeous," Cistine breathed.

"And very peaceful." Maleck lowered himself on the cliff, and Cistine—keeping a healthy distance from the edge—sat beside him. Ashe crouched next to her. "We'll eat here, then go back."

They divided the berries and ate, and while they did, Maleck mapped the terrain for them.

"This is the lowest part of the Izten Torkat," he explained, "the Throat of God. This gorge runs through the lower passes of the Vaszaj Range, until the branch of the river feeds the sea."

"I don't remember this from our journey with the merches," Ashe said.

"Most caravans keep well north of it, traveling the Vingete Vey. We're far from the safe roads. The caravans here choose more clandestine paths."

"I wonder if that has anything to do with a certain curly-haired warrior making trouble for the last caravan," Cistine said, "and getting herself shot."

Maleck nodded. "It's very likely they're taking the dangerous road to avoid a guarantee of trouble on the Vey."

"Good luck to them. You people bring trouble wherever you go." Ashe wiped her hands on her thighs, drew her blade from its sheath, and cleaned it in smooth, loving strokes with a cloth from her pocket. Maleck was silent, and Cistine ignored them both as she drank in the sight before her—the mountains and trees, the foaming, gurgling river below. It wasn't until Maleck leaned around her to speak to Ashe, interrupting her view of the valley, that she snapped back to attention.

"That is a fine weapon," Maleck said. "Does it have a name?"

Cistine laughed, but Ashe said seriously, "All my weapons do."

Cistine gaped at her. "I didn't know that!"

Ashe shrugged. "It's a joke in the Cadre. Every new initiate is given a sword, and every Warden tells the recruit to name it, or else they'll name it themselves. And it's never flattering."

Maleck bobbed his head slowly. "Names are very important in Valgard. The names we give our weapons. Our lands. The names we give each other.

What do you call this one?"

"Echelon," Ashe said. "Lord Rion gave her to me himself, after the...after we came back from Valgard."

After the war. Like every Warden who'd fought in those days, Ashe usually spoke of that victory proudly and without pretention. But here in Maleck's presence, it felt wrong to be so casual.

Maleck extended his hand. "May I?"

"No one touches Echelon except me." Ashe's tone was as uncompromising as the steel she cleaned.

"Wisdom. I'm sorry I kept her from you when we first met." Maleck drew the swords from between his shoulderblades, laying them at a cross before Cistine, where Ashe could see them. "These are Starfall and Stormfury. Thorne gave them to me when I swore my allegiance to him. To his Court."

"The one where he was High Tribune?"

Maleck shook his head as Ashe slid the blades closer to herself. She nicked her thumb on the edge of one and stroked her knuckles down the length of the other. Cistine wasn't certain what she was reading from the metal's weight and tang. The broader details of weaponry were a language like Old Valgardan; Maleck and Ashe spoke it fluidly, but Cistine was years behind in learning.

Finally, Ashe said, "They're good swords."

"They have been my faithful companions for many years." Maleck took the weapons back and sheathed them, and as they clicked into place, Cistine shuddered. The motion reminded her that she'd watched Maleck kill with them; that before she'd known the quiet he was capable of, the calm, she'd believed he was nothing but a death-god bent on slaughter.

Cistine pointed to the birch dagger on Maleck's hip. "Did you name that, too?"

"Yes," Maleck said. "Remany."

"Is that Old Valgardan? What does it mean?"

Maleck squinted across the gorge. The mist burned away as the sun climbed higher, and several gem-sleek birds took flight from the treetops below, swooping over the rapids. Cistine almost wished she had one of Tatiana's lightboxes so she could capture this sight...these hues and tones, and the mist soaring up from the valley.

"We should return to Villmark," Maleck said. "I must report to Thorne."

With Maleck, it was difficult to tell if he was avoiding answering questions, or simply keeping his focus where it so often was: on his duties. Cistine wiped the berry juice from her hands and slowly rose, stretching the kinks from her limbs. "Lead on, then."

"No. You lead. Use the skills we showed you."

The journey back to the camp went much slower than the one out from it. Cistine slinked between the trees, searching for her own footprints. But Maleck had sent them across a stream at one point, and that disoriented her. Maleck and Ashe offered no advice along the way except once, in unison, "You're about to lead us off the cliff."

"You're both enjoying this, aren't you?" Cistine snapped, guiding them away from the ledge she hadn't even seen.

"Immensely," Maleck deadpanned.

"I always knew you were going to be the death of me," Ashe added.

They were all sweating—and despite her endurance training, Cistine's lungs were ruthlessly sore—when the way became familiar again. At last, they ducked under the lichen shroud and into the camp.

The moment they entered, Cistine knew something was wrong.

The cabal had gathered before the shelters, and Tatiana was shouting. Quill had a hand around her elbow, restraining her. Thorne's arms were crossed, and Ariadne rested her hand on her sword.

And the person Tatiana was shouting at, who was shouting back at her...

"Julian?" Cistine strode across the camp, drawing the eyes of the archers who'd wandered from their own beds to observe the dispute.

Hopeless busybodies.

Julian spun around at the sound of Cistine's voice, his hair disheveled, clothing askew, face still red from yelling—all contrasting with the shock of his open mouth and fever-bright eyes as he beheld her.

And then he stormed toward her, and Cistine almost came to a halt. She'd never seen him walk like that before—had never seen him look so *furious* before.

"Where *were* you?" Julian roared.

"On patrol! I told you before we left!"

"Did you make sure I was awake? Gods, Cistine, I thought something happened! I thought maybe the Vassora snapped you up, or Thorne and his people tossed you off a cliff!"

"As if they would," Cistine said. "Julian, calm down. Shouting won't help anything."

"Well, forgive me for being *agitated* when my princess goes missing in a camp full of strangers! *Never* do that again."

Cistine slammed to a halt. "Excuse me?"

Quill's lips rounded in a soundless whistle. Slowly, Thorne tipped his head.

"Don't go on patrol without me while we're here." Julian halted before her, his clipped voice enunciating every word into a blade's jab. "Not if you can't be clear about where you're going. I thought you were dead, Princess!"

"Clear?" Cistine seethed. "Let me be *clear* then, Julian: don't you ever, *ever* command me. Suitor or not, you're still my subject, and I'm your princess. That isn't just a name, it's a title, and you will respect it."

Julian's jaw dropped again. Hurt flashed through his features. "Is that how you're going to treat me while we're here? As your subject?"

"If you're going to act like my jailer, then yes!"

Maleck stepped forward to Cistine's side. "She was never in any danger, I assure you."

Julian's eyes snapped to Maleck, and his face reddened again. "She's been in danger ever since your *friend* found her in that tavern. I'm starting to wish he'd just minded his own business that night."

"Julian!" Cistine's fury pounded out the pain of knowing she'd hurt his feelings.

"These people are corrupting you, Princess! They're turning you into something you're not...something you were never supposed to be."

"*I* decide what I'm supposed to be!" Cistine stabbed a finger against his chest. "Whether that's cosseted and useless or this cabal's student, it's *my* decision. Not theirs, or *yours*."

"You would never have chosen this if we hadn't come here."

"But I came for Talheim," Cistine said. "I will never regret this choice, no matter where it leads me."

"Well, I'm starting to regret coming with you. Maybe I should've reported you to your father instead. I can't stand watching them mold you into their perfect pupil. You care more about patrols and weapons now than you care about your own kingdom!"

Rage stifled Cistine's breath. "*What?*"

"Tell me I'm wrong! We're facing down time against the lies you told your father so we could come here. But if I didn't know any better, I'd say none of that matters to you anymore. Morning patrols? Afternoon training? That's not why we're in Valgard!"

"I know why we're *here*, Julian!"

"Well, you could have tricked me. You're certainly distracted enough with that gods-forsaken garden back in Hellidom."

Cistine opened her mouth, and Maleck laid a hand on Remany. "Walk away."

His tone suggested he knew something Cistine didn't. Perhaps he sensed how close she and Julian were to throwing blows.

Julian stared at Cistine, breathing heavily. Then he turned on heel and stalked back to their shelter.

Humiliation painted Cistine's cheeks as she watched him go. She and Julian had argued before, but they'd never fought outright—and certainly never in the middle of a camp, with everyone shamelessly eavesdropping.

Quill clapped his hands suddenly, and Cistine winced. "All right, that's the end of that! Don't some of you have training to do? Patrols to muster?"

"Move your haunches, or you can groom the pelts in every shelter with a fine-toothed comb!" Tatiana yelled.

That threat sent all the archers scuttling away.

"That was something else." Ashe stepped to Cistine's side. "Do you want me to talk to him?"

"Yes," Cistine said shakily. "Please."

Ashe squeezed her shoulder and ducked into the shelter, leaving Cistine facing the cabal.

"What happened while we were gone?" she asked.

"He woke in a panic," Ariadne said. "And nearly tore the camp apart searching for you and Ashe. Mostly for you."

"He refused to believe you were with Maleck," Tatiana added. "Or that you were safe."

"He called Mal a few choice names," Quill said—then winced as Tatiana slammed an elbow into his ribs.

"It doesn't matter what he said, it was all baseless," Ariadne growled. "But things certainly escalated from there."

Cistine pressed her hands to her cheeks. "I'm so sorry. You didn't need our...you didn't need *this* in the middle of your battle camp."

"Of course not," Thorne deadpanned. "Because with all these people stacked on top of each other, there are never angry words exchanged here. Or blows."

Quill hooked his thumbs into his belt. "That's us. The picture of sophistication and restraint."

Cistine knew they were trying to make her feel better—to ease her shame. But what she really needed was to be alone, to grapple with just how suddenly sour her day had gone.

"I have to relieve myself," she blurted out, for lack of anything less humiliating to punctuate the mortifying exchange. Ignoring Quill's spurt of laughter and Tatiana's smile, she walked back into the trees, then broke into a run.

She was crying before she'd taken a dozen steps. By the time she'd sprinted almost a quarter-mile, she gasped with tears. She caught herself against a thick tree and sank down to her knees in the tangle of its upraised roots. Even when she pressed a hand to her mouth, she couldn't stifle her sobs.

Julian was right. She *had* changed. She'd tried to make herself fierce, make herself like steel that could face whatever awaited her in Stornhaz. Even today, she'd decided to turn empty gossip and useless knowledge into strength for Talheim.

But she hadn't considered how becoming that person and doing those things might make her someone Julian despised.

Cistine couldn't hear anything over her throbbing heart and hacking sobs; so when a dark-clad figure swung onto the tallest root above her, she sucked in a breath and sat back hard on her heels, swiping an arm across her damp face.

Thorne propped his back against the tree and slid to his seat, draping his arm on his cocked knee. His other foot stirred the air in a soundless current.

"I need to be alone," Cistine mumbled.

"These forests are dangerous," Thorne said. "If you prefer, I'll keep my distance. But none of us travels alone here."

Cistine glanced up at him. He didn't look at her—didn't take in her blotchy cheeks or her red, damp eyes. "Not even you?"

Thorne's jaw clenched. "This was an exception."

His presence brought some relief to her sobs, though the silent tears didn't stop. Cistine curled into the dip of the roots, burying her face in her hands.

"I told you I nearly forged the *valenar* bond once," Thorne said. "When I left Stornhaz, she chose to stay. Our paths separated, not because I chose to leave, but because I wouldn't become a man who abandoned everything he believed just to cling to her love."

Cistine sniffled deeply, laying her head back against the tree. "How did you keep from hating yourself for it?"

"I didn't apologize. Don't *ever* apologize for who you are. When you make mistakes, when you harm someone without meaning to...apologize for that. But never for who you are. This life will try hard enough to put out your fire. Don't hand it a cup of water."

His words stopped her tears like a spigot. For a moment, Cistine watched the scene from afar: a girl with her heart shredded by an argument with her suitor, weeping because he didn't appreciate the ways she'd changed for her kingdom and her people. To save lives.

And for herself.

Get up. The pull was insistent, as loud as the call that plucked her spirit so often in this kingdom. *Dry your tears. Don't apologize for this choice.*

Cistine dragged in a shuddering breath, pushed herself to her feet, and wiped her face on her sleeve again as she looked up at Thorne. "Any future arguments we have, I'll make certain they take place outside the camp."

Thorne swung upright, balancing on the root. "Quill wants to train with you whenever you're ready." He leaped down and walked away—giving her the choice to stay and cry, knowing he'd keep watch nearby, or go back to Villmark and face the aftermath of the fight.

Keeping some distance between them, Cistine returned to the camp with Thorne.

⤸⤷

The cabal and the archers were gone on patrol by the time Cistine returned and Thorne slipped off to his hovel. Only Quill remained in the center of Villmark, perched on an upturned spike of rock as he wound fabric around his palms and knuckles. When he spotted Cistine, he raised his chin in greeting, but she didn't return the gesture. She stared past him, at the pelt spread out at the camp's boundary and the satchel on top of it.

Julian's things. He'd moved from their shelter—to be away from her, maybe. Or to sleep where she couldn't leave without waking him.

She didn't know which possibility filled her with the greatest rage as she stormed toward Quill. His eyes narrowed, brows pinching downward at the look on her face. He hopped off the rock and slid a hand under his hair, flopping it from one side of his head to the other. Then he put up both hands. "Hit me."

Plowing forward with a bark of rage, Cistine slammed her knuckles into his palm so hard she shoved his arm back.

He held his other hand out to her. "Again!"

Cistine drove blow after blow into his hands, and he took each one—each slam of her anguish and anger, over and over, absorbing them as if he had a limitless well for her to pour herself into.

So she did. She pounded his hands with cross-hook after cross-hook until green bruises lodged in the skin at the hinge of Quill's thumbs, until her own arms trembled from the strain of landing blows. Her hands, unwrapped, were sore and bleeding from the first and second knuckles, and she tasted the salt of her own tears by the time she buckled, eyes blurry and chest heaving with exhaustion.

Quill snared her forearms and looked deep into her eyes. "More?"

Cistine flexed her fists. "I don't know. I don't know what I need."

He released her and stepped back, holding up his bruised palms. "Don't hold onto it. I can take it. I've taken worse blows from bigger people."

Cistine bent with her hands on her knees, catching her breath as she stared at him—at his relaxed face and the concern in his eyes. He cared...he *truly* cared if she was all right, if she was bottling her anger or releasing it, if it was eating her alive. Just like he'd cared in the tavern, when he'd saved her from the slavers—a day Julian wished had never happened. Or at least he wished it had never been branded by Quill's appearance.

She knew he hadn't thought of it that way. He hadn't thought of what it would've meant to her, *for* her, if Quill hadn't been there. Just as Julian and Ashe hadn't been there.

He truly didn't comprehend what she owed to these people.

Cistine passed by Quill's wounded hands and wrapped her arms around him instead. And though his breath rushed out in shock, she didn't let go. He was surprisingly solid for all his leanness, blooded with that same power she'd first felt when he'd tucked her against his side in that tavern, safe from Matthias and Roosha.

After a moment, Quill's arms circled her, too. "*This* is how they relieve anger in your kingdom?"

"Shut up," Cistine muttered against his armor. "And thank you."

Quill chuckled, resting his chin on her head. "My pleasure, Stranger."

CHAPTER
THIRTY-ONE

DURING THE THREE days they spent in Villmark, Julian didn't sleep in the shelter again; he always dozed on the camp's edge when Cistine slipped out for patrol with Maleck and Ashe in the mornings. Whether Ashe's presence on these outings was some arrangement between her and Julian, Cistine didn't care to ask. She was glad to look for scat and markings while Maleck and Ashe trailed her through the underbrush, murmuring about Courts and constellations—a lesson so familiar by now, Cistine could easily ignore it.

She liked to keep focused, not giving herself time to think of how Julian hadn't embraced her, hadn't kissed her, hadn't even spoken to her since their fight.

She trained with Quill in the afternoons, making certain to wrap her knuckles now. In the evenings, Tatiana showed her how to lay snares and cook her own food, and that proved to be the greatest and worst distraction of all.

The first time she watched the warriors skin the meat, Cistine vomited into the nearest pile of brush. There was too much blood, too much sinew, too many slick, dangling things for her to bear.

Ariadne found her heaving in the bushes that night. She didn't offer a hand to her or a cloth to wipe her clammy, sweaty face. Her tone was stern as she hovered over Cistine: "Not everything you eat is plucked from a flowerbed. You respect the life that was given for yours...every life. Go back to the camp and *watch*."

And because it was Ariadne laying a challenge and taking a jab at Cistine's gardening, she went. She watched the rest of that night and the next, chewing on her knuckles when she tasted bile. By the third night, the skinning no longer left her nauseous, but she still didn't take up the knife when Tatiana offered it to her. This was a small step, like jogging before she ran.

She ate with Quill and Tatiana that evening, letting their banter soothe the pain in her heart as she stole glances at Julian and Ashe—off by themselves around another firepit. Maleck and Ariadne sat one fire closer, both angled slightly toward the Wardens.

Cistine dragged her attention away from them when Thorne sauntered into the small pool of firelight. His armor was sprinkled with stone dust, gleaming like starlight in the blackest night as he crouched on his heels beside Tatiana, across from Quill and Cistine. "The scouts have reported back. The three carts should enter the Izten Torkat in two days."

Quill sat up straighter. "We need a day and a half to lay the trap. We leave at dawn."

Cistine groaned, wiping off her hands as she stood. "In that case, it's bed for me. All these early mornings are awful for my health."

Thorne's brows peaked. "Are you coming along?"

Embarrassment warmed the small of Cistine's back. "I assumed you wanted our help. Ashe's sword, at the very least. And Julian's."

"It isn't my choice. The hunt is Quill's."

Quill sat forward, prodding the fire with a stick. Tatiana looked between him and Cistine, propping her elbows on her knees and folding her fingers under her chin.

"We could send them higher up the trail," Quill mused. "The carts will descend past them. Cistine can send Faer down the Throat to let us know when they're approaching...and if there's anything we ought to be aware of before they reach the ambush point."

"Clever," Tatiana said. Quill flashed her a broad smirk.

"Why them, and not one of us, or the archers?" Thorne asked. The question wasn't cold or angry—merely searching. But Cistine still wanted to hit him for it.

"I need my warriors with me," Quill said, and Thorne smiled, as if the words were an old joke he couldn't help appreciating. "And the archers have to close both ends of the trail. We only have forty to divide between the upper and lower passes. I can't risk posting less than half at each."

"Besides," Cistine added, "you can't leave us here. We need something to do, or we might tear each other apart."

Thorne glanced up, and something in his posture, in the way he looked at her through his lashes, made Cistine's breath hitch; as if he saw her, and understood how desperately she wanted to do something useful, and not be trapped here with Julian, waiting for the others to return.

Finally, Thorne nodded. "Then we break camp at dawn. From now on, follow Quill's command."

Villmark disappeared rapidly below them the following day, its inconspicuous hovels and stone spans hidden under a thick wreath of predawn fog. When sunlight finally trickled down through the mountain peaks, burning away the mist, Villmark was gone. The terrain around them consisted of nothing but thick pines and a bald path winding between the sap-riddled trees.

They crossed a long stone bridge after several hours and parted company with the last archers there; the others had gone to lie in wait at the trailhead, leaving Cistine, her companions, and the cabal to make the steep ascent along the narrow ledge that wrapped the gorge.

After only a half-hour of hiking, Cistine understood why Ariadne had been so reticent to make a stand on this pass. It was only wide enough for two to walk side-by-side, and to their right there was nothing—no guarding fence, no hindrance to prevent a perilous fall into the river below. The whitewater foam raged over ancient debris that had fallen from the mountains in long-ago landslides.

"Do you remember what this river is called?" Tatiana drilled Cistine as they walked.

Cistine did her best not to look off to the right again. "The Muunvat, wasn't it?"

Tatiana smiled, slapping her between the shoulderblades. "That's right. Old Valgardan word for *spit*, because it will carry you straight down the Throat to the True God's belly if you fall in."

"Stop telling tales, Tatiana," Thorne said behind them. "No one is going into the Throat."

Tatiana flashed him a wicked smile. "Assuming the surgeons cooperate, you mean."

They camped along the path that night, everyone in a row up the slope, but Cistine didn't sleep. She was too nervous at the possibility of having nightmares that would send her flailing over the cliff. Instead she sat up, watching the stars wheel slowly overhead, churning Skyygan's constellation from its roost one night at a time and ushering in the time of Kanslar Court.

She was still sore with Julian, but she knew he was right. They had little time before Kanslar rose—and then, prepared or not, she would have to make the journey to Stornhaz.

The thought woke her up as fully as a splash of cold water to the face.

It was almost dawn when Ashe sat up beside her, kneading her thigh as she leaned against the rock next to Cistine. "I knew you wouldn't sleep up here."

Cistine shut her tired eyes. "Am I really so predictable?"

"To me, yes. I know heights terrify you."

"They certainly aren't my favorite place." Cistine turned her head, peering at Ashe in the dimness. "How's your leg?"

"Stiff. It's going to need a good, long rest after this little adventure."

"I'm sorry for dragging you along."

"You didn't drag me. I chose to come, because my place is at your side—even when you go rushing off unprepared into enemy kingdoms."

Ashe tipped her head against Cistine's. "And for whatever it's worth...as angry and hurt as Julian is, he knows it's where he belongs, too."

"I wish he would talk to me. But I don't want to fight again."

"Give him time," Ashe said. "You're both so young, and you're still navigating the waters of courtship, in a foreign kingdom, with matters of life and death hanging over your heads. You'll survive this, Cistine. You just need time to breathe."

Cistine nodded, accepting her Warden's wisdom as a balm on her throbbing heart. Together they watched the stars stow away, one by one, to usher in the dawn.

CHAPTER THIRTY-TWO

THE SUN HAD crested the gorge, scattering late-morning rainbows through the spray of mist that almost touched the path itself, when Quill called for a halt again. While everyone quenched their thirst and gathered their breath, Quill caught up to Cistine, walking just behind Thorne in the lead.

"This is where we part ways," Quill said. "Hold out your arm."

Cistine obeyed, her pulse speeding up as Quill clicked his tongue. Faer floated from Quill's shoulder to Cistine's leather vambrace, and Quill stroked a hand from the back of the raven's head to the base of his tail feathers.

"You listen here," Quill said sternly. "No name-calling. No teasing. You heed Cistine like it was me talking to you. And when she sends you, you come straight back. Understood?"

Faer cocked his head, beady eyes gleaming.

Quill turned his attention back to Cistine. "Remember all the whistles I taught you. How to call him back, how to send him to me."

Cistine nodded. "I remember."

Quill took her shoulder and turned her to face up the path. "About a hundred yards ahead, there's a niche in the rock behind some brush. You and your friends can fit into it easily. As soon as the carts roll past, send Faer."

Cistine swallowed, her breath lodging around a lump in her throat. "Ashe, Julian, it's time."

When they both nodded, Cistine hurried up the trail, pausing beside Thorne. Together they gazed up the perilous road where the carts would appear.

"Are you going to kill them?" Cistine asked.

"No," Thorne said. "Surgeons are servants of Valgard. They do as they're told."

"And the Vassora?"

Thorne glanced down, and Cistine looked up into his icy blue eyes. The answer was already there, calm, needing no voice.

But Cistine remembered how he hated this.

"Make sure you're the ones who survive that fight," she said.

And with Faer perched on her shoulder, his talons pricking her armor, Cistine walked up the path, away from the cabal—into her own mission.

The niche in the rock face was precisely where Quill said it would be. Cistine wondered how he'd known that, and known they would all fit comfortably in it, as she crouched inside the cleft and watched the trail.

They were masked behind a stunted shrub, its tangle of hardy branches covering the jagged lee. Outside, the river raged, and sunlight beat relentlessly on the path. They'd taken shelter for nearly two hours, and Cistine's thighs were cramping. Ashe and Julian crouched silent as corpses beside her, and Faer had gone to sleep on a branch with his head under his wing.

Nervous energy blazed in Cistine's body, rattling her focus. She found herself constantly grazing Nail's handle, assuring herself it was still there.

"It's so hot." Ashe wiped her brow. "Maybe the cabal all went into the river for a swim and left us to work."

Cistine dug her elbow into her Warden's ribs, but the thought still made her smile. "Who do you think would be the first to suggest swimming without any clothes on: Quill or Tati?"

"Maleck." Ashe shrugged when Cistine revolved to stare at her. "It's the quiet ones you have to watch out for."

"You're being ridiculous," Julian muttered.

Cistine opened her mouth to retort, but Ashe shifted suddenly, laying a hand on her arm. "Do you hear that?"

Cistine pressed her right hand to the cleft's chilly wall and rocked forward on the balls of her feet. After several seconds, she did hear it, above the humming rapids, across the narrow path and down the gorge's pouting lip: the creak of wagon axles, the trundle of wheels, slow and deliberate, through the ruts, and the clop of horse hooves on dirt and stone.

"Wagons," Julian said.

They receded deeper into the lee, and Cistine coaxed Faer off the branch and onto her wrist. Shadows fell across the path, blocking their view as the carts labored by: three in a line, each pulled by a team of four horses, swaying heavily with Vassora and surgeons bound for Stornhaz.

Cistine stroked Faer's plumage with shaking fingers, watching the final wagon pull past. Then she whistled softly and tossed Faer from her arm.

The raven took flight, squeezing out above the bush and dipping below the cliff's edge. Cistine sat back on her heels, feeling a strange stab of disappointment. "That's it. Now we wait."

"Again," Ashe muttered.

Cistine tapped her fingers on the rock, leaning her head back and shutting her eyes. With her role in the mission completed, the exhaustion of a sleepless night crept over the corners of her mind, coaxing her almost into a doze.

Then Julian sat up sharply, jostling Cistine's arm. "What was that?"

Cistine pried her eyes open and saw how pale he was, his dark hair a slash against his bloodless brow. He braced his hand on the stone, staring past Cistine. Ashe tensed as well, rocking forward on her knees. "That sounds like another wagon. Are they coming back?"

Cistine scrambled to the cleft, bracing her hands on the walls and peering up the winding trail.

There was not one wagon coming—there were several, descending from the upper path. The first three in the line were riddled with arrows, but the carts behind them were unharmed—as if the archers had spent their quivers too quickly, because they hadn't expected these wagons to appear.

"This is the real trap," Cistine hissed.

"They sent more carts," Ashe said. "A fleet to crush Thorne's cabal."

Thorne.

Cistine grabbed Julian and Ashe by their sleeves, heaved them from the hollow, and ran down the trail, fighting the tug of their descent with skidding feet. Her toes jammed into the front of her boots, and when she stumbled, Julian caught her elbow. His face was grimly set, all traces of grudging dislike gone. Whatever he thought of Thorne and his cabal, this would be a slaughter—the same kind they'd feared for Talheim.

They couldn't stand by while it happened.

When they rounded the curve in the trail to reach the ambush point, Thorne already had the Vassoran leader down on his knees, his twin blades pressed to the man's throat. His voice carried thinly above the roaring river below: "*Tell us where the flagons are!*"

Cistine caught herself on the branch of a jutting mountain shrub, slamming to a halt, her feet crying for relief. She screamed for Thorne, and his eyes shot to her above the man's head. The cabal, holding the other Vassora at bay with their blades, tensed but didn't turn.

"This is the trap!" Cistine cried. "There are more wagons coming down the pass!"

The Vassoran leader lunged suddenly to his feet. A blade dropped from his sleeve, raking Thorne's wrist, and then the fighting broke out—turning the trail all at once into a bloodbath.

Cistine recoiled as Thorne decapitated his attacker and turned immediately to guard Ariadne's back. Faer took flight from the clefts, swooping and screeching as six Vassoran guards leaped at Quill all at once, and Tatiana ran to his defense. Ashe drew Echelon and stumbled down the trail, sweeping in at Maleck's side and knocking out the legs of a guard who charged him from behind. Maleck pushed Ashe's head down beneath a second blade.

Panic choked Cistine when Julian drew his sword as well. She grabbed his hand. "Don't."

Julian looked from their entwined hands to her eyes. His mouth softened, but steel flashed in his gaze. "Stay here. Keep out of this."

He kissed her brow, and then he was gone—sprinting into the fray.

Cistine's legs gave out. She dropped to her knees as the cabal battled across the pass. Death-gods, every one of them, and her friends fit perfectly at their sides. Maleck matched the hitch in Ashe's stride as they plowed into the Vassoran ranks, and though Julian fought alone, Thorne watched over him. He plucked enemies away from Julian's back three times in as many minutes.

And then, with a great cry, twenty archers charged up from the southern pass, laying into the flanks, forcing the Vassora to cluster, and the cabal whirled through them like a single, vicious blade.

How many battles had they fought together this way? How many enemies had they destroyed—here, and on the Vingete Vey—like this? They could handle these guards. They'd prepared for it.

But the other wagons would come around the trail any minute. And if the archers from the upper pass hadn't come down to warn the cabal, it could mean only one thing: they were all dead. Killed by whoever was in those other carts.

Cistine stared at the three wagons below. The surgeons huddled together in one, weeping as the battle rocked across the path outside. Their sobs echoed with the same terror Cistine had felt when she'd watched Maleck and Quill cleave through Rolf's entourage.

And now they were fighting again, and she *wanted* them to win.

Because they were her friends. Savage, brutal, incomprehensible. But they had trained her and saved her life. They'd helped Ashe walk again.

They were her friends, and they were about to be slaughtered.

Cistine's gaze lit on an archer's body, cut down by the Vassora only a few meters ahead of her, between the carts and the cliffside. She bit her fist, whispered a prayer, and charged from hiding.

She ran faster than she ever had in her life, conquering the meters in a few long bounds and sliding to her knees beside the archer. With shaking fingers, she unbuckled his quiver and plucked his bow from his hand; and as she slipped the quiver's strap around her own chest and cinched it tight, some of the fear tumbled from her body.

She could feel her mother's hands on her shoulders. Queen Solene's voice whispered reminders in her ear—things Solene's own mother had taught her, and her mother's mother before her. A skill passed down through the women of Solene's family for generations, from the time they'd been huntresses on Talheim's plains, all the way down their lineage to the Middle Kingdom's princess, on this pass, with this bow in her hands.

Cistine drew one of the arrows and thumbed the shaft; resin-dipped. Perfect. She wouldn't have to be close to the fighting to make this work.

Not if she had fire.

Sunlight licked the edge of steel, jerking Cistine from her reverie, and she toppled backward as a Vassoran guard rounded the cart and charged her.

Before she could even touch the quiver, a black shape dropped from the sky, slamming into the guard's face. He screamed as blood poured from his eyesocket. Faer flapped back, circled, and plunged again. This time, his assault sent the guard reeling off the path into the Muunvat River.

Cistine stared up as the raven perched on the cart's edge, ruffled his feathers, and called out to her. If he was as clever as he seemed, then maybe he was all the help she needed.

"Faer, listen to me," Cistine said, "I need some way to start a fire!"

Faer tipped his head. Then he took wing again.

Cistine turned and tore up the trail. A throb of movement pulsed in the small rocks under her feet, but she wasn't certain if that came from the battle or the advancing carts. She ran with all her might, feeling how her muscles gloried in the familiar motion, eating up the path like a sprint around Hellidom.

Faer bawled as he swooped on her left. He carried a sharp flintstone and a wedge of steel in his talons, the same kind Tatiana used to start fires in the camp.

"Good, Faer!" Cistine put out her hand. "Give it to me!"

The raven dropped the tools, and Cistine lunged to catch them before they bounced off the trail. She checked her stride, looking back over her shoulder; she'd put a healthy distance between herself and the fighting.

When she looked ahead again, she saw the carts and the Vassora in them—clusters of men who'd rolled up the wagon sidings. Cistine had a clear view of their vast numbers and the tall wooden crates in the footwells between the seats.

Perfect.

She raked the flintstone against the steel, creating a shower of sparks that caught a dry shrub alight. Slipping the stone and steel into her pocket, Cistine drew the bow from over her shoulder and notched an arrow. She plunged the resined shaft into the fire until the sturdy wood caught aflame. Then she turned, sighted on the wagons, and let the arrow fly.

But her arm wasn't used to the weight of the string anymore, and the arrow arced wide, soaring into the gorge. Guards shouted when they spotted her. Cursing, shaking even worse, Cistine notched and lit a second arrow; and as she did, she felt the strength again, as if her mother propped her elbows up. The Queen's gentle voice whispered in her ear. Whispered her name—

No. Shouted it.

Someone *was* shouting her name.

Cistine glanced over her shoulder just as she loosed the second arrow, hearing it skim the nearest wagon and clatter away. She drew the third the same instant she made out the shape charging toward her.

Thorne. With one sword gone and the other in his hand, he sprinted up the trail. "*Cistine!*"

She didn't need him to rescue her. She didn't need him to face this band of Vassora alone, with only one blade, for her sake.

She could do this—and she would.

She notched and lit the third arrow, turning back to the carts. They had reached the trail's narrowest part, where the horses had to slow. Exactly where Cistine wanted them to be.

"Cistine, stand down!" Thorne bellowed. "The flagons are in those carts!"

She let the arrow fly.

It slammed into the nearest wagon bed. A guard danced backward from the flames, reeled, and fell into the footwell. Something shattered under his weight with a sound like fracturing glass.

Thorne's hand caught Cistine's shoulder. He spun her toward the mountain face with her stomach pressed to the chilly stone and planted his hands on the rock on either side of her, leaning the hard, muscular planes of his chest against her back—shielding her with his body.

And the first cart exploded.

Cistine had never felt such tremendous heat, or seen such a bright light, or heard such a loud, concussive blast—as if every symphony in the three kingdoms clashed all at once. Fire roared through the gorge, and a furious *crack* rent the air like a lightning strike on the trail above them, shaking the mountain to its foundation. When that fiery blast took the second cart, it threw shrapnel down the trail—cart posts and metal and gore as the horses and Vassora blew apart. Thorne's hand slid around Cistine's middle, hitching her against him so no inch of her body was outside his protection, and he snarled in her ear as something struck his back, flinging them both flush to the mountainside.

When the third explosion sounded off, the narrow trail buckled out from under their feet.

Cistine screamed as the ground vanished. Her stomach soared into her throat, and she and Thorne pitched backward as the ledge crumbled to pieces beneath them. The mountain was ripped up into the sky above—

No.

They were falling. Falling together, with Thorne's arms still around her, and the fragmented carts raining like a starshower on every side. Straight into the Muunvat River.

Cistine screamed again—a prayer. A plea to the gods to save them.

And they slammed into the water.

CHAPTER THIRTY-THREE

THE TIDE RUSHED—a gentle, steady, in-and-out sound, breathing as it surrounded Cistine, filling her senses with the echo of water in motion, a churning, unstoppable force.

The river.

Cistine's eyes flipped wide, and she gasped—then retched. The taste of fish waste and silt and soaked, rotten vegetation clogged her mouth. She rolled onto her side and heaved into the rushes and cattails growing along the riverbank.

She was out of the water. Only her legs still dangled in a shallow, lazy whirlpool, where an overturned tree and several sharp stones gathered the river in their gentle embrace. Thick, white foam surged along the log, and just beyond that, the Muunvat stormed by.

Cistine remembered nothing after the fall but the impact against the water snapping her head back, knocking her unconscious in a split second. She rolled onto her belly again, the base of her skull throbbing, her limbs weak and limp as she scouted the underbrush. There wasn't much of it between her and the gorge's stone walls, which overshadowed the bank, the river itself—and the sodden figure draped among the reeds, submerged to his chest in the water. Even as Cistine watched, he slipped farther away, his chin bobbing under the current.

"Thorne." Cistine crawled toward him. He didn't stir when she laid a hand on his silver hair, or when she gripped the back of his armor and hauled at his enormous, muscular weight, digging her heels into the silt as she fought to free him from the sucking mud.

When that effort proved useless, Cistine wrapped her hands under his arms instead. With better leverage, she slid them both from the mire and further up the bank to the sunbaked dirt. Laying Thorne out on his back, she pressed her ear to his chest.

"Don't be dead, please, please," she chanted—and yelped with relief when she heard the labored rush of his lungs and the thud of his heart. "Thank *God.*"

A cool wind swept through the gorge, and Cistine shivered as she straightened. She was grateful it was still summer. They wouldn't freeze to death, but it was going to be a long, uncomfortable night while they waited for their clothes to dry. Dusk encroached the gorge, and there was no way of knowing where they were without the sun—or how far the Muunvat had carried them.

All she did know was they hadn't washed ashore by chance. Somehow, Thorne had dragged them both out. He'd saved them from her reckless mistake.

Teeth chattering, Cistine pocketed her hands, wincing when her fingers brushed something hard and damp.

The flintstone and steel had survived the fall.

Hysterical, sobbing chuckles escaped Cistine as she dragged herself upright and stomped to the nearest tree. She broke off a small branch, quartered it the way Tatiana had showed her, and gathered several handfuls of dry pine needles. She built a small fire, and by its light, turned Thorne onto his stomach to observe his wounds.

The shrapnel from the carts hadn't pierced his armor—a testament to the durability of those reinforced threads. But when Cistine removed the chest-piece, shoulderplates, and vambraces and undid the armor's clasps, rolling his shirt up along his back, she caught her breath.

Whatever had slammed into him on that path, it had painted a grisly milieu for his scars. Those old craters swam in a sea of vivid bruising. The contusions beneath his skin were forked branches of red-and-pink lightning traveling from between his shoulders to just above his hips. She couldn't imagine how sore he would be when he woke...or how much worse the wounds had been made when he'd hit the water, still shielding her.

If that debris had struck her finer training armor instead—if she'd been in the way of that blast rather than under his protection—she would be dead.

Sourness filled Cistine's mouth, and tears budded in her eyes. She carefully rolled Thorne's shirt down and scooted away to sit across the fire. Pulling her knees to her chest and sheltering her face against them, she gripped her ankles and waited for the nausea to ebb.

She hadn't meant for the carts to explode, only to catch fire. She'd come so close to losing her life, and she hadn't even realized the gamble in the moment. Now that knowledge felt like a hand holding her head under the river; she could barely breathe with the weight of shame and panic as she relived that terrifying plummet over and over in her mind.

When the fire banked at last, she heard a low, heavy groan, the cracked sound of her name on abused lips.

Cistine picked up her head, wiping her eyes on her wet sleeve as Thorne rolled to face her. His gaze flashed with pain at the sharp movement, his attention alighting on her like a brand.

"Are you hurt?" he rasped.

She shook her head. "Not badly. Thanks to you."

Thorne's damp hair straggled water down the side of his cheek and neck, his eyes blazing with some unfathomable emotion. "You pulled me from the river."

"Of course I did. How do you feel?"

"Unpleasant." Thorne wrapped an arm under his body and touched his tender side and back. His face twisted in a scowl. "And you?"

"Better than I should. I wasn't the one who struck the water first."

"But you were the one it knocked unconscious." He sat up slowly, sliding both hands to the small of his back this time and arching with a low moan.

"And you were unconscious when I found you."

"Swimming half a mile against a raging current is no easy feat, especially while towing someone else's weight."

Cistine sank her chin back to her knees. "I'm sorry."

She didn't know which thing she was most sorry for: the harm she'd unknowingly caused, or the mistake she'd made.

"Apology accepted." Thorne's reply covered every possibility. "Have you slept?"

"Does being unconscious count?" Cistine joked weakly.

Thorne shook his head. "Sleep. Your body needs rest to heal."

"So does yours."

"It needs less," Thorne said. "And I've been sleeping for several hours."

"I thought unconsciousness didn't count."

"I wasn't unconscious. I was dreaming. Now lie down."

Now that Thorne was awake and moving, Cistine gave up the struggle against her exhaustion, the weight of emotion and the day's chaos. It all swarmed her at once when she curled up beside the fire, fighting a few lingering shivers in the cold canyon breeze, dragging out the only question that mattered now: "Are we going to die here?"

Thorne held his silence, and Cistine was glad he didn't reassure her with empty promises. He pondered the question instead.

"The wounds we can see are nominal," he said. "If either of us is hemorrhaging, we'll know by morning. But assuming we aren't, and that we can avoid succumbing to the elements, our chances are better than fair."

Cistine shut her eyes and blew out a long, steady breath through her parted lips. "Thank you, Thorne. For saving my life—twice."

"You rushed into battle to save my cabal." His quiet voice was the perfect harmony to the gurgling river. "You fell for them. I could never let you fall alone after that."

And as guilty as she felt for putting them in danger, it was gratitude that brought back the tears to her eyes.

She was glad he hadn't let her go. And she was glad that, if she was doomed to be stranded on foot, downstream from anything familiar in the Valgardan wilds, then at least she was stranded with Thorne. In this wilderness, his presence felt like the safest place she could be.

∽⌒∽

Cistine slept hard and deep, and woke to a cool wash of daylight through the river mist, the fire's dead fumes tickling her nose. She sat up, brushing gravel from her cheek and tugging the rat's nest of her tangled, filthy hair.

All of this was enough to confirm that the destroyed path, and their fall into the river, hadn't been just another nightmare.

She spotted Thorne at once: crouched on the whirlpool's edge as he bathed dried silt from his skin. He'd removed his armor and the dark shirt beneath, and the bruises were even worse by daylight than firelight. Cistine pressed a hand to her throat at the sight of them.

"Poultices," she said, and Thorne raked his head around to look at her. "There are poultices that can help distribute the blood from those bruises."

"You know them?"

"Ashe has been teaching me ever since Tatiana came back. I can keep an eye out for herbs while we walk. I assume we'll be walking?"

Thorne nodded, straightening and tugging on his shirt, then buckling his armor back into place. Without his wounds visible, he almost seemed unscathed. But Cistine had watched him move through the Den, through Hellidom, enough to know there was a hitch in his stride as he kicked apart the fire's bones. "Are you ready to move?"

"Move where? Do you even know where we are?"

"The Muunvat travels through the Izten Torkat for many miles before it spills into the Agerios," Thorne explained. "Judging by the height of these cliffs, we're still three days' walk from where they end. If we circle around there, we'll have only a few small foothills to cross. Within five days, we could reach Starhollow. I have no doubt Quill will have taken the others there. He's already been pestering me to visit for weeks."

Cistine remembered the note Faer had brought Quill the day Tatiana left Hellidom. If this Starhollow was the place he'd been so eager to go that day, he would certainly wait for them there. "Well, if that's where we need to go, then I'll find a way to make it there. Even if my feet hate me by the end of it."

Thorne offered his hand, and Cistine let him draw her upright. He turned her to face along the gorge—south, Cistine assumed. He led her confidently in that direction, his stride sure despite a subtle limp.

"You seem so comfortable in this slice of Valgard," Cistine remarked.

"These lands are part of Blaykrone. I know them better than my own name."

And somehow, it was that—seeing his face, and hearing his voice when he said the name this time—that made Cistine understand. "Blaykrone was your territory when you were High Tribune."

Thorne nodded. "When I abandoned my position in the Court, I had to make them believe I hated my territory and everyone in it. But I've made certain the people know I would leave everything behind to help them if trouble arose."

"Is that the mask you told Ariadne you wear?" Cistine asked. "You let everyone else in Valgard believe you're a bloodthirsty scoundrel so you can protect the people you care about?"

Thorne grimaced as they clambered over a mound of fossilized wood. "That wasn't intended for your ears."

"But is it true?"

Thorne sighed. "I'll trade you a question for a question while we walk. Fair?"

Cistine considered the offer. "On one condition: you can't ask me any of Talheim's secrets."

"I have no interest in them." If Cistine's surprise showed on her face, Thorne made no mention of it. "To answer your first question, I let people believe I'm a vicious *bandayo* because it's easier to create a reputation than to control one."

"How do you mean?"

Thorne stayed silent—either pondering her question or stymieing his pain. "When a High Tribune leaves Stornhaz in disgrace with lashes on his back, there's bound to be talk. For a brief moment, I controlled what was said about me. I chose to take advantage of that."

"And you chose to make yourself wicked."

"To them, I already was. And it's better they see me that way. The less they believe I have to lose, the less they can take from me."

Shivers cavorted along Cistine's spine. He spoke so quietly, but with so much anger, about these faceless people he was fighting in Stornhaz, with their surgeons and imported wagons full of *Svarkyst* steel. "Who are you fighting, Thorne?"

"It's my turn to ask a question." He brushed aside a curtain of creeping moss, waiting for Cistine to step through. "You didn't tell me you could shoot."

In his usual style, it wasn't a question—more of an invitation for honesty. "I don't like to. But I'm fairly competent."

"Who taught you?"

"My mother."

"Why the bow, and not the sword?"

"That's two questions," Cistine remarked. Thorne's brow sketched upward. "But, all right, I'll allow it. Swordplay was too...active. It required too much effort to prepare every day. Archery was something I could do in a dress and bracers."

Even as the words slid from her mouth, she wanted to swallow them back. How shallow and bothered she sounded—too lazy to be inconvenienced, while people like Thorne and his cabal had no choice but to pick up their weapons or die on their knees.

"Anyway," she murmured, "the first time I told my father I didn't want to train, he never forced me to lift a sword again. But Mama wouldn't take no for an answer. She dragged me kicking and screaming by my skirts to the archery range every other day."

"A woman of sheer determination. Much like her daughter."

Cistine smiled grudgingly. He was doing an excellent job of wheedling more truth from her by asking questions that weren't really questions. "All the women in her family are trained with a bow. It's an ancient tradition I continued."

"And that was your choice."

"My reluctant, complaining, arguing choice," Cistine laughed, wiping her nose on her sleeve. "It's my turn. Are you going to tell me who you're fighting?"

"I've already told you," Thorne said. "Injustice."

It was barely an answer, but that was clearly a closed subject. So Cistine settled for the second most-burning question on her mind: "Before we...before we fell, you told me not to shoot the carts because the flagons were inside. What is a flagon?"

Thorne's stride hitched—barely a misstep, and she couldn't be certain if it was because of his injuries, or because she'd mentioned the flagons. "Your father never told you?"

"Should he have?"

Thorne said nothing for almost a quarter mile as they picked their way over small, shallow streams that trickled from the cliffs to their left and poured into the Muunvat River on their right. They crossed dense pockets of undergrowth, each step puffing insects up from the dirt in quiet, fizzing spirals. Cistine brushed her hands over the waist-high reeds, concentrating on scouring the undergrowth for herbs rather than watching Thorne as he moved ahead of her.

"Flagons are weapons," Thorne said at last. "Volatile ones. That was the trap: not that the Vassora were there, but that they moved in a divided formation with the flagons coming in behind. Once we captured the weaker carts, the stronger ones were free to move down the trail unimpeded."

"Not entirely unimpeded." Cistine could still see the arrows freckling the cart, telling the story of a bloody battle at the trailhead. "Do you suppose the merch in Hellidom knew what the trap really was?"

"If he did, Baba Kallah will have dealt with him already."

Cistine tried to mimic his cool, questing style—asking a question without really asking it. "And she's...capable of that. Because she's part of your cabal."

"I wouldn't have left her in charge of Hellidom if I didn't trust she could handle *all* its affairs."

And of course he trusted her: the grandmother who'd helped raise him—the only one who'd showed him genuine love as a child. He had broken impossible bonds for her, had left his life behind when someone attacked her. Entrusting everything he cared about in her hands must've been a simple choice.

Cistine wondered if she would ever trust anyone that much. The closest she could think of was Ashe, but not even she understood why Cistine was training.

"I take it by your silence it's my turn again," Thorne said. "What are your favorite books—and why do you love them?"

He could have asked no better question to pass the time. Cistine had three books, always close to her heart, that she chattered about while she and Thorne picked their way along the shore. Cistine plucked herbs and leaves from the underbrush whenever their blooms struck her as familiar; when hunger pangs took hold, they foraged for berries and fruit trees, and ate as they walked. The shade kept them cool, and while Cistine's limbs were still sore from the plunge into the Muunvat, talking kept her mind off the hurts.

For his part, Thorne truly listened, and asked questions about the story plots as she unraveled them. It wasn't until they stopped to make camp at sundown that Cistine wondered if he'd kept her talking so he could save his energy. He was pale and weary when he sank down and put out his hand for her flintrock; they built a fire, and for the first time in hours, everything was quiet.

The silence made Cistine self-conscious of how much she'd talked that afternoon. "I'm sorry for rambling in your ear all day."

"Don't apologize," Thorne said. "I asked."

Cistine picked up a handful of brown pine needles and sprinkled them gently over the fire. "It's only fair if you tell me some of your favorite stories now that you know the intimate details of mine."

Thorne cocked his knees and pressed a hand to his back, leaning against a fallen tree. The small fire grew between them, and he stared into it. "I haven't taken the time to read anything but reports or maps in...stars only know how long."

Cistine frowned. "That's everything I've been afraid of about becoming a queen. A life without time for books sounds so dull."

Thorne eased his breath out in small increments. "Have you ever noticed what your three favorite epics have in common, Cistine? Adventure. A hero with something to conquer."

Leave it to Thorne to notice such things. "That's true."

"Wouldn't you rather live an adventure than read about someone else's?"

"That depends. Are these the kinds of adventures where I plummet from cliffs?"

Thorne's cheek dimpled with a crooked smile. "Possibly. But in your epics, does the heroine ever die from those things?"

Cistine chucked the pine needles at him this time, laughing. "This isn't a story, Thorne! It's our lives."

"Precisely. And life is meant to be lived. Books and storytelling have their place, but don't forget to look up at the world around you every once in a while, Cistine. You may miss something extraordinary in this life while you're buried in someone else's."

Cistine folded her legs as Thorne tilted his head back, fingers still splayed against the small of his back. "You didn't answer my question about *your* favorite books."

"I only remember one," Thorne said. "A collection of truncated Valgardan epics Baba Kallah read to me when I was a child. I used to revisit it even when I was supposed to be doing my schoolwork."

"It must've made quite the impression on you."

Thorne's lips twitched upward as his eyes fell shut. "That was where I found the name for my Court."

Cistine remembered Maleck mentioning the subject—and how he'd avoided elaborating on it. Perhaps more intentionally than she'd credited him for. "What do you mean, *your* Court?"

Thorne's boots slid against the leaves as he stretched his legs out around the fire. His feet nearly touched her knees. "Sillakove. That's what the cabal calls itself behind closed doors. Sillakove Court, unbound by the constellations. We rise in every season. Our crown is Kiralay, the king of all stars."

A shiver of excitement wormed down Cistine's back. "Sillakove. That must be Old Valgardan. What does it mean?"

"Starchaser." Thorne's voice shook slightly, and his eyes fixed on her, the piercing blue dulled some by the pain he'd kept from her by distracting them both. Cistine couldn't look away.

The silence was broken only when her stomach gurgled, and they both blinked, sitting back.

"I just remembered the herbs," Cistine said. "I'm going to make a poultice."

"Take your time." Thorne let his head fall back again. "I'm not going anywhere."

That was what concerned Cistine, but she didn't tell him so before she went to the shore. She turned out her pockets, surveying the herbs she'd managed to collect as they walked, and she began to plan.

It was after dark when she finally followed the firelight back to Thorne's side. Worry stabbed her when she realized he hadn't moved at all— his head still draped back on the fallen tree, hand bracing his back. She knelt beside him and shook his shoulder, and he grumbled, "I'm awake."

"I have the poultice."

"You're going to have to apply it yourself," Thorne groaned. "I can't."

She grimaced. "Bend over, then."

Slowly, Thorne tipped forward, stretching his arms between his cocked knees. Cistine removed his armor and tugged up his shirt, biting her lip as she once again beheld his back. The color had worsened to a dark, angry scarlet-purple all over. The bruising nearly erased the scars completely.

Thorne flinched as she applied the herbal pack to his skin. "Great *stars*, that's cold!"

"Well, we don't have any ice, and mud is the next best thing I could think of. Now hold still."

Thorne grunted a rapid stream of profanity which Cistine chose to ignore as she slathered the poultice over his back. She tried not to dwell on the fact that she was touching him—that her hands were all over this man who had been a stranger less than a month ago, or that her fingers were encountering his scars, over and over again, when she'd been so reluctant to even imagine their texture before he'd left Hellidom.

She concentrated on the task, and nothing more. When the bruising was covered under a mud mask, Cistine tugged down Thorne's tight shirt. "Lie down on your side."

Thorne stretched out, pillowing his head on the bend of his arm. "Tell me more about the books you've read in Talheim."

"No." Cistine folded her arms on her belly as she rocked back against the log. "No more books. You need to sleep. *I'll* keep watch tonight."

Thorne's eyes were already shut. "Wake me if anything stirs."

Cistine hummed noncommittally, but if Thorne realized she hadn't really affirmed, he didn't mind. In minutes, he sank into the same deep-breathing slumber as the day she'd found him slumped at the kitchen table in the Den.

Alone for the first time that day, Cistine studied her fingers—mud-caked and smelling strongly of fish and herbs—and let herself remember the feeling of Thorne's scars. Those small, chiseled craters where he'd been whipped for defiance. The blows he'd taken for withstanding injustice. Now he wore bruises like a cloak above those scars, for *her*.

Fierce determination arced through Cistine like the sizzling trail of a shooting star. She would sit watch as many times as she had to, carry on forever if she must, and she would walk out of this gorge beside Thorne. They would survive this together, just like they'd fallen together. He was going to make it back to his people...to his cabal. *His* Court.

She would make as many mud-packs and take as many night watches as needed to guarantee that.

CHAPTER
THIRTY-FOUR

THORNE WOKE SLOWLY the next day, and Cistine left just as he began to stir. She was determined to make another poultice and slap it onto his wounds before he was awake enough to protest from pure machismo.

At the riverside, after she towed up handfuls of mud for the pack, Cistine tried to finger-comb the tangles from her hair. She hadn't bathed in days, and she knew it showed: shavings of river scum and sweat tack flaked off under her fingernails as she scratched her scalp. She was afraid to lean too far over the river, to catch even a distorted glimpse of herself. She did her best to feel through the snarls in her hair as she stared absentmindedly across the Muunvat, reflecting on everything Thorne had told her the day before.

Sillakove. His reputation. They were in *his* territory, yet few knew it was still under his protection. Tatiana had told Cistine some people would wait an entire star-cycle to appeal to their favorite Tribune with special requests, or to ask for favors.

She wondered if Thorne had been a Tribune worth waiting for.

She picked at the ends of her hair, gazing at the opposite wall of the gorge. It was barely visible through the early-morning mist, the shadows of its stunted growth on shallow shores frolicking along the dark brown stone in a mesmerizing twist.

A hand closed around her mouth from behind, another around her shoulder, pushing her sharply toward the water. Thorne's voice warmed her ear: "Do not make a sound."

Cistine froze. His voice was as cold as the mud under her clothes as he pressed her into it, his arm circling her back and holding her down. When she stopped struggling, Thorne gave a chin nod across the river.

Though she'd already been staring that way—however absentmindedly—it took Cistine a moment to realize the thin shivers of shadows on the rock didn't only belong to the trees bowing in the gorge's perpetual breeze.

There were men prowling the opposite bank.

Cistine stiffened, and Thorne's hand tightened on her shoulder, bringing her closer into the shelter of his broad frame. His eyes were fixed across the river's treacherous rapids, watching as these armored men parted the foliage with their swords, searching for something.

Thorne released Cistine and crooked a finger. He crawled on his belly back into the brush, and Cistine wriggled from the mud after him, leaving all hope for cold poultices behind. She waited for Thorne to get to his feet before she dared climb to hers. When she did, she was shaking. "Who was that?"

"The Vassora," Thorne growled. "They must've found a safe way down from the pass."

"The cabal?"

"They're not dead." Cistine wondered if he said it so firmly to convince himself. "This band must have come from further up the pass, after the others moved on."

"Are they looking for us?"

"Most likely. But there's nowhere to cross this part of the river. The nearest land bridge is miles south. With any luck, they'll give up the hunt before they make it that far."

Cistine studied his face—eyes still dimmed with sleep, cheeks sprouting a strangely dark stubble that clashed with his colorless hair. "But knowing *our* luck, the danger is still there."

Thorne rubbed the back of his shoulder as he looked toward the Muunvat. "My head would be a fair prize in Stornhaz. If they're desperate enough, they might cross rivers for me."

Cistine tossed up a silent prayer and brushed past him. "Then let's make sure we're no longer near any rivers when they decide they're that desperate."

It was an unpleasant start to the day that Cistine couldn't shake from her thudding heart or quivering hands as they traveled south. The foliage that had seemed so beautiful the day before, so fertile and welcoming with its offerings of herbs and berries, had sprouted eyes. She could feel herself being watched, as if the Vassora were directly behind them while they slowly trekked along the Muunvat's lazy turns through the canyon.

Finally, she couldn't stand the quiet—from herself, or from Thorne. She hopped up on an ancient, rotten tree, gripping the sapling branches beside it as she turned to look down at him. "Why is your hair white?"

Thorne's eyes widened—as if, of all the questions she could've asked to jolt life back into yesterday's game, this was the last one he'd expected. Cistine's lips twitched despite her bad mood as she dropped down on the other side of the log.

"I'm waiting," she added. "Impatiently."

Thorne reciprocated that small smile and slid over the tree. He placed a hand to his side when he straightened, stiff as a Citadel elder who could only make it to the glass courtyard to warm his skin every afternoon. Those people were Cistine's favorite gossips—before today.

"Augmentation left scars. Some are unseen: Maleck's hollowness, like a withdrawal that's never ended. And then some..." Thorne trailed a hand through his hair. "Some scars are visible."

Cistine stared at the gentle feathers of his hair laying against his neck. In the sunlight that curled lazily through the trees, the ends glimmered like freshly-mined ore. "Augmentation did this?"

Thorne nodded, raking his hair back again, and if it had been anyone else Cistine would've thought the motion was self-conscious. "When I was a boy, there was some punishment...stars, I don't even remember what it was for. I did something, and this was my father's retribution."

"Was it a burn?"

"A shock of some kind. Baba Kallah thinks it blanched the hair follicles. It's never grown back its natural color."

This time, there was no mistaking the edge in his voice. It hovered somewhere between nervousness and anger, fighting against both.

And now Cistine knew High Tribune Thorne—the calm, collected leader of Hellidom, the warrior striving against injustice, raiding wagons on the Vey, fearlessly fighting in the mountains—was embarrassed about his hair.

"It was fuchsia, wasn't it?" she said, and Thorne stared at her in disbelief. "Your hair."

"No."

"Honeydew? Lapis-lazuli?"

"Neither!"

"Oh, Thorne, we both know you're too unique to have a hair color like anyone else's," Cistine teased. "Look at you...strutting around with a white crown, the envy of men three times your age."

Thorne pushed her head down, and Cistine laughed.

"It was black," Thorne growled playfully, "if you have to know."

Cistine rubbed her own tangled rat's nest, squinting up at him. The sunlight haloed his head, and she tried to imagine him looking like Julian: that wing of dark locks, and those captivating eyes.

"I can't see it," she admitted. "This look suits you."

Thorne dipped his head, saying nothing as he brushed through a hedge in their path. Cistine skirted wide around it, fidgeting her fingers against her thighs.

"Besides," she added, "it would be too dramatic. You, with your black hair, and your black armor, sulking around everywhere."

"I believe it's my turn to ask a question."

"Wait, I'm not finished." Cistine ignored his longsuffering sigh. "Quill's hair. It's white on top, too."

She knew she'd replicated his slippery way of asking a question that was not a question this time. Thorne peered ahead as they walked, his face stroked with sadness. "That was an accident. Maleck's doing. Before the war."

Cistine's feet snagged in the undergrowth so hard she nearly stumbled. "Maleck? *Why?* I know they wrestle sometimes, but...but *that?*"

"Maleck was not in a good place at the time," Thorne murmured. "He and Aden were arguing. Quill got between them, and when Maleck swung..."

A chill tumbled through Cistine, setting the hairs on her arms tingling.

"If Maleck hadn't pulled his strike at the last instant, the augment in his hand would've killed Quill." Thorne rubbed the back of his neck. "Even from a glancing blow, the scar's never gone away."

Cistine expected to feel horror, but it was sympathy that swelled in her chest. "Maleck must feel so guilty."

"He didn't come back after that until the war was nearly over," Thorne admitted. "And he's been careful with Quill ever since. Maleck never starts fights with him. He swore he wouldn't raise his fists against Quill unless Quill asked him to...and he's kept his word."

Her mind riddled with notions of a younger Quill, augment-shocked and sobbing, falling away from the horror in Maleck's eyes, Cistine let the subject drop. "It's your turn to ask."

Thorne's question came swiftly, as if he'd been aching to ask it: "Why are you afraid to become queen?"

Cistine winced. "Ask a different question."

"The ones we're reluctant to answer are usually the ones we most need to face. Besides, I told you about my hair."

She scowled at him, but his face remained impassive—a stone wall. She wanted to claw the calm from his features, to show him just a morsel of the chaos his question had thrown her into.

"That throne is a prison," Cistine finally said. "I've known it ever since I was a little girl. It's all dresses and books and balls when you're a princess. But the moment the princess becomes the queen, she's shackled to that life. Endless processions. Everyone demanding your time. Your life is no longer your own."

"That's true," Thorne said. "It's about something larger than you. It's about your people's needs and how your position allows you to meet them."

Irritation raised her temper in a flash hotter than flame. "And this was why I didn't want to discuss it. I knew you would tell me I was selfish."

"I didn't say that. Not everyone has the temperament to sit on a seat of judgement. I would trust my life to less than half of Valgard's Chancellors."

"So it's my *temperament* you find flaw with?"

"When you're snarling at me."

"Well, forgive me if I'm furious when you imply I'm unqualified to rule!" Cistine snapped. "You don't know Talheimic law, or what *Talheim* needs."

"And you do?"

"I've read the books! The entire library, in fact."

"But have you sat with the people? Have you truly listened to *their* needs and not just what the books tell you?"

Cistine scowled, looking away from him. "When I have time."

But she'd rarely made time for anyone outside the Citadel. She knew the biddies and court gossips like her own mind, knew the things they craved; but the rest of Astoria, and the rest of Talheim, were in some ways as foreign to her as the Northern Kingdom.

"Books offer pure facts," Thorne said. "But a man can tell you much more about his family's needs when he has a broken leg and six hungry mouths to feed."

"Well, if you're such a paladin of greatness," Cistine muttered, "why are you leading a cabal of savages in hiding rather than a real Court of your own?"

It was a blow aimed too low, and Cistine knew it. But he'd made her feel furious and humiliated, and she ached to hit him back.

"I lead Sillakove from the shadows because the change I tried to effect in Stornhaz was far before its time," Thorne's tone was steady, unaffected by her jab. "Most of the Chancellors didn't want to listen. But for all my mistakes, I've learned that bringing about change requires you to step forward. To sit in that uncomfortable place...to be the leader the people need."

"And what if you know in your heart you're incapable of being that?"

The breeze lifted Thorne's hair as he looked down at her. "Then you pretend. You pretend you're in control, that you know exactly what you're doing. And usually, somewhere along the way, you realize you actually do."

"Is that how *you* lead?"

Thorne smiled. "You've followed me this far, haven't you?"

Cistine punched his arm. "You don't know where we're going?"

"I do now," Thorne chuckled, massaging his elbow. "Yesterday, I wasn't certain if we were north or south of Starhollow."

"But then you saw which way the Vassora came from?"

Thorne nodded, and the moment of humor evaporated. Silent, they foraged deeper into the trees—escaping the feeling of being watched.

Cistine couldn't think of another question to ask Thorne until they made camp that night. She was too focused on the journey, on finding more herbs, and on her sore feet and the hunger pains in her belly. She was relieved Thorne offered to hunt—and as famished as she was, watching him skin and cook the goose he'd trapped didn't make her feel sick this time. She was ravenous as she listened to the bubbling fat plop and sizzle on the cookfire stones.

"You've been quiet all afternoon." Thorne handed her a spit of meat, and Cistine tore into the breast, groaning with satisfaction. "Should I fear for my life the next time I sleep?"

"Maybe." Cistine wiped her mouth on her sleeve. "Actually, I've been thinking up another question."

"Ask it."

"You and Maleck have both mentioned how important names are in Valgard. Why is that?"

Thorne ate several bites of his own portion before he said, "Valgard's heritage remains mostly unchanged from how it was before there were

Courts, when we were still ruled by a king. Most able-bodied men and women train as warriors. Once they've sworn fealty to a Court, they learn its methods of warfare. They become capable of defending it from any onslaught."

Cistine's scalp prickled. "Everyone in Stornhaz is a warrior?"

"The majority are. The elites prefer gossip and good food, but most could easily peel the skin off your bones if you gave them a reason to."

"Noted," Cistine said. "But what about the names?"

Thorne finished his spit of meat, broke it down, and tossed it into the fire. "Every warrior, every elite, is born twice and dies twice. The First Birth and Death are the child's life. At the time of that First Death, the warrior enters the House of Visions with his Chancellor. He drinks from the Dreamwater Chalice, and the gods grant him a vision of his future. When he emerges on the other side, he's broken open. There's nothing left of him but his training. Like the Chalice, he's empty. The Chancellor fills this empty vessel with a Name—something that suits the warrior's life, his personal journey. That's the Second Birth, when he becomes a true warrior of Valgard."

"And the Second Death?"

Thorne dusted off his hands. "That's the day he arrives at the Sable Gates of Nimmus."

Gooseflesh raced down Cistine's arms and thighs. "What name does the Chancellor give them, exactly?"

"Every Name is different. And every one is a secret." The flames popped and danced in the reflection of Thorne's gaze. "It belongs to the warrior and those he trusts...those he chooses to share it with. Some share it with close friends. Some only share it with their *valenar* and *selvenar*. And some never tell anyone at all."

"Why not?"

"Because it carries weight. There's power in the Name...the power to command the warrior. Speaking the Name can draw them from mindless rage or dispatch them to kill in a heartbeat. It can even tempt a man to act against his better nature."

"How is that possible?"

"Something to do with the Dreamwater," Thorne said, "the way it affects the mind. When the Name is spoken, as the warrior reaches the end of all he is, it creates a mental bind. The Name is like a key to the innermost spirit."

Cistine chewed her next bite much slower, giving herself time to think. "The warrior has to trust their Chancellor absolutely, I imagine, to give them that much power."

Thorne nodded. "The Name-forge is an act of utmost allegiance. Because the Chancellor knows the Name of every warrior under his command, those warriors must place their faith in him not to abuse or endanger them."

"Do you think the Chancellors deserve that trust?"

"No."

Cistine winced, finished her goose, and broke down her own spit. "Did you Name the cabal?"

Thorne slowly nodded. "It was one of the last things we did together before we left Stornhaz."

"And who Named you?"

Thorne's eyes narrowed slightly. "Baba Kallah."

The scars on his back. Baba Kallah's broken leg. That hadn't just been the Chancellor's retribution for Thorne's rebellion when Salvotor dragged him before the Court: it had been punishment, because someone else had taken something that was rightfully his. Baba Kallah had forged a bond with Thorne that no one else ever could.

Cistine wondered if a single person in Talheim would ever trust her that much. She wasn't even certain they should.

"You should get some rest," Thorne said after a long bout of silence. "I'll keep watch tonight."

Cistine didn't protest this time. She was too tired, her head spinning too much to make an argument. She curled up with her back to him, and Thorne snuffed the fire. The moment darkness pressed against her eyelids, Cistine felt peace wash over her.

On the cusp of sleep, she heard Thorne speak—a last, quiet question: "Why did you shoot that cart? Even if the flagons hadn't burst, you were still drawing their fire. Why risk your life for us?"

Cistine had to reach deep into herself to find her drowsy voice: "Because you're my friends. What else could I do?"

Thorne said something else, but it grazed by Cistine. She'd already tumbled over the edge into slumber.

She dreamed that night that she was being led to the House of Visions, and in her mind, it was a great library. She thought it was her father taking her there, determined to give her a Name that would bind her to the throne of Talheim forever.

But when the Chalice was placed in her hands, it was Thorne whose fingers she touched. Thorne, his eyes limpid and playful, like they had been that morning when she teased him about his hair.

"Drink it," he urged. "Forge the bind."

And Cistine didn't look away from him as she put her lips to the cup, and drank.

THE
HEART
OF
FLAME AND WILD

CHAPTER THIRTY-FIVE

CISTINE'S DREAM KEPT her quiet the next day. Even while they walked, she could still feel the Chalice's cold silver edge biting into her lower lip. She could taste the Dreamwater's herbal, ashy burn on her tongue.

Thorne didn't comment on the silence. He seemed as focused as she was on scaling the rocky terrain that sprouted along the Muunvat's southern shores. It was nearly midday before Cistine noticed the stone walls growing shorter. She slowed, and Thorne pulled ahead of her; Cistine watched his back, wondering what the skin beneath that armor looked like today, and what it would look like once they reached Starhollow and Thorne's wounds became someone else's concern.

She was about to ask him how he felt today, but he preempted her with a tilt of his head, motioning her to join him as he parted a thick knot of undergrowth with his hands.

When she reached his side and beheld the beauty before them, her breath snagged in her chest.

The Muunvat poured in a violent jettison over the rocky cliff to their right, filling a basin far below. Its flow over the years had eroded the landscape, creating a great crescent in the stone. Judging by the echo below their feet, Cistine suspected it was several meters deep. The foothills stepped down on both sides of the river into dense, hilly foliage, and from the basin itself, the river continued in a thinner, slower eddy that Thorne had said eventually joined to the Agerios Sea.

"Beautiful, isn't it?" Thorne leaned his temple against the tree to his left. "That means we've reached the end of our southern journey."

"We made it," Cistine sighed. A three-day trek, without a cot to sleep on or a second change of clothes, would've seemed impossible even a month ago. And yet, not only had she survived, she felt *stronger* for it—just knowing she'd prevailed.

Thorne let the branches fall. "We still have days to go."

Cistine propped herself against the tree to her right and lifted her foot to massage the abrasions on her heel. "I can hardly contain my enthusiasm."

"You seem to be containing it quite well, actually. You almost have me convinced you aren't fond of foot travel."

"Was it my screaming blisters that gave it away? Or all the limping?" When Thorne laughed, Cistine couldn't help but smile. "We'll manage. I know we will."

They descended onto the basin's narrow rim. The pool sparkled a mystic blue-green under the torrential waterfall, and as they picked their way down the bulbous, slippery rocks, Cistine glimpsed the depths of the hollow sink, a sharp turn in the stone that created a broad ledge. Small peninsulas of rock jutted out into the basin itself, ripples cavorting on their edges.

"I've never seen any place like this." Cistine leaned forward to peer into the basin, and Thorne caught her arm.

"It's better seen from a distance," he warned.

Cistine jutted her tongue at him as they resumed their descent. If she hadn't known he was in pain from his last fall into the water, she would've pushed him in just to show him how little she cared about the distance.

When they reached the round shore and sidled toward the smaller mouth of the Muunvat, Cistine watched her reflection, toe-to-toe with herself. "I hope there's a bath where we're going, with real soap. Lavender would be preferable, but I'll take what I can get."

Thorne covered her mouth suddenly with his hand. Cistine's last sidestep pressed them arm-to-arm against the stone, and if not for his grip on her face, she would've toppled forward into the water.

Cistine didn't have to ask why he'd silenced her or what he was staring at.

The opposite bank was populated once again not only with foliage, but with Vassora.

There were eight of them, strapped in armor, twin swords crossed on their backs, prowling the riverbank. Here, they could make it across. They wouldn't need a land bridge.

One by one, like enormous, glittering black vipers, they slid into the water.

Thorne turned to Cistine, wedging his shoulder against the stone wall. "Stay here. To reach you quickly, they have to swim. That will give you high ground and an advantage. You still have Nail?"

Cistine nodded. "What are you going to do?"

"I have to kill them. Quill will never forgive me if I lead them to Starhollow."

Cistine drew Nail with shaking hands and offered it to him. "Take this. You're unarmed."

"Not for long." Thorne curled her fingers back over the hilt, pushing the knife away. "If one of them gets past me, put your knee in his groin and this knife into his eye at the same time. *Do not* run—these cowards are as likely to wedge a blade into your back as to chase you down."

Fear lodged itself in Cistine's throat like a bone swallowed sideways. She didn't offer him Nail again...she didn't think her rigid fingers would part from the antler handle if she tried. She couldn't remember the last time she'd been this terrified.

Quick and light, Thorne crossed the shore. He bent briefly to pick up a rock from the basin, and then he halted beside the river.

Clutching Nail to her heart, Cistine watched the exchange unfold.

The Vassora fanned out before Thorne in a deadly falcate fuming with power, each man thick and vicious with a hand to one sword on his back. Thorne faced them, tossing the rock and catching it close to his hip.

"That was a clever trick in the pass," Thorne said, "separating the wagons. Whose idea was that? None of you have the alacrity to devise an ambush like that."

Most of the men bristled, but one said, "Devitrius sends his regards."

Thorne tensed. "I wish I could say I'm surprised. But after the underhanded feat he pulled off with Rolf, I think I'm beginning to understand how all this works."

"Well, we congratulate you on your cleverness. Unlikely you'll live to witness the culmination of it, though."

Thorne's voice was calm, unaffected: "That remains to be seen."

Cistine thought she'd been afraid before, but her bowels clenched and bile branded her throat when the man turned his attention straight to her. He cocked his head, slow and lazy, enhancing his likeness to a viper. "She's not one of us, is she? Talheimic? That's very interesting. She wouldn't happen to be a princess, would she?"

Thorne said nothing.

The man chuckled. "What a fine catch *she* would make."

Cistine wavered on the stone. Perhaps Thorne's head was a prize in Stornhaz, but the way the man looked at her, how he spoke *of* her, like she was some priceless artifact—

He wanted her. She could see it in his eyes.

And so could Thorne.

The High Tribune's body vibrated with a low growl. "Back away."

The Vassoran guard stepped forward instead.

The rock sailed from Thorne's hand, straight and sleek as rainfall, and smashed into the man's forehead. He plunged into the ferns, his brow cracking open, and Thorne tore the swords from the man's back and stepped forward to meet the rest of the pack.

Cistine couldn't have moved if she'd wanted—to flee, or to help. She was stunned, rooted to the rock as she watched the battle the banks.

If Maleck and Quill were death-gods, then Thorne...

Thorne was death itself.

Cistine had never known death to have a face before. Before today, slaughter had not had a name. But here—today—in this forest grove, in this river basin, under the broad, brilliant brushstrokes of sunlight, death unleashed itself. It was here, cutting between the Vassora, frolicking in their blood. Slaughter's sword was a silver flame, and the battlefield gave him a name.

It screamed it, they *screamed* it—

Thorne. Thorne. Thorne.

He was merciless. Fearless. Thorne hacked the Vassora apart like a weaver separating the threads from a tapestry. One by one, he severed the cords of their lives and dropped them—headless, limbless, laid open—onto the riverbank.

This was the man the merches had feared. The reputation he'd created for himself...for the first time, Cistine saw it was truly not without merit. The man who loved his grandmother and feared for his warriors was also a warrior himself, burning like a fallen star through the Vassoran ranks.

Cistine didn't realize how loud those few seconds of combat had been until the quiet returned to the glade, bereft now of even birdsong or the hum of insects. Absolute silence descended as Thorne faced his back toward her and slowly lowered his swords.

No one had gotten past him. None had even come close.

Thorne stabbed his right-handed blade into the soft soil, his back and shoulders rising and sinking in deep, measured breaths.

And then he crumbled to one knee.

The heavy thud of his weight, as if he'd had no strength to slow his descent, freed Cistine's boots from the stone. She scrambled onto the riverbank and eased toward him. "Thorne?"

He kept his head bowed, and when she grazed a hand along his back, he flinched—*flinched*—beneath her touch. Cistine knelt beside him and saw his eyes were open and fixed on the soil. He breathed heavily through his open mouth and wouldn't look at her. He didn't stand. Cistine wasn't certain he could.

But she *was* certain they couldn't stay here, surrounded by these corpses. She wouldn't be able to keep from vomiting at the sight.

So she took Thorne's arm and pulled it across her shoulders, and when she dragged him to his feet, he took some of his own weight and used the sword to prop himself up. The other blade knocked against Cistine's side as she led him slowly away from the shore—away from the blood that ran into the basin, chumming its numinous waters with the taint of battle.

It wasn't strength that kept Cistine walking; it was numbness, the sheer inability to feel any strain in her back or legs, or in her shoulders as she helped Thorne along. It was emptiness, with her mind still in that beautiful basin, watching the battle happen over and over.

It wasn't the first skirmish she'd seen since she'd arrived on Valgard's shores. It wasn't even the bloodiest. But it was the first that had been fought, in part, for her. Because that man had threatened her...because he'd taken a step after Thorne warned him not to.

"Cistine." Thorne's voice was quiet. "Here is good."

Camp. They needed to make camp for the night. Somehow, time had gotten away from her, and the wooded foothills had grown dark. In her head, it was still daylight-on-water bright, back in the basin. Back on the shore.

She slipped out from under Thorne's arm, and he caught himself against the nearest tree. He dropped the swords and gripped the thin trunk with both hands, digging his forehead against the wood, and concern pierced Cistine's numbness. "Did you strain something?"

"I don't know."

"Is there a stream nearby?"

"More mud packs?"

Cistine couldn't tell if he was teasing her. She didn't want to be teased. "Water. My head is throbbing."

Thorne's powerful shoulders rose and fell. "There's a stream a quarter mile north. Keep your hand on your knife."

Cistine didn't want to touch or look at Nail, or think of what she might've been forced to do with it today if Thorne hadn't been death's divine agent. It wasn't until she found the stream, rinsed her hands, and brought several scoops of water to her mouth that she became sharply aware of why she was shaking, and why her stomach ached with tension.

It escaped from her, a whisper aloud into the black-bathed trees: "You've killed people, too."

The Vassora in the pass were dead because of her. If she'd killed today, it wouldn't have been the first time. And Thorne hacking those men to pieces was no different than her setting the wagons aflame to protect the cabal. He had done it, not for pleasure or for fun, but from necessity to protect Quill's haven. And to protect *her*.

The Vassora had wanted them dead or captured, and they were alive and free because of Thorne. Alive to fight for Talheim. Alive to prevent more bloodshed, and to find ways to protect what mattered most.

Grimacing, Cistine yanked off her boots, then her thin socks, and washed them in the stream.

She picked her way back to Thorne in darkness. He'd settled himself with his back to the tree where she'd left him leaning. Cistine waited for some clarity in the clouds scudding the moon before she built a fire.

Thorne's eyes dragged open as the warmth bathed his face. He winced when Cistine knelt in front of him, between his knees, and took his chin in her hand. "What are you doing?"

"Your face is covered in blood," Cistine said. "So unless you want to face a barrage of questions the moment we see the others, let me clean it off."

Cloth in hand, she wiped the blood of other men from the High Tribune's face and hair, and he submitted without protest. Cistine wondered if he understood this was done in gratitude for his sacrifice, for saving her life. She didn't know how to thank him for killing those men, for not leading them to the others or letting them reach her. She had endurance now, stamina, and she could sling a punch at Quill, who never hit back. But she knew she wasn't ready to defend herself in battle.

She'd needed him today. And he'd been there.

Thorne's nose wrinkled when she blotted his brow. "Where did you find a cloth?"

"It's my sock."

"What in the *stars?*" Thorne knocked her arm aside, coughing. "No wonder it reeks."

"Excuse me!" Cistine snapped in mock-offense. "Women do not reek. We give off a delightful, feminine odor."

"Then I regret to inform you that judging by the stench of your sock, you have the feet of a man."

Cistine slapped the wet sock against his knee. "Fine! I was finished, anyway."

Thorne picked up the sock as Cistine retreated across the fire. He studied it like a poisonous adder and then, grudgingly, laid it over his brow. "I wasn't sure you would come back after what you saw today."

"You know who my father is, and you've met Ashe. You can imagine the kind of battle stories I've been told ever since I was in the womb." Cistine hesitated, choosing her next words carefully: "Seeing it...seeing it is different, yes. But it's not the killing that concerns me, it's *why* someone kills. Someone like King Jad, or...someone like you."

Thorne's eyes softened. "Then this corrupted *bandayo* doesn't frighten you?"

"Don't call yourself that," Cistine scolded. "I was frightened today by what you could do, yes. But I'm glad we're friends. I'd rather have you fighting for me than against me."

Thorne grunted, and his eyes fell shut again. "The people you fight for are fortunate to have you on their side, as well."

The compliment warmed Cistine to the marrow of her bones. "Thank you."

"We should kick out the fire," Thorne added. "If the Vassora divided their forces like before, some of them may be prowling these hills."

Cistine stomped and scattered the kindling, then settled on the hard ground, wrapping her arms around herself as a chill from the shadows burrowed into her muscles.

"Your kingdom," Thorne said. "Would you tell me about its plight? The reason you came to Valgard."

"I already told you why. That night you taught me about the constellations and Courts."

"You gave me the diplomat's answer. I didn't know you then. The sort of woman you are, or the lengths you would go to in fighting for what's yours to defend."

Cistine wondered what he could really do with that information. A disgraced High Tribune was in no position to ally with King Jad, even if he'd hated her enough to try.

And she no longer believed he did.

"Tell me," Thorne murmured, "in your own words. What are you fighting for, Cistine?"

Perhaps it was nothing more than the hitch in his voice—that subtle snag that told her he was searching for a distraction from his pain, just as much as for the truth—that loosened her tongue.

Cistine told him everything: the southern barracks, King Jad's threats, the history between the two kingdoms and the uncertain fate they faced. The more she talked, the more they both relaxed, until she wasn't even certain Thorne was awake.

But she didn't mind if he'd fallen asleep. She talked until she was hoarse. And in telling him, she felt as if her kingdom was a bit closer—and in some way, she was closer to Thorne, too.

CHAPTER
THIRTY-SIX

Their progress slowed after they left the basin. Thorne limped more and spoke far less, his energy focused on climbing the steep hills, and he often leaned heavily against the trees that pocked them. Cistine gladly matched her pace to his. Her feet, sockless now, burned with new blisters.

Two days passed with no sign of the Vassora. If not for Thorne's wellbeing, Cistine would've been relieved. But her stomach still knotted every time she looked at him, and she didn't even feel hungry when they stopped to make camp the second night.

"We must be close to Starhollow by now." She yanked her fingers through the hopeless snarls in her hair.

"Fairly," Thorne said. "Tomorrow we turn our course northwest."

"That will put us back into the taller hills."

"What did you think the *hollow* in the name implied?"

"You Valgardans and your names!" Cistine crossed her arms and leaned against a moss-covered stone, watching Thorne shift and stretch out. "Can you make it?"

"Even if I have to crawl."

But he didn't crawl. In fact, he seemed stronger at daybreak, as if the prospect of facing the last leg of their journey invigorated him. It was Cistine who struggled to keep pace now as they banked northwest, climbing the steeper foothills again.

"How did Starhollow come by its name?" Cistine puffed during the uphill trudge.

"Legend has it that the True God hurled down a star in judgement against the Elder Kings," Thorne said. "A devastating blow to the Northern Kingdom itself. Starhollow is the wound it left behind."

"Doesn't anyone ever come to see the star?"

"That heap of ore was mined for weaponry centuries ago. The legend lost its intrigue not long after. No one ever bothers to visit Starhollow anymore."

They crested the hill, and Thorne stumbled as he halted, gripping the limb of a short, gnarled tree for support. Cistine looped a hand into the crook of his elbow, propping him up. "No one except fools like us, you mean...chasing fallen stars to their resting places."

"True. Only fools and star-chasers."

Thorne led the way down the slope, to the treeline and into the meadow beyond.

Starhollow was the most beautiful god-wound Cistine ever imagined: a wide-open space fringed with distant mountains and elegant pines like the tall, straight backs of queens adorned for festivals. Summer emeralds and wildflower pallets blended with the purple-gray granite and sheer white of the snowcapped peaks. The sky was such a deep, cloudless blue, it was almost violet overhead. Cistine had never seen it so clear.

"This," she stammered, "*this* is Quill's...*haven?*"

"In a sense. It isn't that he calls it home, but...someone very precious to him does."

Cistine stepped out from among the trees and laughed as the grass wound around her calves. "Gods, this is such a perfect place."

Thorne nodded. "Over those hills, you'll find what you're looking for. Go ahead. I'll catch up."

Though Cistine's heart drummed at the prospect of seeing the others, she shook her head. "We started this journey together, and that's how we're going to finish it."

They walked through the meadow at Thorne's pace, and Cistine drank it all in as deeply as she could: the crisp, clean air, the bountiful sunlight, and the places where the ground sloped gently up toward the foothills and into the mountains themselves. In the distance, she spotted planting fields and game paddocks where cattle grazed and tamed deer bedded on the hillsides. "Is there a village here?"

"No. Starhollow only has two permanent occupants," Thorne said. "Quill's chosen certain archers he trusts to come and go occasionally, tending the animals. And during the harvesting season, there are others who help shuck the corn and plow."

Looking up at his face—at the easygoing way he took in his surroundings—Cistine suspected some of those people were the cabal themselves.

They climbed several small, rolling dells before they reached the center of Starhollow and came to a halt once again.

This was what they had been walking toward all this time: a cottage with gently-rounded gables and numerous windows of all different-colored glass that peered out over the meadow. Ensconced between garden plots, the homestead gave off the tantalizing smell of fresh basil and lavender shoots. Behind it, fed by a river winding through the trees, was the purest, clearest pond Cistine had ever seen.

Tears of relief burned her lashes. Even reaching Starhollow, she hadn't been certain how much travel still lay ahead, how many more steps they would have to take before they could finally rest. But there it was, no more than a quarter mile away: shelter. Sanctuary.

As if to assure them of that, a lonely call split the air, and Faer's unmistakably sleek, dark shape swooped from a weeping willow tree on the pond's bank, vanishing into one of the open windows. Cistine moved to follow him, and Thorne gripped her shoulder, pivoting her around to face him. His expression was stern, but his eyes impossibly soft, like the still water below.

"Everything I told you on this journey," he said—then grimaced, gripping his side.

"It's safe," Cistine promised. "I'll never tell a soul. Not even Ashe and Julian."

And now Thorne truly smiled at her for the first time—a crooked, left-handled smirk that turned the pained pools of his eyes to bright blue again, and Cistine knew he was as relieved as she was. And that they were finally safe.

The cottage door flew open, and Cistine heard her name cracking the cool mountain breeze. Thorne let go of her shoulder. "Go. Before Julian loses what's left of his sanity."

Cistine swatted him gently on the chest before she ran, feet scraping raw against the insides of her boots as she slid down the hillside and sprinted toward the cottage. Julian stepped through the doorway, his hair tossed against his brow, eyes wide. When they settled on her, he swore. And then he ran, too.

When they collided, a bleeding fissure in Cistine's heart knitted itself closed. The strength of his arms, the solidness of his chest, the strong thud of his pulse under her ear...she couldn't press herself close enough to him. She couldn't keep herself from crying as he kissed her hair, her cheek, her shoulder. And when he pulled her head up, when he stared into her eyes, she stopped breathing.

"I'm sorry," Julian stammered. "God, I'm...I can't believe we almost...when I saw you fall over the edge of that path, all I could think of was the things I said, how I...in the war camp, *gods*..."

"I know." Cistine's vision blurred with tears. "I treated you like a peasant, and I'm sorry."

"No, I'm the one who should apologize. You're my princess, you're *everything* to me." Julian gathered her close against him again, resting his cheek on her hair. "I'll never leave you alone during a battle for the rest of my life."

Even as Cistine buried her face against his chest, her elation fizzled. It wasn't quite the reunion she'd hoped for...not quite the message she'd hoped he would glean. But he'd apologized, and they were together again.

It was all that mattered.

Quill was the first of the cabal to emerge from the cottage, and he didn't pause to greet Cistine. He sprinted up the hill behind her, and Cistine heard a scuffle, and a curse, and Quill's agitated shout: "*Thorne.*"

Maleck passed them then, nodding to Cistine as he jogged up the hill to join his friends. Moments later, the two warriors descended past Cistine and Julian, supporting Thorne between them. With his arms cast over their shoulders, he sagged. His feet scraped the ground as if he was too exhausted to step for himself anymore. All his strength from that morning was gone.

Cistine peeled herself back from Julian to watch them pass. "Thorne?"

His head bobbed at her voice, but he didn't speak.

"He'll be all right." Julian's tone was low and soothing, but that didn't reassure Cistine. She looked to Quill for his assessment, and the knot in her chest loosened only when the warrior nodded and flashed her a smile.

Ashe reached them then, half-stumbling from the cottage on her injured leg. She collided with Julian and Cistine, wrapping her arms around them both. Cistine expected herself to cry again, but her tears had spent themselves quickly. She could only smile as her Warden kissed the top of her head.

"*The trail gave way,*" Ashe growled. "That was all the cabal would tell us when we asked what happened. Quill's bird tracked that gorge for hours, and he didn't spot you. We were worried your bodies washed out to sea."

"Not quite that far."

Ashe pushed her out, gripping the sides of her neck. "Your *bodies*, Cistine. We thought you were dead."

And in Ashe's stormy gaze, Cistine saw how badly that notion had scared her, and how close her Warden must've come to cracking apart as she'd been forced to sit and wait. A woman of action, with no choice but to pace in one place and pray for the best outcome.

"Besides the fall itself," Cistine said, "I was never in any real danger, I don't think."

"Because Thorne took care of you," Julian said flatly.

"We looked after each other." Cistine watched as Thorne's warriors bore him into the cottage. "We brought each other home."

"We're not home quite yet," Ashe warned her. "And according to the cabal, Kanslar rises in two days."

"They'll sit the Judgement Seat for months," Cistine said. "We can spare a few days to catch our breath, at least. My blisters are growing blisters of their own, and I'm famished, and..."

She broke off, heat warming her cheeks. She'd hugged Julian, pressed herself into him, and only now did she remember the state of her hair and the filth on her body. She stank like river scum, and probably looked no better.

Julian didn't seem to care. He took her hand as they walked toward the cottage. "Food first, for the starving royalty."

But they were intercepted in the doorway. Tatiana, blending with the bright light in her peach-colored shift, leaned against the wooden frame with her arms folded. Her eyes glittered like topaz reflecting flames.

Cistine grimaced. "I know. No more foolish maneuvers."

Tatiana arched a brow.

"To be fair," Cistine added, "I didn't know the path was weak."

Tatiana's heel tapped an executioner's beat on the floor.

"I can't say it will never happen again." Cistine ignored the way Julian's hand tightened around hers at the confession. "But I can promise if it does, I'll consider my options more carefully. And I'll make sure I pull *you* in with me next time."

That sculpted brow slid slowly back into place. Tatiana's mouth quirked to one side as she considered the best Cistine could offer: not an apology for saving their lives, but an ultimatum for peace.

"You did look magnificent with that bow in your hands," Tatiana sighed, "before we heard the trail give out."

Cistine grinned as the warrior strode forward, long sleeves flapping, and brushed aside Ashe and Julian to embrace her—a hug that smelled like cumin and dust. Comfortable, domestic things, as if the cabal had been baking and cleaning while they waited to see if their High Tribune and their prodigy would return.

"Come inside," Tatiana said. "We just finished baking a loaf of bread."

Cistine loved the cottage the moment she laid eyes on its interior. Freckled with light, it sported a small alcove to the left for shoes, a hat-rack, and various coats and cloaks—most of which, judging by their fine design, belonged to Tatiana. To the right, nestled between the windows, was a round, lace-draped reading nook, its deep recess promising hours of uninterrupted time with a good book. A vat of stew bubbled on a great, pot-bellied iron stove next to it, and along the left wall across from the stove, just past a silk-draped mirror, was a bookshelf absolutely splitting with volumes. Their spines sported every hue imaginable, organized by color.

"Whose home *is* this?" Cistine asked.

Tatiana pointed to the enormous table in the middle of the room, large enough to seat at least four warriors at once. Ariadne sat there with a wide-eyed girl who stared up a set of steps beside the stove.

"Tati," the girl said, "what's wrong with Thorne?"

Tatiana motioned Cistine to stay in the doorway. Then she laid a hand on the back of the girl's chair: "I don't know, Pippet. He probably went off wrestling bears in the forest. But look, he brought home company."

The girl twisted in her chair to study Cistine. She was young, ten or so years old, and the angle of her face and her shrewd eyes made Cistine think of ravens and cinnamon sticks and mismatched hair, though hers was a soft collision of brown and black gathered in twists and small braids. "Does Quill know her?"

"Yes," Tatiana said. "And I think he'd like her to stay with us."

The girl nodded to Julian and Ashe. "You're from the Middle Kingdom, aren't you? Like them?"

"I am," Cistine replied.

"All right, you can stay. *If* you'll tell me stories about your kingdom."

"I think I'm growing used to that." Cistine edged into the room. "Thank you for letting me into your house, Pippet. I'm Cistine."

"Oh. You're the girl Ariadne's been praying for when she prays for Thorne every night."

Ariadne's eyes jumped to Cistine's face, and Cistine hoped none of the shock in her chest slithered into her features. Only the gratitude.

"I suppose I am," Cistine murmured, and Ariadne lowered her gaze again.

"I don't know yet if I'm pleased to meet you, but Helga says that's the polite greeting. So, pleased to meet you, Cistine." Pippet pointed to Ariadne. "You're supposed to show me how to draw swords, remember?"

"I'll show you the room where all the girls are staying." Tatiana grabbed Cistine's arm and towed her to the staircase. A narrow doorway opened behind it, and Cistine inhaled the powerful aroma of fresh basil from inside.

"How many rooms are there?" she asked as they climbed the steps to a short, rug-coated corridor.

"Three on this level, and an attic room above," Tatiana said. "The women have one. We gave the one down the hall to Julian. Quill, Thorne, and Maleck share the loft, and the other room on this level belongs to Helga, Pippet's nanny."

"Pippet is Quill's sister, isn't she?" Tatiana nodded. "How old is she?"

"She'll be eleven this year."

"Has she been here ever since you left Stornhaz, then?"

Tatiana's gaze sharpened. "That's not my story to tell. Ask Quill. But you should know it's a sensitive subject for the whole cabal. Pip is like a little sister to all of us. We would do *anything* to keep this place safe for her."

She opened the door, and Cistine dared to dream of collapsing straight into the mattresses spread out on the floor. One was enormous, capable of fitting three people. There were two more crowded around it, leaving only a small walking area to the closet and a wide wall of windows. Through the blue-tinted glass, Cistine could see across the meadow as far as the mountains. The pond glimmered to the right.

"This is Pip's room," Tatiana said. "She and I share the largest mattress. Ariadne has another, and Ashe has been using the third. You two will have to squeeze in together."

"I could sleep anywhere right now, as long as it isn't on the ground."

Tatiana laughed, shoving her aside. "I keep some of my wardrobe here. Clothes I outgrow, or ones that won't fit in the closet in the Den anymore or ones I think Pip will like once she fills out." She flung open the closet door and buried herself inside. "I'm going to give you something fresh, and then you're going straight down to the pond to scrub yourself clean."

"But I'm starving," Cistine complained.

"Trust me, *Yani*, you smell awful enough that you're going to put everyone off their appetites if you set foot in that kitchen right now."

Cistine scuffed her boot on the floor, flaking crumbs of mud against the faded wooden boards. "Tati, did Ariadne really pray for us?"

"Oh, don't sound so surprised. She may be pricklier than a Kroaken cactus, but she doesn't actually want you *dead*."

"I didn't mean it like that. She just...doesn't strike me as the praying sort."

Tatiana emerged with some green-and-gold threads slung over her arm and swiveled to face Cistine. There was a guarded light in her eyes. "You know why Valgard and Talheim have the same beliefs—the True God and his vassals? Northern pilgrims brought their beliefs to the Middle Kingdom and blended teachings with them. So I'd assume you have some concept of temples and the people who serve there."

"Priests and priestesses? Of course we do. I have a cousin who serves in the Temple of the True God in Astoria."

"Well, that was almost Ariadne's life. A long time ago. Some habits lie deeper than others, especially when it concerns life and death." Tatiana draped the dress across Cistine's arms. "These look to be your size. Now wait here while I fetch some soap from the pantry."

She disappeared into the hall, and Cistine followed her to the threshold. She watched Tatiana all but dance to the staircase, where she nearly collided with Quill. They exchanged a rash of words, and then Tatiana clattered downstairs while Quill hurried up a second set of steps chiseled into a wraparound stairwell across the hall.

Curiosity took hold of Cistine's feet and marched her quietly to those steps. At the bottom, she paused to listen. A door creaked open above, and voices rumbled—Maleck thanking Quill for something he'd brought. And then Thorne growling profanely, the words all blurring together.

Cistine climbed the staircase swiftly—moving in and out of pockets of sunlight where windows gleamed down on the steps—to the door at the top which was faintly ajar. Through the seam, she glimpsed Thorne on the bed, flat on his stomach, with Maleck leaning over him to examine his back.

"With these injuries, you shouldn't have been walking," Maleck murmured. "*Allet*, you should not have even been *standing*."

The Old Valgardan word pricked Cistine's ears. *Brother*. She'd never heard Maleck sound so concerned.

"I know," Thorne growled.

"You hit that water like a battering ram," Quill added from somewhere outside Cistine's narrow field of vision. "We could hear the bones break from the pass."

"Fracture," Maleck corrected. "Not break."

"I don't need you to ruin my analogies."

"No, you do that well enough yourself," Thorne said.

"Thorne, stars above, this isn't a joke!" Quill snapped. "Why didn't you wait for us? Let us come down and get you?"

"The Vassora were on the move. I couldn't let them find her."

Cistine caught her breath as Maleck swiveled to the left, looking at what she could only assume was Quill.

"You're not going through with it, are you?" Quill murmured.

"What in Nimmus do you think?"

Cistine frowned. This conversation made no sense to her, except that Thorne had walked with fractured bones and worse wounds than she'd realized just to keep her safe.

"I understand why you did it," Quill said. "You know I do. She's my friend, too. But you can't *fight* right now, Thorne. We have to make it all the way back to Hellidom without the strongest weapon in our arsenal. It's a bad situation, you know that?"

"Just give me the herbs," Thorne grunted. "Let me sleep on a bed for once. I'll be all right."

Maleck dipped his head. "As you wish."

Footsteps brushed toward the stairs. Cistine slid rapidly back down to the level below, running on silent feet down the rugs—glad they absorbed the sound of every stride. She skidded to a halt at the top of the next staircase, where she nearly collided with Tatiana.

"Why are you so out of breath?" the warrior asked.

"I've decided I'm excited for this bath, after all." Cistine plucked the soap bar and clothing from Tatiana's hands and smiled at her. "Thank you."

Tatiana wrinkled her nose. "You can thank me by washing the river scum from your hair. Before we decide you're better off sleeping under the stars."

CHAPTER
THIRTY-SEVEN

ALMOST THE ENTIRE cabal gathered for dinner that night: Cistine, Julian, Ashe, Pippet, and Helga squeezed in together at the table. Maleck leaned against the window, a bowl of stew balanced in one hand, and Ariadne settled cross-legged on the floor at his feet. Quill and Tatiana sat on the reading nook's round edge.

Only Thorne was absent. And Cistine felt that absence like the pain of striking the Muunvat's surface all over again.

She tried desperately to ignore it as she dove deep into the mercy of a true meal again. She couldn't bite back a groan of pleasure when that first bite of soft carrots, celery, and venison slid down her throat. Everyone at the table laughed—Pippet loudest of all—and Quill exaggerated the sound with his next bite.

"Enough of that," Helga said crisply when Pippet laughed so hard she almost choked. Cheeks and ears hot, Cistine smiled gratefully at the woman, who winked back.

She'd met Helga before the meal, at the cook stove in the enormous kitchen behind the staircase. Though she looked to be Baba Kallah's age, Helga was strong and straight-backed, unglimpsed by the rigors of passing time. Her frequent smiles were bright like a sunrise, and she'd offered the first one when Quill had come sliding down the banister to the table and grabbed Cistine in an embrace, swinging her off her feet with a shout of, "Thank God you're all right—whoever's been giving you lessons on the dramatic, I need to have words with them, Stranger..."

After that, he'd begged her to tell them about destroying the wagons—twice—before Helga had rounded them all up for supper.

Now there was nothing but the sound of spoons scraping bowls as they ate. Cistine was clean, swathed in layers of silk thanks to Tatiana, and her belly was near full. She finally felt human again—and even moreso when Helga announced there was dessert.

Cistine had never watched a band of ruthless warriors fight over fresh lemon pie before, but she thought it might be her new favorite sight to behold.

"Tell us about the wagons again?" Quill said as he flopped back onto the nook, sporting a bruised cheek where Tatiana had elbowed him away from the pie plate.

"Give it a rest, Quill," Ariadne snapped. "We know how it went. The flaming arrows. The carts. All of it."

Cistine pierced her pie slice and circled the air slowly with a forkful of custard. "*I* want to hear about the surgeons. At least tell me my maneuver was good for something other than almost breaking Thorne's back."

Maleck's eyes narrowed slightly, but he said nothing.

"The surgeons are gone," Quill said.

"Meaning you..." Cistine trailed off, glancing cautiously at Pippet.

"We can discuss it later." Ariadne's quiet command put an end to the conversation—and to Cistine's appetite. She pushed her pie toward Julian, and he ate it without complaint.

The silence was more subdued while the others finished their dessert, the heaviness broken only when the top of a curved window swung downward and Faer nudged into the cottage. He groomed his plumage for a moment, then took wing—not to Quill's shoulder, but to Pippet's.

"Hello, handsome!" she crooned. "Oh, who's the biggest, bravest, *strongest* raven in all Three Kingdoms? Is it you? I think it is!"

Faer fluffed his feathers with utmost dignity while she scratched his chest, eyeing the room as if to ensure they all knew he was, indeed, the biggest, bravest, and strongest raven.

"Do we have a plan?" Cistine asked when Pippet got up from the table, crawled onto the reading nook and wedged herself between Quill and Tatiana.

"Going forward?" Quill wrapped an arm around his sister's shoulders and leaned them both back against the pillows in the nook. Tatiana laid down beside them, tangling her legs with Pippet's and stroking her long hair. "It's being made."

"We must return to Hellidom, and soon," Maleck said. "It's a great burden Baba Kallah carries in our absence."

"But Valgard is going to be in upheaval for a few days," Ariadne said. "We're better off waiting for the roads to quiet down."

"Would this have anything to do with Skyygan setting?" Cistine asked.

Maleck and Ariadne exchanged a glance. In the shadow of the nook drape, Tatiana grinned.

"Yes," Maleck admitted. "Yes, it would."

"And Kanslar rises," Julian muttered.

Cistine slid the last slice of pie onto her empty plate, gathered the dirty dishes, and followed Helga into the kitchen.

The room's perpetual warmth enveloped her like a hug. The hearth still blazed, though they'd scraped the soup pot dry. Slabs of cured meat hung from the roof beams on either side of the chimney. The shelves along two walls were stocked with dried herbs, and Cistine inhaled their perfume as she spread out the dishes on the preparation table taking up the middle of the room.

"Ready to dirty your hands?" Helga nudged hips with Cistine in passing, and Cistine smiled gratefully.

"Anything to take my mind off the Vassora." She helped Helga lift an enormous tub of soapy water onto the table. "If I never cross ways with one of them again, I'll die happily."

Helga nodded as Cistine started to soak the dishes. "I'm not eager to send this cabal back into the wilds again after what everyone has suffered…particularly you and Thorne. It was a surprise when they all arrived at the door, dusty and bloodied up to the last, but it was you two they fretted over. Now I can see why."

Cistine smiled wider, scrubbing the bowls and stacking them neatly off to one side. "I'm glad we had such a lovely place to come to. I don't think my ribs and hips could take another night sleeping on the ground."

"We owe Quill and Thorne for this place," Helga said, "for this life. It's a good life…a hard one, no doubt. But the two aren't always opposed."

"I'm beginning to understand that. Do *you* have any idea how long we'll have to stay?"

"Thorne needs a few days' rest, at least, to let the herbs and poultices do their work."

Cistine glanced at the slice of pie on her plate. "Is he allowed to have anything other than tea?"

Helga rolled up her dishcloth and snapped Cistine on the backside. "Go take him the pie. I can finish up here."

"I don't want to leave you with all this work!"

"Nonsense. Work keeps me young and fit to chase after Pippet." Helga rolled her sleeves and nudged Cistine aside, plunging her arms to the elbows in the sudsy water and leaving Cistine no chance to argue.

The cabal had left the cottage already, and the front door hung open, ushering in the sounds of laughter from the lawn. Even Julian and Ashe had gone with them; and it was good to hear them enjoying themselves, and to be in a place where there was more than just her voice and Thorne's and the rush of the river through the gorge.

The angle of light had shifted in the wraparound staircase to the loft, painting the stairwell lavender and salmon by the time Cistine climbed to Thorne's door. It was shut, and she wondered if she should even bother him. But she knocked anyway.

There was no sound from inside. Curiosity nudged Cistine's fingers down to the handle, and she quietly slipped into the room.

The large attic space was still brightly-lit, bracketed with windows that ushered in the waning daylight. Thorne was fast asleep on the bed where she'd spied him earlier, face pressed into the pillow, blanket tangled around his hips. He'd cast his shirt into the corner, and his bruises popped against his tan skin like dark lilypads on calm water. One arm crushed the pillow to his face; the other hung off bed, his knuckles brushing the floor.

Cistine tiptoed to the bedside table and replaced his empty stew bowl with the pie.

As the plate rattled slightly on the wood, Thorne's hand snaked up suddenly, catching the back of her calf, and Cistine froze. For just a flash, like sunlight on a basin's surface, she remembered him tearing the Vassora apart.

But when Cistine looked down at him, she couldn't see the viciousness in his face—the ferocity with which he'd faced down the Vassora. His eyes were dazed and drowsy. "What do you need, Cistine?"

Cistine let out a slow breath. "For you to rest and recover so we can go back to Hellidom."

Thorne's eyes fluttered shut as he lost the battle against the herbs coursing through his body. "You stand watch, then."

Cistine stared at him as his hand slackened, falling back to the floor. By the time she mustered a quiet, "I will," he was already asleep again.

She picked up the soup bowl, hurried to the door, and paused, glancing back at Thorne's inert form. Here in this sanctuary—here among his cabal— his guard was down. And he trusted her to keep watch while he healed.

Cistine smiled. "Sleep well, High Tribune."

The encroaching sunset did nothing to dampen the cabal's wild spirits. Maleck and Ariadne were grappling in the grass when Cistine stepped from cottage, and they didn't even look up as she passed. Shading her eyes in the glorious light, Cistine spotted Tatiana and Pippet in the thickest clot of wildflowers they could find, dancing to welcome the night. Faer circled above them, occasionally diving to snatch strands of Pippet's hair.

Quill wasn't difficult to spot, either. He sprawled on one of the hills, watching Tatiana chase Pippet. Cistine gathered her skirts—a motion she'd almost forgotten to do as she'd grown used to wearing her training armor—and hurried to join him.

"How's Thorne?" Quill asked by way of greeting as she stalked—soundlessly, she'd thought—behind him.

Cistine flopped down at his side, gathering her knees under her body and smoothing her skirts over them. "Asleep."

"Helga's corpse brew," Quill said. "That's what we used to call it when we were younger. Witch hazel, poppy, and valerian, and something that dulls pain. She'd force it into us every night after a hard day of training."

"And you never offered it to me? You're cruel."

Quill's brows peaked with feigned innocence. "I didn't know how to make it!"

"Liar." Cistine pummeled his ribs with her elbow, and he laughed.

"It's good to have you back, Stranger. When we heard you fall...I thought Ashe was going to jump in after you. It's a good thing Maleck was there. It took him and Ariadne both to keep hands on her."

"And Julian?" Cistine had finally spotted him and Ashe on the other side of the hill, slowly limbering up to wrestle. Ashe was taking special care to stretch her mended leg.

"I've never heard a man scream like that before," Quill said. "I had to tackle him down...hold him until he stopped thrashing."

Cistine winced. "I wasn't thinking of what it would mean to him or Ashe. I just knew I needed to stop those wagons."

"It meant you saved all our lives. Including theirs."

Cistine watched Quill pick up a small stick from the grass and twirl it between his fingers. "I don't think the cabal blames you for what happened in the pass, Quill. I certainly don't. The Vassora were clever. Maybe even Devitrius was clever, too."

The stick halted, balanced between his middle and ring fingers. "I should have anticipated that, but I was ready to spill blood after what they did to Tati. I got them into danger because of that."

"But you got everyone *out*, Quill. You brought them here."

He smiled. "But I did that for selfish reasons."

That selfish reason was currently rolling in the grass, trying to escape Faer's attacks. Cistine tugged up fingerfuls of grass, then trickled them down into the soil. "About Pippet..."

"You want to know why she lives here, and not with us."

Cistine bit the corner of her bottom lip, saying nothing.

"My sister," Quill began, "is the greatest thing that's ever happened to me. And keeping her safe has been my responsibility ever since she was born. But I almost failed, and after that...I knew I wasn't fit to raise her. She was just an infant when she was taken, and I almost didn't get her back in time."

Cistine glanced up at him. "Taken? By whom?"

Quill didn't answer at once. When he finally spoke, his voice wasn't much louder than a whisper: "Slavers."

Cistine's heart plummeted, and her supper rose up in her throat. "Like Matthias and Roosha?"

Quill nodded, snapping the twig in half as he watched Tatiana pounced on Pippet, tickling her sides until she begged for mercy. Cistine studied his face—the planes as calm as ever, but the quiet fury storming his eyes. "Do you want to tell me?"

"It isn't a happy story."

"But it's your story. And it's Pippet's. So I'll listen, if you want to tell it."

Quill hurled the sticks down with the precision of a knife-thrower, embedding them tips-first in the soft soil. "Pip was just a few months old when we left Stornhaz. I'd had enough public disgraces with my parents by that point, I thought my family would be safe if the Chancellors ever found out what we were doing. I didn't have much to lose when they threw me in the Lightless Pit."

He swept a hand along the side of his head—palming the scar.

"Tati freed me. She told me my parents were dead...the roof of their apartment collapsed. An unpredictable accident, everyone said." His voice was brittle as thin ice. "And my sister was gone. Someone snatched her from her cradle and sold her to slavers."

Cistine buried her mouth between her hands. "She was a *newborn!*"

"If they're too young, slavers raise them. Train them in the business, either to perform or to lure in other people who will. There's a market for flesh of every age, every color, every kind you can dream of." Quill paused, his breath hitching, anger framing his usually-laughing mouth. "It stretches much higher than just your common tavern criminal. People you wouldn't expect to indulge in that kind of debauchery...important, powerful people. Elites, and...even High Tribunes."

He was quiet again, his eyes distant and dark with memory.

"You wouldn't expect it from them, but they do it. And they kept her hidden from me," he said. "It took me two months...two *months* to hunt them down. But when I did..."

He trailed off, and Cistine was glad. Her mind supplied the bloodsoaked caravan, the way she'd seen Quill hack his enemies to pieces. What she imagined he'd done to Matthias and Roosha that night in Veran.

Not only for her, she understood now...but for Pippet. For the memory of the life she'd nearly been enslaved to.

"We were lucky Tatiana managed to sneak Helga from Stornhaz," Quill continued. "She was my nanny, and then Pip's. Our parents were never particularly invested in us. Helga was an anchor, and she's raised Pippet right. But she's never gone to school, never had friends her own age. And even though I try to protect her, keep her away from what we do in Hellidom...she knows there's a bigger kingdom out there. She asks to leave Starhollow now, and I'm running out of excuses for why she can't, without telling her it's her brother's mistakes that keep her captive here. So either she learns how cruel this kingdom is, or she learns to hate me."

Cistine looked across the meadow, this place she had been so glad to find at their journey's end—she looked at it through Pippet's eyes. Starhollow was a refuge, and a sanctuary for the girl; but in time, if this struggle between the cabal and the Courts didn't end, it would become a prison. Pippet would feel like a prisoner, and Quill her jailor.

"I'm sorry," Cistine said. "Quill, I'm so sorry."

"So am I," he said. "But I do what I can. I bring her things. I send Faer to keep her company...that bag of feathers is more interested in her than me, anyway. And I make sure to visit whenever Thorne can spare me, so she knows I'm here for her however I can be."

"She knows." Cistine watched Pippet cartwheel through the meadow, checking with every turn that her brother was watching her perform. "And I think it's good for her that you all came here. She obviously trusts Tatiana."

"Tati is a better sibling to her than I am, sometimes. Always bringing her new clothes to try on. I haven't spent a mynt on threads in years."

"For whatever it's worth, I don't think Pippet could ask for a better brother than you. You've surrounded her with the best kind of people."

Quill grunted, breaking another stick in pieces. This one, he simply laid out on the ground. "I'm glad you were able to meet her before you made your way back to Talheim. Pip's never met someone like you. A princess. A royal girl who isn't selfish or greedy or hardened by this kingdom."

Cistine laughed. "Well, I'm more than happy to dress in beautiful gowns and weave flower crowns with her while I'm here. It's a nice reprieve."

"Enjoy it while you can. It won't last," Quill warned. "Tomorrow morning, Thorne's called a session with the cabal."

"And?"

"And *you're* invited, Stranger." Quill drew a cinnamon stick from his pocket and jammed it between his teeth, laced his fingers together in a stretch, and got to his feet. "Your Wardens, too, if you think they're ready for it."

Cistine stared after him as he swaggered down the hill to join his sister and Tatiana, the sunset limning his white locks bright gold.

A slow smile crept over Cistine's face. "We'll be there."

CHAPTER THIRTY-EIGHT

Although he was still confined to his bed, Thorne was no less strict on timeliness than usual. It was barely after dawn, the upper peaks not yet kissed by the sun, when he summoned the cabal to the loft—and Cistine and her friends joined them.

Cistine had fallen asleep quickly the night before, and slept deeply—too deeply. She was still yawning and leaning heavily against Julian's side when Quill trailed into the room. He was the last one to join them after patrol, shirtless, barefoot, sweeping his hair away from his scar as he kicked the door shut and settled against it. "What's the word, Thorne?"

Thorne folded his arms, looking between the cabal. His appearance was almost amusing—blankets around his hips, pillows behind his back, and still in command of the room. Cistine bit back a smile as she settled her weight into Julian, and he wrapped his arm around her shoulders.

"We need to discuss what happened in that pass," Thorne said.

Ashe frowned at Cistine. Julian's fingers dug into her shoulder as if he was afraid she would topple away from him again at any second. But Cistine watched Thorne's gaze flick to her, then settle on Quill instead.

Quill scratched his scar. "It was crawling with Vassora even after the pass collapsed. Twice the amount our scouts told us."

"A traitor?" Ashe asked.

"More likely, the Vassora kept tight lips about their numbers," Maleck answered. "They were warned ahead of time not to give away their position or clout."

"Someone anticipated an attack," Julian said.

Tatiana grimaced. "Someone always seems to, these days."

"And the surgeons?" Thorne asked. "What were you able to pry from them?"

"Before the Vassora plucked them from our clutches and sent us running with our tails tucked, you mean?" Quill muttered. "Not much."

Thorne's eyes never left his face. "But enough."

Quill stared back at him. The silence throbbed with tension. "It's the Chancellor of Kanslar Court. That's who they've been meeting with."

Cistine's heart sank. "Is he dying?"

"They wouldn't say," Quill admitted. "Even with knives at their throats, we figured they wouldn't. But with the number of surgeons coming and going from Stornhaz, I'd say that's a bet even a frugal man could safely make."

Thorne had gone very still. The breaths that lifted his crossed arms along his chest were markedly shallow. "What is he dying *of*?"

"I wish I had details to give, but we didn't have time to force a confession before the Vassora arrived, and then we had to turn and flee. Like cowards."

"We can be certain of one thing," Ariadne said. "There's too great a risk to make another frontal assault. The Courts are determined to ensure these surgeons arrive safely."

"It was a bad hunt," Thorne said to Quill. "Let's make certain the next one is better."

Quill snapped his bare heels together. "Without a doubt."

"There's another reason I called you all here." Thorne's eyes swept the room, hanging on Cistine longer than the rest. "The Vassora know there's a Talheimic presence in Valgard again."

Julian tensed. "What?"

Cistine kept her gaze on Thorne. "We faced a pack of them on our journey here. They suspected I was the princess."

"Is this going to be a problem?" Ashe directed the question, and her focus, toward Maleck—as if she trusted his assessment more than anyone else's in the room.

Maleck shrugged. "It all depends on who told them, and why."

"It could've easily been the Guide," Cistine said. "He knows who I am."

Thorne nodded, slowly and stiffly. "And given the Chancellor of Kanslar Court is fascinated with Talheim, if the Guide told him of your presence here, he may deploy the Vassora to hunt for you."

"Which wouldn't end well if you were found with us," Tatiana added.

"What do you mean, he's *fascinated* with Talheim?" Cistine demanded.

Maleck tipped his head. "It isn't a murderous fascination, if that's your concern."

"I don't care! Why didn't any of you mention this *fascination* before? Isn't that something I ought to know about before I meet with him?"

"I assumed you knew," Thorne said. "Why else would you have chosen to meet with him, of all the Chancellors?"

Cistine frowned. The cabal's secret exposed a flaw: her own ignorance yet again. She'd simply assumed the Guide knew best when he'd suggested she meet with Kanslar's Chancellor. And given her own kingdom had offered her nothing, not even the most basic formal training about Valgard's culture or the Chancellors, that had been an easy assumption to make.

Whatever the reason for these gaps in her education, intentional or not, she supposed it truly was a gift of the gods that she'd met this cabal, after all.

Cistine struggled to return to focus. "Would a journey to meet with Kanslar's Chancellor be dangerous right now, with him sick and the Vassora knowing about us?"

Thorne stayed silent, and the cabal watched him. Quiet energy hummed through the room.

"The guards who know you're with us are dead," Thorne said at last, "but I would suggest biding your time and continuing your training for now."

"We don't have time to wait," Julian protested. "Kanslar's about to rise. Why does it matter if they know we're with you?"

Ariadne scowled. Thorne's face paled slightly, and he stared at Julian for a moment. Then he looked again at Cistine.

"Kanslar's Chancellor is my..." Thorne broke off, rubbing the side of his neck. "Mentor. The one I was groomed to succeed. Ever since I left the City of a Thousand Stars, it's been a game of chase. That man would break open Nimmus and Cenowyn to find me."

"And what do you want with him, Thorne?"

"I want peace," Thorne said. "But it's been out of my reach all this time. We've been deadlocked in this pointless struggle for a decade."

"Then you and the Chancellor have at least one thing in common: patience."

Thorne's eyes flashed with pain as if she'd stabbed him. "True."

Before Cistine could truly fathom that look—or apologize for whatever she'd said to cause it—Maleck interceded: "We must move quickly back to Hellidom, where we can regroup and dispatch our assets."

Thorne nodded. "I can be ready to leave tomorrow at dawn."

"Helga says you need three more days at least," Quill argued.

"We'll see about that," Thorne said. "Once we reach Hellidom and rendezvous with Baba Kallah, we'll have a clearer idea of how the winds are blowing."

One by one, the cabal surmised the meeting was over and left the loft, muttering among themselves. Ashe trailed after them, and Julian gave Cistine an insistent tug toward the door. She resisted, turning back. "You go. Meet me in the kitchen. I'll be there soon."

Julian glanced between her and Thorne, his jaw flickering with tension. But he was wise enough to say nothing as he followed Ashe from the room.

"Are you all right?" Cistine asked when the door closed softly on Julian's heels.

"My back is mending. Tomorrow—"

"I don't mean your back. The Chancellor. Your old mentor. He's dying, Thorne. Are you all right?"

Thorne blinked. "Do you think I'm mourning for him?"

"I don't see how you couldn't."

"Our bond was never...we were not friendly, Cistine," he said. "At best, he tolerated me because of our positions. And I didn't rebel because his *kindness* was such a burden on my heart."

Cistine frowned. "Then why did you wait so long to leave?"

Thorne shifted, turning his focus to the windows. "If you live long enough with something, no matter how terrible it is, you may begin to question who you are without it. If you *are* that thing. If it's somehow crawled inside and made its home there. That fear can make you do terrible things. Or not do things you know you ought to do, because you're afraid people will see that darkness in you."

Cistine shivered at his quiet, inflectionless tone. "I doubt you're like him: some sickly, vengeful Chancellor who drives his own Tribunes away."

When Thorne said nothing, Cistine knew she'd spent her welcome. Perhaps he was still irritated with her for whatever pain her words had inflicted.

She went to the door, and had just opened it when Thorne's voice reached her again—a quiet parting, heavy as a storm's shroud against a mountain: "You shouldn't go to Stornhaz."

Cistine froze, her hand resting on the door as she looked back.

Thorne still didn't face her. A rut cleaved between his brows, his mouth trembling as if he wanted to say more but couldn't bring himself to.

Or as if he was about to weep.

"I told you before, you can't discourage me from this," Cistine said. "The risks are worth it for my kingdom. I have to go."

"No, you really don't. The Chancellor is more than my mentor, Cistine, he's..." Thorne flexed his fist against the blankets and swallowed. "The Chancellor is my *enemy* because of who and *how* he is. Whatever the Guide in Veran told you, you're better off treating with Yager or Traisende than with Kanslar."

Was he trying to delay her? Cistine couldn't fathom why, after everything she'd told him about Talheim's plight and her own fears on their walk to Starhollow. "Julian is right. I can't wait that long. Talheim needs aid *now.*"

"Kanslar's Chancellor is not the man to give that aid. There's something dangerous in him...something you aren't prepared to face yet."

"Well, maybe I'm dangerous, too. So we'll be an even match after all." The cool doorknob bit into Cistine's tightening fist. "I told you to respect my decision, Thorne. And I'd like it if you remembered that."

She shut the door before the worry in Thorne's face could make its way into her chest and inspire her own.

It was a cloudy day, but a clear night. Cistine retreated to the hills surrounding the cottage, wrapped up in a blanket, watching the sun sink between the mountains.

Heaviness settled across her shoulders—fear and concern and irritation an unwelcome blanket in and of themselves. And not just her own; the cabal had been quiet all day, and growing tenser as dusk approached. Cistine had finally escaped the cottage when the weight of their unhappy glances became too much to bear.

She tried not to dwell too much on that, or on her conversation with Thorne that morning, as she gathered her knees to her chest and watched the stars wink to life above the hollow. There was so much peace to be found here, but her thumping heart didn't know it. Her pulse tingled in her elbows and as she sought out one cluster of stars among the many.

Light footsteps, gentle as spring rain, pattered through the grass. Cistine looked over her shoulder as Pippet climbed the hill to join her. "Ashe is looking for you."

"Oh. Thank you, Pippet." Cistine mustered a half-smile. "Would you tell her I'll be back soon?"

"No, you tell her." Pippet dropped cross-legged beside Cistine. "I don't like being inside on nights like this. Everyone is so sad. And Thorne and Helga are arguing."

Cistine frowned. "About what?"

"She says he's not leaving. She won't let him." Pippet pulled out threads of grass one at a time, echoing her brother's flighty movements the day before. "And he called Quill a turncoat and Quill says he has a pig's head and now they aren't speaking to one another."

"Children." Cistine muttered—then slapped a hand over her mouth. "I'm sorry, I shouldn't have said that."

But Pippet was laughing, her eyes crinkling at the corners exactly like her brother's. "You're funny. I like you."

"Well, thank you, Lady Pippet." Cistine affected her most royal tone. "I'm told I'm *quite* likeable."

"Because you're a princess?"

Cistine tipped her head. "Do you know what that means?"

Pippet shrugged. "Not really. I just know everyone here likes you. Even Ariadne, and she doesn't like everyone. But she prayed for you." Pippet flaked the grass off her hands. "Thorne likes you, too. I'm glad he's staying...I know he's hurt. He looks like he fell out of a tree and hit every branch falling down."

Cistine's heart clenched at the girl's rueful tone. It was no wonder Quill struggled to keep secrets from her; Pippet was just as perceptive as him. And by the pain in her eyes, Cistine thought she felt just as deeply. "I can tell how much they all love you, Pippet. You make them happy on nights like tonight. Especially Quill."

Pippet's face brightened as her eyes flashed to Cistine. "Why did you come out here all alone? Are you sad, or are you hiding?"

"Maybe both." Cistine shook out the blanket and fluffed its corner. "Do you want to hide with me?"

Pippet scooted over and tugged the blanket around herself, folding close to Cistine's side. "Do you know why everyone's sad?"

Cistine bit her lips together at the corner and turned her gaze to the night sky. "I think I can guess."

For there, far across the meadow at the crown of the mountains, the Conquering King's constellation began to rise.

CHAPTER THIRTY-NINE

IT WAS PROOF of Helga's mettle that the cabal did not leave the next day—or for several days after that. Cistine hardly saw Thorne during that time; she was still too annoyed with him for trying to talk her into waiting for another Court to rise to power before entreating aid for Talheim, and for not respecting her decision to address Kanslar. She let him keep her at arm's length, and she kept him at hers.

Still, Cistine was glad they stayed, and Thorne had more time to recover. She knew at once he would need his strength when, five days later, she jolted from sleep to Julian's hand on her shoulder and the sight of his unhappy face swimming into focus above her.

"We have visitors."

Cistine was awake at once, sitting up and yanking on her robe— another gift from Tatiana. "Are they friendly?"

"They look like the archers from Villmark," Julian said as Cistine staggered up, lashed the robe around her hips and flipped her hair from the collar. "But Thorne doesn't seem pleased with them, whoever they are."

The moment Cistine and Julian descended the steps into the main room, Cistine could feel the rage seeping from Thorne's pores. He stood by the table, arms folded, without a hint of pain in his posture. Ariadne leaned against the wall, angled slightly between Thorne and these visitors. Quill lounged at the table, propping his chair back against the wall. Six archers faced them from the doorway, stiff-backed like Thorne, their heads bowed.

"You know better than to come to Starhollow without my permission," Thorne growled. "Only approved patrols are allowed here."

"Yes, High Tribune," one of the men mumbled.

"This had better be well worth the intrusion, Magnus."

Cistine's nape prickled at Thorne's deadly calm—the same voice with which he'd addressed the Vassora.

The archer raised his head, his eyes cutting briefly to Cistine and Julian. "This matter should be discussed privately."

If Thorne knew they were behind him, he gave no sign of it. "I'll be the one to decide that. Is this about the Vassora?"

Magnus nodded. "They've congested the roads. Caravans and foot patrols are being searched. In the last two days, they've come dangerously close to Villmark. We've had to abandon camp for now."

"That explains the intrusion." Quill's dark scowl belied his easygoing tone.

"It's no coincidence this came with the advent of Kanslar," Ariadne murmured. "You know what they're searching for, Thorne."

Thorne traded his weight. "No one leaves the hollow without my permission. Magnus, take your men and establish a camp at the mouth of the river. Send out patrols in constant rotation."

Magnus saluted with an arm across his chest. His eyes flicked back to Cistine, swimming with some unreadable emotion. Then he led his archers from the cottage.

"Quill," Thorne said the moment the door shut, "call Faer. I have a job for him."

Quill let his chair fall forward on its legs. Grimmer than Cistine had ever seen him, he loped out after Magnus and his men.

"You intend to send word to Baba Kallah?" Ariadne asked.

Thorne nodded. "She'll have to fortify Hellidom herself this time."

"Thorne, what's wrong?" Cistine slid her hand from Julian's and approached the High Tribune. "You knew this would happen, didn't you?"

"This isn't the usual congestion. This is Kanslar searching for something. And they've wasted no time doing it. Their constellation just rose four days ago."

"That suggests a long game," Ariadne said. "They intend to use every second of their time in power to conduct a thorough hunt."

"And they've been planning for this while the other Courts were in session."

"But we already suspected that."

Thorne cut Ariadne a swift glance. "We have no guarantee Magnus and his men were cautious on their way here, or that the other archers won't come to join them. Ariadne, help Maleck keep watch on their camp."

Ariadne dipped her head and retreated through the door.

"What can we do?" Cistine asked.

"I'll find Ashe," Julian offered. "She and Maleck should know about the archers so they don't stumble across them and start a fight."

Cistine squeezed his arm. "Hurry."

With Julian gone, Thorne raked out a chair and dropped into it, rubbing his face with both hands. "Kanslar has never managed to trap us here before."

Cistine pulled out a chair for herself and sank down across from him. "Do you know what the Chancellor is doing, exactly?"

"No." Thorne folded his hands against his mouth. "But it isn't like him to move this swiftly. That worries me. It makes me worried for Hellidom."

"Maybe the Chancellor is desperate. I think sickness...even dying...can make men do desperate things."

Thorne nodded, his throat bobbing with a hard swallow. "But we don't know what he's being treated for. That's obviously a well-kept secret among the Courts, and now they know we're searching for it."

Cistine folded her arms on the table. "What are you going to do?"

"We have decisions to make." Thorne gripped his side, grimacing. "Other options open to us. It's clear the Courts are preparing for something. They've rallied the Vassora. They're patrolling the Vey. They're searching all caravans and traveling parties. And we know they're transporting weapons of...particular make. None of this bodes well for us."

Cistine silently weighed honesty over privacy, knowing he was flirting with the edges of a secret she was already privy to. "I know about the *Svarkyst* steel. I...I listened in to your meeting the first night we were in Hellidom."

Thorne's brows rose. "Of course you did. We were strangers to you, and not particularly welcoming ones, barring Quill. You had to think of your people's safety. I understand that."

"Do you?"

He shrugged. "In your place, I would've done the same. And never apologized for it."

Cistine slumped in her chair. "I'm not apologizing, either. But I wanted you to know I knew. In case I...form an opinion on some things. On your plans."

"Which I have no doubt you will. Do you want to know more about what's transpiring on the Black Coasts? What an attack against them would mean if it came down to that?"

Cistine parried a stab of excitement and truly considered what he was offering her. She'd learned by now that the truths this cabal told were never without cost, and often that price was some sort of bad feeling or another nightmare. "I want to know, but not yet. I need to focus on other things for now. My training. The Courts."

"I agree."

Grateful that he didn't try to dissuade her again, Cistine found it easy to smile. "When I *am* ready to know, will you be the one who tells me?"

Thorne drummed his fingers on the table. "As you wish."

CHAPTER FORTY

WITH THORNE'S LETTER dispatched to Baba Kallah, there was nothing for the cabal to do but keep up their guard, patrol Starhollow, and maneuver around Magnus and the archers, keeping them apart from Pippet. Quill was adamant his sister not know why they were staying so long—or how much danger they'd face when they finally escaped.

The knowledge that Kanslar's Chancellor was on the hunt passed through the cabal like a shooting star, leaving a brilliant trail of unease that brightened their faces day by day.

Cistine longed to alleviate the strain however she could, so she flung herself headlong back into patrol. She and Julian always went together, keeping to the fringes of the archer camp. Their ranks swelled the day after Magnus and his men arrived, from six to almost thirty. According to Tatiana, that was everyone from Villmark who had survived the ambush in the Izten Torkat.

They weren't an unfriendly bunch, but they were rowdier than Cistine liked. She was always glad to move past them on patrol—and doubly glad it was Maleck's duty to walk among the makeshift cots and small shelters on the riverbank, watching the archer ranks from within. Even necks-deep in their wine pots and huddled around fires, the men showed deference to him as much as they did to Thorne himself.

"I think they're afraid of him," Julian remarked one night as they watched Magnus and Maleck confer over a fire. "They must know what he was capable of as an auger."

Cistine frowned, tucking her hands into the sleeves of her coat. It was still late summer, but mountain nights were chillier than the lowlands. Helga had loaned her the bulky fur parka, which made her feel like a predator lumbering on the fringes of a herd of deer.

Julian, at least, didn't seem to mind holding the paw of a bear.

"Everyone except the cabal treats Maleck like he's going to chop off their heads," Cistine observed. "But he never even puts a hand on his swords if he's not in combat."

"And a viper doesn't bite until you step too close to it. It doesn't hurt to have your guard up."

Julian's words resonated in Cistine's head while they trekked back to the cottage under a thick curtain of clouds. She watched distant lightning flicker over the mountaintops and felt the crackle of its energy in her fingertips as if she was about to throw a punch.

It had been weeks since she'd had her guard up around Maleck. Or around any of the cabal, for that matter. They were spirited and wild, but they didn't frighten her the way they had at first. Because they'd laid hands on her jumbled pieces since then and built something up from that. They'd seen her at her worst—her most selfish, her most defensive, her weakest— and found something to work with, not someone to hate. Someone who could survive a fall into a river, and a perilous journey back to safety afterward. Someone who could keep herself, and a wounded High Tribune, alive with poultices and filthy socks and campfires.

A warm glow of pride bloomed in Cistine's chest, chasing out the cold. She gripped Julian's hand tighter, and he squeezed back. "Vipers or not, they don't frighten me. I want to thank them for everything they've done."

"How would you do that, short of killing all their enemies for them?"

Cistine swatted him on the arm. "The same way you reach the hearts of any group of people: through their stomachs."

The most difficult part of Cistine's entire plan was keeping Helga from the kitchen the following day—something she practically needed a polearm and a chain across the kitchen doorway to manage.

"Go read with Pippet!" Cistine shooed the older woman away from a pot of broth bubbling on the iron stove. "Or find something to lecture Quill about. I have everything under control, I promise!"

Helga harrumphed, dropping the ladle back into the stewpot. "No one ever cooks in this kitchen except me."

"Well, it's like Tatiana says," Cistine laughed, pushing Helga's shoulder, "we have to be...*flexible*. Helga, *please!*"

Helga tossed up her hands. "Oh, stars above! All right, if you're certain you know what you're doing."

Cistine wasn't entirely certain of that; she'd plucked a random recipe ledger from the bookshelf and decided to cook the most aromatic and savory-sounding dish on the list. But if she couldn't cook by heart, at least she had the acumen to follow a book's simple directions—with a few personal embellishments for flavor.

That was how she passed the day—chasing away random visitors, squirming from Julian's arms more than once, and running frantically from shelf to pot to iron skillet. Between bouts of baking and cooking, she scrubbed the entry room until the wooden floors and table glowed. And then, snagging Ashe and Julian for help, she transposed the kitchen's larger preparation table with the table from the main room.

"Are you feeding barbarians, or royalty?" Ashe chuckled as she and Julian positioned the table by Cistine's careful instructions.

"Both, really." Cistine perched her hands on her hips, surveying their handiwork. "Will one of you find Thorne and ask him to rally the cabal? It's almost time to eat."

Her friends swapped incredulous smiles before they slipped out, and Cistine busied herself numbering the stacks of plates she carried to the table, the amount of cutlery she laid out, and the pitchers and wooden cups she placed; aside from a few times in the Den, she'd never set a table before.

She'd barely set down the last steaming dish when the door opened, and everyone streamed inside: Julian and Ashe first, then Thorne, with the cabal behind him. They were all dressed casually except Maleck and Ariadne. Even Helga wore a sun dress, showing the deep tan of her time-folded skin. Quill carried Pippet on his back as effortlessly as if she was five years old.

And they all came to an immediate, quiet halt at the sight of the table, and the meal there.

Cistine twisted the cooking cloth between her hands into a rat's tail. "It's nettle soup, whipped potatoes, basted lambsquarters, and honeyed root vegetables. Oh, and mint and blackroot tea. I've never tried it myself, but it sounded interesting."

Tatiana whistled lowly. "A princess of many talents."

Quill let his sister slide to the floor. "I didn't know you could cook."

"I never have. At least, not without help," Cistine admitted. "This was a new experience for me. My way of thanking you."

"What could we have possibly done to deserve such a magnificent feast?" Helga chuckled, wrapping an arm around Pippet. The girl grinned at Cistine, and Cistine smiled back.

"You cared enough to look twice," she said. "In a tavern. On the Vey. When I was in your house. What's waiting in the Courts is…larger than I thought. Larger than anything I was prepared to face when I first came here. And you may all be dark-hearted fallen stars, and death-gods, and cold killers." Cistine looked among them, one by one. "But I consider you my friends as well as my mentors. And to show how much I appreciate what you've done…well, feeding you seemed like a good way to start."

To her surprise—and unease—no one spoke. They shifted their feet. Ariadne cleared her throat. Tatiana stared at the table as if she wasn't certain the dishes were edible.

Thorne was the first to speak: "Thank you, Cistine."

The others mumbled it too, and Cistine had the horrible feeling that in her effort to express her gratitude, she'd made everything awkward for everyone else.

Maleck finally moved toward the table, and Cistine winced at the squelch of his filthy boots on the floorboards. Ashe shot him a glare worthy of any battlefield. "Wipe off your feet before you take *one more step*. My princess spent all day scrubbing these floors, and we don't need *you* muddying them up again."

Maleck froze, gaping at her.

Then he burst out laughing.

The entire cabal turned to stare at Maleck as he cackled into his cupped hands until he was hoarse; and Cistine realized she'd never heard him laugh before, not even once, in all the weeks she'd known him. It was a strange, husky, raspy sound...but pleasant.

Cistine perched her hands on her hips. "You heard her. Take off your boots. *Now*."

And just like that, the awkwardness shattered. The cabal kicked off their boots and dove toward the table, yanking out seats and elbowing one another away from the dishes. Cistine stood back, wiping off her hands and grinning as she watched them spar for first bites of everything.

"Don't forget your prayers!" Ariadne called to Pippet above the din, halting her fork and knife above her portion.

"Great God of all we know, I hope everyone leaves their soup for me!" Pippet trilled, and Ariadne tickled her neck in passing.

Julian curled an arm around Cistine's waist and kissed the hollow beneath her ear. "Not bad, Princess."

Stomach fluttering, Cistine shoved him toward the table. "Don't compliment me until you've tried it."

Julian grinned, pushing Ashe's arm aside as he helped himself to a heaping portion of potatoes. Ashe retaliated with a punch to his ribs.

Watching her friends fight over the meal she'd prepared—the labor of preparation still caked on her hands—filled Cistine with a warmth she'd never felt before.

"Are you going to stare at us all night?" Ariadne asked. "Or should we try to save a portion for you?"

Cistine waved a hand. "I'd rather you all ate your fill."

"That's generous of you." Quill had a strange look on his face, as if he thought she might steal his portion from him. They all attacked their plates with the vigor of starving wolves, not even lifting their eyes as Cistine settled into the chair between Julian and Ashe.

"It finally makes sense to me," Cistine said to Ariadne, "why you made me do all that grueling labor in the Den."

The warrior swallowed her bite, jaw working furiously. "Oh?"

"It's...comfortable, having everything done for you. But there's no feeling quite like someone else walking into your clean house or eating the meal you prepared with your own hands."

"Mmm," Ashe mumbled in the affirmative, sipping her tea.

Pippet made a face and twisted toward Helga. "I don't like this food."

Hurt stabbed Cistine's belly, but Helga waved her hand. "You don't like anything but stew and venison sandwiches these days. Go make yourself something in the kitchen."

Pippet scampered off, and Thorne cleared his throat. "Don't mind her. It's a stage of life."

Cistine flashed him a grateful smile. "As long as everyone else likes it."

Thorne raised his brows and nodded.

"So...you made all this yourself?" Quill asked.

Tatiana hurled a root vegetable at his head, slathering honey into his eyebrow and across the bridge of his nose. "Less talking. More eating."

Pippet returned with a bowl of cold stew in her hands and burst into laughter. "Your face is sticky! What *happened*?"

Quill dipped his knuckles into the vegetable pan and smeared honey on his sister's cheek as she scampered past, eliciting a high-pitched giggle from her. "*That.*"

"Not at my table!" Helga warned when the siblings both grabbed for the dish of potatoes at the same time.

"And not my potatoes, either!" Cistine cried in mock-offense.

"How old are all of you, anyway?" Julian grumbled as he hacked his lamb into bite-sized pieces and swirled them into the honey.

"That's a good question." Ashe gestured across the table with her fork.

"We've been brushing elbows in close quarters for weeks now, and we barely know anything about any of you."

"Did you ever think we might prefer it that way?" Ariadne asked.

Cistine snorted. "What could it hurt to tell us? Surely you're not *that* old."

Thorne gestured to himself, then to Quill, Tatiana, and Ariadne. "All of us, twenty-eight years old, or thereabouts. Maleck is…"

"Unknown," Maleck finished. "Roughly thirty-four, I believe."

"Really?" Ashe's brows leaped. "Here's to being the elders at a table of wild children."

"I'll toast to that," Helga chuckled, and Pippet poked her in the side.

"You don't look that young," Julian said to Maleck.

Maleck rubbed his face with one hand. "Augmentation has unexpected effects."

A tense silence descended, broken when Ashe said crisply, "Raise your fork if you're an only child."

Tines caught the brilliant candlelight from the windowsills, and Cistine sighed. "Quill and Pippet, put your forks down."

The siblings swapped smiles, but they obeyed.

"Maleck, Ariadne, I didn't know you had siblings," Cistine added.

"Mine are of no merit to mention," Maleck said. "They are not good people."

"And my sister is preoccupied with her own life," Ariadne said.

Thorne set down his fork and stretched, cracking tension from his neck.

"What of you, Ashe?" Maleck asked. "You have no siblings?"

"Childbirth was difficult for my mother," Ashe said. "She was too afraid to try for another after I was born."

"Julian?" Thorne asked.

Predictably, Julian muttered, "I don't want to talk about it."

"Julian, *please?*" Cistine curled her hand into the crook of his elbow and laid her chin on his shoulder.

"Who's going to resist those eyes?" Quill snorted. Someone hit him under the table with a loud *thump.*

Julian sighed, towing a hand back through his dark hair. "Well, my father was away at war when I was born. My mother raised me the first year alone, and I think she decided enough was enough. They never wanted children, anyway...I was a wartime necessity."

Cistine's jaw popped open. "I didn't know that."

"It's rare in Talheim for someone not to want heirs, given the laws of succession." Julian shrugged. "But my father is close with his brothers, so he didn't mind the estate going to one of them. It was because of my mother they even tried for me. If my father died in the war, he didn't want her to be alone. They were lucky enough she was pregnant when he followed your father up here to Valgard."

"But Lady Eboni and Lord Rion adore you," Cistine said. "I always thought they'd planned to have a family."

"You don't always plan for the things you fall in love with." Thorne's gaze flicked to Cistine. "That doesn't mean you love them any less."

"I don't doubt they love me," Julian added. "But some of us are born out of strategy."

"And perhaps that makes us stronger," Thorne said.

"What about you, Tati?" Cistine asked, eager to spare both men the whole table's quiet attention. "You don't have any siblings?"

"My mother died when I was young," Tatiana said. "It was only Papa and me after that. He was too distracted to marry again, and hardly rich enough to keep just the two of us alive."

"He isn't a Tribune?"

Tatiana stuffed her cheeks with potatoes, coughing as she shook her head and gestured with her fork. "Quill and Thorne are the only ones who come from good stock around here. Well, and Aden."

There was something profound in the sadness of the silence that followed—something Cistine, holding Tatiana's gaze, thought she understood.

"Aden?" Ashe broke the stillness. "Who is that?"

"Thorne's cousin," Quill said.

Thorne pushed his plate away and did not meet any of their eyes.

"The rest of us come from common heritage," Maleck added.

"Which gave us lofty aspirations, unfortunately." Ariadne stuck out her hand. "Pass the tea, would you, Mal?"

"Anyway, it's been years since most of us have seen our families," Tatiana said. "They've probably disowned us."

"Or we already disowned them," Quill sighed.

"I could never disown my parents." Julian's voice was low, and Cistine wondered if he was thinking of his father—still stationed at the southern barracks, awaiting some sort of attack from King Jad.

She took his hand under the table.

"The Middle Kingdom is fortunate to have known peace and happiness since the war," Helga said. "Meanwhile, we've seemed to climb down from one poor choice to the next. In the Courts, in the territories, amongst ourselves…"

"And who knows where we'll find the bottom," Quill said.

Quiet descended again, and it seemed everyone ate more slowly after that. Cistine studied their faces, weary despite the good meal, and tightness banded her chest. She didn't know if it was empathy or shame. "I'm sorry that what my kingdom did here didn't bring you any peace."

"It brought peace of a different sort," Maleck said. "It brought calm amidst the storm that was advancement in augmentation's uses."

Thorne finally spoke up, his voice grave: "Calm might not be the right word. It froze the world as we knew it. But the heat is still there, under the surface. Someday, something may melt that frost. Valgard's heart may awaken again."

He held Cistine's gaze as he spoke, and she had the strange sense he was trying to convey something important with that look.

"Listen to him, being so cryptic," Ashe scoffed, breaking the wordless tension between them. "What is it about royalty that makes them think they need to sound so pretentious?"

Cistine batted her lashes innocently at her Warden. "Just because *you* have the vocabulary of a drunk fox."

"Do you see what I put up with?" Ashe groaned to Maleck.

"You have it no worse than I do." Maleck toasted his cup of tea to her. "Cistine, at least, has patience and kindness to spare."

Quill spat out his drink. "Patience? *Kindness?*"

"Excuse me!" Cistine snapped.

"Was that a joke?" Tatiana demanded. "Are *you* making jokes now, Maleck?"

"Only following my High Tribune's years of glowing examples."

"That explains why it was such a poor joke, then," Ashe quipped.

Thorne smirked at Cistine. "I think we were just ganged up on. By a pair of drunk foxes, no less."

"Ashe terrifies me, so I'll let it go this time," Cistine laughed.

Ashe winked at Maleck, and once again, he chuckled. Cistine was beginning to like that sound.

"Has everyone finished?" Helga asked.

"I'm bursting at the seams," Tatiana said.

"Couldn't eat another bite, really," Quill agreed.

Julian pushed his plate away. "I give up, too."

Thorne excused himself and vanished outside, mumbling that he was full. Helga got to her feet. "I'll take these dishes, then."

"Wait." Cistine held up a hand to stop her. "Don't throw away the scraps. I want to take the rest of the food to Magnus's camp."

Tatiana's brows flicked up. "Why don't you let *us* handle that? I think you've worked hard enough today."

"She's right," Quill said. "We'll deliver the food as soon as I grab my swords. Tati?"

"I...left something in the kitchen. I'll be right behind you."

They both broke away at the same time, hurrying from the room. Maleck, Ariadne, Ashe, and Julian quickly excused themselves outside, and Helga tugged Pippet upstairs to get ready for bed, whispering in the girl's ear as they went. In moments, Cistine was alone with the remnants of her first successful meal.

A happy glow spread through her chest, chasing out all the stress of the day's cooking. Grinning, she hopped to her feet and gathered the food into one of Helga's empty satchels from the trunk under the window. Then she filled two skins with tea and nettle soup and hurried from the cottage.

She didn't need Quill and Tatiana to make deliveries on her behalf. She could easily cook and serve a meal to two groups in one day. After all her training, this was nothing.

It was a fine night for a walk, the air a bit warmer than usual, the sky full of stars, and Cistine was content to make the long walk to the archer camp alone. Everything was quiet aside from the brush of her slippers on the grass. The world was so large, and everything so infinitely far from her grasp.

Talheim seemed very far away.

She wondered what her parents were doing tonight...if they were thinking of their only daughter and wondering what sort of trouble she was getting herself into at the Bartos estate on the coast. Or if they were so completely occupied with the Southern Kingdom, with King Jad and his advances, they didn't have time to wonder after her.

Some part of her hoped for the latter. It would buy her a bit more time to negotiate.

She reached the archer camp just as her arms began to tremble from the weight of the food sacks, and a pair of men accosted her there. Their focus was on her face, not on the food.

"You're the girl from Talheim," one of them said. "The one who broke open the Throat of God."

Cistine stifled a groan. "Yes, that was me."

"Thank you." The man shocked her by bending low and crossing an arm over his chest. "You avenged our brothers who died riddling those wagons with arrows."

"We're forever grateful to you, *Logandir*," his companion added. Then they both tucked aside to allow her passage into the camp.

The unexpected exchange crowded Cistine's thoughts as she wound between the straw nests and makeshift tents, searching for Magnus. She'd been granted reverence all her life from Talheim's people; they bowed in the streets whenever she passed. But that was the decorum she'd been born into, the veneration her title deserved. She'd never been bowed to in gratitude for her deeds.

And that name they'd called her, *Logandir*—it was familiar, but she couldn't place where she'd heard it before.

She was still puzzling over it when she spotted Magnus seated at one of the camp's many fires with his men, laughing as he thumbed pebbles into the flames. Cistine halted behind him and cleared her throat. "I have a gift from the cabal."

Magnus twisted around, his eyes alighting on her with surprise—and something almost like suspicion. "What's this all about? Thorne's sending servants to appeal to us now?"

Cistine's cheeks warmed with disgust. "We thought you and your men might like something *not* cooked on a spit. But if you're going to be rude about it..."

"Ah...wait." Magnus got to his feet. "Let's see what you have there."

Cistine bit back a smile as she laid out the offering—the lamb, the vegetables, the heaping bowl of potatoes, and the skins full of nettle soup and tea. The men murmured appreciatively, crowding around her and Magnus.

"I haven't had lamb since the farm!" one of them called. "Give it here, Magnus!"

"Wait your turn!" Smirking, Magnus picked up a quarter and bit into it.

Eyes bulging wide, he gagged and almost retched on Cistine's shoes. Hurling the piece of meat into the fire with a furious scowl, he shouted, "Is this the High Tribune's idea of punishment now? Serving us rancid food?"

"I beg your pardon?" Cistine snapped. "It's not *rancid!*"

"It tastes like the Undertaker's toe hairs! Is this some sort of cruel joke?"

Cistine picked up one of the remaining quarters and nibbled it—and forced herself not to recoil.

Gods. It *did* taste awful, like overcooked, overspiced *char.*

She'd added a few extra ingredients to the mixture—herbs she was fond of eating straight off the plant—but she'd never known them to taste like *that*.

Though, granted, she'd never married them with a spice rub before.

Cistine's eyes and cheeks burned as she watched the men pry at the potatoes, sip the nettle soup, and gag. This was worse than a joke. It was a lie. The cabal hadn't enjoyed the meal at all.

Humiliated, Cistine threw down the lambsquarter and stalked away.

She'd been foolish to think she could learn this skill—to think the cabal *believed* she could. Cooking had always been as far beyond her grasp as swordplay; and what if the cabal was merely propping her up with pretty words when it came to training, too, or learning about Valgardan borders and politics, just as they'd propped her up with their lies tonight?

Heat stung Cistine's eyes, and she felt as if someone had scooped out her guts with a spoon. Her belly was hollow with shame.

If she couldn't even master a simple meal, how could she hope to negotiate a peace treaty with Kanslar's Chancellor? If she couldn't discern when the cabal was lying to her, how would she navigate the Courts?

Useless. Underprepared. And Kanslar's constellation was already high in the sky, winking ruthlessly down at her, reminding her that this was all just wasted time.

Cistine was so entrenched in embarrassment and indignation, she didn't realize Magnus had followed her until he was jogging at her side.

"Don't feel poorly," he said. "You were only the messenger. This scuffle between us and the cabal has been going on for years. At Villmark, we welcomed them with mountain roaches in their pelts. This little trick certainly escalates things, though."

His words couldn't have jabbed any deeper into her chest if they'd been a blade. Cistine folded her arms tightly beneath her breasts and sped up. "Please leave me alone."

"There's no need to act this way! Why don't you join us around the fire? We'll have some meat cooked on a spit, like you said. I can promise it'll be better than that swill, at least."

"*No*, thank you."

"Come, I insist! We'll make you forget your troubles for the night."

"I said no," Cistine snapped, "and I won't say it again."

"That's for certain," Magnus chuckled, resting a hand on the back of her neck.

His touch towed her back through miles of mountains, to Veran, to that tavern where the slavers had trapped her. Two moments clashed within her, helplessness against helplessness, drowning her in the sensation that she was still that cosseted child, out of her depth in the tavern.

And then Quill's training blew through Cistine. It slammed the hurt and rage from her body, slammed out the panic at the touch of fingers against her neck. She grabbed Magnus's hand, plucked it from her shoulder, and jammed it backward on the hinge, spraining it with a snap. She kicked his legs out from under him and thrust him to his seat on the dusty ground, then stomped his groin so hard he vomited.

"Don't you ever," she snarled while he retched and writhed before her, "*ever* touch me, or any other woman, without permission. Do you understand me?"

Magnus coughed and gasped. He didn't seem to know which place to grab—his battered groin or his wounded wrist.

Footsteps pounded the dirt. Cistine looked up, breathing raggedly, as Thorne skidded into view through the camp's firelight. His icy eyes skipped between her and Magnus, and his brows vaulted with a look that almost passed as shock.

And for a flicker of an instant, as pride.

"I take it you've learned your lesson, Magnus," he said. "But if you choose to forget it again, I will happily stand back and watch Cistine teach it to you again and again, until you don't have an unbroken bone in your body. Is that understood?"

"Yes, High Tribune," the man moaned.

"Good. Now go soak your groin in the river. Cistine?"

She halted on the verge of storming off again. As Magnus crawled to his feet and limped away, Cistine faced Thorne and folded her arms. "*Yes?*"

Thorne's gaze swept over her. Then he smiled. "Walk with me?"

And because it was a question—because he had the decency, at least, to ask—Cistine waited for him to fall into step beside her before she left the camp.

"Your cabal are a pack of filthy liars," she said hoarsely as the darkness closed around them. "I know about the dinner."

Thorne sighed. "They were trying to be gracious."

"By not telling me my food tasted like *rot?*"

"You tried," Thorne said. "For their sake, you tried, which is far more than most have done in more years than we can count."

"But they didn't have to be cruel about it."

"They didn't eat it to mock you, Cistine. They didn't want you to feel badly." Thorne glanced back at the archer camp. "Now, what they intended with the archers was uncalled for. And they should be reamed for it."

"Then why didn't you stop them when they said they'd take the food?"

Thorne pulled a face. "Because I was busy vomiting all over Helga's flowerbeds."

Cistine hit him on the shoulder. "You were not!"

"Forgive me," Thorne's smile was a pale flash in the dark. "But I really was."

"Wonderful!" Cistine tossed up her hands. "You save my life twice, and I repay you by serving you the worst meal of yours!"

"Hardly the worst. There's no denying Quill and Ariadne are worse cooks than you."

"I doubt that's possible."

"If you don't believe me, ask Maleck," Thorne said. "He claims he still can't eat Ariadne's fish because it tastes like betrayal."

Cistine squinted up at him in the dim moonlight. "Is that really true, or do you just not want me to feel like a failure?"

Thorne's brow furrowed. "There's no reason you should feel that way, Cistine. None of us is a master of all things, and we don't expect perfect mastery from you. Not every swordsman is a baker. Ashe would gladly tell you that, I suspect."

Cistine frowned. "How did you know her parents were bakers?"

"Maleck mentioned it."

It was so strange to her—Maleck laughing. Maleck knowing these details of Ashe's life. "He seemed in good spirits tonight."

Thorne pocketed his hands, a casual posture belied by the dip of his head as he watched the ground beneath their feet. "Before tonight, I hadn't heard him laugh in...stars only know how long. *Too* long. Months. Maybe a year or more. And I can only guess how long it was before that."

"What was different today?"

"It isn't just today. It's ever since you and your Wardens came to Hellidom. He's always gone where I've told him, done whatever I've asked. But when I caught up with you in that meadow, and I saw Maleck with his blade against Ashe's throat...I knew something had shifted."

"Do you know what it was?"

Thorne hummed thoughtfully. "Ashe has never been afraid of him. Furious with him, ready to rip out his lungs, but not afraid. I think that's something Maleck hasn't known, outside this cabal, in decades. Everyone he meets perceives him as a threat."

"And perception is everything, I suppose," Cistine said. "Some people are perceived as murderous *bandayos*, but they're really protectors."

"And some are perceived as cosseted royalty, when they're made of steel underneath."

Cistine wound her hair behind the shell of her ear, searching the horizon until the cottage came into view. "Back at the archer camp, they called me *Logandir*. Do you have any idea what that means?"

Thorne slowed his stride. "I do. It's from the stories Baba Kallah read to me. Logandir was the leader of the Traisende. They called her *The Wild Heart of Fire*."

Cistine frowned. "Did they call me that because of what I did in the pass?"

"It would seem so."

"And...is that the same as being Named by someone?"

Thorne chuckled. "No. But it does mean you're beginning to make quite the impression."

Pippet and Helga were still upstairs when Cistine and Thorne strode into the cottage side-by-side. The cabal was gathered at the table, their faces drawn with unease. They all sat up at attention when Thorne appeared.

"Cabal," he said, "on your feet. Cistine has something to say to you."

The warriors rose slowly and faced her. Cistine nodded to Ashe and Julian. "You, too."

When they rose, Cistine took a deep breath. She'd rehearsed this on the last quarter-mile from the archer camp, but she still feared her voice would shake.

"I appreciate that you all lied to me about the meal to spare my dignity," she said. "But I don't ever, *ever* want to be the brunt of your jokes that way again. If you can't think of a better way to jab back at the archers, ask me for help. I'm sure I've read enough books that I could offer a few ideas."

"Fair enough," Tatiana said.

"And if I make rancid food, then for God's sake, be honest with me about it. I can't improve when I don't know I'm failing."

The cabal exchanged heavy glances, filling the air with doubt-dusted silence.

Ariadne, unsurprisingly, took the first stab. "Cistine, your food tasted like licking a bloated corpse."

"It's true," Quill admitted. "I've scrounged from pig troughs that tasted better."

"The next time you want to pamper us, try infesting our beds with lice," Tatiana said. "I think we'd suffer a little less."

Cistine perched her hands on her hips. "Is this your way of apologizing?"

They all watched her, quiet and curious, and Cistine let them stew in it for a bit.

"Apology accepted."

Quill and Tatiana loosened up with relief. Ashe smiled, pushing out the chair beside her. "Care to join us for some cards?"

"Later," Cistine said. "I was just on my way to make dessert."

"Oh, no, you don't!" Quill grabbed her around the waist and slung her down in the chair, and Julian anchored her in place with his hand on her shoulder. "You're going to sit here and learn a card game with us."

"Consider that *your* penance for that meal." Julian nuzzled her temple and kissed her hair.

Across the table, Cistine met Thorne's eyes.

Thank you, she mouthed.

He dipped his head, and a flash of intention crossed the space between them—what his actions, if not his words, conveyed. *The hunt was yours.*

And judging by the levity at the table as they dealt out the cards—and the lightness in her chest—Cistine thought she'd done all right.

CHAPTER
FORTY-ONE

THERE WAS A disadvantage to being Talheim's most renowned court gossip. While Cistine was never short of juicy morsels to share with her friends, there was always a handful of revelations she wished she'd never stumbled across: friends' suitors being caught in closets with the new maids; the diagnosis of an elder's terminal bloodcough; the first time her mother had suffered a miscarriage...and the second.

By the sunset following the disastrous supper in Starhollow, she had a new reason to vow never to go snooping again. A reason that changed everything.

It passed as most days in the cottage had: helping Pippet do chores and weave flower crowns under Helga's watchful eye, and then swimming with Julian, Ashe, Pippet, and Tatiana to escape the afternoon heat. And when Quill took his sister on a walk one way, Cistine and Tatiana went the other.

They talked for hours, traversing the meadows, plucking flowers for more crowns and discussing Talheimic fashion, Valgardan weaponry, and books. Endlessly, books.

"I wish I had your freedom with libraries," Tatiana said wistfully as they waded through a particularly high meadow of grass. "Stornhaz limits access to its larger ones."

"Are they hiding something?"

"I think the elites just like the feeling of holding on too tightly to things—whether it's mynts, or food, or knowledge. In a way, leaving Stornhaz was the best thing that ever happened to me. In Hellidom, I have no station. I'm not a poor tinker's daughter. And Thorne doesn't care what we read, so long as it doesn't keep us from patrol."

"But Hellidom can't be your entire future," Cistine said. "Don't you ever dream of doing anything besides patrols and spying on wagons?"

"And completing my collection of bloodied knives?" Cistine flung a handful of clover at her, and Tatiana batted it aside, laughing. "I don't know. I rarely think about it."

"Why not?"

"Because there is no *end* to this." Tatiana gestured with a spread of her arm to Starhollow, the cottage far behind them, and the mountains beyond that. "We've been on the run for ten years. If Thorne has a better plan, he hasn't shared it yet. It's always him and the Chancellor at each other's throats across the distance. We ransack a caravan, he kills our archers. We spy on his surgeons, he puts an arrow through one of us. Neither one has managed to bring the other to his knees."

"There has to be *some* end in sight," Cistine said. "Something has to give eventually."

Tatiana rubbed her shoulder. "It rarely gives out in our favor."

"But what if it did? Would you stay in Thorne's cabal, or would you want something else?"

Tatiana groaned. "Oh, I don't *know*."

"If you could be anything! I want to know."

Tatiana blew her curls from her brow, frowning thoughtfully as she walked ahead of Cistine. Her mother-of-pearl dress blurred around her bare feet as she plucked up a meadow sunflower and pressed her nose into its black heart.

"A barmaid."

Cistine groaned, sweeping Tatiana's shins in passing, and they settled back into banter rather than soul-bearing on the long walk back to the cottage. But the conversation left Cistine restless when they returned. The notion of endless conflict, dead archers, and wounded warriors nipped her fingertips, sending her dusting and cleaning just to give her hands something to do. She avoided the kitchen, where Helga was pottering around—no doubt cooking something to erase the lingering aftertaste of the previous night's meal—and paused to place several of Pippet's books back on the shelves while the girl sketched furiously at the table.

"Cistine, look," Pippet announced. "I made you something!"

Cistine braced her hands on the back of Pippet's chair, squinting at the drawing. "It's lovely. Is that me?"

It had to be—Pippet had captured the hickory shade of her hair perfectly, and with a crown perched askew on her head.

Pippet nodded and pointed to the drawing's other occupant. "And that's Quill, destroying you in training like he always does."

"Hm. I think I need to have a word with your brother. He's telling you tall tales."

Helga laughed from the kitchen, then summoned Pippet for help. The girl leaped up, pausing long enough to wrap her thin arms around Cistine before she chased after her nanny's call.

A shard of warmth pierced Cistine's worry as she stared down at Pippet's drawing. Earning her acceptance was different from the cabal's. It brought the same kind of warmth as summer afternoon in a teahouse—but it also awakened a strange, protective fire in her. A need to keep this place and this girl secret at any cost.

Cistine smiled as she turned toward the windows—and nearly leaped with shock.

Faer perched on the windowsill, ruffling his wings and cawing indignantly to be let in. Cistine hurried to the window, undid the latch, and brought him inside on her wrist. The cold, damp wind followed him in; a storm was threatening the valley, hanging low over the mountains. Cistine shivered as she stroked Faer's damp plumage.

"Oh, God, please tell me the note wasn't damaged." Cistine freed the scroll from Faer's leg and unrolled it. To her relief, the ink hadn't run.

But now she was holding it—and looking at Baba Kallah's elegant, tidy handwriting...

Cistine glanced toward the kitchen, then toward the stairs. She hadn't seen Thorne all day. She didn't know where he was or how much longer he would be gone, either patrolling Starhollow or plotting with Magnus. And if this was an important note...if Hellidom was in danger, or if Baba Kallah needed their help for any reason...

There was really no harm in reading it.

Cistine had told herself this before.

The memory was vague. She recalled opening the door to her father's private study and slinking inside to look for him, and finding herself staring at a large, official-looking letter on his desk instead. Not at all like the one she tucked herself into the reading nook with now. She remembered picking up that letter and seeing Lord Rion's signet on it.

Thirteen. She'd been almost thirteen that day, when she'd learned Lord Rion, Lady Eboni, and Julian were leaving Astoria.

My Thorne,

All is well here. No sign of attack. I've vetted Orrin's story—I am convinced he was unaware of the finer points of the trap in the pass, and Hellidom has not been compromised.

The harvest is growing. The people are quiet. We are safe...as I hope you are, Stornjor.

Baba Kallah's handwriting was so neat and cramped—making room to say more.

The letter from the commander of the King's Cadre had looked so much more official than this. Of course it had...because, through it, Lord Rion had made his resignation official and informed King Cyril they would be taking up residence in their family lands in Practica.

I know you asked me to wait until we saw one another face to face. But I feel I must address your other concerns now. I know if I wait, these matters will devour you like a Viperwolf, and that would certainly complicate our reunion.

Cistine remembered the cold tide of reality smashing over her that day, like the Agerios would bash itself apart on the rocks whenever she and her family picnicked on the shore.

As a child, she'd asked why it kept doing that…heaving itself up and throwing itself forward, only to be broken in foamy pieces again. She remembered her mother telling her that was what the sea did, because it didn't know any better. It didn't know how not to be broken.

She'd thought of the sea when she'd realized Julian was about to leave. That the dashing boy she'd glimpsed shyly around corners for years and years—the playmate she'd started to hope might take notice of her fletched dresses and bejeweled gloves instead of the toys they shared—would soon be gone.

She'd felt like a wave then, knowing she should let go of him, but not knowing how to do it. How not to be broken.

She felt like a wave now.

My answer is yes. As much as it pains you. Whatever it destroys. You must tell Cistine why you truly helped her when she first came to Hellidom. Even the ugly bits. Even the parts that were lies and deception.

She was honest with you about the Svarkyst steel. Now you must be honest about the rest. Even that you knew the Chancellor would come for the Talheimic princess.

Cistine was in the study, and in the reading nook—her lungs squeezing, her breaths wobbling, her eyes sparkling with hot tears of shock, and disbelief, and rage…

Tell her you intended to use her to lure the Chancellor from Stornhaz. It's better she learns it from your own mouth than anywhere else.

Cistine was a wave smashing into the rocks—the letter falling from her hand as her fragile heart cracked in pieces.

And then she was moving.

She staggered up from the nook, waving Faer off as he plucked at her shiny sleeve in passing. Her dress—a gift from Tatiana—suddenly felt like a hunter's net, like boning that squeezed her organs to bursting. She wanted to be free from it, but she didn't have any other clothes. She didn't have anything here that Thorne and his cabal hadn't given to her—these gifts, these placations...

These lies.

She stormed up the stairs, hating her skirts and sleeves, hating the slippers on her feet. She hated every step down the hall to the room she shared with Ashe and Pippet, and Tatiana and Ariadne.

Lure. She didn't wonder if they knew—she was certain they did. The cabal kept no secrets from each other. Only from the people they used and had purposes for. The ones they pretended to befriend when they were really grooming them for slaughter.

Lies.

She burst into the room, and Ashe sat up sharply on the mattress. She'd been dozing, judging by her cloudy eyes and the state of her hair, and she shuffled her appearance into something respectable at Cistine's arrival. "What's wrong?"

"We're leaving," Cistine said. "We're leaving Starhollow, right now."

Ashe scrambled to her feet. "Thorne's orders?"

"Mine!" Cistine snapped, incensed at the sound of his name. "Leave anything you don't need. I'm going to find Julian."

Cistine picked up her training armor and hurled it into the corner—

those threads Tatiana and Quill had helped her choose. She wondered if they'd truly cared about making her proficient, or if they'd all been simply helping Thorne entertain her by her own wishes, to keep her complacent and close by until Kanslar Court rose to power and he could use her to tempt his sickly mentor from safety. To lure him into the open.

Lies on top of lies.

Cistine slammed her fist into Julian's door twice, and he answered it bedheaded as well, and shirtless. For once, that sight did nothing to stir Cistine's nerves. They were already raw, fizzing with fury. There was no room left for anything else.

"Something happen?" Julian mumbled.

"Put on your shirt. We're going."

Julian's eyes widened. "*Finally.*" He ducked back into the room and reemerged before Cistine had mustered enough clarity to turn away from the door. He walked with her to the top of the steps, meeting Ashe with Echelon in her hand. "Do either of you want to tell me why you finally decided to go?"

"Not now," Cistine growled. "Once we're out of the mountains."

They walked out into the rainstorm's tendrils, the faint whisper on the grass like the world's dullest lullaby. Cistine tucked her head and walked shoulder-first into the mist, and her friends—her true friends, her Talheimic companions—walked beside her without question.

Their loyalty, she could trust. Their hearts were beyond question.

They walked north, across the river from the archer camp, past the pond where Cistine had wasted away the days even after Kanslar's constellation had risen. She'd let herself become complacent, distracted— allowed her focus to shift from her home and its needs. She'd welcomed this interference with open arms when she should've marched straight to Stornhaz.

The moment the cabal had left Hellidom, she should've gone.

But she'd taken Thorne at his word. She'd let him trick her into believing the danger was in Stornhaz, even in the Chancellor's household, rather than in his own hands.

No longer. Never again.

Julian's warning shout sliced the cool air, and Cistine picked up her head just in time to catch a faceful of feathers. Faer banked and swooped back toward them, tangling his talons in Cistine's hair this time, grabbing and tugging and making a mess of things, just like the man who commanded him. Cistine swatted upward as hard as she could, cracking the side of her wrist against Faer's sternum. The raven faltered and flopped into the grass, squawking indignantly at the blow. But he'd done his job.

"Cistine!" Quill's voice was unmistakable even before she caught sight of him jogging after them. He had the audacity to be wide-eyed, as if he hadn't sent his watchdog of a bird ahead to stop them—to prevent her from leaving.

Just like he did to his sister.

Julian started forward with a low curse, and Cistine slung an arm across his front. "Don't stop. Just keep walking."

They trudged up the riverbank, pretending Quill wasn't following them. Pretending they'd never heard of such a man before and couldn't hear him shouting their names now.

Until his hand descended on her shoulder.

"*Get away from me!*" Cistine hurled his arm aside as she whirled to face him. "How dare you touch me, how dare you even *look* at me after what you've done? What all of you did!"

Ashe and Julian halted several paces up the bank, listening with blatant curiosity as Cistine faced Quill, heaving with rage. Quill stared at her in shock for a moment, then with a face full of calmness that was somehow more infuriating. "Would you mind telling me what it is I've done? I lost a bet with Tatiana, so I have to keep a ledger of all the times I fail."

"Don't play coy with me," Cistine seethed. "Like you played into Thorne's games. Deceiving me...giving me gifts. Pretending we were all friends! As if Talheim and Valgard could ever be anything but enemies after what we did to one another!"

Quill's brow wrinkled with concern that almost seemed sincere. "Cistine, you aren't making any sense."

"Don't condescend to me! Don't pretend you didn't know what he wanted…how he intended to *use* me."

And Quill's eyes finally betrayed him. They skipped away from her, searching the rain as it intensified. "It isn't what you think."

"Despite what your cabal believes, I'm not a silly, vapid little princess. I'm sure you all enjoyed playing me for one, like you did with the archers. But the deception is over, Quill. I know who you truly are."

He looked up at her with the nerve to seem wounded, eyes flashing painfully. "Let me find Thorne. He can explain what's really happening here."

"You mean he can lie!" Cistine shouted. "I'm not going to give him the chance. As far as I'm concerned, in this struggle between Thorne and the Chancellor, the Chancellor is a *far* better man."

Quill blanched. "You don't know what you're saying."

"I know exactly what I'm saying!" Cistine stepped closer to him, filling the slim space between them with the heat of her furious breath. "The Chancellor is the only one who hasn't lied to me or used me. And the *only one* who can actually help me and my kingdom!"

"Cistine, no—you know what he's capable of! Thorne and Baba Kallah—"

"Enough!" Heat raged in Cistine's head and heart, her temples throbbing as she fought the angry tears. "I'm done believing the cabal's stories. Go tell them to your sister, Quill. I'm leaving. And if you try to force me to stay here against my will, you'll be no better than a slaver."

Quill's mouth hung open, and this time Cistine believed the hurt in his eyes. Believed that if nothing else, he finally understood how she saw him…what he had done to her. What he had helped Thorne do.

"Cistine," he said as she turned away, "you should know, if you're going to go, the Chancellor is—"

Cistine turned and struck past Quill's guard—straight into his face. His nose crunched under her knuckles, and he staggered backward, falling dazed on the ground and smashing his head on the shore. He doubled over on his side, clutching his temple in one hand, over his scar. Cistine fought down a stab of guilt at the concussed look in his glassy eyes. She would not apologize for silencing him when he'd violated her command to stop feeding her stories.

So Cistine left him there and joined her friends again. When Julian took her hand, she almost wept. But she forced herself to keep walking, one sodden, miserable, freezing step after the other—away from Quill. Away from the cottage. Away from the cabal.

Back into the Valgardan wilds.

CHAPTER FORTY-TWO

By THE TIME they reached the Vingete Vey, some of Cistine's wrath had cooled. She'd spent enough nights awake and enough days in choked, furious silence to parse out where the blame was due: what she owed to herself, what she would have to pay Thorne back for if their paths ever had the misfortune to cross again, and what belonged to the cabal.

They'd walked along the Vey for less than a full day before a wagon slowed beside them, and the driver offered them a ride. He was an older man, a trapper named Jaius, with long braids nestled in the tufts of his silver beard. Rosy cheeks embraced his blue eyes, which watered constantly despite the heat. The back of his cart was crammed with furs and barrels of treated meat for trade in Stornhaz. Julian and Ashe took turns sleeping in the back of the wagon and riding in the seat—keeping Jaius company.

According to the trapper, Kanslar's season was the greatest for Valgard; the Chancellor, it seemed, had a soft spot for fine pelts and game meat. Cistine listened to him discuss this with Ashe and Julian from the back of the wagon, since she couldn't bring herself quite yet to carry on a civilized conversation with a Valgardan.

The man's blue eyes were too much like Thorne's, his accent too much like Tatiana's, his face too much like Maleck's. These were marks against him.

As the days passed, Cistine's fury cooled into caution. Lulled by the swaying wheels and the tug of the tired horses against the cart's hitching rails, she reflected on the truths that lay ahead of her, not behind. Whatever else the cabal had lied about, it was still true the Chancellor was fascinated with Talheim. She had the Guide's word and the Vassoran guard's crude hints to confirm that. She would still have to go cautiously and choose her words carefully before him.

Ashe's voice broke into her thoughts: "Do you think Maleck knew?"

Cistine lifted her head from the pillow of animal hides, looking at her Warden where she perched on a trunk of furs nearby. "What?"

"The things Thorne was doing." Ashe's voice was brittle with anger on Cistine's behalf, but also soft with curiosity. "Do you think he knew?"

Cistine flopped back down. "Does it really matter?"

"Yes."

"*Why.*"

"I don't...I don't know, Cistine." Ashe's sigh was filled with something less than disappointment, but more than annoyance. Something softer. "Because Maleck and I have more in common than I...than *either* of us wants to admit. And I need to know I'm not capable of something like this. Of hurting someone I claim to care about this deeply."

Cistine swallowed. "Maybe you're right. Maybe Maleck really thought he was helping a useless princess."

Ashe's grateful smile made the concession worthwhile—even if Cistine didn't believe a word of it.

The cart flap peeled back suddenly, and Julian crawled in among the furs. "Your turn to keep the trapper awake."

Ashe slipped out to join Jaius on the seat as Cistine settled back into the furs, burying her face in her arms, and Julian rubbed her back with his knuckles.

"Just a few more days," he said. "Then we'll be on our way home."

The notion jumped tears to Cistine's eyes. Right now, she wanted to run to her mother, like she had after she'd found Lord Rion's note. She wanted that warm embrace to piece her back together again.

Julian stretched out beside her, propping his head on his hand and draping an arm around her waist. "Do you want to talk about it?"

Cistine rolled over, facing away from him. "Not really."

He was quiet for several minutes before he touched her hip. "We knew this might happen, Princess. Staying with them was always a risk."

"I said I don't want to discuss them, Julian." Cistine's voice shook. She was so tired of people ignoring her wishes and testing her boundaries.

"All right. But when you do, you know I'll listen."

She knew he would—and he would feed her anger. He would agree with her offenses and console her with his complaints. And she would feel justified, and she would simmer, and it would lead to nothing. A pot uselessly boiling over. It wouldn't change anything if she kept looking back...back to Hellidom. Back to Starhollow.

So she told him nothing. She kept to herself, and slowly pulled the pieces of her composure back together as the days wore on. She didn't even bother to look outside the cart as they crossed a tributary and moved along the banks of the Ismalete River, tumbling north to south.

They followed it deeper into Blaykrone territory. Through Eben.

Sometimes, Ashe or Julian tried to coax her to look at the landscape, to behold the mountains in the west or the southern edge of the enormous lake where Cassaida's family lived, or the Sotefold Forest that marked the beginning of Erdotre territory. She declined each time. She didn't want to know. She didn't want to love Valgard's hills and valleys, its lakes and rivers—or its people.

She wanted to appeal to the Chancellor, and then she wanted to go home.

A day finally dawned when Cistine was shaken awake by Ashe's hand on her shoulder to find Jaius had driven them through the night.

Cistine sat up, her hair storming around her face. On the other side of the wagon, Julian stirred as well.

"We're here." Ashe announced. "Come and see Stornhaz."

The City of a Thousand Stars wasn't accessible by any roads. They had to dock the cart on the river's shore and load the pelts and meat barrels onto a barge, which sailed upriver through a slotted gate into the confines of the city's encircling outer wall.

At the sight of its interior, some of Cistine's anger faded and a hint of wonder returned. Stornhaz was splendid: enormous, yet insular. Several tall towers and gaudy domes, draped with flower-studded lichen, were almost tall enough to peer over the flat, white stone wall around the city. There were dozens of docks sprouting into the water from the ends of the streets and the backs of the alabaster homes, decorated with banners and pennant-chains and garlands of flowers, which loomed over the channel. Draped in balconies, the homes seemed expensive by common standards—and that, at least, verified Tatiana's tale of the rich and powerful who dominated Stornhaz.

And that was good. Those were precisely the sort of people Cistine needed to meet with.

They traveled below several roads built almost to the top of the wall, balanced on stone struts. These were framed with strange posts, all with a single arm that hung out over the roadway.

"Streetlamps," Jaius explained when Cistine gestured to the poles. "Lit with augmented bulbs that could burn all night, every night. But they've been dark some twenty years now."

Cistine's belly dropped as they sailed below one of those towering bridges. She was glad to pass out from under the shadows of its struts and poles into smaller, more familiar streets. Avenues that reminded her of Astoria—of home.

The sweet music of bells filled the air as the barge passed by a particularly wide dock at the edge of a broad, column-wrapped terrace. Children kicked a ball across the open flagstones in front of what seemed to be a school. When they spotted the barge, the children whistled and waved. Cistine fluttered her fingers in reply and tried not to think of Pippet, who must have been their age, trapped in Starhollow with her lying brother.

She tried not to feel guilty that even to Pippet, who was innocent in all this, she had not said goodbye.

The streets widened as the pole barge moved upstream. Jaius guided them effortlessly among the docks, until he pushed into port seemingly at random. Workers in dark blue livery swaggered from the nearby buildings to unload the barge.

"Where are you off to now?" Jaius asked as Julian helped Cistine onto the dock.

"The courthouse," Cistine mumbled. "Could you point us in the right direction?"

Jaius took her shoulder and gestured up the avenue. Even in the darkness of the overcast day, it glowed with a mosaic of pink stones. "This street is called the Rouge. Follow it until it intersects with the Fogway...you can't miss it. Turn right, follow the Fogway until it crosses over the channel. Then you'll find yourself at the courthouse gate."

"Thank you." Cistine beckoned her friends to follow her down the Rouge.

"Have you thought of how you're going to appeal to the Chancellor without anything to trade?" Ashe asked while they hurried up the street.

"Short of falling on my knees and begging...not really," Cistine admitted. "I'll have to see the sort of man he is."

"Hopefully less of a bastard than his protégé," Julian growled.

Ashe slapped the back of his head. "Not helpful, Julian."

Cistine pretended she hadn't heard them. She slowed to a halt at the mouth of the Rouge, where the pink tiles gave way to an avenue of silver blown glass under some hard shell that allowed foot travel without cracking the designs below. People hurried up and down the street, most wearing heavy ankle-length coats with trimmed edges and tasseled hoods.

"Stornhaz fashion," Julian noted. "Maybe we should shop while we're here?"

Cistine knew he was trying to cheer her up, but she wasn't in the mood to be cheered. She turned right, stepped out over the blown glass, and started toward the courthouse.

She could see it from a distance: rain-wrapped, the tallest and most impressive building in Stornhaz thus far. It was also the largest, with a sprawling complex of apartments or studies or gods-knew-what spread out in its wings. The muraled walls glittered in vibrant gemstone shades, dazzling Cistine's eyes as they crossed the winged bridge over the channel. It dead-ended in a gilded gate, guarded by a pair of what could only be Vassora.

Cistine's feet slowed almost of their own accord. Staring at these men in their matching armor, she couldn't help but see their friends in the basin, the ones Thorne had butchered for her...*because* of her.

Because he hadn't wanted to share his bargaining tool.

But that wasn't the explanation he'd given Quill and Maleck in the loft, when he hadn't known she could hear him. When he'd had no reason to lie.

You're not going through with it, are you? Quill had asked.

What in Nimmus do you think?

Cistine shrugged away the memory like an ill-fitting coat, lifted her head, and lengthened her stride.

"That's far enough," one of them said. "State your name and business."

"My name is Cistine Novacek, Princess of Talheim. I've come to request an audience with the Chancellor of Kanslar Court."

The men exchanged a glance, and Cistine felt a faint blaze of pride that warmed away the chill in her numb fingertips. Let them wonder what she knew—let them puzzle out for themselves if she was aware the Chancellor had an interest in Talheim. In *her.* She'd proven she wouldn't be hunted. She'd presented herself fearlessly, and now she waited for them to decide if it was worth denying her entrance if she truly was who she claimed to be.

Julian and Ashe lurked a respectable distance behind her, but Cistine knew they were tense. Prepared for anything.

One man turned and spoke softly to a guard inside the gate. That man scurried away through a wide arch in the courthouse façade.

And now Cistine waited, washed in rain, backlit by lightning, her bones rattled by thunder. The Vassora offered them no shelter. They simply stared at Cistine as her clothing dripped and her hair ran wetly down her back, erasing any trace of royalty from her bearing and bringing her low before she could even present her case to the Chancellor.

At last, the other guard returned, bringing with him a woman of striking beauty, bedecked in a gold-fringed white dress that married with her tan skin and the gold paint on her lips and eyelids.

"Is this how we've decided to treat those who appeal to Kanslar Court?" the woman barked. "Open the gate at once!"

The Vassora scurried to the bushes that shrouded the wall. They turned a large crank there, and the halves of the gate pulled apart from the inside, allowing Cistine and her companions entrance to the courthouse of Stornhaz.

The woman stepped aside to let them pass and bowed at the waist. "They tell me you're Talheim's princess. The Guide of Veran sent word some weeks ago that we ought to expect you. I take it you were delayed?"

Julian opened his mouth, and Cistine treaded lightly on his foot. "We were being held captive by a man named Thorne."

The woman's eyes, black as night under her filigreed lids, flickered. "A name we are, unfortunately, far too familiar with. I hope you don't consider any ill treatment you suffered in his hands a reflection on Valgard itself...and certainly not on this Court of which he was once High Tribune."

"Not at all. He made it abundantly clear you stand opposed."

"In every way." The woman dipped her head. "My name is Rakel. I am stewardess of the courthouse in the time of Kanslar." Cistine opened her mouth to speak, and Rakel interrupted, "These terms must all seem strange to you. No matter, the servants will explain them as they lead you to your room."

She clapped, and from the hedges themselves, from around the fountains and under the shelter of the columned arches, servants appeared— dressed in the same white-and-gold livery as the stewardess. They enclosed Cistine and her companions, laying gentle hands on them and turning them to the left.

"Where are you taking us?" Cistine demanded.

"All visitors are given quarter in the western wing," Rakel said. "I will inform the Chancellor of your arrival. Once you've changed into fresh clothes, I'll fetch you."

"As long as we can stay together."

Rakel dipped her head. "Of course. However you feel comfortable. This is a Court, after all. We are made to serve the people."

Cistine wasn't certain how much she believed that, but perhaps her suspicion was really the cabal's grudge whispering in her ear. There certainly didn't seem to be a trace of ill intent in the way the servants treated them: guiding them to the west wing, leading them up a flight of steps, and portioning out an enormous room for them.

The rich rose-and-honey wall accents blended beautifully with the pale wooden furniture inside. Twin hearths burned on opposite walls, warming the high-roofed chamber as the servants showed them the closets. One was full of women's clothing, the other with men's.

"The stewardess will return for you shortly," one servant said, and they all bustled out together, shutting the door behind them.

"I wish there was time for a bath." Cistine snagged down a dress at random. "I don't like the thought of meeting with the Chancellor looking like this."

"At least you'll be dry." Julian disappeared into the other closet to change.

"He's right, it's a start," Ashe said while she and Cistine changed rapidly from their sodden clothes. "But, God's bones...don't they have anything other than dresses here?"

"You say that like it's a bad thing."

"You know I don't like being choked by a dress." Scowling, Ashe selected a gown of pale silver dappled in black. "But if that's what's demanded of me to save Talheim..."

"Then it's worth it," Julian concluded from the doorway. Cistine knotted her bodice as she turned to face him, but it was not the tight jerk of the cords that stopped her breath.

That black shirt. The dark trousers, tucked into the inky boots.

He might as well have raided Thorne's wardrobe.

Julian's brow creased. "Not good?"

Before Cistine could stammer out an answer, there was a knock at the door. Rakel glided inside without waiting to be summoned. "I've spoken to the Chancellor. He's occupied with private matters today. Tomorrow afternoon, he can meet with you. I hope you're willing to stay with us that long."

Cistine nodded. Though she was relieved to have time to cobble together a plan and smooth out the state of herself, she wondered if the Chancellor's poor health was preventing him from seeing them immediately.

She wondered what else it might prevent him from doing.

"If you'd like, we could tour the courthouse," Rakel offered. "It's nearly time for afternoon tea. You look as if you could use a warm cup."

Cistine sagged. "Yes, *please.*"

With Rakel as their guide, they left the room—touring the west wing first, where merches and visitors from all the territories came and went. The halls circled around the courthouse interior, where numerous rooms looked down over the largest peristyle Cistine had ever seen. It was mostly open space, dotted with trees and tables and lounging furniture. But in the center, accessed by four separate bridges over a circular pond, was a glass-domed island. Inside, Cistine spotted brightly-colored flowers, and people milling around in attire just as bright.

"The teahouse," Rakel explained, "or the gossip den, if you will. This is where all the Court ladies and their children meet with visitors to discuss matters in and out of season."

Cistine politely feigned innocence at the terms, and they spent the long descent from the west wing into the peristyle with Rakel explaining the Court system all over again. There were flickers of new revelation that caught Cistine's attention—particularly how each Court had its own wing where its Tribunes and Chancellor and some elites lived, holding full control over who came and went, but the teahouse and the peristyle were factionless.

Here, the Courts met peacefully. They ate meals together on occasion, and welcomed visitors with open arms.

Cistine certainly found that to be the case. When they crossed the western bridge over the hoop of still water and entered the glass dome, more than a few friendly shouts greeted them. Three women rushed to kiss Rakel's cheeks and then exclaim over Cistine's appearance, as if she wasn't mud-caked and filthy from the road and still mussed with rain.

"Come and sit with us," one of them begged. "We've just ordered lobster bisque up from the kitchens, and we can't possibly eat all of it ourselves!"

Cistine glanced at Rakel, and the stewardess smiled. "Why do you suppose I brought you here? Go, mingle. Enjoy yourselves. I'll return for you at sunset."

Welcoming the unexpected, lighthearted distraction with open arms, Cistine followed the women to their glass-topped table. It was surprisingly warm inside the dome, with woven braziers burning every few feet. The windows dripped with condensation, and children chased one another around a fountain that burbled in the dome's center.

"So," one of the women drew out the word as she sat. "I'm Ingrid. My companions are Liv and Astrid."

Their appearances clashed wildly. Astrid was dark-skinned like Tatiana, and plump, with large, gentle features. Liv was pale and slim, and every angle of her body and face was sharp. Ingrid was somewhere between them...copper-skinned, black-haired, and unexpectedly muscular. In fact, they all were. Besides that, the only thing noticeably alike about them was their smiles.

Cistine introduced herself and her companions as Julian drew out a seat for her. He and Ashe sat on her right and left, protective as ever, but Cistine felt herself relax for the first time in days as she watched Astrid fill a cup with steaming jasmine tea.

"Are you visitors, or part of a Court?" Cistine asked as she cradled the cup, warming her fingers.

"We're from Yager," Ingrid said. "Such a shame it's Kanslar's time now. We were enjoying ourselves so much during Skyygan's season."

"Some of our favorite shops aren't licensed to sell under Kanslar rule," Liv added. "It's a pity, really. They fell out of sorts with the Chancellor long ago."

"Now we wait until Traisende takes power," Astrid pouted.

Ashe rolled her eyes. Cistine knew she had dismissed these women already as shallow and self-secured—no better or worse than Cistine had been when they'd first come to Valgard.

Cistine refused to resent them for it.

"There must be some good shops left alive," she offered. "Maybe you could show me a few while my companions and I are here. We have until tomorrow afternoon before we meet with the Chancellor."

"That would be lovely," Ingrid said. "Tell us what you'd like to see!"

They discussed bookstores and teahouses and tailors for the next hour, during which a servant delivered a massive tureen of lobster bisque to the table. The more food they ate and the more tea they drank, the more at ease Cistine felt. Even her companions let down their guard once their bellies were full.

There was a brief lull in the conversation after Liv poured them all dessert tea. It was like nothing Cistine had ever tried before, with flavorful pearls bobbing in milky liquid. The sweetness was a bright offset to the savory bisque. She found herself growing sleepy as she reclined in her chair, and Julian stroked her hair.

"So, Cistine, we're all fainting of curiosity," Ingrid said. "We heard the servants whispering in the halls that you've been kept hostage by that dreadful bandit leader who roams the wilds."

"Kanslar's former High Tribune, Thorne," Liv whispered, "and his cabal of outlaws."

Julian's hand froze, and Cistine's pulse stammered. She slowly sipped her tea. "Yes, I was."

"Simply horrifying." Astrid shuddered. "They call him a savage. They say his hatred for our way of life here is outmatched only by his hatred for the territory he once ruled—Blaykrone."

"Its people still fear him," Liv agreed.

Cistine frowned. Thorne had lied to her, and he'd certainly used her, but as for Blaykrone...she'd heard him advocate for a different strategy whenever plans put his old territory in danger. He'd pushed for the siege in the Throat—and nearly died there—to keep the battle as far from his people as possible.

All the time she'd silently raged against the High Tribune, she hadn't thought of his people who he would've rushed into any battle to defend. The ones he placed before himself...before his cabal. Before Cistine and her companions.

She was almost relieved when Rakel returned, interrupting the conversation. Everyone stood, and the women embraced Cistine, promising to find her in the morning.

"It seems you've made friends here already," Rakel remarked as she led them back toward the west wing.

Aloud, Cistine agreed...and she privately hoped they were more trustworthy than the ones she'd made before them.

CHAPTER FORTY-THREE

EVEN FRESHLY BATHED and dressed in soft pajamas, after feeding her old dress to the hearth, Cistine was wide awake. She couldn't stop thinking of Blaykrone, of all the reasons Thorne had done what he did. In the quiet, with Ashe sharing the bed beside her and Julian drowsing in a nest of pillows on the floor, Cistine's anger receded. Hurt took its place.

Hurt was an uncomfortable companion, jabbing her with sharp elbows and harsh knees, keeping her awake through the night. She watched the moonlight trace its fingertips lower and lower on the wall, and she wondered why Thorne's betrayal was so painful.

That question dampened a dawn that should have brimmed with wonder. Rakel knocked on the door shortly after sunrise, and Cistine and her companions inhaled a quick breakfast of porridge before Ingrid, Liv, and Astrid arrived.

The five women, and a reluctant Julian, spent the morning perusing the intersecting streets of Stornhaz within sight of the courthouse. There was more to see than they could take in on a single day: hat shops and haberdasheries, weavers and artisans, and endless thread shops. Not even one sold training armor, much less clothing for battle—or weapons.

When Cistine made casual mention of it to Liv, the woman laughed. "Those are in a different district. Why would you want to shop for armor?"

"I suppose I don't." Cistine thumbed along the racks of dresses without truly seeing them.

"May I ask you a question?" Cistine shrugged, and Liv turned, dresses forgotten, to face her. "What was it *really* like, being held captive by High Tribune Thorne?"

Again, that uncomfortable prickle along her spine. "What do you mean?"

Liv raised her shoulders several inches. "Here in Stornhaz, it's always the same: one Court sits in session. The others drink and make merry for months. Nothing ever changes. The thought of a bit of excitement, even being whisked away by a handsome former Tribune...well, the entire notion is a bit of a blood-stirrer, isn't it?"

"My blood wasn't stirred."

"Not even once?" Liv teased. "What's he *really* like? Is he just as brutal and rugged and chiseled as the stories say?"

Cistine choked. "Chiseled?"

"Tell me!" Liv laughed, seizing her arm.

Cistine tugged away. "I wiped his face with my filthy sock."

She left Liv blinking—clearly unsure of how true that was—and stalked away to bury herself in more dresses.

Despite those occasional questions from all three women—which gave Cistine the overall impression they were simply bored and playing at friendliness because they thought Cistine's story was exciting—the day was a welcome distraction. At least she could walk hand-in-hand with Julian and side-by-side with Ashe, and though she didn't buy anything, staring at the dresses kept her mind from wandering.

Except when they made her think of Tatiana.

It was past midday when they returned to the courthouse, Ingrid, Liv, and Astrid mourning as they passed their favorite shops lying dormant for Kanslar's season. Melancholy panged in Cistine's chest at the sight of their dark windows and the signs proclaiming closure until Traisende rose.

Talheim's monarchy had its flaws, she knew, but at least there'd been no shops forced to shutter their windows when her father had taken power;

and there would be none like that when she sat the throne, either.

Julian squeezed her hand, interrupting her thoughts, and Cistine glanced up as they crossed the bridge to the glass dome. Rakel waited for them at the door, hands folded at her waist. She wore a deep scarlet dress today, with lids and lips painted to match. In them, she looked less like a vassal of light and more like a specter of blood.

"The Chancellor is prepared to see you now," she announced.

The breath dropped through Cistine's body, tumbling from her lungs to her ankles as her stomach soared into her throat. The girls collectively pouted, and one by one they swept forward to embrace her.

"You should have supper with us," Astrid said. "We'll be waiting here in the dome."

"Dumpling stew tonight," Ingrid added. "You can't miss it."

"We'll do our best," Ashe said.

Cistine embraced Liv last—and stiffened as the woman's lips brushed her ear. "Look at his skin. The Chancellor's skin."

Cistine pushed her out at arm's length, meeting her gaze shrewdly. But Liv was still smiling as brightly as ever, and she took Ingrid and Astrid by their arms, flouncing into the dome.

Through the peristyle's northern gate, they entered another courtyard. Walled in by colonnades and arches, the enormous expanse of open yard touted several statues of what Cistine could only assume were the Court symbols: four women circled on one base, holding a chalice aloft and letting its contents run over the edge. Several yards away, a tall man in a shroud and cowl pulled his hood low across his cheekbone, half-turning as if to break free from his stone castings. Across the courtyard, the statue of a man took the knee, bending a bow and aiming his arrow at the sky. Beyond him was a carving of great plumes of vapor, rendered in precise detail as if the billows had simply been turned to stone mid-waft.

Then there was the conqueror, a man with a mace in his hand and chiseled pelts falling back from his shoulders. His stone eyes stared in quiet benevolence over the courtyard. But the rendering of his clenched knuckles over the grip of that mace...pure venom. Pure violence.

"Each of these statues demarks the entrance to the private wing of a Court," Rakel explained. "Those people you see gathered around them are members of the Courts themselves."

No one paid the visitors a second glance, too consumed with drinking wine, lounging on fainting couches, and laughing without a care for whatever was happening outside the courtyard.

Rakel led them up a short flight of steps to the jutting, rounded-out face of the tallest edifice in the courthouse. The peaked roof loomed some seventy feet overhead, and the sheer height of these columns and walls left Cistine breathless as she took her first step up toward its doors.

Something ripped through her body as her foot contacted the stairs, a sensation icy and visceral, dizzyingly weightless. Nausea poured through her, and with it the sudden, vivid clarity that she was *here*, that she'd come at last, that she stood at the door.

In a moment, she would step through it. She would begin negotiating for the future of her kingdom, and it all rested with her.

Cistine's knees buckled, and she almost plunged down. She gripped Julian's elbow to keep her feet, and he clutched her arm in turn. "Princess?"

Come. The call surged through her. *Come and see...*

"I'm...I'll be all right," Cistine croaked. Her legs still felt like sand, and Julian and Ashe exchanged a glance over her head.

Bristling at their concern and fearing they might try one last time to wrestle this negotiation from her hands, she forced herself to climb those steps, to silence that strange call in her body and bones, and to think of nothing but the Chancellor she would soon entreat.

A pair of guards met them at the double doors, putting out a hand toward Ashe and Julian. Rakel grimaced, turning to face them. "I'm afraid there are no weapons allowed within the courtrooms themselves. They don't facilitate peaceful negotiation."

Ashe fingered Echelon. "I'm not turning this over to strangers."

"Then you should stay," Cistine said. "Julian and I will go on ahead."

Ashe's eyes cut to her, and Cistine stared back at her Warden, silently willing her to go along with it.

She didn't want Ashe unarmed. Not here.

After a long, tense moment, Ashe removed her hand from the sword. "Mind your tongue in there, Cistine."

She nodded and took Julian's hand again as they entered the building, stepping into a market that encompassed the entire lower level. The domed roof sheltered a long-windowed chamber where people milled in regalia, eating at small tables or shopping from vending carts and booths. Some gathered around potted plants and chattered, and their voices soared in the high-ceilinged antechamber. The polished marble floor echoed the clack of dozens of feet, Rakel's among them, as they crossed the market.

"What is this?" Julian towed Cistine close to his side.

"Sometimes, Court business takes a great deal of time," Rakel said. "We like to keep our people occupied and well-fed during the proceedings, so tempers run low."

Cistine inhaled the fragrance of food and strong wine and looked up at the banners hanging from the walls—long cloths that sported the markings of each Court, the same renderings as the statues outside. Even as high as the ceiling was—where the dome ended and the roof flattened out above a broad balcony Rakel set them climbing toward—Cistine knew there were still levels above them.

Her stomach wriggled at the sheer height.

They climbed the steps to the balcony, where a small fountain churned into a marble basin. More people were gathered there, reading on benches or watching the market below. Everyone seemed at ease. They were simply waiting for their affairs to be attended.

"Some of them are here for the Tribunes," Rakel explained when she caught Cistine's curious glance. "Most, in fact. You're the only ones who will have the pleasure of the Chancellor's personal regard today."

"Aren't we lucky," Julian said under his breath. Cistine knew crowds put him on edge the same way they'd put Ashe on edge in Veran. She hadn't understood that as well before she'd trained with the cabal, but now she recognized how difficult it would be to struggle free among so many bodies if something happened. If something demanded they run.

They walked some distance down a polished, pale hall, past a series of doors and stairwell mouths, leaving the bustling market behind. The silence thickened, and the resonance of their feet on the marble descended tightly against Cistine's ears as they climbed a long flight of stairs and reached a guarded door at the top. Six guards this time.

"The princess may enter," Rakel said to the guards. "But only she, I'm afraid."

Julian tensed. "We're going together."

"No," Cistine said. "It's all right, Julian. This is for me to do."

"Cistine…"

"Trust me. This is how royalty negotiates." Just like Thorne had showed her in his loft: he'd taken her aside and treated with her as equals, and Cistine was prepared to do it again. She'd told her plight to Thorne twice: once as a diplomat, and once as a princess with everything to lose.

Somewhere in the balance between the two, she knew she could sway this sickly Chancellor to her side.

Julian's midnight eyes glimmered with distress. "I don't like this."

Cistine's ears burned at his defiance. "Do as I say, Julian. Wait for me."

"I'll wait with you," Rakel offered.

Cistine extracted her hand from Julian's and smoothed down her dress. Glad she was washed, with her hair brushed and her clothing clean, she faced the guards with her chin raised. "I'm ready."

A pair of them pulled open the doors, and Cistine walked inside to meet the Chancellor.

The room itself was as impressive as the market, if smaller in scale. Its roof was low everywhere except in the center, where a steep, circular vault allowed light to fall in a perfect sphere in the middle of the room. Balconies banded the beige walls and dropaway floor, with a door leading out from the one across from Cistine. To her right and left, steps led down to the sunken floor, with its long red desk, plush seat, and a pair of lounging couches.

Seated on one of those couches, bent with his head in his hands, was the Chancellor of Kanslar Court.

There was no mistaking him, not only for his presence, but for his stately attire: a well-trimmed shirt, pants, and boots, all fletched in silver. He wore a cloak joined across his clavicles by a chain of moon-colored discs, its dark folds decorated with threads of silver like falling stars. Cistine didn't know how he could bear it; the room was unseasonably hot. She was already sweating in her dress as she cleared her throat. "Chancellor?"

He dropped his hands from his face, and Cistine saw he was only fifty years at most, not the ancient, sickly old man she'd anticipated. With dark, silver-threaded hair brushed back from his eyes, broad-jawed and thick-browed, and thinly mustached across the width of his sumptuous lips, he radiated normalcy and benevolence like a kindly uncle.

Except that he also wore a bandage over one half of his face. And it was spotted with blood.

"Please, come down." There was a musical quality to his voice, calm and careful, almost familiar.

Cistine descended to the sunken floor, where the Chancellor gestured to the couch across from him. Cistine lowered herself onto the edge of it with a furtive glance at the desk; she'd expected to meet on much more formal terms than these.

"You'll have to excuse my face," the Chancellor said. "Medico's orders, you know."

"Please, don't think anything of it," Cistine said. "I'm just grateful you agreed to meet with me...especially on such short notice."

"Well, when Rakel told me Talheim's princess was in the courthouse..." the Chancellor chuckled. "You are Cistine, yes?"

"I am. Princess Cistine Novacek of Talheim. I understand you have some fascination with my kingdom."

That was her first strategy—to clear the air and make it known she knew she already had his interest. And why she had it.

The Chancellor's visible eye narrowed slightly, casting lines into his face. "It's true. I've been intrigued by Talheim ever since our war with them."

"I didn't come to make war. I came to prevent it."

The Chancellor fingered his bandage. "Interesting. I'll hear your terms. But first, I'd like to know about the perils you've faced in my kingdom. I've heard rumors that you were held captive by a man named Thorne. Is that true?"

Cistine swallowed. This man, with his tanned complexion and bandaged face, wasn't precisely who she'd envisioned as Thorne's former mentor. Yet there was no denying the intrigue in his voice when the High Tribune was mentioned. "It's true, Thorne captured me. He intended to make use of me before I escaped."

"What an ordeal," the Chancellor sighed. "I assume his intention was to use you to bait me from my city, that he hoped my interest in Talheim would be enough to coax me from behind the safety of these impregnable walls."

"Something like that."

"Well, he was right. I would've come." The Chancellor pushed himself slowly up from the couch, and as the light caught the planes of his face...

A flicker. Something strange in the tone of his skin.

Swallowing became difficult. "Chancellor, I don't want to discuss my...ordeal with Thorne. I came to plead for aid."

"Mm." He walked to the desk. "But you see we have our hands full with troubles of our own. Ransacked caravans. Devastated flagon shipments. Bandits and thieves on the loose."

Thorne, Thorne, Thorne.

Cistine tensed.

"There's an infestation in the belly of Valgard." The Chancellor plucked at his bandage, slowly separating it from his brow. "The other Chancellors have chosen to ignore it during their seasons. But now that Kanslar is in session, it's time we dealt with this infection once and for all."

Cistine curled her fingers over the sofa's edge. "I *don't* want to discuss my time as a prisoner."

"Of course not. Not in the hands of that wicked boy."

He yanked off the bandage and let it flutter onto the desk. Cistine saw it was barely bloody, and there were no weeping sores beneath it.

Liv's words arrowed through her mind: *Look at his skin.*

She shifted until the sunlight caught the man's profile: a slick, strange, silver edge to his cheekbone and the sweep of his brow. It traveled almost to his neck, where the skin was plain and tan once more. Where the bandage had covered, the flesh was angry and inflamed, but not marred with illness as she'd expected.

"Ah, Thorne." The Chancellor shook his head slowly. "I tried my very best with him. But some people have the taint of defiance in them, and it can't be beaten out. Or whipped out, as it were. My father drove it from me, but I could never quite seem to destroy it in my own son. And now, here we are, with you caught between us. The perfect prize."

His words drove a fist into her gut, and Cistine swayed forward as the implication struck her—not just what he'd said, but the reason his voice was familiar. And the reason Thorne had told her not to go, and why he hadn't been able to bring himself to explain *why.*

She knew this Chancellor's name.

A name of scars and broken legs and whippings.

"Salvotor," she whispered.

The Chancellor's voice hung rich with a smile Cistine was glad she couldn't see: "That is my name, yes. Chancellor Salvotor of Kanslar Court."

Maleck had been right. Names truly did carry impossible weight in Valgard.

Chancellor Salvotor, the head of Kanslar Court, the man she'd come to plead for aid, for the *salvation* of her kingdom...

He was Thorne's ruthless father.

CHAPTER FORTY-FOUR

CHANCELLOR SALVOTOR WAS no friend to Talheim, no one Cistine could bargain with...no one she wanted to strike hands with even on the brink of war. He was the sadist who abused his wife and child. Who scarred and intimidated his son for years. Who broke his own mother's leg.

Cistine couldn't catch her breath. Sense abandoned her, leaving her head spinning.

Run.

She was alone in a room with the man who gave Thorne those hideous scars. Not the man who *allowed* his son to be whipped, but the one who pushed the sentence through and carried out the lashes himself. Not the one who allowed the cabal to be driven from Stornhaz...the one who put his boot to their backs.

Thorne had been right. Quill had been right. She hadn't known what she was up against, who she'd intended to appeal to.

And now she knew why Thorne had written to Baba Kallah. What he'd been prepared to do before she'd run away. What Quill had been about to tell her, foregoing Thorne's sacred trust, before she'd knocked him senseless on the riverbank.

He'd been bracing himself to tell her who the Chancellor was. Who he was to Thorne. To all of them.

Run.

"I understand your reluctance to help us." Cistine's voice shook as she forced herself up from the couch, turning toward the stairs. "Perhaps once you've rooted out that infestation, we can discuss terms again."

"Not another step," Salvotor said, "or I'll send for your companion and snap his neck."

The threat froze Cistine in place.

The tempo and tenor of his voice didn't change, but Salvotor was suddenly the only one with sovereignty in the room. He was a man speaking to a child as he went on: "I do think I can make time for my...small Talheimic *obsession.*"

His tongue curled around the last word, and a chill burrowed up Cistine's spine and lodged in the base of her skull.

"I know what Thorne has been trying to do," Salvotor continued, "why he's kept you away from me this long. He knows full well what it meant to me the moment I received word from Veran that Talheim's own *princess* had set foot on our shores. And he knew exactly what would happen when I found you."

Salvotor stalked toward her with the slow, steady grace of a predator. Not sickly—not ill in any way. They'd been wrong about that, too.

"If you lay a hand on me," Cistine said, "my father will bring down *Nimmus* on your head."

"That's the idea." Salvotor's fingers flashed out, squeezing the column of her neck, and Cistine's whole body unlocked.

This was what the cabal had been preparing her for—this moment, and this room, and this hand around her throat.

She cocked her fist—thumb outside her fingers, foot coming forward, shoulder rolling, stepping into the punch—and she slammed her hand straight into the side of Salvotor's face, into the red scarring where he'd worn his bandage.

It wasn't like punching Quill. It was like punching a boulder.

Cistine *heard* her knuckles crack. She screamed, doubling up, clutching her hand as a tide of nausea pounded through her body, and Salvotor didn't even flinch. Her blow didn't so much as tip his head to one side.

His skin was diamond-hard, glittering in the light. It had fractured her knuckles.

He lifted her by the throat, backing her against the wall. With their faces inches apart, Cistine saw the strangeness of his flesh through her watering eyes: lined with thread-like rivers crafting a pale, gossamer sheen that wavered like a snake coiling under his skin.

"A short bout in Detlyse Halet will do wonders for that temper," Salvotor purred, "while I send word to your father: Talheim's only heir in exchange for the Key. A fair trade, don't you think?"

Cistine fisted her unbroken hand and swung weakly into his ribs. The Chancellor's retaliatory backhand was everything Cistine feared after Baba Kallah's stories. It whipped her head to the side, opened up her cheekbone, and burst tears from her eyes. Gods, her head—her *face*—everything spun into cobwebs. A ring on his second finger had sliced open her cheek, and she was weeping into the cut, burning it with the salt of her panic and horror—

A door slammed. Cistine heard the chaos of weapons clashing out in the hall, and then a deadly roar above the catastrophe: "*Salvotor!*"

The grip on her neck loosened. "Hello, Thorne."

The Chancellor tossed Cistine onto the floor, and the marble cracked her elbows and popped her left ear and the hinge of her jaw. She couldn't get up, couldn't find her hands or feet as air rushed back into her lungs, and one ear rang. Hot blood, thick, abundant, coursed from the pinna, sliding down her neck—

Thorne shouted her name. Cistine looked up at the balcony, and there he was. Somehow, he'd found his way into the city of his disgrace, and he'd come for them, for *her*, just as he had in the pass: swords in hand, pale hair slanting into his eyes, and those eyes fixed on her as she dragged herself up on the arm of the couch.

Salvotor snatched the back of her dress, and Cistine bawled with frustration and fear. She kicked backward—her slipper sailed off—her bare heel connected with *something* that wasn't hard like his face. The Chancellor released her, and Cistine flung herself toward the stairs.

She was halfway to the top when she collided with Julian. He thrust her behind him and charged the Chancellor, and Cistine tried to yell, but her aching jaw blocked her voice. She managed no more than a weak croak as Julian swung a stolen sword straight into the Chancellor's ribs.

It rebounded as if he'd slammed it against stone.

Salvotor grabbed Julian by the throat and hurled him toward the steps, where he landed with a thud on his shoulder, cursing. Cistine crawled back down and propped him up with her hands under his arms, and he picked up his sword and bundled her up the steps to the balcony. Thorne stepped in front of them, facing Salvotor.

These two men...Tribune and Chancellor. Father and son. They matched one another for murderous glares.

"How did you manage to find your way back into Stornhaz?" Salvotor said. "I thought I sealed all your holes a decade ago."

"It was never a matter of getting in, and you know that," Thorne growled. "It was always about you coming out."

"And you couldn't even accomplish that. All those years you managed to mask your movements on the Vey, all those carts you robbed for nothing. You even had a princess in your hands, and you couldn't use her properly! You only ever made it this far because I ordered the Vassora to stand down and let you pass. You truly are an unmitigated disgrace."

Thorne sheathed one blade and gripped the railing, and Cistine knew he would leap down and go to war against Salvotor, here and now. But he would get no further than a fist to that man's iron cheekbone.

"Thorne!" Cistine shouted. "You can't kill him. You saw what happened—his skin!"

Salvotor's eyes swung to her, and there was such hatred there, such an abundance of rage, Cistine saw who he truly was.

Not the diplomat. Not the leader of Kanslar Court, but the man who'd beaten his son and broken an old woman's body. He stood unarmed below them, and yet Cistine could envision him perfectly with a whip in his hand. With a belt. With a cudgel aimed at Baba Kallah's thigh.

The Chancellor reached into his pocket and withdrew a small, glittering emerald bottle. It reminded Cistine of the jars Tatiana had taken with her to Villmark.

"Boy," Salvotor growled, and the word was a taunt flung at Thorne, who winced as if he'd been slapped. "I am going to add to those marks on your back."

The Chancellor slammed the glass bottle against the side of his face.

And Cistine would never forget what happened next.

Serpent tongues of lightning spewed down the Chancellor's sleeve and wrapped his fist in a glove. When he clapped his palms together, the lightning transferred between his fingers like confectioner's taffy and raced up his other arm.

Thorne whirled, and there was fear in his eyes as he flung himself at them, pushing Julian to the floor, shoving Cistine's head down.

The lightning ruptured and roared into the marble doorframe. Great chunks of it broke apart, hailing down on the floor, and Cistine heard them strike Thorne's bruised back. His breath hitched against the side of her neck as he spread his arms, shielding them both.

When the tongues of lightning lashed out again, Thorne didn't wait to be struck: he hauled Julian to his feet and drove him through the doorway. Then he snatched Cistine by her arm and pushed her ahead of him, out into the long hall. The arch collapsed behind them, sealing off Salvotor's furious roar as his own incomprehensible power blocked off his route to them.

Rakel was gone, the hall riddled with Vassoran bodies. More were charging toward them already. Maleck, Tatiana, and Ariadne stood with swords in hand, ready to meet them.

Thorne shoved Cistine toward Julian. He caught her, holding his sleeve to the flow of blood from her ear. She still couldn't hear anything through it, and the whole side of her head throbbed as they ran straight toward their enemies.

A strange calm stole through Cistine when her feet touched the hallway's lower level. She knew what would happen next, and it made more sense than whatever had just happened in that room.

The cabal surged forward, slamming into the wave of Vassora. Their weapons gulped blood greedily and without mercy. Cistine saw they had no grace to spare for these people who rose in defense of a man who wore sleeves of lightning, a charlatan of blood and power who would be at the cabal's heels any moment as they forced their way to the mezzanine that looked out over the market.

Chaos reigned below. More guards pushed their way between the confused, flighty people, running toward the same thing.

Toward Quill, who stood like a dark boulder in the bright stream of fleeing Valgardans, thumbs hooked casually in his belt.

Cistine tasted the bitterness of terror in the back of her throat, but Thorne was calm as he stepped forward—as he pulled a glass jar just like the Chancellor's from a pocket on his armor.

Thorne whistled a familiar, two-beat note, and Faer's answering call was unmistakable. The raven tucked away from the banners above and fell straight toward Quill, choosing his armored form from the crush of bodies. The moment the raven alighted on his shoulder, Quill planted one foot and skimmed the other, twisting toward the balcony, catching sight of them— of Thorne brandishing the jar. Quill's chin jerked down in a swift nod, and he gripped the collar of his shirt, rolling it up over his nose and mouth like a mask.

For the second time that day, Cistine witnessed the impossible.

Thorne threw the jar. Quill leaped, caught it in one fist, and smashed it against his thigh as he landed. His armor started to glow; the inlaid threads lit up in a wash of silver-blue, illumining the reinforcements. They blazed with ephemeral radiance as Quill whirled back to face the guards.

Bright, hot flames scythed the air, catching the banners alight, clearing a crescent of space around Quill with the guards at the forefront. His armor smoldering, Quill launched through a series of spinning kicks, handstands, and blows that sent gout after gout of flame toward the Vassora. He punched through their defenses, rendered their steel useless, and sent them running like firelit foxes through sheaves of wheat, setting the potted plants, carts, and tables alight.

Thorne bolted toward the steps, and the cabal streamed after him down the stairs, where Faer landed on Cistine's shoulder. Quill dealt with the last two guards before the fire whispered out of existence, turning to nothing but skeins of steam curling up from his back.

Tatiana reached him first. She wrapped an arm around him and hustled him toward the door, and Cistine didn't know if she was imagining how Quill's feet dragged on the marble.

The outer courtyard stormed with Vassora. Thorne cursed, and Julian swept Cistine behind him with one arm. "Tell us you have a way out of here!"

Before Thorne could answer, Cistine heard a whistle from the direction of Kanslar's statue. The sound turned back half the guards who were moving toward the cabal.

Ashe perched on the conqueror's shoulder. Knees cocked, elbows resting on them, wrists hanging loosely between her legs, she peered down at the Vassora like an oversized buzzard spotting carrion. "I take it you didn't expect the likes of me."

Maleck shot forward like an arrow, piling into the ranks of distracted guards. The others followed, and Ashe lunged down into the fray. Echelon rang against Vassoran steel, and as the guards scattered from its wicked edge, Cistine spotted the doors to the peristyle: shut and barred, trapping them inside.

Cistine pushed Julian's shoulder. "Help them."

"I'm not leaving you undefended, Princess!"

"If you want to save me, then help them clear us a path!" Cistine was already running toward the door. Julian chased after her and fell into the fight by sheer necessity as the Vassora swept in to intercept them. With Julian's borrowed blade hacking at anyone who pursued her, Cistine stumbled to the door and grabbed the bar, pushing up against it.

Useless, like pressing on a mountain face and expecting it to move. Two men at least had to have lifted the bar over its hooks.

"Faer!" Cistine screamed—and whistled for good measure. When the raven alighted on her elbow, Cistine brought him on level with her eyes.

"We need a way out!"

Faer revolved his head. Intelligent, beady eyes blinked slowly as he studied her face. Then he took wing toward the western edge of the courtyard, gliding over the chaos of combat where death-gods battled Vassoran guards in a whirl of blood and steel. Cistine ran after him, lungs burning, legs pumping. When a guard stepped into her path, she dropped and slid under the edge of his blade, shredding her dress on the cobblestones. She rolled to the base of the walkway that fringed the courtyard, where Faer had alighted, flapping and crowing.

There was a runoff grate fastened to the ground. If it joined the channel cutting through the heart of Stornhaz, then it would do.

Cistine grabbed the grate with her unbroken hand, heaving with all her might, but it didn't budge. She pulled until her face broke out in sweat and the veins swelled in her forehead. Blood continued to snake down her neck, renewing its flow with the strain.

Hands suddenly joined hers over the slats. Thorne was grim and silent as they dragged the grate back together, exposing the dark plunge into the drain below. Thorne shouted for his cabal, and they came running—Ariadne in the lead, Tatiana and Quill and Julian behind her, Maleck and Ashe bringing up the rear with a last swipe at the guards.

Ariadne took the plunge into the sewer as if she'd done it countless times before. Tatiana sprang in after her, and Quill whistled Faer away before he took the leap. Julian skidded to a halt, grabbing Cistine's hand. "You first, Princess."

Cistine sucked in her breath as she stepped over the edge and dropped through a short, chilly cavern of open space, straight into Quill's arms. He set her on her feet and nudged her aside as Julian leaped down to join them.

Cistine pressed herself to the wall, wincing at its slippery, mildewed texture as Thorne dropped down next, and then Maleck. And Ashe...

Ashe did not appear.

"Ashe?" Cistine pushed away from the wall, back into the light from the open grate. Maleck swiveled to look up as well.

The overcast daylight framed Ashe's head as she stared down at them.

"More guards will be here soon. Someone has to lay a trail away from this rancid hole."

"*Ashe*." Cistine's voice cracked with frenzy this time as she grabbed Maleck's arm for balance on the slippery slope. "Get down here!"

"You should've let me go first, Princess. You made me draw the short lot."

Maleck snarled under his breath, grabbing the wall, preparing to hoist himself back up.

"Maleck. Stop."

He hesitated, fingers digging into dark stone, head cast back to look at her, braids tumbling from his brow.

"You have to get them out of the city. You told me no one knows the way in or out better than you. Now prove it." With her eyes still fixed on Maleck, Ashe added, "Julian, our princess is in your hands now. Take her home."

"Ashe, don't you *dare!*" Cistine screamed.

Ashe opened her fist and dropped Echelon into the sewer. Maleck reached up, catching the sword by its sheathed blade as Ashe fitted the grate back into place and ran.

"*No!*" Cistine jerked forward, and Julian caught her around the waist, cursing against the shell of her damaged ear.

"*Asheila!*" Maleck roared Ashe's full name, slung Echelon over his back, and started up toward the grate.

"Maleck! Come back here!" Ariadne snapped.

Quill snared his friend by the leg. "Mal, we have to go!"

Maleck kicked free and started to climb again.

"*Darkwind.*"

Thorne's voice boomed through the shaft—a quiet, deft command. Maleck stopped as if an invisible hand had flattened him against the wall.

Cistine stared through tear-stained eyes at Thorne. His own face was bloodstained and cut with lines of distress, but he was staring at Maleck, and only Maleck.

"Come back," Thorne said. "This was her choice. As Cadre—as cabal."

Maleck's fingers loosened. He dropped back onto the slope, staring at Thorne with bruised, sunken eyes. Hating the decision. Hating the Name that had pulled him back.

And if he started climbing again, Cistine would be right behind him.

But Maleck didn't climb. Feet braced, he pushed Quill, then Tatiana, down the slope into the water. Then he turned those deep, anguished, wild eyes onto Cistine.

She didn't know how she'd ever believed they were cold, or without emotion, like twin graves in that wounded face. How she'd ever let herself think Maleck didn't feel anything...didn't feel *everything*. With Ashe's sword strapped to his back, Ashe's last command bearing on his shoulders and her full name still framing his lips—a name Cistine didn't think anyone else in the world knew, except her family and Ashe's—Cistine saw her own agony, her own shock, those same first blows of grief reflected in Maleck's face.

So when he put out his hand to her, she took it. And she took the plunge with him into the filthy water.

CHAPTER FORTY-FIVE

FIRE BURNED INSIDE the courthouse walls when the cabal swam down the channel and stowed away on a barge. That, Cistine assumed, was the only reason the orders hadn't reached the gate yet to keep it from being opened. She didn't know who to thank—God, or Ashe, or pure luck—for the distraction as they floated out from Stornhaz's impregnable wall and rode the outgoing barge for miles downstream.

They followed Thorne's cue to dismount when darkness suffocated the world. They slid through the black water to the shore, and then they ran east, into the arid, dry fringes of Kroaken territory.

Little flourished in Kroaken but scrub brush, hardy trees, and dirt mounds piling up and shifting down beneath their feet with every step. Cistine's calves screamed by the time they'd climbed and descended two dozen of them. Her head throbbed, an earthquake of pain radiating from the drum of her ear. She was relieved Julian walked on that side, keeping anything from startling her. She was afraid if she was jarred, if her emotions were prodded even the slightest bit, she would start crying and never stop.

Numb. That was the word she repeated to herself in time with the plod of her feet on the dirt. Numb. Unfeeling. Composed.

The night was deep when Thorne finally called for a halt, and the cabal quietly set about making a small fire and tending their wounds. Cistine stared at Quill through the flames as Tatiana examined a slit in his armor.

"Dangerous," Tatiana muttered. "If this had been there before you used that flagon…"

"I know." Quill shot a swift glance toward Cistine.

Flagon. The carts. The *Chancellor's* carts…

"Don't do that again," Tatiana warned. "Not until I fix your threads."

Quill's face softened slightly as he focused on her again. "I won't."

Maleck knelt before Cistine, interrupting her view. He still wore Echelon across his shoulders. His fingers, surprisingly gentle, took Cistine's chin.

"Get your hands off her," Julian spat.

"Unless you know battlefield triage," Ariadne said, "I suggest you be quiet."

Julian opened his mouth but gave no retort. Cistine stared into Maleck's eyes, and he stared back. Then he turned her head and examined the blood on her neck. He brushed his thumb just below her ear, pressing the skin until she winced and groaned.

Across the fire, Thorne looked up. A deep divot appeared between his brows.

Maleck let go of Cistine's face and took her hand instead. He examined her knuckles, splaying her fingers with his and examining the swelling and the stippled skin. He brushed away the hair above her ear and tested the tender skin over her skull.

"Your eardrum is ruptured," he said at last. "Your knuckles are fractured, and you have a concussion. Nothing fatal."

Ariadne tilted her head, and a strange expression crossed her face. "He struck you."

"And threw me." Cistine hated how small the words emerged. How feeble.

"What about your hand?" Quill asked.

Cistine cleared her parched throat. "I punched him in the face."

Quill burst out laughing. It didn't sound amused. "You *punched* Salvotor in the face?"

"Yes, and his skin was like adamant. There was something wrong with it. The women in the Court warned me about that."

Quill's laughter cut off sharply. The cabal all looked at Thorne. He continued to watch Cistine across the fire.

Cistine knew it was coming. She knew they had to have this conversation, even if she longed for nothing more than to curl up in the sand and dream Ashe was with them again. Her Warden—her brilliant, clever, and powerful protector. The closest friend she'd ever had.

Gone. Because of Cistine's choices. And because of Thorne's.

"All of you should go hunting," she said, "or patrolling."

Tatiana frowned, but Thorne said, "She's right. Quill especially needs to eat. Maleck and Ariadne, on patrol. Quill, Tatiana—"

"And Julian," Cistine added. "You've hunted plenty of pheasants."

"Not tonight, Princess. I'm not leaving your side."

"I'm telling you to go as your friend, Julian," Cistine said flatly. "Don't make me order you as your princess. *Please*."

Julian scowled, looking between her and Thorne. Then he stood, dusted his hands on his trousers, and walked away among the small knots of hardy trees. Maleck, Tatiana, and Ariadne moved swiftly behind him. Quill was slower to rise, and stiffer than Cistine had ever seen him, as if char coated his bones from that impossible fire of his.

He walked over to Cistine and reached into his pocket, and for a terrifying instant she thought he would offer her one of those jars. Those *flagons*.

"I don't let just anyone into my sister's life," Quill said hoarsely. "I wouldn't let someone as trivial as *bait* into Starhollow."

He dropped a crumbled note in her lap and walked away. Even before Cistine unfolded it, she knew what she was holding, but the tears still gathered on her lashes as she stared at the picture Pippet had drawn: Quill and Cistine fighting, her in a crown, and him absolutely thrashing her.

Thorne picked up the bristly branch of a scrub tree and prodded the fire. "I'm sorry for what I did. And for what I didn't say. Whatever you want to ask, ask it. No questions for questions this time. This interrogation is yours."

Cistine crumbled the drawing gently in her fist and removed her only slipper, giving her sore foot some relief. When she realized she'd already worn a hole through the thin, impractical sole, she tossed it into the fire and watched the embers dance.

It was difficult to sort out her thoughts from the day's horrors—to untangle the anger from the confusion, the confusion from the calamity, and calamity from the grief.

"Is there a chance Ashe is alive?" It was the most important question.

"Yes. A small one. Salvotor likes to play with his victims."

"Salvotor. You mean your father."

Thorne's shoulders trembled with a deep, unhappy breath. "Yes."

"I understand why you didn't tell me," Cistine said. "You didn't want to face him. Out here, or...in there." She gestured vaguely to Thorne's head and chest, his mind and heart. "But if you're so terrified of him, why did you come to Stornhaz?"

"Because you're my friend," Thorne said, "a friend I've hurt. A friend I want to make amends with."

She stared at him, and she knew by his ashen pallor that *he* knew she'd seen the letter.

Cistine hiked back her good arm and hurled the wadded-up picture straight into his face. Thorne took it in the eye and barely winced. "How could you *use* me that way, Thorne? How could you lie to me and plot all this time to use me as bait against the Chancellor?"

"If you had given me the chance to explain myself, you would know it hasn't been that way for me for some time."

"But it was in the beginning!"

"Yes." Thorne picked up the picture, smoothed it out, and refolded it along its creases. "Just as you had your companions to think of when you listened in on our meeting about the *Svarkyst* steel, I had my cabal to think of. I thought that by using you to draw my father out, I'd finally bring them peace. Are you surprised I chose them over you?"

Cistine had no reply. She hadn't cared for the fate of his cabal until she'd realized their peril was in part her doing after the Vey. How could she expect him to have cared for hers? "Why did you ever strike a bargain with me, if you only ever intended to use me as bait? I was weak, Ashe was injured…you could have held us captive."

"I am not Salvotor. I planned to use you as bait to lure him from Stornhaz, but I wanted you competent enough to stand against him by that time. I allowed the cabal to train you because I wanted to give you a fighting chance when that day came. And then, as time passed and things changed for me, in how I saw you—as a fellow ruler, and as a woman—I knew you would go to him whether I wanted you to or not. So I was determined to continue that training for a day like today."

Cistine glared at him. "How long since things changed?"

Thorne shifted his jaw. "The night I told you about our Courts and constellations. You asked me if I had ever been a child, and I remembered why I first began Sillakove Court, under my father's nose and within his own halls. Because I didn't want to become the very sort of man I was with you: the kind who would use women as bait. Who would place innocent, trusting lives in the Undertaker's hands to accomplish his own ends."

The memory of his face in the darkness that night, as he'd held the door shut and studied her by the moon's light, raised the hair on her arms. "You wanted to tell me then, didn't you? About what you'd planned with me—and about your father."

Thorne nodded. "But I didn't know you well enough to trust you with the truth of what I am. I only knew that you told me not to discourage you out of respect, and that you'd go even if I begged you not to, because you didn't trust me yet, either. So from that day on, your training was about nothing more than preparing you to face the Chancellor whenever *you* chose to go."

Cistine bent her knees and rubbed the chill of the desert night from her bones. "I wasn't prepared."

"I know, Cistine. That was why we came after you."

"And the Chancellor isn't sickly," Cistine added.

"I noticed." A biting edge crept into Thorne's voice. "I don't know what his play has been with these surgeons—whether he's paid them off to keep up appearances, or if there's something more at work here."

"It *is* something more. He was wearing a bandage on his face where I hit him, and there was blood on it. I think there have been surgeries. Not invasive ones, but...cosmetic."

"Changing his appearance?"

"I don't know. The texture of his skin...it was like scales under the surface."

Thorne sat up straight. He stared at her, his lips parting in a soundless breath of shock. Cistine saw the blood drain from his features. "He *didn't*. That clever stars-damned *bandayo*."

"What?" Cistine crawled around the fire to sit closer to him. "What did he do? Does this have anything to do with...with the lightning?"

Thorne stared at her with inscrutable eyes. "The lightning was an augment."

A chill wrapped through Cistine's body. Then came the shock, dropping down through her like a stone plummeting from a cliff. She swayed, clutching her belly. "That isn't possible! Augmentation was driven from the kingdoms two decades ago! The lids—the Doors to the Gods—"

"Sealing them prevented any more augments from being mined, yes, but there were still troves already gathered. Already bottled."

"Flagons," Cistine whispered. "That's what they're full of. That's why the carts exploded when the guard I shot fell on them."

Thorne nodded. "Fire and lightning augments destroyed the path that day."

"This...this violates the truce," Cistine said. "If my father hears about this—"

"King Cyril knows." Thorne's words struck Cistine like a kick to the throat. "Valgard was too dependent on augments when the war started. Like a drunkard taken off the bottle without weaning, the Chancellors knew we would die from it. So King Cyril agreed we could keep our hoards and slowly deplete them over time as we adjusted to life lived like the Middle and Southern Kingdoms."

"My father knows? He *knows* augments still exist here?"

"On a much smaller scale than before, but...yes."

"Did *Ashe* know?"

"Maleck doesn't believe so. Flagons were used carefully during the war to keep Talheim unfamiliar with our battle tactics. There are some who think that reticence is why we lost the war..." Thorne's words surged louder and softer as waves of nausea battered Cistine's belly.

This was why her father had kept such a tight fist around all mention of Valgard in Astoria, and especially the Citadel. Even from *her*. Maybe he was ashamed—maybe he felt guilty—and maybe he'd feared his gossiping daughter would spread word to the people of Talheim that their benevolent, powerful king had allowed the North to retain a cache of weaponry their people had fought and bled and died to destroy.

"Then, that," Cistine rattled out, "what the Chancellor did..."

"He unleashed a lightning flagon," Thorne said. "Each Court has its own store of flagons, and they've cut into them sparingly in the past twenty years. For Salvotor to have used one today, to try and trap us in that room...it shows his desperation."

Cistine covered her face with her hands and reminded herself to take slow, deep breaths. The revelation of augmentation's lingering existence...of its lingering *use*...

"Quill," she gasped as the thought struck her. "You gave him a flagon. *You* have flagons?"

"Yes." Thorne's tone was tense. "When we escaped Stornhaz, we stole as many as we could carry. We use them *exceptionally* sparingly. Maleck doesn't use them at all, because of the risk they pose."

Cistine could hear in the heaviness of Thorne's words that there was a story to that. "What exactly do you mean?"

Thorne rubbed a hand over his mouth. "Certain augments are harsher than others. There are some, like the ones we use in battle, that a man can only endure for a minute at most before the sheer energy burns through flesh and bone...until it consumes everything. You've seen the markings of that: Maleck's chest. Cassaida's face."

Cistine pressed her lips together, breathing deeply through her nose. She remembered Ashe telling her this their very first night in Hellidom. Only now that Thorne mentioned it again did she realize the strangest thing about her encounter with the Chancellor today. "Salvotor wasn't wearing any armor."

"I know. And that's what concerns me." Thorne bent forward, clasping his hands together. "Years ago, before we left Stornhaz, he was obsessed with hunting the last dragons who dwelled in the halls of Spoek's mountains. I wonder if this was why: another of his experiments."

Cistine stared at her fractured knuckles. "You think he's forgoing the armor entirely?"

Thorne nodded. "Plating himself with reinforcements directly beneath the skin, so he's never unprepared to use a flagon."

Cistine grimaced, looking up at him again. "None of this would've happened if your people had just given up augmentation altogether."

"I'm aware. But we didn't. And the augments themselves aren't evil. It's men like Salvotor who must be stopped. My father is everything *your* father and grandfather feared, Cistine."

And though Cistine was certain she would regret it—certain she didn't want to know—she forced herself to ask: "What does he want?"

Thorne slowly curved his arms around his cocked knees, beholding the fire with an unfathomable gaze. "We don't know the finer points. Not yet. But we've suspected for years now that Salvotor is no longer respecting the boundaries of Court sessions. We've heard rumors and accounts suggesting he's planted spies in high-ranking positions in most of the other Courts, impressing his will on them. We didn't have any proof of that until you came along."

Cistine blinked. "Me?"

"You gave us Devitrius," he said. "A man we've known all our lives as a private, confidential informant to my father. But there he was, treating with the Black Coasts for *Svarkyst* steel during Skyygan's time."

"That would also explain the Tyve poison that almost killed Tatiana," Cistine murmured. "If Salvotor has a road into their Court, he has access to their shadow poisons."

"Precisely."

"But what does he want with the other Courts?"

"We're not sure of that, either," Thorne said. "The only thing we do know is Traisende and Yager have dodged his influence...so far. They're the ones who leaked information about the spies to us."

"I know you, Thorne. You have *some* idea of what he's doing."

Thorne picked up a stick and poked the fire again. "As I said, the Courts all have a private store of augments. It wouldn't surprise me if my father was trying to influence them so he could force the Courts to unite into one, with himself at the head and all the flagons under his disposal."

"Gods. *No.*" Cistine had only spent a handful of minutes in the man's presence, and already she knew how dangerous that power would be in his hands. To imagine him with a *kingdom* at his disposal, and a self-declared Talheimic obsession, was more terrifying than the threat of King Jad himself.

"You see my dilemma," Thorne said. "Why I've been in this conflict with him for so long. Why I was willing at first to do anything to bait him from that city. He's surrounded by guards there. More importantly, he has ears and eyes in every Court. Hidden loyalists who report to him. Apart from Devitrius, we don't know who they are, so we don't know who we can trust."

Cistine shivered. "You should have told me from the beginning he was never going to treat with me."

"I know." Thorne's eyes fluttered shut in a sharp wince. "My fear, my own disgrace over the blood I share with him...they're no excuse. My reluctance to face him, to face what *I* am notwithstanding, you deserved the truth." Now his eyes found her face, haunted with shame. "I know I can't change what happened. I can't bring Ashe back to you. But I'm sorry, Cistine. I swear on my grandmother's life, I'll be honest with you from now on. In all things."

After everything that had happened that day and in the long weeks before—after everything they'd endured together and apart—those words made Cistine's eyes burn with tears. "What do you want from me?"

"Nothing. You've already given me more than I thought anyone could. When you came to Hellidom, you showed me something I'd struggled to find for ten years."

"Devitrius?"

Thorne shook his head "A future."

Cistine stared at him, agape. He snapped the branch into pieces and tossed them one by one into the fire.

"The others don't know this," he said, "but ever since I sent Aden away...stars. I've been treading water, Cistine. Seizing everything that's come my way if it so much as looked promising. But I've had no plan. No idea of what would happen if I won this struggle. Even if I exposed Salvotor for everything he is, and my position was restored...what then? Where would I even begin bettering my kingdom?"

"How were you going to do it before you left Stornhaz?"

"That was the problem. I had notions, ideas...dreams. But enacting them was always my greatest struggle, knowing I would fight a battle to effect any change at all." Thorne clasped his hands loosely, a heavy sigh rolling through him. "Valgard is directionless. Our campaign for progress ground to a halt twenty years ago. Even if I became the Chancellor of Kanslar Court, I could change laws here and there, but what could I do for Valgard that would truly matter in the end?"

Cistine said nothing, knowing he was really asking himself.

"But then you came along," he continued, "and at first, I didn't care for your plight...for Talheim's plight. The more I listened, though, I began to understand what you said, and what you were fighting for. I heard you, Cistine...I do hear you."

Thorne's eyes sizzled between fire and ice.

"You asked me in Starhollow what I wanted from the Chancellor. I want his position. I want to break my father's plans, his Judgement Seat, at the foundations. And then I'm going to convince the other Courts to stand with Talheim against the Southern Kingdom."

His words knocked the breath from Cistine's body. She stared at him, heart thundering in her chest, unable to believe. "You're lying to me again."

"I would swear a blood oath on this. I'm not lying to you. Ever since I was a child, Baba Kallah has told me to dare greatly, to do something worthwhile with a lineage that's been nothing but beatings and lies and bloodshed for countless generations. And what better way to do it—what better way to make up for what I've already done—than to help you and your kingdom? If we forge peace and establish honest trade between Valgard and Talheim, perhaps we'll better both our homes. Valgard will find a way toward progress again through an alliance with the Middle Kingdom. Not just a truce, but a treaty to unite our kingdoms. And Talheim will find safety again."

Cistine hardly dared to hope, after all her dreams had been dashed today, that the help she'd been looking for all along didn't sit on a Judgement Seat, scheming and infiltrating and making friends and enemies in low places. But that it was here. That it had always *been* here, as close as a seat across from hers. As close as a calm face beside a waterfall, as the hovel beside hers, as the body sheltering her from raging fire. From *augmentation*, which her father *knew* lived on; and he hadn't told Ashe, his trusted Warden, or even Cistine, though she'd been groomed to become queen.

But Thorne had told her. He exposed everything now, when he stood to gain nothing from her if she chose to walk away.

"You're right," Cistine said at last. "That's how you'll repay me for what you've done. You'll take the Judgement Seat and you'll convince this kingdom to stand with Talheim. And I'm going to help you do it."

Thorne arched a brow. "Really?"

"This struggle became personal for me today. That...that *bandayo* broke my hand. He threatened my friends and he took Ashe." Her voice cracked, and she paused to compose herself. "I'm going to find her. And I'm going to help you destroy the creature who sired you."

Thorne's mouth twitched. "I'd welcome your insight. You have more to offer than you can imagine."

"I'll have to offer it carefully," Cistine said. "I know why your father wants me now, and for Talheim's sake, not just my own, I can't let myself fall into his hands again."

Thorne frowned. "You learned why he's fascinated with you?"

"As bait," Cistine said. "Just like you. But he wants to use me against my father, to force a conversation with him. Something about a...a Key. Does that mean anything to you?"

Thorne rested his head in his hands, and that, more than anything they'd discussed so far, made Cistine fear she was going to be sick. "Unfortunately, yes. The Key is a legend...a young one, but already infamous. Almost as soon as the Doors to the Gods swung shut, the rumors started that King Cyril helped forge a Key when they sealed the wells. Something that could throw the lids open and allow augmentation back into Valgard."

Cistine's lips were numb. Her breaths came out short—shallow. "But it's just a rumor, isn't it? A silly story to keep the elites occupied? There can't possibly be a Key to the Doors."

Silence.

"*Thorne.*"

He wouldn't look at her. He stared at the fire. "There's a Key. And Salvotor is right: Talheim hid it after the war. Your father knows where it is. The only reason Salvotor hasn't rushed to the Middle Kingdom to demand it face-to-face is because King Cyril defeated him personally in battle. Salvotor fears him. He would never face him without holding some advantage—and that advantage is the princess as a captive."

Cistine fisted her unbroken hand. "How can you be *sure* the Key is real?"

This time, his eyes did slide uneasily to her. "Because I've been searching for it, too."

A Key to the Doors to the Gods. A Key to undoing everything Cistine's grandfather, her father, Lord Rion, and Ashe had fought for. The things her grandfather had *died* for.

A Key no one in Talheim had ever mentioned to Cistine, but one that would allow augments of all kinds to slither back into the world and wreak havoc unimpeded. A Key *Thorne* wanted.

Cistine didn't know what to say.

So she punched him in the jaw.

EPILOGUE

ASHE TASTED BLOOD, felt it pumping from various points in her body, soaking her ridiculous silver dress. The cold stone beneath her had grown pliant somehow. She could push her hands into it and sink straight through, into the dust, into that Mad Kingdom, whatever Maleck had called it...*Nimmus.*

Ashe grimaced as a boot pressed between her shoulders, bringing her back to the world, flattening her to the courtyard stones. Those Vassoran bastards had taken their time, and taken turns pummeling her guts and face once they'd finally cornered her by a side door on the courtyard's west wing. For the past ten minutes, at least, she'd had some relief while a bearded, sneering Valgardan rat had her pinned under his foot.

He was important. All the Vassora backed away the moment he strode out from the courthouse. But he wasn't smart enough to realize she'd sent the guards on a fruitless chase to the west, so maybe she'd bought Cistine enough time to get to the channel...to escape.

Someone was approaching—someone even more important than her captor, it seemed, because he bent a knee in reverence, sinking his weight down between Ashe's shoulders until her entire sternum creaked in protest. She squinted one eye shut, picking up her head enough to see who'd joined them.

This newcomer—this bastard. She knew who he was immediately.

She'd spent enough of her life guarding royalty to know by his fine threads and swaggering stride that he was a Chancellor.

No...he was *the* Chancellor of Kanslar Court. The one Maleck had always changed the subject away from when Ashe mentioned him.

The one Cistine had come to see.

"Devitrius," he said smoothly to the man who climbed from Ashe's back. "I trust you've combed the direction she sent her companions?"

"No sign of them," Devitrius said. "Seems they escaped through the channel before orders reached the gate. Someone set fire to the teahouse."

Ashe grinned bloodily up at the Chancellor. She hadn't been the one to set the fire, but she wanted to kiss whoever had done it, because they'd spread the enemy ranks thin and slowed the descent of information down the channel.

Cistine was free. She was out of the city. Julian would take her home.

Ashe let go.

But a hand on her jaw jerked her back to agonized focus as the Chancellor drew her head up, sending a fissure of pain breaking along the bend of her spine and into the small of her back. "Tell me where Thorne's taken the princess, and I might let you rejoin her."

Ashe knew better than to answer. The first lesson Lord Rion had ever taught her was not to goad an enemy when she was disadvantaged. She had to be the better person, the cleverest in the room, if she wanted to survive.

"You know," the Chancellor purred, "he was right to use her as leverage against me. And he was right to take her back. We're going to play a little game, Thorne and I. Let's see who's holding the princess by the leash at the end of it."

Ashe surged up against the boot in her back, and the other man lurched away and kicked her in the side. Water swarmed Ashe's eyes as the steel toe dug into her abused ribs. A tear slipped down her cheek, and the Chancellor brushed it aside with his thumb.

"This is your last opportunity to end this swiftly. Tell me where Thorne is hiding the princess."

Ashe gritted her teeth. She'd let Cistine's idealism and their long days in quiet Hellidom lull her into forgetting what Valgardans were—what treachery and viciousness this kingdom was capable of. All of Rion's teachings about the horror that made up the heart of it. But Thorne's cruel manipulation had knocked her back into focus better than a kick to the head.

He'd used Cistine as bait. Lied to her and manipulated her. And in the siege on the courthouse to steal her back from the Chancellor, Ashe had seen him use an augment, breaking the truce as effortlessly as he'd broken Cistine's heart.

He'd spat in the faces of Ivan and Cyril Novacek today. In Lord Rion's face. In *hers*.

Thorne was a dead man. And thanks to him, Ashe would never trust a Valgardan again.

The Chancellor's eyes narrowed at the conviction that curled Ashe's mouth into another ruthless smile. He released her and straightened. "Do what you do best, Devitrius. Stir the waters and show Thorne my face in his reflection."

As Devitrius bound her wrists behind her back, Ashe slowly peeled the fingers of darkness away from her mind. She concentrated on the pain: her damaged ribs, her broken face, even the lingering pang in her leg.

Cistine was in danger. The Chancellor would not let her go. And when the princess and Julian escaped from Thorne's cabal, they would be unguarded. Exposed. Hunted.

Cistine needed rescuing. Thorne had to be punished for what he'd done. And Asheila Kovar, Warden of the Princess, would not die until she'd accomplished these things.

There was still work to be done.

End

A GUIDE
TO OLD VALGARDAN

Words:

Allatok – Heathen

Bandayo – Bastard (roughly)

Tajall - Infant (roughly)

Storfir – Big One

Stornjor – Great Love

Izten Torkat – Throat of God

Muunvat – Spit

Yani – Sweet

Sillakove - Starchaser

Selvenar – Blended hearts

Valenar – Blended blood

Phrases:

Eisken kas korvat – Worthless little barmaid

Items:

Rifandi – Paralytic poison

ACKNOWLEDGEMENTS

THE JOURNEY INTO Valgard and Talheim started long ago with a different face, and it floundered. Twice! It was not until a song, a roadtrip, and a big green notebook that everything changed. And now you hold the book of my heart in your hands.

Thank you first and foremost to God. For the inspiration at 2:30 a.m., and the bravery to tell the truth, and the lessons for me to learn along the way. So. Many. Lessons. I'm the person I am today because You taught me the way—a lot of it through these books. Whatever I asked, You gave: energy, wisdom, courage, inspiration, motivation, strength, endurance, vision, truth. You kept all Your promises, even when I doubted in my wilderness. You were right—whatever I thought was lost, You redeemed. I am forever changed.

To Dustin and Danny: who first suggested a world governed by stars, who took time on the long drive to York Beach to brainstorm the Court system with me. Who read the book and loved the characters and then said "Don't change it," when that was what I needed to hear.

Especially to Danny—my sweetheart, my *selvenar*, my happy ending. Thanks for being my rock and shield, my one and only. From now to the end of time. <3

To my parents: for encouraging the craft and pushing me to stick with it. For supporting every dream, every time, no matter how crazy. For being there through query letters and rejections and the new path to self-publishing. To

Dad for teaching me to throw a punch all those summer walks ago (you probably thought I wasn't listening, but lookie, I was!!!!) and Mom for the 5 a.m. hotel conversation when depression told me I had to fix everything, and you reminded me I just had to walk it out. As always, you were right!

To Pam, whose goofy Snapchat game led me to a song that threw the doors to this story wide open. I've listened to the song a thousand times since, and each time is like the first I saw Cistine, Thorne, and Baba Kallah so clearly. I can never thank you enough for that—and for the sleepovers, and the jam sessions, and for always me keeping just the right amounts of insane.

To Atty, Chief, Joy, Holly, and Jen, who met me when I was just starting Cistine's journey, and who have gone across Valgard and back with me, from the depths of Unsverd to the peaks of the Isetfells and beyond. You are MY cabal, always and forever. <3 Special thanks to Atty for being my critique partner, for telling me you loved it from Chapter 1, for showing me not just the writing, but the craft; and to Chief for taking my Excel sheet of Old Valgardan and helping me build a language from it that makes sense.

To Miranda and Cassidy. There are hardly any words. For every Snapchat and call and every message and every comment (especially the ones that helped me save one very important arc); for the Vine scripts and memes that made me almost cry laughing. For the encouragement and reviews and feedback that ACTUALLY made me sit down sobbing on the kitchen floor. For the face-to-face adventures and video chats and for loving the cabal and loving ME. For being much more than just beta readers. You two are my dream team, my sounding board, my heart's first line of defense between this book and the world it lives in now. I don't think our language has words for what you two mean to me, but: malatanda. I can no longer imagine this journey without you two.

To Maja Kopunovic for every stunning cover, for being the visionary who brings the face of THE STARCHASER SAGA to life. I can never fully express how much my heart sings with every opportunity we get to work together. You are more than just an artist who brings my books to life; you are a true friend.

Special thanks to Savannah Goins and the team of Bookstagrammers for the magical cover reveal that helped bring this book into people's worlds!

To every single person in the Cabin in the Woods Discord chat (I'd name you all, but our tribe keeps growing!!!): for all the love, for all the encouragement, and for playing Cards Against Humanity and making me laugh until I cried about licking things to claim them as your own. <3

To Karen and Mina, who opened their homes to me at different times during crucial parts of this series. I always think fondly of autumn car rides to the apple stand and warm summer mornings of brainstorming, of crying at your houses while I wrote hard scenes and talking about themes that blended this story into our own lives. Mostly, I am forever changed by and grateful for your love. <3

To Maggie. For everything. For growing up and growing wise with me. For being my soul sister, always. For believing.

To David & Roberta and Jeff & Pem, for asking me what my function was and digging into it with me, making me say it out loud for the first time: I tell stories because God gave them to me. You opened my eyes to the realization that He gave me this gift, and THIS BOOK, for a reason. I refuse to waste it.

To all the Dreamers who've been part of this journey. To Katie, Meaghan, Sydney, Dani, the Brittanys, Leeva, Piper, Maverick, Tiffany, Hannah, Holly, Heather, Becca, Bethany, and everyone else—I could fill a whole book just thanking those who have gone on this road with me, who've laughed, shrieked, raged, cried with me, and in these and so many other ways, kept me going, one foot in front of the other. My life would be empty without you.

To Christina Rojas and Ingrid Salinas for bringing the faces of this cast to life. I still do a little dance every time I look at them!

To Lina for the amazing song you wrote about this book, for reminding me why I do this every single time I start to forget. And to Elsie Bean—for polishing my princess up for her debut ball. For teaching me and guiding me and being so loving and professional through the whole process. For never thinking less of me while we learn together. <3

Special thanks to the DARKWIND STREET TEAM and everyone who participated in the cover reveal, giveaways, and hype train! You guys are boss and I am so privileged and proud to have worked with you on this book. Thank you for helping spread the word and the love!

To Annelisa for asking the hard questions about love, and Meagan for putting that love into art I will always adore. You guys will always be part of my team and precious in my heart. Long live the Three Musketeers!

And to you, dear reader. For picking up DARKWIND. For taking a chance on diving into a world that means more to me than any story I've ever written. Cistine's journey had barely begun, and I'm excited beyond belief to share all of it with you.

See you in the next one! <3

Read On For a Sneak Peek at

THE STARCHASER SAGA
BOOK II

CHAPTER ONE

SOMEWHERE IN THE crossing between Kroaken territory's pale sands and the hard-baked dirt mounds of neighboring Lataus, Princess Cistine Novacek of Talheim lost the last threads of her fury. Where trees prodded the sky again and the surroundings became more familiar, relief eased the snarl of emotion that lived in her heart ever since she'd left her Warden and closest friend, Asheila Kovar, in the City of a Thousand Stars, and escaped into the wilds with a disgraced High Tribune and his cabal.

It was toward him that all her fury had been directed. But after days of walking, it finally simmered away; perhaps because there was only the two of them now. Thorne had sent the rest of the cabal ahead to Hellidom, the Sanctuary City below the Nior River's falls, days ago. Cistine could still see their faces as they'd gone: Tatiana and Quill wearing matching scowls; Ariadne, even quieter than usual; Maleck, his eyes sunken, with Ashe's sword Echelon strapped to his back. And Julian...

Cistine's suitor had fought her every step when she sent him away, and she'd been just as reluctant to see him go—fearing how much she'd miss the touches and warm glances that never failed to set her heart aflame.

Except they hadn't lately, eclipsed by fury. It was from that endless spool of rage unwinding through her body that Cistine had urged him, then ordered him, to leave with the cabal.

There was a conversation she had to have with Thorne, and Thorne alone.

In the dimness of midday under a sky masked with clouds, Cistine risked a glance at the High Tribune walking on her right side, where she could hear him. Her ruptured left eardrum kept the world out of balance, and the broken knuckles on one hand ached only a sliver more than the bruised ones on the other, which she'd smashed against Thorne's jaw several days before.

He'd taken that blow like he took most things: silently, and without flinching. Only his watering eyes afterward had made her regret lashing out with her fist. Hitting people had never been her retort of choice before she'd traveled north to Valgard in search of an alliance to protect her kingdom from the threat of war. But now that Thorne's cabal had trained her, she had more in her arsenal than witticisms from countless books mined in her father's library. And Thorne had made her so furious, stacking one betrayal on top of another, she hadn't known what else to do.

She caught him looking back at her now, his silver hair wind-tossed, blue eyes pale chips of ice in a faintly-stubbled face. He looked just enough like his father—the Chancellor of Kanslar Court, the man Cistine had hoped would help stymie a threat of war from Talheim's southern neighbors in Mahasar—that it sent a chill burrowing down the backs of her arms.

She'd found obsession, not aid, at the end of that desperate road. Chancellor Salvotor was no benevolent judge, he was a ruthless abuser with dragon scales under his skin and a lust for power in his heart. Cistine was only free of him because Thorne and his cabal had chased after her and her companions into Stornhaz and exposed themselves to the very man who'd driven them out a decade ago.

They'd risked everything for her, though she had run straight to the City of a Thousand Stars without so much as bothering to speak with Thorne when she learned his initial plan for her—a lure to draw Salvotor from within the impenetrable city walls.

But matters were different now. She understood that...understood *Thorne*.

As if he sensed the shift in her thoughts, he asked, "Does that look mean you're finished resenting me?"

Cistine let the slap of her feet—bound up in the rags of Julian's shirt, since she had no shoes—answer at first. Then she cleared her throat. "It means I'm ready to ask questions."

Thorne squinted ahead into the pale gray light. "I've been waiting for that."

Of course he had.

She opened her mouth to ask her first burning question, and Thorne held up a hand. "There's a reason I brought you this way alone."

They mounted a short incline in Lataus's hilly terrain and halted at the edge of a steep basin, its center a broad hole traveling deep into the flesh of the world. Cistine's stomach plummeted at the sight of it—and of the creatures crouched around it on broken haunches or fallen completely.

There was nothing like these great metal beasts in Talheim. Vegetation grew along their bellies and bird droppings painted their faces in war stripes. Spiraled siphons with sparkling glass bowls on the ends drooped from their rusted arms.

Cistine pressed a hand to her middle, nauseated by their strangeness.

"These are harvesters." Thorne sank to one knee, balancing his wrist on his leg. "And this is one of the smaller augment fields."

Cistine stared down at him, lips parting in shock. "That hole..."

Thorne nodded. "An augmentation well. Like the others, it was sealed after we lost the war, when Talheim offered the truce."

Cistine's father had fought in that war, had ascended from Prince to King during it, and as conqueror he'd forced Valgard to seal the Doors to the Gods and halt the mining of augments—the god-like energy blooming in the Northern Kingdom's core. But her father never told her the entire truth: the scars that war had left, or that there were still augments, already mined, in this kingdom—and its people used them.

People who were not so profoundly wicked as men like Julian's father always claimed.

Thorne gestured into the basin. "These harvesters are a kind of machine fed on augments. Lightning, mostly, that kept their moving parts in motion."

"Like a clock?"

"In one sense. But instead of winding them, we filled their depositories with an augment and sealed the door. They ran for hours, sometimes for days, tilling up more energy from Valgard's core."

Cistine sank to her knees beside him, grateful to give her feet some relief. "Why are they still here? Their parts must be valuable."

"The depositories were," Thorne said. "They were removed to house more augments in Stornhaz when the war ended. But moving these machines required augmentation, and with the Doors sealed, it was a waste to return them to the city."

Cistine stared at the peculiar machines, their angles too sharp, their design too rigid for this plain wilderness, and that burning question finally made it past her dry lips. "You said you've been searching for the Key to wells like this one. That you wanted to use it to open the Doors to the Gods and let augments flow back into the world. Why?"

"Not for the reasons you're thinking. Not for power or pride, not even to unseat my father," Thorne said. "For the people. The ones being treated by the medicos, the ones who relied on augmentation to help their crops in times of drought, after forest fires, during the harshest winters."

His answer cooled the fire in Cistine's belly. If she'd had such resources to preserve her own kingdom, would she reject them?

"I'm telling you the truth, Cistine," Thorne said when she didn't speak. "I wanted the Key for my people. I won't say it doesn't still interest me, but it isn't my focus now. The Key is only a legend. What we have if you and I stand together is more tangible. Knowing what you do now, are you still with me?"

Cistine couldn't muster an answer through the tightness in her throat. She ached to believe the promise he'd made—that he would find a way to expose Salvotor for planting his own men in the other Courts, replace him on the Judgement Seat, and put an army behind Cistine to push back the threat of King Jad of Mahasar and protect Talheim.

"I'm with you," she said. "To help you find a way to unseat your father, and to find Ashe. But I won't help you open the Doors, Thorne, and I won't help hand that Key to the Courts either."

She meant every word; but she hadn't gained reputation as Talheim's greatest court gossip by keeping her curiosity in check. During their days of walking, she'd been wondering about this Key; how it had been forged, *why* it existed, and who among Talheim's own people—even in the Citadel where

Cistine was raised—knew of its existence and location.

"Understood." Thorne pushed himself up slowly, gripping the small of his back where he'd struck water shielding her from a fall. "And I'm grateful...for your help, and your understanding."

Cistine rose and dusted her hands on the tattered dress she'd worn since Stornhaz. "I know I burned my share of bridges when I left Starhollow, but I'm glad we mended this one."

"Some small comfort," Thorne chuckled.

"It means more than you know." Cistine rubbed her sunburned face and winced. "I just don't know how I'll manage with the others. Quill and Tatiana will hardly look at me."

"Remember what I told you when you and Julian argued at Villmark. Apologize for the harm, not for what you felt. Your hurt...that rests solely with me."

"Not solely. You shouldn't have kept the truth from me, but I didn't have to lead Julian and Ashe into danger just because I was angry. We carry that weight together, Thorne."

A familiar croak split the air, and Cistine turned south to face the sound—and the great raven who flapped across the basin's rim and alighted on her wrist. "Hello, Faer," she whispered, stroking the back of his head with one finger.

"Quill and the others must have reached Hellidom safely, then." Thorne stepped closer, running the palm of his hand down Faer's sleek plumage. "And now it's our turn, *Logandir*."

Wild Heart of Fire. The name, given to her by Thorne's allies after a disastrous battle in the Izten Torkat, poured new strength into her veins. She smiled up at Thorne and found him already gazing at her, a small smirk crooking his mouth in turn.

And Cistine thought maybe he did understand how much it meant to her, knowing he'd determined long ago never to use her as bait. That even if fear had kept him from being honest, he'd abandoned cruelty and truly sought to help her.

Faer brushed out from under Thorne's hand, ascending to Cistine's shoulder, and only then did she realize how close she was to the High Tribune—

sharing breathing space while they stroked Quill's trained raven.

Cistine turned her face into the wind, sharply cooler now and smelling of rain. Thunder murmured between the tattered clouds, the quiet voices of the True God and his lesser vassals discussing the fates of Cistine and her friends.

The gods seemed to be betting against them.

"I always thought it was more than coincidence," Thorne mused, "how the storms increase whenever the Court of the Conqueror sits in session."

"Do you think we're ready to face this one?" Cistine asked.

Thorne shifted his weight. "I don't know."

At least he was being honest, just as he'd promised. Even if such an unhappy answer, from someone as confident as Thorne, made the wind's bite seem much colder. "Let's go. The others are waiting."

With Faer on her shoulder, Cistine led the way toward Hellidom.

ABOUT THE AUTHOR

Renee Dugan is an Indiana-based author who grew up reading fantasy books, chasing stray cats, and writing stories full of dashing heroes and evil masterminds. Now with over a decade of professional editing, administrative work, and writing every spare second under her belt, she has authored *THE CHAOS CIRCUS*, a portal fantasy novel, and *THE STARCHASER SAGA*, an epic high fantasy series. Living with her husband, son, and not-so-stray cats in the magical Midwest, she continues to explore new worlds and spends her time in this one encouraging and helping other writers on their journey to fulfilling their dreams.

Find Renee Dugan online at:
Reneeduganwriting.com

And on social media: **@reneeduganwriting**